PRAISE FOR THE BESTSELLING NOVELS OF JO GOODMAN

"Goodman has a well-earned reputation as one of the finest Western romance writers. Her strong plotlines, realistic, colorful backdrops, deep sensuality and engaging characters are only part of her appeal. The winning combination of toughness and tenderness are what enthrall readers."
—*RT Book Reviews*

"This first-rate tale easily measures up to its predecessors and will make readers eager for their next visit to Bitter Springs."
—*Publishers Weekly* (starred review)

"A tender, engaging romance and a dash of risk in a totally compelling read . . . Gritty, realistic, and laced with humor."
—*Library Journal* (starred review)

"Jo Goodman is a master storyteller and one of the reasons I love historical romance so much."   —The Romance Dish

"Fans of Western romance will be thrilled with this delightful addition to Goodman's strong list."   —*Booklist*

"A wonderfully intense romance . . . A captivating read."
—Romance Junkies

"Exquisitely written. Rich in detail, the characters are passionately drawn . . . An excellent read."   —*The Oakland Press*

"For the pure joy of reading a romance, this book comes close to being some kind of perfection."   —Dear Author

Berkley Sensation titles by Jo Goodman

KISSING COMFORT
THE LAST RENEGADE
TRUE TO THE LAW
IN WANT OF A WIFE
THIS GUN FOR HIRE
THE DEVIL YOU KNOW
A TOUCH OF FROST

A Touch of Frost

Jo Goodman

BERKLEY SENSATION
New York

BERKLEY SENSATION
Published by Berkley
An imprint of Penguin Random House LLC
375 Hudson Street, New York, New York 10014

Copyright © 2017 by Joanne Dobrzanski
Excerpt from *The Devil You Know* by Jo Goodman copyright © 2016 by Joanne Dobrzanski
Penguin Random House supports copyright. Copyright fuels creativity, encourages
diverse voices, promotes free speech, and creates a vibrant culture. Thank you for buying
an authorized edition of this book and for complying with copyright laws by not
reproducing, scanning, or distributing any part of it in any form without permission.
You are supporting writers and allowing Penguin Random House to continue to
publish books for every reader.

BERKLEY and BERKLEY SENSATION are registered trademarks and the B colophon
is a trademark of Penguin Random House LLC.

ISBN: 9780399584275

First Edition: June 2017

Printed in the United States of America
1 3 5 7 9 10 8 6 4 2

Cover photo by Claudio Marinesco
Cover design by Rita Frangie

For Chloe, Jack, Mother, Mojo, G,
and the Handler

Chapter One

Frost Falls, Colorado
April 1892

"He's got eyes for you. I know about these things, and I'm not wrong about this. Just see if he doesn't."

Belatedly, Phoebe Apple's attention was drawn from the window where the landscape passed at a measured, hypnotic speed, to the fellow traveler on her left. "Pardon?" she asked, turning slightly in her seat to address the older woman. There had been precious few words exchanged since they had boarded together in Denver, and Phoebe had a desire to keep it that way. As a rule, she favored conversation, but found it more comfortable when it was going on around her.

She offered an apologetic smile. "I'm sorry. Woolgathering. I didn't hear what you said."

"I see that plain enough. You've had your nose pressed to that window for the better part of the last hour. Like a beggar at the bake shop." She presented this with a hint of amusement, no reproof. "Deep thoughts, I take it."

Phoebe presented a light shrug but made no comment about the depth of her thoughts. She required a moment to recall the woman's name. There had been introductions at the point of taking their seats, but Phoebe found herself struggling to bring forth a name.

"Amanda Tyler," the woman said. "Mrs. Jacob C. Tyler."

"Of course." Having been caught out, Phoebe felt herself flushing. "Phoebe Apple."

"Oh, I remember." Mrs. Jacob C. Tyler leaned a few degrees

toward Phoebe and whispered in confidential tones, "Don't look now, but he's glancing your way again."

Startled, Phoebe's chin came up a fraction and she cast her eyes in every direction except behind her. It was the hand suddenly covering one of hers and squeezing gently that grounded her. She dropped her head and stared at her lap, aware now of the softness of Mrs. Tyler's palm, the pressure of plump fingers, and that comfort and admonishment were being offered simultaneously.

Under her breath, Phoebe asked, "Who is watching me?"

"I didn't exactly say he's watching you. More like he's got an interest."

"Why would he be interested in me?"

Mrs. Tyler sat back again and released Phoebe's hand in order to give it a few light taps. "You have a passing acquaintance with a mirror, don't you?"

Phoebe turned fully sideways to regard Mrs. Tyler and was confronted by the woman's clearly entertained expression. "I know what I see in the mirror, Mrs. Tyler, but that is neither here nor there." She wiggled the fingers of her left hand, drawing attention to the gold wedding band. "I am married." She widened the opening of the pale gray cape she was wearing, modestly exposing her rounded belly. "And then there is this." She splayed her fingers across her abdomen. "There is every possibility that I will give birth before I reach Frost Falls. It is that imminent."

Mrs. Tyler chuckled appreciatively. Creases radiated from the corner of her eyes like rays of sunshine, adding lines to what was otherwise a seamless face. Her smoothly rounded countenance made her a woman of indeterminate age, certainly north of forty given that there were silver threads in her sandy-colored hair, but how far north was impossible to know.

"He entered this car after we were seated," she said. "I can't imagine that he saw your ring or took note of your condition. The way he looks at you suggests to me that neither would be an impediment. I have the sense that he's a man who enjoys looking."

Phoebe frowned, troubled. It was difficult not to seek out the man.

Mrs. Tyler's smile faded along with the lines at the corner of her eyes. Two small vertical creases appeared between her eyebrows. "Oh, I see that I've done harm. Nothing I said was meant to worry you. I thought you would be flattered or at least diverted. It seemed to me you were in need of a bit of diversion, but clearly I mistook the matter." She twisted the brilliant cut pear shape diamond ring on her finger. "My husband will tell you that I frequently say what's on my mind with no sense that my observations might not be well received. I do apologize."

"There's no need that you should." Force of habit had Phoebe responding quickly, too quickly perhaps to give her words the weight of sincerity. "Truly. You aren't wrong that I am in need of a bit of diversion."

"Well, if you're sure." Mrs. Tyler said the words uncertainly, but she did not wait for confirmation before she plunged ahead. "Four seats in front on the left. He is in a seat facing this way, though how he can ride backwards on the train is something I will never understand. He's wearing a black duster and a black, silver-banded hat. Quick. Look now."

Phoebe did. It was only possible to glimpse him in profile before his head began to swivel back in her direction. She could not be sure that he meant to look at her again—if Mrs. Tyler's observation could be trusted—but she did not want to take the chance that she would be spied studying him. The wide brim of his hat shaded his face, making it difficult to see much more than sharply carved features set in a fashion that could most kindly be described as grim. She had the impression of dark, unkempt hair, overlong so that it curled at the collar of his duster, and at least a day's growth of stubble defined his jaw.

Oddly, neither his hard, forbidding expression nor his lack of interest in barbers diminished Phoebe's sense that here was an attractive man.

"Do you know him?" asked Phoebe, speaking out of the side of her mouth.

"No. Never saw him before, but then maybe you don't recall that I told you right off that I'm not from these parts. Saint Louis born and raised."

"Yes. I remember now. You're going to Liberty Junction. That's farther along the line than Frost Falls."

"That's right. My son and daughter-in-law just settled there. He's managing the hotel and gambling house."

"Hmm."

Mrs. Tyler surreptitiously nudged Phoebe with her elbow. "I take it you don't know him. The man watching you, I mean. Not my son."

Phoebe shook her head. "I think I might have seen him at the station in Saint Louis, but I don't know him."

"Don't know as you could have any question one way or the other, so it probably wasn't him. His good looks stick in my mind the way hot porridge sticks to my ribs."

"I suppose."

Mrs. Tyler shrugged. "Maybe it's different for you. Maybe you only have eyes for your husband, which is nice on the face of it. You're young. Time yet to discover that there's no harm in looking or being looked at."

Phoebe risked another glance four rows up and on the left. The gentleman—and Phoebe was resolute in naming him as such—had reclined in his seat as much as space would allow. He had shifted his long legs into the aisle and rested one boot across the other. His arms were folded against his chest and his head was bowed. She imagined that beneath the brim that obscured his face, his eyes were closed. Phoebe felt completely at ease studying him until she noticed the bulge under the duster at his right hip.

"He's carrying a gun," she said.

Mrs. Tyler nodded and amusement crept into her features again. "I do believe you're right, but I hardly imagine he is alone. Surely you've read some of the popular dime novels. Nat Church is a favorite of mine, and I don't mind saying so."

"Mine also, but I believe the tales of gunfights and entanglements at high noon are exaggerated for dramatic effect."

"Perhaps." One of Mrs. Tyler's eyebrows arched in its own dramatic effect. "And perhaps not."

Phoebe's quiet laughter changed the shape of her mouth, lifting the corners, revealing a ridge of white teeth resting on her full lower lip. Her eyes darted to the beaded bag wedged between her hip and the side of the train car. She slipped a hand through the reticule's strings and pulled it onto her lap.

"That's a beautiful bag," said Mrs. Tyler. "May I?"

Phoebe held it up for the woman to examine more closely but she did not release it. "Seed pearls and jet beads. It was a gift."

Mrs. Tyler tentatively ran her fingertips across the beadwork. "It's exquisite. Wherever did you find it?"

"Paris. But I didn't find it. As I said, it was a gift." Phoebe regarded the bag with more careful study than it deserved and said in a low voice, "He's looking this way again, isn't he?"

"Mm-hmm."

"Perhaps he's admiring the bag," she said.

"Lord, I hope not. It would be so disappointing."

That made Phoebe laugh again. She lowered the reticule and Mrs. Tyler withdrew her hand. She was still smiling, carefully avoiding eye contact with the stranger, when she felt a subtle change in the train's rhythm. "Did you—" Her question remained unfinished because the next variation in the clackety-clack cadence was not at all subtle. Engine No. 486, a powerful workhorse of Northeast Rail, regularly carrying passengers, mail, and cargo from New York to points west by way of Chicago, Saint Louis, and Denver, jerked, juddered, stuttered, and squealed, and began to slow at a rate that threw people forward or pushed them back into their seats.

Mrs. Tyler threw an arm sideways in aid of protecting Phoebe and Phoebe's swollen belly. It was of marginal helpfulness, keeping Phoebe from becoming a projectile that would have landed her with considerable force against the empty bench seat across the way, but not keeping either of them in place. They both dropped to the space between the forward and rear seats, banging their knees and landing in an awkward brace of limbs. Mrs. Tyler's arm was squeezed between the lip of the forward seat and Phoebe's abdomen. There was time enough for her to give Phoebe a curious look before the train bucked and buckled and they were thrown sideways into the aisle. Mrs. Tyler took the brunt of the fall, supporting Phoebe's slighter weight in the cushion of her plump bosom, arms, and thighs.

"Don't try to move yet, dear," Mrs. Jacob C. Tyler said. "I'm fine. You're fine. No sense—" She stopped because men were shouting, a woman was weeping, and at least two children were caterwauling in a forward car. There was no point in talking when action was what was called for. She held Phoebe close, keeping her still until she realized that Phoebe was not moving. "We need some help here!" she shouted. "Help here!"

She was in no expectation that help was coming. She could not be sure that anyone had heard her above the din. The train was moving but still slowing; the floorboards vibrated against her spine and backside. "Mrs. Apple?" She raised her head as far as she was able in an attempt to reach Phoebe's ear. "Mrs. Apple?"

Phoebe groaned. Her eyelids fluttered. "I'm here. I'm fine."

"How's that? Did you say something?"

This time Phoebe nodded. It was more effective than trying to speak. She managed to place her hands on either side of Mrs. Tyler's shoulders and push herself high enough to create some space between her and her comfortable cushion. She slid a knee between Mrs. Tyler's, found more leverage, and was finally able to sit up. She scooted backward, took Mrs. Tyler's hands in hers, and pulled her to a sitting position as well.

They stared at each other for what felt to be several long moments but was probably no more than a couple of pounding heartbeats. Nodding simultaneously, they yanked at their skirts, untangling them from under their knees so they could rise unimpeded. Using the seats for purchase, they lifted themselves just far enough to collapse into their respective places.

The train stopped. The silence was eerie. It was not that people were no longer shouting or weeping or caterwauling, it was merely that the train had ceased to be the steady, comforting percussion that meant there was forward progress. There was none of that now.

Phoebe looked around to see where she could help. Behind her, passengers were getting to their knees or coming to their feet. One man held a handkerchief to his nose. Blood speckled the white cotton. He waved her on, indicating he was fine or that he would be. A mother was huddled in one corner of a bench seat, her young daughter in her lap. They were locked in a fierce hold that looked to be reassuring for both of them.

Phoebe moved her gaze forward, four rows up and to the left. Her lips parted on a small, sharp intake of air. He was not in his seat. "He's hurt," she said, no question in her mind that Mrs. Tyler would know to whom she was referring. Without communicating her intention, she sidled past Mrs. Tyler and stepped into the narrow aisle. She started forward, felt a tug on her skirt, and looked back and down to find Mrs. Tyler holding a fistful of mint green broadcloth. "It's all right. I think he's unconscious. Someone needs to attend to him."

Mrs. Tyler unfolded her fingers. "Fine. But have a care. Handsome doesn't mean he's not dangerous. Sometimes they go hand in hand."

Phoebe knelt at the stranger's head and put one hand on his shoulder. She shook him gently. There was no response. Out of the corner of her eye, Phoebe saw his hat lying under a seat. She leaned sideways, pulled it out, and set it on the flat of his abdomen. His duster lay open, and what she had suspected was a gun was exactly that. Without knowing why she did it, she raised the right side of the duster and drew it across the weapon, then secured the coat by tucking part of it under his hat.

"Ma'am?"

Phoebe raised her head. The man who had addressed her was peering over the back of his seat. His bowler sat at an angle on his head that might have been jaunty once but was now merely askew. He regarded her out of widely spaced gray eyes that indicated he was experiencing some pain. He did not ask for help. There was a trickle of blood at one corner of his mouth and another just below his left ear. He alternately dabbed at the wounds with two fingertips and then patted the breast pocket of his jacket for a handkerchief. He merely shrugged when he came away empty-handed.

"He was trying to move toward your end of the car," he said. "Perhaps to go to that mother and her child. I don't know what he hit when he went down, but I heard a crack. Or at least I think I did. You might want to look for a bump. I'm going to go forward. Seems to be the heart of most of the commotion."

Phoebe reached into her reticule, felt for her handkerchief, and passed it to him. "For your lip."

He thanked her for it and smiled unevenly as he pressed it to his mouth. He got to his feet, wobbled a bit before he found his bearings, and then began to move to the forward car.

Phoebe watched his progress to make sure he didn't stumble and fall. At the same time, she made a careful search of the stranger's thick thatch of dark hair. She found no obvious lump and her fingertips were clean when she removed them from his scalp. She located the contusion at the side of his forehead, just above the gentle depression of his temple. There was no laceration and that made her suspect that he had not fallen against anything sharp. More likely he had banged his head on a wrought iron armrest.

She was on the point of trying to rouse him again by taking his shoulder in the cup of her palm when she heard the first shot. She remembered thinking that the sudden silence of the train had been eerie, but that silence was nothing compared the dead quiet that followed the gun blast. Phoebe quickly looked over her shoulder at Mrs. Tyler. That worthy was wide-eyed but still as stone. The man who had been nursing a bloody nose was sliding back into his seat. The mother and daughter continued to clutch each other. Phoebe could not see the child's expression, but the mother was clearly terrified.

Another shot.

Phoebe jerked. While the sound echoed in her ears, the man under her hand never stirred. Oh, to be unconscious. She envied him his oblivion and could not call herself a coward for wishing that state had been visited upon her.

Two male passengers at the very front of the car had taken cover under the seats and were now belly-crawling toward the rear. As a strategy for escape, it was not a bad one. It lacked speed and dignity, one of those being infinitely more important than the other.

Phoebe gestured to Mrs. Tyler to flee the car, and when the older woman stood and turned, Phoebe believed she had been successful in encouraging her. It was not the case, however. Mrs. Tyler took only as many steps as necessary to reach the mother and daughter and slipped in beside them.

"You really should wake now," Phoebe whispered to the stranger. "Whatever is happening is coming this way. I can feel it." The words had barely left her lips when the forward door to the car was flung open.

The first man to enter was not dressed so differently from the unconscious man she was trying to rouse. Black hat. Black duster. Black boots. All of it was a little more battered, more weather-beaten, but essentially indistinguishable. She wondered if there was a uniform for men in the West or only men on trains in Colorado. Phoebe recognized the absurdity of the errant thought but that did not help her tamp down the nervous laughter that bubbled to her lips.

The man's broad shoulders filled the doorway, but he had enough room to bring up his gun and point it at her. The way he did it was not a menacing gesture, merely a casual one. Phoebe instantly felt cold and the placement of her lips was frozen on her face. That was perhaps unfortunate, but at least she was no longer laughing.

Chapter Two

Mr. Shoulders—that was how Phoebe thought of him—
stepped into the car and moved to the left. He was followed
by two men, similarly dressed but with less imposing figures. Sweat-stained blue bandannas folded into triangles
covered their faces from nose to chin. Mr. Shoulders used
a black scarf to achieve the same masking effect.

Phoebe looked to their eyes for differences, but all three
pairs were brown. At her present distance she could not
make out any variation in the coloring. It was the same with
their hair. All brown. Plain brown. Mr. Shoulders had very
little of it showing below his hat, but the Blue Bandannas
wore their hair longer so that it covered their ears. It made
her wonder about their ears. Small? Large? Jug handles or
pinned back?

It occurred to her that the three men might be brothers
or at least related, and her mind wandered to gangs like the
James boys or the Youngers. Regardless of their affiliation,
there was no question in Phoebe's mind that Mr. Shoulders
was their leader.

"What do we have here?" Mr. Shoulders asked.

At first Phoebe thought he was addressing her, but then
she realized his stare had shifted and encompassed the car
as a whole. He jerked his chin toward the row of seats on
her right. "Seems like two sidewinders are making their
getaway. Can you see them?"

Phoebe understood that he was referring to the men on
their bellies under the seats. They had already squirmed

past her and were likely only a few feet to the rear of where she knelt.

Neither of Mr. Shoulders' companions had the same vantage of height or position to glimpse the sidewinders, but that did not keep them from acting. They strode down the center aisle in tandem, careless of the injured man blocking their path. Phoebe was able to shift to avoid them, but her patient was summarily pushed out of the way, and what wasn't pushed was stepped on. Phoebe winced when the stranger's right hand was ground under a boot heel.

The pair under the seats did not require encouragement to come out of hiding. They gave themselves over without guns being drawn. Phoebe understood, but she was disappointed with their immediate surrender. Apparently it was the same for Mr. Shoulders. Out of the corner of her eye, Phoebe saw him shake his head in what she thought was a disgusted, pitying gesture. She would have known for sure if she could have seen the placement of his lips.

Mr. Shoulders lowered his gun but did not holster it. "Get their valuables," he told his men. "And their guns if they're carrying, though that doesn't seem likely. Put them down if you have to, but I'm not thinking that will be necessary. Get the farmer with the bloody nose next and then see to the women behind you. Go gentle. Don't alarm the little girl."

Before she could think better of it, Phoebe snorted. It was perfectly audible in the quiet of the car and immediately garnered the attention of Mr. Shoulders.

"There's something you want to say?"

Phoebe lifted her chin, met his eyes, and said, "Where I come from, the snort speaks for itself. Anything I could add is simply gilding the lily."

"You don't say."

"You are correct, sir. I *don't* say." Phoebe held her ground when his eyes narrowed and bored into hers. He was smart enough to know she was poking fun at him and clear in his own mind that he did not like it one bit. She was not surprised when he changed the subject.

"How about you empty that little bag hanging on your wrist? You probably have a reason for holding it so close. Leastways that's been my experience with women. What do you have in there that will make taking it from you such a pleasure?"

Phoebe began to slowly unwind the reticule's strings. A cry of distress behind her made her stop and turn her head. Even before she looked, she recognized the cry as coming from Mrs. Tyler.

"Not my ring!" Mrs. Jacob C. Tyler placed her hand over her heart and covered the pear shape diamond ring protectively with her other hand. "I cannot surrender it." Her voice was touched by defiance now. "I could not forgive myself. It's engraved. It can be identified. You don't want it."

The Blue Bandannas exchanged sideways glances and without a word passing between them came to a decision that satisfied them both. One of them said, "That's thoughtful of you, ma'am, thinking we wouldn't want to be connected to a piece that might mark us as thieves."

The second man nodded and finished the thought of the first. "But we know our business. Won't be the first diamond we plucked or gold that we melted to a little nugget."

Mrs. Tyler actually wailed then.

"Stop bullying her!" Phoebe said, rising her to her feet. "What you are doing is unconscionable. It makes you small men and even smaller-minded."

Mr. Shoulders said, "You got the small-minded part right. I've been telling them that for years now." He addressed his men. "Get the ring, boys. No more foolin' around. Ma'am, you best lower yourself to the floor again or take a seat. Seems to me you're bent on some foolishness."

Phoebe had no response to that except to obey the edict. She did have a plan in mind, and he had correctly divined it. It *was* some foolishness. The best she could do as her knees began to fold was give him the benefit of a narrow-eyed stare. She thought he might have chuckled behind his scarf.

Mr. Shoulders stepped forward until he was standing at

the boots of the man Phoebe was tending. He held out a hand toward her, palm up. "Might as well surrender your ring. Doesn't seem fair to take from one and not the other."

Phoebe set her lips mutinously, but she complied, twisting the ring until she was able to slide it off her finger. She dropped it in his palm and quickly retracted her hand.

"A mite tight, wasn't it?" he asked, folding his fingers around the band. His eyes dropped to her belly. "That'd be because of the baby, I imagine. I recollect womenfolk talking about fingers swolled up like little sausages when they're in the family way."

Phoebe protectively placed her hands over the curve of her abdomen, interlacing her fingers.

Mr. Shoulders jerked his chin at his companions. "You done there?" When they nodded, showing him the trinkets they had collected, he indicated the last car. "Check it out, and do it quickly. Folks there have had some time to consider their situation so have a care you don't walk into an ambush."

It occurred to Phoebe that the passengers to the rear had had enough time to flee. She hoped they had. Dusk was upon them and soon they would have cover of night, but regardless of cover, she did not think these train robbers would want to run them to ground. It was difficult to imagine the reward would outweigh the risk.

Thinking about the reward-to-risk ratio had Phoebe inquiring in practical accents, "Shouldn't you be robbing the mail car? There is one, I believe. It probably has a safe. Don't you want to blow it up?"

"You have some experience with safes?"

"No. Robberies. This is my third. First on a train, though." When Mr. Shoulders used a forefinger to tip his hat brim a fraction and cock an eyebrow at her, Phoebe took it as an invitation to explain. "I was standing at the teller window at the bank on Fifth the first time I witnessed a robbery. The second was at the theater. The thieves were after the opening night take, but the performance was a benefit for the policemen's widows and orphans fund, so it did not end well for the robbers. They had to sit through the play, which I believe was its own form of punishment, and then they were frog marched to the station."

"I see." His eyes dropped to the beaded bag hanging from her wrist. "Now about your bag there. Seems to me it would be easier to open than a safe. Why don't you toss it here?"

"There's no money. I have a comb. An etui. My spectacles. A notepad and a stub of a pencil. Oh, and a photograph of my husband. I can show you, if you like." She saw him hesitate, and while he was thinking it over, she used the opportunity to slip the strings off her wrist and open the bag. "See?" she said. The reticule was lined in black satin so that even when she offered him a look inside, the contents were barely visible.

"Just a moment." Phoebe told herself it was nerves that made her smile just then, but it might also have been that she meant to communicate an apology. She had never shot anyone before.

Remington Frost opened his eyes. He could not orient himself immediately in the dim light. He blinked several times before he realized he was lying flat out on the floor of a train car, and what light there was, was coming from lit candles in two wall sconces. Outside it was dark. It came to him slowly that someone near his head was bending over him, shaking his shoulder.

"Mister. Wake up, mister. You're not dead. Mama says you're not dead."

In response, he groaned. It was not enough for her to stop shaking him. He recognized the girl as the one who had been sitting beside her mother when the train ground to a halt. The train. Oh, yes. It was coming back to him. It explained what he was doing on the floor. He remembered leaping to his feet and never quite getting them under him. He had stumbled, staggered, and finally dropped. The memory of the ignominious fall had him searching for the source of the throbbing near his temple. He gingerly explored the injury with his fingertips, wincing once when he found it and pressed too hard.

"Are you going to cry, mister? Don't cry."

He wasn't, but he thought she looked perilously close to tears. Looking up and past her, Remington saw her mother hovering and recognized that she was similarly poised to weep. To avoid that end, Remington asked the child, who had flirted shamelessly with him while playing peek-a-boo, what her name was.

"Madeleine," she said. She pointed to her mother. "This is Mama. And that"—here she pointed to a second woman hovering nearby—"is Mrs. Tyler. Can you sit up? You should sit up and tell us your name."

Remington discovered it did not hurt too much to smile, although the placement of his lips felt more like a grimace. He made the effort because it was not in him to disoblige a fair-haired coquette, especially one under the age of six. He swept his hat off his chest and returned it to his head as he sat up. He drew his knees forward and swiveled around in the narrow aisle so he was not presenting his back to Madeleine, Mama, or Mrs. Tyler.

Touching a finger to his hat, he nodded once in way of acknowledging them. "Remington Frost, ladies." He placed his palms on the armrests on either side of him and used them to lever himself to his feet. Getting his bearings, he looked around. They were alone in the car. "Where are the others?" He asked the question more sharply than he meant to. Madeleine scrambled to her feet and clutched her mother's skirts. He was sorry for that. He hadn't meant to frighten her, but he didn't apologize. Perhaps he would later. There wasn't time now.

Because Mama was attending to soothing her daughter, Remington addressed Mrs. Tyler. "Where are the other passengers who were in here?"

"I can't say about the man wearing the bowler. He went forward early. If you're talking about the farmer and sidewinders, they're working to repair the track so the train can move on."

"The farmer and the sidewinders." He had no idea what that meant. "What happened to Phoebe Apple? Why isn't she here?"

Mrs. Tyler regarded him narrowly. The severity of the expression did not favor her rounded features, but it clearly communicated suspicion. She did not answer his questions; she asked one of her own instead. "How do you know her?"

"I don't." Impatient, he asked, "Where is she?"

"She doesn't know you. She told me so."

"That's right, but it has no bearing on what I'm asking. I need to find her."

Mrs. Tyler's suspicion shifted to confusion. "I don't understand, but the answer is that I don't know where she is. They took her."

"They?"

"Who else? The robbers. They took her, or she went with them, I'm not sure any longer. It was all a muddle the moment she shot the leader."

Remington closed his eyes briefly and rubbed his forehead with his fingertips. The ache on the side of his head was nothing compared to what was forming behind his eyes. "She shot someone?"

Mrs. Tyler nodded. "Him. The big fella."

"The big fella."

"That's right. I figure him for the leader. Others thought the same."

Remington tapped into a well of patience that he thought had gone dry. "Mrs. Tyler. I believe I need to point out that—" He stopped because she was shaking her head vigorously, one hand raised to her mouth, her eyes no longer suspicious but sympathetic. "I'm sorry. I wasn't thinking that you were unconscious for all of it, but it seems you were. Is that right?"

"I was *not* playing possum," he said dryly.

"Oh, I did not mean to imply that you were. That would demonstrate extreme cowardice in the face of Mrs. Apple's actions."

There was a steady thrum in his head that Remington was manfully trying to ignore. Behind his eyes, a hundred little men were all marching to the same drummer. "*Mrs.* Apple? You're speaking of Phoebe Apple?"

"Yes. They took her wedding band same as they took my

ring." Mrs. Tyler's eyes were instantly awash in tears. She blinked them back while she searched for a handkerchief. "They have my bag, too. I have no—"

Remington dug his handkerchief out of a pocket and gave it to Mrs. Tyler. It was not the gesture of a gallant, more like the thrust of a combatant.

Madeleine, who had finally stepped outside of her mother's skirts, took a step closer. In spite of that, she said, "They took Mama's ring. One of the blue men said they would melt it into nuggets with the others."

Remington looked to Madeleine's mother for verification. When she nodded, he asked, "Blue men?"

"She's referring to the blue scarves two of them wore to hide their features. I'm Mrs. Bancroft, by the way. My husband is Lieutenant Avery Bancroft. We're on our way to Jackson to be with him."

Madeleine knuckled her eyes. "And now Mama doesn't have her ring. We are all very sad about that."

Remington did not know what else to do except nod. Not for the first time he had cause to regret being in receipt of his father's telegram. If only he had left Chicago when he planned, the message would have arrived too late for him to take any sort of action. He would have shown up in Frost Falls ignorant of his father's request, and while Thaddeus would have been disappointed, he was not one to assign blame where none was warranted.

Thaddeus Frost was accounted by all to be a fair man, but Remington could not say how his father would view this. Remington had promised to see that the last leg of Phoebe Apple's journey—in her case from the connector in Saint Louis through Denver and on to Frost Falls—was without incident. Here, then, by any measure, was failure on a grand scale.

Cursing softly so only his lips moved around the blasphemous words, Remington lifted his hat, plowed four fingers through his dark hair, and then resettled the Stetson on his head precisely as it had been. It was only then that he took notice that all three females were watching him with unnatural interest.

"What?" he asked, looking briefly at each one in turn. "What is it?"

"Nothing," said Mrs. Jacob C. Tyler, though her audible sigh indicated otherwise.

Lieutenant Avery Bancroft's wife blinked once and flushed pink, but she offered no explanation.

It was Madeleine who showed no inhibition in giving voice to what was on her mind. "You're very pretty."

"Oh." A small vertical crease appeared between Remington's arched black eyebrows as they drew together. "Well, thank you, I suppose."

Madeleine nodded gravely. "My father's handsomer."

"I'm sure you're right."

Mrs. Bancroft placed a hand at her daughter's back and gently rubbed it. "That's enough, Maddie." She raised her eyes to Remington. "Are you steady on your feet now?"

He was afraid to nod, afraid the motion would make his head swim, so he answered instead. "I am."

"Then shouldn't you go forward and help the men do what is necessary to move this train?"

Before he could answer, Mrs. Tyler interjected, "I believe Mr. Frost has more immediate concerns. Isn't that correct? You were inquiring about Mrs. Apple. I would like to understand your intentions."

One of his eyebrows kicked up. "My intentions? My intentions are simply to find her, effect a rescue, and deliver her unharmed to the Twin Star spread outside of Frost Falls."

"*Frost* Falls," said Mrs. Tyler. "That's you?"

"My great-grandfather. He settled there, ranched, the town came later. To your point about my intentions, my father remarried a while back. Phoebe Apple is his wife's younger sister. I think you're wrong about her being *Mrs.* Apple."

"I did not mishear her. And then there's the child."

"Child?" Remington looked from Mrs. Tyler to Madeleine. The little girl's eyes widened and her golden ringlets bounced as she shook her head. "Whose child?"

"Her husband's." Mrs. Tyler ignored Remington Frost's impatient sigh and put her hands together, extending them about four inches from the cinched waist of her skirt. "Seven months gone would be my guess, although she told me birth was imminent."

Remington was reckoned to have a better than fair poker face at the card table. Some remarked that it was excellent. At the moment, though, what it was, was astonished, and he could not make it otherwise. He braced himself by placing his hands on the seat backrests on either side of him. "She's pregnant?"

"I suppose that knock to your head accounts for you being slow on the draw. That's what I am telling you. It certainly appears she is carrying a child."

As quick as that, Remington's astonishment was replaced by suspicion. He did not think he had mistaken the almost infinitesimal pause that Mrs. Tyler took before she answered him. His dark eyes narrowed as he studied the older woman. He thought she was trying to tell him something without saying it straight. He could not be sure unless he asked. So he did. "It *appears*? You have reason to doubt it?"

Another pause. "Perhaps. I don't like saying so, especially as she showed such courage."

"Mrs. Tyler. I need to know. I wasn't there when she boarded in Chicago, and I barely caught sight of her when she changed trains in Saint Louis." He opened his duster, reached inside his jacket, and produced a photograph. "This is all I had to identify her."

Mrs. Tyler regarded the photograph with a critical eye while Madeleine craned her head and stood on tiptoe to see it. "It's a fair likeness. Why didn't you introduce yourself to her? You said she's family."

"I'd be curious, too, if I were you, but I hope you will believe me when I tell you I had my reasons and they would take too long to explain. I need to find her, and I can't imagine that it's not important for me to know whether or not she's carrying a child."

There was yet another hesitation, this time a long one while Mrs. Tyler looked Remington up and down.

"Well?" he asked.

"The truth is, I just don't know. I had no reason to doubt her until she fell on me when the train jerked and jumped. My forearm was wedged between us. Right here." She showed him by placing her forearm against her abdomen. "Mrs. Apple felt . . . well . . ."

"Yes?"

"She felt lumpy."

Mrs. Bancroft's lips parted on an indrawn breath. Madeleine giggled.

"Lumpy," Remington repeated without inflection.

"Yes. It struck me as strange. In other circumstances I might have inquired, but the circumstances being what they were, I did not."

"All right." Remington accepted this bit of intelligence without making judgment. He would have to learn the truth for himself, but at least he knew there was a truth to uncover. The pregnancy could explain why his father thought it necessary to shadow Phoebe. If it had been possible, Thaddeus would have asked him to chaperone her from the moment she boarded in New York, but business had only taken him east as far as the Chicago stockyards. After receiving the telegram, and armed with the photograph, he bought a ticket for the first train available to him and the two thoroughbreds he had purchased. Shipping the horses complicated his departure, and that was how he came to miss connecting with Phoebe Apple in Chicago. It was a piece of luck that he crossed her path in Saint Louis. And then again, maybe it wasn't.

He considered another possibility and addressed Mrs. Tyler. "Did she strike you as"—here he tapped his temple with a fingertip—"as slow?"

"Slow? No, not in the least. A bit distracted, I thought. She spent a great deal of time staring out the window, but you know that since you were watching her. Perhaps she was fascinated by the landscape, but I supposed she was simply thinking, daydreaming. I don't know that for a fact; it was just my impression. But slow? No. There might be cause for some to say that she showed a lack of good judgment, but I would not be one of them. And neither should you be. It was the act of assisting you that put her squarely in the sights of that awful man." She fell quiet, thinking. "Well, that and the fact that she snorted."

"How's that again?"

"She snorted." Mrs. Tyler attempted to demonstrate but could only manage a disdainful sniff. "Something like that. It was an elegant expression of derision."

"I see," he said dryly. "And she was tending to me? Do I have that right?"

"Yes. The farmer was looking after his own injury, and the two sidewinders were bent on escaping. Mrs. Bancroft was comforting her daughter, and I freely admit I did not yet have my wits about me."

"You said she shot him."

"Yes. Winged him, actually." She touched her upper left arm with her right hand. "Here. Caused him to take a step back, but I think it was more in surprise than from the injury. His companions reappeared from the rear car, saw what happened, and pointed their guns at her. He—the big fella—stopped them and ordered them to bring her along."

"Did she resist? Snort?"

"That is not amusing, young man. She had the good sense to go with them and saved the rest of us. I imagine he wanted her to attend to his wound."

"How long ago?"

"There was still light then." She looked to Mrs. Bancroft for help. "An hour, would you say?"

"That seems right. Perhaps a little more."

Remington exhaled long and deeply. He raised an eyebrow and pointed to the bank of windows on his right.

Mrs. Tyler shook her head. "Other way. I watched until they disappeared over a ridge. I can't possibly know where they went after that."

"And Phoebe Apple? You're sure you saw her riding out with them?"

"Yes." Although her answer was firmly given, it was followed by the gradual, thoughtful appearance of a frown.

"What is it?" asked Remington.

"Well, I can't say that it's anything, it's just that . . ." Mrs. Tyler worried her lower lip. "I didn't think of it before; it didn't occur to me, that is, but she rode alone, and none of them was walking. It's peculiar now that I think on it. Almost as if they had a spare animal just for the purpose of taking a hostage. Peculiar, like I said."

"Peculiar," Remington repeated under his breath. "And no one tried to stop it?"

She shrugged. "Didn't seem that way, though I wonder what you think anyone could have done. Even if any of the passengers were allowed to keep a gun, I don't imagine they wanted to fire for fear of hurting her."

Remington could feel the weight of the Colt at his side. They hadn't relieved him of his weapon, but then he had not exactly been a threat to them. Annoyed with himself as much as this turn of events, he flattened his mouth as he considered his options.

There were the two thoroughbreds he had purchased in one of the rear cattle cars. If they had not been injured when the train was forced to a stop, it was possible he could ride out, provided he could locate tack and one of the animals would accept him as a rider. Seemed like a lot of *if*s.

"Mister."

Remington's attention was caught by the insistent tug on his long coat. He looked down at Madeleine, who was clutching his duster. "Yes, Madeline?"

Her fingers unfolded and she smiled at him guilelessly. "I can ride a horse."

Mrs. Bancroft touched her daughter's shoulder. "Not now, Madeleine."

"But I can. A pony anyway. And I have a good seat. Father says so."

"Madeleine, please." Mrs. Bancroft smiled apologetically. "I don't know why she thinks that is important now."

Remington didn't either, and he surprised himself by hunkering in front of the little girl. "Is it important?"

Madeline returned his direct gaze and nodded. "The big

man wouldn't give her the reins. He had to lead her. She doesn't have a good seat; she was wobbly."

"Good to know." He ruffled her hair as he rose and looked to the adults for confirmation. When they both nodded, he said, "Unless they get impatient with her and force her to ride with one of them, she'll slow them down."

Mrs. Tyler regarded him hopefully. "Then you're going after her?"

"I am."

Mrs. Bancroft frowned deeply, not at all optimistic. "Alone? On foot? Shouldn't you wait for help? Form a posse?"

Remington Frost thought she posed good questions, but since he hadn't worked out the answer to any of them, he simply touched a forefinger to the brim of his hat, offered a grim, parting smile, and turned to go. He could almost feel them staring after him as he went in search of the engineer.

Chapter Three

"Excuse me," said Phoebe. When no one responded even so far as to look in her direction, she repeated herself in a louder, more strident tone. This time Mr. Shoulders, who was in control of her horse's reins, slowed just enough to bring her mount abreast of his. She noticed the two reprobates riding side by side in the lead did not pause or deign to glance back. That was just as well. What she had to say was not meant for the entertainment of the entire party.

"What is it?" Shoulders asked impatiently. The scarf he still wore over the lower half of his face muffled his voice, but it did not make the words he barked out any less severe.

Intent on whispering now, Phoebe nearly unseated herself as she leaned toward him and rolled her eyes in a significant way to indicate the sparse scattering of greenery on her left. "I need a moment."

Shoulders quickly closed the gap between them and extended his injured arm to keep Phoebe in her saddle. He did not have to push her back into position. His touch accomplished that.

"For God's sake, woman," he growled. "Watch what you're doing."

Phoebe settled more firmly in the saddle, but the effect was the opposite of what she wished. The warm leather under her nether regions reminded her how urgent her need was. "Really," she said. "I need a moment."

"We're not stopping. You've slowed us down enough already."

She felt compelled to remind him, "I told you at the start that I'd never ridden before."

"Uh-huh. And you're not riding now. You're sitting. More or less. And she's doing all the work."

"She? What's her name? Perhaps I would do better if she and I had a conversation, became better acquainted."

"Lady, your bag is missing a few marbles."

That gave Phoebe pause. "My bag is . . . oh, you are referring to my mental acuity, implying that I am, if not precisely brainless, at the very least a slow top. Do I have that right?"

Shoulders stared straight ahead. He shook his head slightly and swore under his breath. "Give it a rest," he told her.

She sighed. "That is the very thing I should like to do, but if you will not stop, then I must find distractions. There is *urgency*, you see."

Shoulders halted his mount and kept Phoebe's mare in check. He called out to the men in the lead. "We're stopping. Call of nature. You go on and we'll catch up." He paused and then added with a thread of sarcasm, "Eventually."

The pair nodded as one and maintained their forward progress. Shoulders waited until they were fifty yards away before he dismounted. He growled at Phoebe when she did not wait for his help. He managed to catch her before she completely unseated herself.

"Jeez, woman. Have a care." His fingers pressed hard into either side of her waist. "Where's the percentage in you breaking your neck?"

"My name is Mrs. Harriman Apple," she said, mustering her dignity. "Not *lady*, not *woman*. And unless you mean to carry me to those bushes, I would be grateful if you would remove your hands from my person."

He removed his hands, even held them up as he stepped away in a show of surrender. "Butter damn well doesn't melt in that mouth of yours, does it?"

Phoebe merely flattened her lips in response.

Mr. Shoulders jerked his chin in the direction of a thicket. "Go on. Attend to your business."

It was harder to maintain any sense of poise when she had to pick her way over rocky ground to reach the sparse covering of thorny bushes. She circled the thicket, found it unsatisfactory because she could see through the spiny, leafless branches, and called out that she was going to higher ground for relative privacy behind a small outcropping of rock.

Mr. Shoulders did not object except to warn her not to try to make a break for it.

Phoebe raised her skirt a few inches to make the climb easier. "And he thinks *my* bag is missing a few marbles," she muttered to herself. "Where does he think I can go?"

"You say something?" he called to her.

"No!" She thought she might have heard him chuckle, but the thought that he was laughing at her was so unpleasant that she dismissed it from her mind. When she finally reached the rocky perch, she ducked behind it and squatted low, making herself invisible to Shoulders. She wondered how long she could stay where she was before he became suspicious, and then she wondered if he would check after her to see if she had done anything except waste his time. She adjusted her skirt, petticoats, and knickers, closed her eyes, and put the image of a narrow stream of rapidly running water in her mind before she made her own.

Well, at least now there would be evidence. When she had finished relieving herself, she straightened her clothing and stood, and was not entirely surprised to see Mr. Shoulders had covered half the distance to reach her. He stopped as soon as she stepped away from the outcropping. She thought that he might offer her assistance during her descent, but he simply turned and headed back to the horses. She was grateful for his lack of attention and wished she were capable of mounting the mare she'd been given without assistance from him.

No words were exchanged as he helped her up and onto the saddle. Her mare remained tethered to his until he was mounted and then he took up her reins as well as his own. Phoebe did not know how to hold herself easy in the saddle.

Her spine was not merely upright; it was stiff. It was not long before she once again felt every movement of the mare as a jolt, not quite painful, but more than uncomfortable. To distract herself, she focused on her surroundings, looking for landmarks that might help her later when she made her escape. And she would escape, she thought. From the moment Shoulders had insisted she accompany him and his men, Phoebe had been plotting how she would get away from them. They had not yet traveled so far that she could not make it back to the train tracks on foot, if not to the train.

She did not deceive herself that there would be a search party. Phoebe concluded that she was on her own when no one from the train stepped forward to help her. Not that she blamed them. She was fairly certain that the passengers had been relieved of their guns, and the one man who was still carrying was lying unconscious in an aisle. Even if someone made noises about following Shoulders and his men, how could they manage it on foot? The telegraph lines had been cut. She knew that because she overheard the men masked by the blue kerchiefs talking about it. It seemed to her that they meant her to overhear, meant her to accept there would be no rescue. She supposed she was meant to embrace hopelessness and therefore be easier to manage.

They didn't know she had been managing situations more hopeless than this since she was thirteen and the actress in the role of the ingénue in *The Tiny House* came down with chicken pox. She had been a seamstress then, a dresser, occasionally moved props, but more often inventoried them. She had been called upon to open and close the curtains when Mr. Bird was so drunk that he was more likely to hang himself in the ropes than pull on them, and she was allowed to give cues to the actors from the wings because her stage whisper was never audible to the theater's patrons. So when the production of *The Tiny House,* a play in three acts written by their most influential supporter—and their leading lady's current lover—was set to open and the ingénue had more spots than a Dalmatian, something had to be done. A generous application of greasepaint disguised the spots but exacerbated the itch. Phoebe pointed out that the actress was going to permanently scar herself with her scratching, which had an immediate but short-lived effect, and when the fevered scratching resumed, it was apparent that appealing to the actress's vanity was not the solution that would see them through opening night.

Phoebe had never had the least desire to move beyond the wings. She was satisfied with whatever work was thrown her way and being backstage suited her just fine, so no one was more startled than she when she announced, quite boldly as it happened, that she would stand in for the ingénue. Everyone in the crowded dressing room gaped at her. She was six years younger than the part called for and more than a decade younger than the actress she was replacing, but none of that mattered. She knew the lines, and at the moment, that was the salient point.

In very little time she was dressed, painted, and turned out in manner that made her unrecognizable when she regarded herself in the mirror. The director pronounced he was satisfied. The leading lady gave her stiff encouragement. The playwright looked her up and down with an interest he had never shown before.

She went on. Her fellow thespians were supportive, the audience warmed to her, and the critics wrote kindly of her performance, if not of the play. Phoebe remained in her role until the afflicted actress recovered and then she played a succession of smaller roles, male and female, as other members of the cast took ill.

The Tiny House stayed open for two months, primarily because the playwright had misplaced pride in his work and the deep pockets to support it. Phoebe never took a role onstage again, which was acceptable to her. She was a manager anyway, and her real strength was in acting as if she weren't.

Phoebe's head turned in the direction of her captor. "You should allow me to examine your arm. That's why you brought me along, isn't it?"

He did not look at her. "Later."

"That *is* why you brought me, isn't it?" When he ignored

her, she asked, "Why can't I see your friends? Shouldn't we be close to them by now?"

"We'd be considerably closer if you hadn't needed to stop."

"And you'd be with them if you hadn't insisted that I come with you. What purpose can I possibly serve? I'm no nurse, which I told you. And we both know you were not grievously wounded. I will be surprised if the bullet from my pistol did more than graze you. I am not a good shot."

"Good enough." He rolled his shoulder, drawing her stare. "That's blood on my sleeve. You didn't miss."

"I was aiming for your heart."

"Oh. Well, then you're not a good shot." Now he spared her a glance. "You had no call to shoot me, by the way. I wasn't going to hurt you."

"Plenty of people got hurt when you stopped the train. That alone made you worth shooting, but stealing Mrs. Tyler's ring . . . that was . . . *wrong*."

"Wrong," he repeated. "You've got me there. But it hardly seemed worth it to stop the train only to get you off it. The effort justified a guaranteed reward. That was their thinking, by the way, but not unreasonable."

Phoebe frowned deeply. She tried to slow her mare by making a grab for the reins, but Shoulders snapped them away and urged the horses to a quicker pace. She had no choice but to grip the saddle horn and keep her eyes on the horizon as a wave of nausea roiled her stomach.

"Slow down," she said. "Slow down or I am going to be sick." She felt his eyes on her, but she did not return his stare. Whatever he saw in her profile must have convinced him she was telling the truth because the horses slowed. She wished she understood how he did it. There was no perceptible movement that she could glimpse. "It's not the baby. It's the motion. It was the same on the train." The headache that was forming behind her eyes was also quite real, but she did not mention it.

"Explain yourself," she said when she thought she could speak without vomiting. "Please."

"You heard me fine. You just don't believe it."

Maybe that was true. "You stopped the train to take me off. That's what I heard." Out of the corner of her eye she saw him nod once. "But why?"

"Figure you're good for ransom. Saw you switch trains in Denver. Made a point to find out where you were headed because I recognized that you carrying a child and all would add to your value. From there it was just a matter of crossing your path again."

"Ransom." She said the word under her breath before she added more loudly, "What makes you think there is anyone who will give you money for me?"

"Just a feeling I have."

"Do you think my husband is waiting for me?"

"Is he?"

"No. I'm a widow."

"Kind of interesting, then, that you're not wearing widow's weeds. You being pregnant suggests he must have died recently, else you made short work of finding another fella to warm your bed."

Phoebe's stomach turned over. "We have to stop. I'm going to be sick." And this time she didn't wait for him to help her. Her dismount was clumsy; she was sliding off the saddle before she had her right leg properly over the mare's back. She might have fallen to the ground if she hadn't been squeezed between the pair of horses. Mr. Shoulders was forced to give her room to move and she slipped out and hurried ten yards to the side and was promptly sick.

Phoebe did not hear him coming up behind her so she startled when his hand appeared holding a canteen. She accepted it without thanking him, sipped, rinsed, and spit. When she took a second mouthful, she swallowed and returned the canteen. He accepted it and thrust a blue kerchief at her. Phoebe's first thought was that it was a match for the ones his men wore. Her second thought was to take it and dab at her mouth. After she was done, she carefully folded it, and held out her hand to give it back. He refused it, shaking his head, and she tucked it under the sleeve of her blouse at the wrist.

"C'mon. Time's wasting, but I think you know that."

* * *

Remington set out from the train alone. He reasoned that in the end it was better that way. There were some volunteers, and as it happened, there were four horses being transported in addition to his pair of thoroughbreds, but when Remington polled the men who stepped forward to help, he judged them to be more eager than experienced and therefore a hindrance. He bartered one of his thoroughbreds for a steel-gray gelding whose owner swore was a surefooted mount who could cut calves from the herd with the precision of a surgeon's scalpel. For Remington the advantage was securing an animal that was used to having someone on his back and could take direction from an experienced rider. The gelding, whose name was Bullet, deserved the moniker because he was swift right out of the gate.

Setting off in the direction provided by Mrs. Jacob C. Tyler and verified by several other passengers, Remington found the trail easily enough. The rising moon, only a few days past full, cast sufficient silver light across the landscape for Remington to keep Bullet moving at a steady pace. There were signs early on that reinforced Remington's thinking that he was making the right choices. Trampled tufts of long grass. Loose rock. A disturbed bed of needles at the edge of a row of loblolly pines. Divots of turf where the horses had made a steep ascent. There were so many signs, in fact, that Remington wondered at the experience of the men he was following. They had chosen to stop the train at least thirty miles from the nearest town, and they had cut the telegraph line. They had set a bonfire to warn the train of approaching danger, so it seemed their intention was not to harm the passengers unduly. They made a good job removing ties and rails on the other side of the bonfire, but they hadn't destroyed them. Remington suspected that within a couple of hours the track would be repaired with enough integrity to support the train moving forward. By that time, No. 486 would be so late for its next scheduled stop in Frost Falls, coupled with the lack of communication, that someone would be sent out to investigate.

What planning there had been appeared to be around the safety of their victims. So why had they taken Phoebe Apple? An impulse? Something motivated by revenge for her actions? Remington could not make sense of that.

The train had been stopped and boarded at dusk, which was better, he imagined, than carrying out the robbery in the full light of day. And yet they had chosen an evening with a nearly full moon. That was hardly wise, so did it mean they had no choice or were so sure of success that they saw moonlight as no impediment to their escape? According to Mrs. Tyler and the lieutenant's wife, the men did not overstay their welcome. To turn a phrase, they came, saw, and conquered.

And now they were gone.

Remington's attention was caught by something fluttering in some scrub brush off to his left. He slowed Bullet to a walk and cut sideways. He could not make out the thing he was seeing because its fluttering folded it in on itself like a wounded bird pulling in its wings. He could not reach it from the saddle, so he dismounted to investigate.

Moonlight had exposed the kerchief but also leached it of its color. It appeared gray, but Remington had no doubt that it was blue. He lifted it to his nose and sniffed. The odors were unmistakable. Sweat. Vomit. And a hint of lavender. That was interesting.

He folded the kerchief and put it in a pocket inside his coat. It would serve as evidence, provided anyone made it to trial, and Remington did not hold out much hope for that outcome. His mouth pulled to one side as he shook his head in derision and disgust. He gave Bullet a pat on the neck before he remounted. "They have the collective sense of a bag of hammers." Then he was off.

Remington estimated he rode for twelve, maybe thirteen miles, circling back occasionally when he realized he had strayed from the trail. He regretted that he had asked Mrs. Tyler if perhaps Phoebe Apple was one bullet short of a six-shooter. He hadn't put it in terms that plain, of course, but it was what he had been thinking. Mrs. Tyler had set him straight. He knew now that Phoebe was not only clever; she was resourceful.

He had no idea how many clues she'd left to mark her passing because he did not believe he had found them all, but what he did find kept him from meandering far from the trail. She had dropped a silver-plated hair comb, the kind that kept her heavy hair tucked neatly in place. She appeared to have snagged the hem of a lacy petticoat or shift on a bramble bush. That little white flag was like a beacon in the moonlight. Clearly her captors were bent on getting where they were going and not paying enough attention to her.

Remington slowed Bullet to a walk again when he caught sight of the rough-hewn cabin tucked in a gentle slope between a narrow stream and a nearly impenetrable thicket of water birches. Dismounting, he approached slowly. Neither he nor the surefooted Bullet made much sound. At a distance of seventy yards, Remington saw movement at the edge of the birches. A horse revealed itself, saddled but tethered to a tree. He waited, expecting to see three more animals, but after two long minutes, none appeared.

Not knowing what he would find when he reached the cabin, Remington left Bullet secured among some junipers and continued alone. The evening had turned cool enough that a fire would have been a comfort for any occupant, but the distinctive odor of wood smoke was absent in the air. The presence of the horse suggested someone was around but did not necessarily mean the cabin was occupied. Remington veered his approach in order to skirt the edge of the thicket and take cover if needed among the water birches.

He saw no evidence that the property was regularly used any longer. No patch of land had been tilled and seeded for a garden. The small smokehouse looked to have been abandoned for some time; the structure leaned noticeably toward the stream.

The tethered horse nickered softly as Remington came upon it. He stroked the mare's neck, quieting her. Her damp coat told him that she had been ridden recently. No one had attended to her, which suggested that time was a more important consideration than the animal's well-being. He laid his hand on the saddle and found it was cool to the touch. There was no lingering warmth from the rider's body heat. The mare did not appear to be injured, and abandoning it while still tethered seemed unnecessarily cruel. Given that cruelty did not appear to be a hallmark of the robbery or the robbers, Remington believed he would find at least one occupant. He examined the mare's tack again. No rifle scabbard. No saddlebag. Perhaps those items had been removed, but if the mare had never carried them, it meant he was standing beside the animal that Phoebe Apple had ridden.

Remington continued his cautious approach to the cabin. If the situation had not demanded restraint, there might have been a spring in his step.

Chapter Four

Phoebe's fingers scrabbled to pluck at the knotted rope that not only bound her wrists together but also secured her to the foot of the cabin's sole bed. She had been engaged in this activity since the men left her and no longer had any sense of the passage of time. Her fingers were stiff and her wrists burned where she imagined they had been rubbed raw by the heavy hemp rope.

Mr. Shoulders had shown no compassion for her condition, ordering her to sit on the floor so one of his men could tie her to a foot leg. She made an effective, if mildly embarrassing, argument for another call of nature, and the men vacated the cabin while she used the porcelain pot. They did not stray far—she could hear them talking just beyond the door—and they did not give her much time. She was shoving the pot under the bed when they stomped back in. Mr. Shoulders made his first order of business to pull the pot out and determine that it was used. His men sniggered at what was now deeply humiliating to her. That lasted as long as it took Shoulders to thrust the pot at one of them. That unfortunate fellow slunk outside to empty it while the other man tied her up. Phoebe wanted badly to yank on his blue kerchief and reveal the face of at least one of her captors. She didn't, though. Perhaps it was good judgment that prevented her from taking action, but she suspected that her courage might have finally failed her.

After she was tied, they had talked for a bit among themselves. She couldn't make out everything they said because their deep voices were like sluggish sash flies buzzing around her head, but she understood there was a disagreement and because of the furtive glances in her direction, it was clear she was the bone of contention.

Phoebe was not flattered. Whatever plan was unfolding, there wasn't enough trust among them for one or even two of them to see it through. They were all in, or all out. That meant she would be left behind. Alone.

Excited by the prospect, her heart stuttered, jumped, and then was still. It was in that brief stillness that she recognized it was not merely excitement that had overtaken her. It was fear.

A succession of calamities immediately sprang to mind: fire if the lantern tipped; darkness if the oil ran out; hunger; thirst; the return of the mad mountain man who likely owned the cabin; unseasonably cold nights; and worst of all to her way of thinking, sitting in her own waste.

Phoebe wanted to believe that she remained stoic as the catastrophes mounted—flood, landslide, high winds that would remove the roof and collapse the timber walls—but it was probably truer that she telegraphed every one of her end-of-life thoughts and her captors simply did not give a damn.

Mr. Shoulders was the last one out the door. He tipped his hat in a mocking farewell gesture. Phoebe waited until he was gone before she called up the first in a colorful string of curses. The theater was fertile ground for blue language and she had paid attention. When she had exhausted her repertoire, she sat quietly, catching her breath and waiting for inspiration. She tried lifting the bed so she could drag the binding rope under the leg. The bed frame was crafted from pine and the legs were square, thick, and heavy. Nothing she attempted gave her enough purchase or leverage. It was then that she began twisting her wrists and plucking at the knot. When she thought she might cry from frustration, she made herself rest. Once, she surrendered long enough to close her eyes and bang the back of her head against the foot rail.

She did not know she was biting her lip as she worked until she tasted blood. After that she pressed her lips together to keep them away from her teeth.

Mr. Shoulders had given her no indication when he expected to return, or even if he would return, so when she heard footsteps confidently crossing the narrow porch from the side of the cabin to the door, she assumed it was Shoulders, one of the Blue Bandannas, or the mountain man. Before she could decide which was the least of those evils, the door opened.

Phoebe's mouth gaped, closed, and fell open again, this last time only slightly parted. She blinked, mostly to clear her watery vision, but also because she was surprised.

"You."

"Mm." He stepped inside and kicked the door shut with the heel of his boot. He wasted no time closing the gap between them. "I was at the window. I had to be sure you were alone."

Even learning it after the fact, the realization that he had been watching her—again—still had the power to make her feel oddly vulnerable. For want of a reply, she nodded faintly. She did not know if he took any notice of it. He was already bending at the waist and slipping his hands under the bed frame. With very little effort, he raised the bed half a foot above the floor. It was much more room than she needed to get free of the leg, but she was too grateful to ask him if he was trying to impress her. And then there was the possibility that he would ask her if he had succeeded. She would have to admit that he had. Or lie.

"How is your head?" she asked when he dropped the bed and hunkered beside her. "I couldn't rouse you on the train." He grunted something unintelligible, which she took to mean that he did not want to be reminded of his humiliating fall. She winced when she felt his fingers brushing her wrists as he plucked at the knot.

"I'm thinking you tightened this as you were trying to work it free," he said.

She had thought the same. "Probably."

"I'm going to use my knife." That said, he spread his duster open and reached inside.

Phoebe could not help herself. She flinched when he

showed her the knife he extracted from a leather sheath strapped to his thigh. That weapon had not been visible to her on the train. Every bit of eight inches long, the finely honed edge glinted in the lantern light. There was no removing her eyes from it. Words tripped over each other in her effort to get them past her lips, "I'm Phoebe Apple, and I think I very much would like to know your name."

He smiled then, just a little. "I know who you are, Phoebe Apple, and I'm not going to hurt you. Stay still."

She didn't breathe until she felt her wrists part ways. Slowly, because her arms were stiff from being held behind her back, she brought her hands forward. Out of the corner of her eye, she saw him sheathe the blade. She took a second breath, this one deeper and more calming than the first.

"May I?" he asked, indicating her wrists.

She regarded him for a long moment, not because she had any trepidation about allowing him to tend to her, but because she simply could not turn away. Looking into his eyes was like staring down into the dark waters of the East River from the height of the Brooklyn Bridge. One could imagine making the leap, disappearing under the surface with hardly a ripple, and never coming up for air, nor wanting to. At least she could imagine it. Phoebe couldn't say if other women were seized by images of drowning in those unfathomable eyes, but it seemed likely as she was credited to be a practical individual who rarely entertained fantastical notions.

She realized she would have to revise that opinion of herself. Tonight, upon being left to her own devices, she had been susceptible to all manner of bizarre images as she contemplated her demise. Now she could add death by drowning in twin bottomless pools to the list.

It was only when he lowered his eyes to where her fingers were threaded against her swollen abdomen that the spell was broken. Phoebe followed his gaze, flushing when she understood that she had never answered his question. She unclasped her fingers and raised her hands, turning them over to reveal her palms and the delicate underside of her wrists.

Seeing the extent of the angry red abrasions, he whistled softly. "You were determined; I'll give you that. You've got some rope fibers embedded in your skin. That will have to wait until later." He looked around the sparsely furnished cabin. "Do you see anything to make some bandages?"

She didn't. There were no linens on the bed and no chest that might hold any. There was a board with three pegs on it next to an ancient woodstove, but nothing hung from it. She stared at her wrists. Tiny beads of blood dotted the skin. Now that she was free of the rope, she was becoming aware of the pain associated with her injury. It was nothing she could not tolerate, but it felt as if she were wearing two thorny bracelets. She turned her wrists this way and that, examining them from all sides.

"What about your petticoat? Your shift?"

Phoebe looked up, startled.

"To make bandages," he said patiently.

"Oh. Of course. I should have thought of it." She lifted the hem of her skirt to a point just below her knees and showed him the lacy edge of her shift. She wasted no time mourning the finest undergarment she owned. She had already snagged it on the trail to leave evidence of her passage. What did it matter if she ruined it beyond repair? Taking the cotton fabric in hand, Phoebe prepared to rend it.

"Let me." The knife was already in his hand.

Her eyes widened fractionally, but she nodded and followed the descent of the blade. In short order the deed was done and he was in possession of two usable strips of cloth. Phoebe arranged her skirt over her legs before she held out her hands. His head bent immediately to the task so she could not be sure that he found her modesty amusing, but it seemed to her that he had. For all the fantastical notions she had entertained tonight, she did not think she was imagining his grin.

"How long ago did they leave?"

"I don't know. It might have been an hour, maybe less, maybe a lot more." She watched him wind the first cloth around her wrist. He had long fingers and a gentle touch.

Whenever he brushed her skin, she felt the rough pad of his thumb.

"I didn't expect to find you alone."

"I did not expect to be left alone. They argued about it. Shoulders wanted one of them—"

"Shoulders?"

"That's what I call him. Not to his face, you understand. Only in my mind. Mr. Shoulders."

He nodded. "Go on. You said they argued."

"Mm. Shoulders wanted one of the others to stay behind. I suppose to watch over me, or at least serve as guard, but I had the sense that neither of the pair wanted to part ways with Shoulders. A matter of trust, I think."

"Did you learn where they were going or what they intended to do?"

"No."

"What about the things they stole?"

She shook her head. "I can't say. What they took from the passengers was always in possession of the men wearing the blue kerchiefs. I rode beside Mr. Shoulders. He kept my horse tethered to his or held the reins himself. The others rode ahead of us and got farther ahead each time I told Shoulders I needed to stop. We never caught up to them until we reached this cabin."

"Ah," he said softly. He tied off her left wrist, but before he began working on the right, he reached into a pocket and withdrew the silver-plated comb. "I think this belongs to you."

Delighted, she smiled fulsomely as she plucked it from his fingertips. "I did not expect to see it again, but it seemed better to sacrifice it than not." Phoebe patted her head and felt the disarray her hair had become. Her fingers deftly brought a semblance of order before she swept back a heavy lock and inserted the comb. Satisfied, she thanked him.

"What about this?" He dangled a blue kerchief from the pincer he made with his forefinger and thumb.

Phoebe wrinkled her nose and waved it away. "That belonged to Shoulders."

He stuffed it back in a pocket. "Was Shoulders sick?"

She frowned. "How did you . . ." Her voice trailed off because she supposed it didn't matter. "No, I was the one who was ill. It was not a delaying strategy on that occasion. The motion of the horse, I think, upset me. It was the same on the train."

He lifted her right wrist to attend to it. "Seems that might account for why you spent so much time staring out the window."

"It doesn't account for why you spent so much time staring at me."

One of his eyebrows slanted upward. "Did I?"

"My seatmate said you did."

"Of course she did. Mrs. Jacob C. Tyler."

"You know her?"

"We are only recently acquainted. She proved helpful. Set me straight and set me on the right path. It was a good start, but it wouldn't have meant much if you hadn't been dropping hints like bread crumbs." He tied off the bandage and made sure it was not too tight before he released her hand. "I'm still trying to decide if Shoulders didn't know what you were doing or if he was so confident no one would follow that he didn't care."

The latter explanation had never occurred to Phoebe. "I prefer to think he didn't know."

"All right. You probably are that cunning."

"Oh, but I didn't mean that I—" She stopped herself. "Hmm. I suppose I did mean exactly that. It's a matter of pride." He smiled then, just as if he understood, and that almost infinitesimal lift of one corner of his mouth fixed Phoebe's attention. He was amused by her, she thought, and in other circumstances she might have taken umbrage, but at the moment she was simply too tired to make much of it. And to give that smile its due, it was an excellent one: a bit sly, certainly a little ornery, and, oh, so thoroughly masculine that she actually had to think about breathing.

A crease appeared between his eyebrows. "Is something wrong?"

"Hmm? No. Oh, no." She could tell he wasn't sure if he should believe her, but she could hardly offer the explanation for her lapse. She did not understand it anyway. The theater was full of handsome men, and the ones who were less so could be made up to be more so. She was acquainted with several, perhaps as many as a half dozen, whose features were more symmetrically placed, and therefore were more beautiful than this man. At the moment, though, she was hard pressed to name one who was more compelling.

Shifting her gaze to a point past his shoulder, she asked, "Did you come alone?"

"I did. Is that a problem?"

"There are three of them."

"And two of us. It hardly seems fair."

"You are awfully confident."

He shrugged. "Do you need help getting up?"

Phoebe looked down at her belly. "Please." She put a hand in his and he brought her smoothly to her feet. It was a more graceful ascent than she could have managed on her own. "Thank you." She smoothed her overblouse, closed her cape, and waited to hear what they would do next. She saw his eyes slip sideways in the direction of the door. "Are we leaving now?"

"Seems best, don't you think? Especially since we don't know when they'll be back."

"Oh, *I* think it's best, but it occurred to me that you were entertaining thoughts of waiting for them and then shooting your way out."

He smirked. "I bet you read those Western dime novels."

"I might have read one or two." She paused. "Or seven."

"Ah. That goes a long way to explaining why you thought you could stop Mr. Shoulders with your little pea shooter."

"I'll have you know it was a .51 caliber percussion model with a five-and-one-half-inch barrel, and the man who sold it to me assured me I could stop a mule with one shot."

"Huh. He probably reads the same dime novels you do. Up close it could have been deadly had your aim been better, but the way it was explained to me, the distance between you and Shoulders made killing him unlikely. Where's the pistol now? Did he take it from you?"

"Yes."

"Mrs. Tyler said you winged him, but you rode alongside him for miles. Could you tell how badly was he hurt?"

It was with deep regret that she reported the truth. "The sleeve of his long coat was damaged more than he was. I thought he meant for me to attend to his injury, but he never asked for help. I had an etui in my reticule. If he had returned it, I could have at least sewn the rent in his sleeve."

"I doubt it occurred to him that you would be so accommodating. You did try to kill him."

"Yes, well, I think I might have been eternally sorry if I had succeeded, but at the time it seemed a most necessary evil. He wanted Mrs. Tyler's stunning ring and his men were frightening the little girl. People were injured, you were unconscious, and I was just so damn riled." Phoebe watched his head tilt a few degrees off perpendicular as he studied her. She stared back, not defiantly, but more matter-of-fact. There was no help for the flush that warmed her cheeks.

"Good to know," he said finally. He gestured toward the door, inviting her to precede him. "Shall we?"

Phoebe hesitated. "I think it's prudent to ask where we are going."

"Probably."

When he added nothing to his answer, she said, "Where are we going?"

"The nearest town is Frost Falls."

"Oh, but that could not be better. My ticket is for Frost Falls." She took a step forward and then stopped. "Wait. What about the passengers on the train? Shouldn't we go back?"

"They were repairing the tracks when I left. I wouldn't be surprised if the train isn't nearing the station about now. It won't be long before people will be looking for Shoulders and his men. You as well."

"All right. If you're sure about the train."

"I am." He took down the lantern and carried it outside.

"Your horse is over there," he said, raising the lantern in the direction of the mare. "You think you can ride?"

She sighed. "I suppose it was too much to hope that the town was within walking distance." She drew a fortifying breath. "I can sit in the saddle, which I understand is not the same as riding."

"No, it's not." He walked with her to the mare, gave her a leg up, and then handed her the lantern while he took the reins and led her to his mount. "This is Bullet. He proved his worth tonight. I traded a thoroughbred for him, and I believe now that I got the better of the deal." He released the reins, put one foot in a stirrup, and threw the other leg over the back of the gelding. "Do you want me to hold on to your mare's strings, or do you think you can manage?"

Phoebe was glad for having the choice, but she knew what the answer had to be. "You'd better hold them."

"That's fine. Give me the lantern." When she passed it to him, he extinguished the light and then tossed it on the ground. "We'd be spotted carrying it from miles away. Ready?"

Was she? She thought she was right up until the moment he put her on the horse.

"Whatever's bothering you, you better say it now," he told her, addressing her silence.

"I don't know your name."

"*That's* what's making you hesitate?"

Rather lamely, she said, "It seems as if it might be important."

"I am going to point out that you left the train with a man you still call Mr. Shoulders. Did you ask him his name?"

"I did. He wouldn't tell me."

"Huh."

Phoebe had rarely heard sarcasm delivered so succinctly. His tone was so dry it was a wonder it didn't scratch his throat. She lifted her chin a fraction and squared her shoulders. "I'm sure he thought I was foolish to ask."

"He had just robbed a train and abducted you. Yes, I can see that."

"You think this amusing, don't you? Well, it's not."
Moonlight made it easy for her to see him raise his hands,
palms out. What she did not know was if he was surrendering, communicating his innocence, or anticipating that he
would need to ward her off. "How do I know you are not
one of them?"

He lowered the hand holding the reins and lifted the other
one to the back of his head. He massaged a spot behind his
ear. "Thought for sure my headache was going away, but
damn if you haven't nudged it awake." He clicked his tongue,
gave Bullet a firm kick, and lightly snapped the reins. "As
much as I'm looking forward to hearing you explain that,
it's going to have to happen while we're on the move. Seems
like asking you if you were ready was more in the way of a
rhetorical question."

Chapter Five

They rode in silence for miles, which suited Remington. He wasn't certain that it suited Phoebe Apple, although whenever he glanced in her direction to assure himself she was still in the saddle, it seemed to him that her expression was more thoughtful than brooding. He favored that. He'd had his fill of sulky women.

"I believe I owe you an apology."

Remington gave a small start as much from the sudden sound of her voice as from what she'd said. "You don't owe me anything."

"I think I do. Clearly you took offense to my question and it's put you in a mood."

"I don't even remember your question."

"Liar," she said stoutly. "I asked if you were one of them. One of the gang. You heard that as an insult, and upon reflection, I do not blame you for brooding about it."

"Brooding?"

"Sulking, then."

"Now I'm insulted," he said dryly.

"No. You're not. You're amused. I can tell. It's all right. I prefer it to petulance."

"Petulance," he repeated, giving the word weight and consideration. He turned to look at her. "Do you really think I petulate?"

"Fool. That's not a word."

"If I'm doing it, it should be." He saw her mouth flatten but decided it was more in aid of checking her own amusement than demonstrating disapproval. "Go on, then. Apologize."

She blinked. "I thought I did."

"No. You said you owed me an apology and told me why. I'm waiting to hear something like, 'I'm sorry.' Or, 'Please, forgive me.' Either is acceptable."

"I am *not* asking for your forgiveness."

"Then it will have to be the other."

"Very well, I am sorry."

"And I forgive you." He thought she might have growled in frustration. Whether she did or didn't hardly mattered. He was prepared to give sound to the chuckle rising in his throat until he looked sideways at her. What he saw made him swallow his amusement.

She had a terrible seat. In spite of the fact that she was hardly more than a willow whip of woman, she sat heavy on her mare's back in all the wrong ways. He also suspected that she was experiencing some pain in certain sensitive parts of her undercarriage. Her skirt, shift, and drawers were insufficient padding for a bottom unused to sitting in a saddle. The leather would be rubbing against her inner thighs, and the heat from the friction was only tolerable for so long. She was bearing up surprisingly well, but he couldn't call himself any kind of man if he let her suffer on.

"You need to put some of your weight into the stirrups," he said. "Dig in a bit."

"What?"

"Bear down and lift yourself up. Sit tall." He slowed the horses as Phoebe attempted to follow his directions. When she was unsuccessful, he stopped Bullet and dismounted. "Here's part of the problem," he said, removing Phoebe's right foot from the stirrup. Her slender lace-up boot dangled in his line of sight until he shortened the length of the strap and told her to try it out.

"That's much better."

Remington saw for himself that it was. He repeated the fix with the other stirrup and was satisfied with the result when she was able to shift her seat. He returned to Bullet's back. "Sit up. You need to be straight but also relaxed."

She tried to do what he said. "So this is what it means to sit tall in the saddle?"

"More or less. I'm more. You're less." Out of the corner of his eye, he saw her nod and then turn her head toward him. Without looking at her, he asked, "What are you doing?"

"Studying you. Most specifically your posture. You move with your horse, not against it. You're easy with him."

"You know, if I weren't leading you, you'd have to spend some time watching where you're going. Like I'm doing."

"Does it bother you that I'm making a study?" Before he answered, she went on. "You were doing that to me on the train. Mrs. Tyler told me. So you might even say that I'm getting some of my own back."

"I wouldn't say that. I would never say that. I might say you were hell-bent on revenge, but not the other." He looked her way, met her eyes. "Mrs. Jacob C. Tyler is a busybody."

"Probably. But she wasn't wrong, was she?"

"No. Did I make you uncomfortable?"

"The idea of it made me uncomfortable. Why were you studying me?"

He swiveled his gaze forward. Her reply intrigued him. *The idea of it made me uncomfortable.* The idea. Not him. That might bode well, although there was plenty of time before they reached Frost Falls for him to make himself insufferable. He'd been told he had a particular gift for it. He heard her clear her throat and realized he had not answered her question.

"Looking out the window had no appeal. I'm familiar with the landscape that had all of your attention, so looking at you was as good a way as any to pass the time. I also played peek-a-boo with Madeleine."

"Madeleine?"

"The little girl sitting with her mother."

"Oh. I didn't know." She hesitated. "So you weren't following me?"

"Following you? How do you mean?"

"I thought I saw you at the station in Saint Louis."

"I'm sure there were plenty of people you saw at the station who ended up boarding the same train."

"Yes. I'm sure you're right."

"It's a peculiar notion, though, that you thought I might be following you. What put it in your head, besides what you've already told me? Were you in anticipation of someone trailing you?"

"No. Well, not really. My friends, people I worked with mostly, had warnings for me when they knew I was set on leaving New York. I suppose I paid more heed to what they had to say than I ought to have done."

"Is that why you bought that palm pistol?"

"Yes."

"Tell me about the warnings."

"Mostly they were about traveling alone. I was encouraged to keep to myself, sit with women, refuse the attention of men. I was warned not to show my money, keep a tight hold on my reticule, and be particular to avoid anyone whose face might be gracing a wanted notice. They said I would encounter confidence men, Indians, card sharps, drunkards, and outlaws." She gave a short laugh. "I imagine they will be pleased to learn that one of their fears came to light." She fell silent a moment, then, "Unless you're a con man, an Indian, a card sharp, or a drunkard."

"None of those."

"Hmm. Then I guess it's just the one thing."

He chuckled deep in his throat. "Disappointed?"

"Oh, no. Did I sound as if I were? I'm not. It's merely that everyone made such a fuss. I think the precautions they advised may have had unintended consequences. Certainly the derringer did."

"And the pregnancy."

Her head snapped around. "What?"

He pointed to her belly. "That child you're carrying. What is it? A pillow? A blanket roll? Maybe you fixed a bustle backwards. That would do the trick."

Phoebe placed a forearm protectively across the bulge of her belly. "It's no trick."

Eyebrow raised, Remington regarded her skeptically. "Does it really serve a purpose any longer?"

Phoebe stared back, but in the end, she was first to look away. Her arm fell. "I've gotten used to it. How did you know?"

"Mrs. Tyler suspected. She said when you fell on her, you felt . . . I think she described it as lumpy."

"Mrs. Jacob C. Tyler is a busybody."

Remington gave a short laugh, and when he replied, it was to echo Phoebe's words from earlier. "Probably. But she wasn't wrong, was she?"

Phoebe shook her head. "I think it was Mavis Wexler who suggested it. Everyone was talking at once so I can't be sure. I might have objected except there was another idea on the table, namely, that I should disguise myself as a man, and the false pregnancy suddenly seemed the better choice. I thought I would end the pretense at a stop along the way. Pittsburgh perhaps. Or Chicago. But there was always someone who came aboard or stayed on board who wished me well and would have noticed the absence of my condition."

"I take it your friends are also avid readers of Western dime novels. Fans of Nat Church, I'd wager. That'd be the most reasonable explanation for their concern."

"Yes. That, and the fact they like to exploit opportunities for drama." She sighed quietly. "They meant well. They would be devastated to know . . ." Her voice trailed away, and she shook her head again.

Curious, Remington asked, "Know what?"

She shrugged.

"You can't shrug it off now," he said. "You started it. What is it they would be devastated to know?"

"That the pregnancy attracted precisely the kind of trouble they wanted me to avoid. Mr. Shoulders told me it was the reason he singled me out. Something about thinking that I would be worth more because of my condition."

Remington frowned deeply. "Worth more? You're talking about ransom."

"He was talking about ransom. I'm just explaining what he said. It was all a bit confusing. I had the impression at the time that he was telling me that I was the reason he and his men stopped the train, and robbing the passengers was almost an afterthought. Something about a sure reward for their trouble. I suppose, in spite of what he said, that he was not confident that he could raise a ransom using me. I told him as much, but he remained set on his ridiculous idea."

"Huh."

"You understand that it's ridiculous, don't you?"

"I'm working that out." He tugged lightly on the reins of her mare, drawing Phoebe closer. "Is there someone out there, maybe in Frost Falls, who would be willing to pay to see you safe?"

"What are you saying? Now *you* want to hold me for ransom?"

"Still working it out."

"If this animal weren't tethered to you, I'd tell you to go to hell."

"Probably better that you don't, then." When he looked over at her, she was gritting her teeth. "Stop it. You're riding stiff as a corpse again. I have no interest in ransoming you or, for that matter, collecting a reward." When she pulled on the reins, he let her have some of the length but did not give them up. "Feel better now?"

She looked straight ahead and didn't answer.

"Mrs. Tyler told me you were Mrs. Apple. Is that true or a detail to complement your disguise?"

Phoebe did not answer immediately. Finally, with no inflection, she said, "A detail."

Remington was hard pressed not to smile in the face of her irritation. If not precisely angry with him, she was definitely annoyed. Because he was curious as to what she would say, he asked, "Is 'Apple' really your surname?"

"I can't think of a single reason to tell you."

"Ah. Tit for tat, then. You'll tell me yours if I tell you mine."

"Yes."

"That's fair." He suspected that response would frustrate her because she was spoiling for a fight, and he knew he was right when he heard a growl rumble deep in her throat. He did smile this time, although he was careful to turn away when he did it.

Once the silence settled between them, Remington concentrated his listening on the sounds around him. The wind swayed pine boughs so they brushed against one another, whispering to him as he passed under them. He never saw the small animals that ran for cover in the underbrush, but he heard them leaping and scurrying. Casting his focus to more distant points, he listened for something out of place, the sounds of snorting horses, hoofbeats, conversation among their riders. He heard none of that.

In consideration of Phoebe's safety, Remington had chosen to take an indirect, meandering route to Frost Falls. He did not expect to cross paths with her abductors, but then he wasn't confident that he knew their destination. Not Twin Star Ranch. In spite of what he had observed or concluded thus far, he still could not believe they would be so foolish as to show themselves at the ranch with any kind of demand. It was perhaps a little more likely that they would go to Frost Falls, but Remington didn't hold out hope for that.

If Mr. Shoulders had spoken the truth, if Phoebe had not misunderstood, then some kind of arrangement had already been made. Remington did not believe for a moment that Phoebe Apple had been plucked at random. She was chosen.

Remington considered his father's request in light of this new way of thinking. Had Thaddeus gotten wind of something he was not prepared to communicate by telegram? Before Phoebe told him what Mr. Shoulders said, Remington's opinion of his father's excess of concern was that it reflected his new wife's apprehensions. Now *there* was a woman who liked to exploit opportunities for drama. Remington typically took it in stride, and on the one occasion he hinted at her predilection to Thaddeus, his father had shrugged it off, excusing it as a consequence of Fiona Apple's life—and success—in the theater.

If Thaddeus's cautions had indeed been prompted by Fiona's fears, then it was unfortunate that those fears had been reinforced. Remington thought they might never hear the end of it. If, on the other hand, Thaddeus had suspected something was going to happen, then Remington damn well wanted to know more about that.

"They took my ring."

Remington required a moment to make sense of what Phoebe was telling him. During the quiet, her thoughts had obviously gone in a very different direction than his. "Perhaps it will be recovered when they're caught. You'll get it back." He could see she was doubtful. "Tell me about the ring."

"It was not merely a detail, if that's what you're thinking."

"I wasn't."

"Of course, I wore it so I could pretend there was a Mr. Apple somewhere, but Mrs. Sweetings gave it to me. It was her wedding band, not that she was sentimental about it because Mr. Sweetings was an adulterer and in bed with a chorus girl when he died, but still, she meant well, giving it to me as a gift. And now it's gone. I suppose I've come around to realizing that I miss her. Miss all of them, actually. My friends."

"If your friends are in New York, what's waiting for you in Frost Falls?"

"Family."

He thought she might elaborate, but she didn't, and he let it rest. "You were right about something," he said instead.

"You'll have to be specific. I'm right about a lot of things."

Her butter-wouldn't-melt reply made him laugh. "Very well. You were right. I *was* peeved."

"I wouldn't say that. I would never say that. I might say you were brooding, sulking even, but not the other."

"You really are getting some of your own back."

"Hell-bent on revenge."

That response, delivered with unexpected saucy humor, set him back in his stirrups. He thought he might catch a wicked gleam in her eye compliments of the moonlight, or maybe a hint of sauce in her smile, but when he looked over, he could only see her in profile. No gleam. No sauce. He made peace with that. He knew what he heard; there was no reason for her to punctuate it.

"So tell me why you thought I might be one of them," he said.

"Oh, you don't want to hear that now."

"I asked, didn't I?"

"Then here it is. You were dressed in a similar manner. The hat. The long coat. You were armed. I know. I know. The same could probably be said of others, but you were the one in my car. When you fell in the aisle, I thought you were unconscious. It was only later that I began to doubt it. I covered your gun with your coat, but it seemed odd to me that no one searched you. They accepted that you were not a threat. In their position, I don't think I would have done that. The men wearing the blue scarves walked right over you. How could they know for sure that you weren't a threat unless you were one of them?"

Remington was thoughtful, offering no argument to counter hers. "Go on."

"I could hardly feel anything save for relief when you showed up at the cabin, but then there was the fact that you *did* show up. I dropped breadcrumbs, as you said, but I don't think they could have been easy to follow, or even to find. It seemed entirely possible that you found and followed because you knew the route we would take. And when I asked about going back to the train, you didn't seem terribly concerned for the passengers. I know what you said about repairs to the track being underway, but could I believe you? I asked you where we were going; you said the nearest town was Frost Falls. But that didn't answer my question. Not really. How could I be sure you weren't lifting me out of the frying pan and leading me into the fire?"

He didn't say anything for a time, waiting. Then, "Is that everything?"

"That, and your reluctance to tell me your name."

"Reluctance?"

"Unwillingness."

Remington nodded. "Might as well call it what it is."

"You're right."

"So what do you think now?"

"Truth? I'm not sure, but at least I'm no longer tied to the foot of a bed."

"Yes, there's that."

Phoebe's mouth quirked. "Is there anything you want to say?"

"Not particularly. There's logic from your perspective; I can see that. Except for that lapse when you shot Mr. Shoulders, your fear did not completely overrun your ability to think."

"And yet here I am with you. The jury's still out, wouldn't you say?"

"What do I need to say that will make you believe you are safe?"

"You know the answer to that."

He did. "'What's in a name?'" he quoted. "'That which we call a rose by any other name would smell as sweet.'"

"Do not flatter yourself. What I smell from here stinks like three-day-old fish."

Remington grinned. "That's worse than bull shit, I'll give you that."

"Keep your bullshit and tell me your name."

"I will, but you are not going to like it."

She waited him out.

"Remington Frost." He expected almost anything from her except what she did. Phoebe yanked her right foot from the stirrup with the intention of giving him a good kick. She missed his leg and jabbed the toe of her boot into Bullet's side. The gelding cut sideways, the mare startled, Phoebe grabbed the reins, and both horses took off at a run.

Chapter Six

Phoebe had no hope that she could stay in the saddle, not a prayer that she could remain on her mare's back. She let go of the reins and gripped the saddle horn with both hands. Every bounce exploded firecrackers of pain up and down her spine. Her teeth chattered. She bit her tongue. She squeezed her thighs together and tried to lean forward. Apparently it was the wrong thing to do. The mare shot ahead again.

Phoebe was aware of the gelding keeping pace, but she did not dare look over. Once she saw Remington's hand cross her field of vision as he tried to grasp the reins. When he failed, she lost sight of him and his horse. The next time she was aware of him was when she felt his arm at her back. Bullet was so close now that she felt his heat. Her leg, the same leg she had used to try to kick Remington, rubbed against his. The half circle of his arm tightened and then she was lifted out of the saddle and held flush to his side while the gelding responded to his direction to ease up and finally stop. The mare ran on, but Phoebe didn't care about that. She was dangling a couple of feet above the ground and Remington Frost did not appear to find that a burden.

Between breaths she managed to wheeze out, "I am going to lose the baby."

"I am reversing my opinion," he said, lowering her to the ground. "There *is* at least one empty chamber in your six-shooter."

"That's just mean." She bent a bit at the waist to catch her breath. Her lumpy belly presented an obstacle. "I'm done with this. Turn your head." Without waiting to see if he complied, she raised her skirt all the way to her hips and began to unfasten the bolster that was tied at the small of her back.

Watching her, Remington just shook his head. "Do you want my knife?"

"Don't say a word. Not a word."

"Hey, you were the one who started this. That was a vicious kick you gave Bullet. I'm only trying to help."

"Uh-huh." She managed to loosen the strings and pulled. "You know I was aiming for you, not your horse."

"I think we've already established that your aim leaves something to be desired. Maybe you should think about spectacles."

"I have a pair. I wear them for close work. I don't need them for distance."

"If you say so."

Phoebe removed the bolster and let her skirt fall in place. She smoothed the material over her hips, transferring the bolster from one hand to the other as she did so. The lightweight wool skirt was ill fitting where it had been stretched, but there was nothing that could be done about that. She looked up at Remington. She held the bolster under one arm; her free hand rested on her hip.

Remington regarded her from under raised eyebrows. She really had no shame. He swore if she had solid wood flooring under her feet, she would be tapping a foot at this very moment. The only thing stopping her was the inability to make a satisfying sound.

"Well?" she asked. "What happens now?"

"We get your mare. She's about a hundred yards ahead. This would be your opportunity to walk."

Phoebe was not sorry about that. She started off. "You can ride ahead. You don't have to provide an escort. I imagine you've had your fill of that."

"I'm not leaving your side."

"Whose idea was it that you escort me at all? Fiona's?"

"My father's."

"I'm thinking it was at Fiona's urging. She doesn't trust me to put one foot in front of the other without specific instruction."

"Seems to me you've mastered it."

"Exactly." She moved the bolster from under her arm so she could hug it in front of her.

"You've removed that thing but is there some reason you're still attached to it?"

Phoebe stopped, turned the bolster over, and held it up for him to see the small row of buttons on the underside. "Jewelry, the remainder of my money, a half-dozen lace handkerchiefs, and an extra pair of spectacles. Inside. Wrapped in cotton batting."

"I see. Explains lumpy."

"It does indeed." She went back to hugging the bolster and picking her way carefully over the uneven ground. "What if the mare bolts?"

"Then you'll have to keep walking."

She did just that. "How long were you following me?"

"Escorting, remember? Not following."

Phoebe did not take the bait. "How long?"

"I was supposed to board the same train as you in Chicago. That's where I was. I didn't make it. I caught up to you in Saint Louis but I kept my distance."

She nodded. "So it was you. I don't know why you thought it was necessary to try to convince me otherwise."

He shrugged. "I decided to join your car after we left Denver."

"So you've always known I wasn't carrying a child."

"Let's say I was surprised when Mrs. Tyler told me you were. I didn't have an unobstructed view of you in Saint Louis or in the car. But Mrs. Tyler also mentioned lumpy and I confirmed that for myself when I helped you to your feet in the cabin."

She remembered brushing against him as she stood. "Oh. How did you recognize me?"

"I have a photograph. Would you like to see?"

"No. I wouldn't. Did Fiona give it to you?"

"My father did. He showed it to me not long after he brought Fiona back from New York. Wanted to introduce me to her family."

"So Fiona was not as forthcoming."

If there was bitterness there, Remington could not hear it. "My father said you turned down his invitation to accompany him and your sister to Twin Star."

"That's right."

She did not elaborate and Remington did not prompt her. There was no more exchange of words until they were within forty feet of the mare. "Stay here," he said. "I don't want you to spook her." When he dismounted, he gave her Bullet's reins before he started to approach their runaway. The mare was grazing on some tufts of grass but came along willingly when Remington took her by the bridle and nudged her to walk. He spoke to her as they closed the distance to Phoebe, telling her all the things she needed to hear, above all that what happened was not her fault.

He walked right into Phoebe's sour look so he supposed she'd heard all of it. He held out his hand for Bullet's reins and indicated she should move to the left side of the mare. "Always mount from the left."

Phoebe did not want to get back in the saddle at all, but she didn't tell him that. The short walk had provided some relief in spite of the fact that the going had been slow. "Hold this," she told him, pushing the bolster at Remington's chest. "I need both hands." She grabbed the saddle, managed to get her left foot in the stirrup on the second try, and hauled herself up and over. There was no helping the soft moan that escaped her lips as she settled in.

"Are you all right?" asked Remington. She gave him a short nod. "I was prepared to give you a leg up."

"I know. At the risk of humiliating myself, I wanted to see if I could do it on my own." She held out a hand to him and pointed to the bolster. "You can give me that."

"I don't think so. You proved you could get on a horse. I need you to prove you can stay on one." He gave her the mare's reins. "Just until I tie this to my saddle. Then I'll want them back."

Phoebe watched him secure the bolster, satisfied that it would not fall off, then watched him mount Bullet with the careless grace of long practice and settle into the saddle. Unlike her mare, Bullet did not stir under his sure command. She returned the reins before he asked for them and then they were moving. She appreciated that Remington set an easy pace. She wanted no part of another wild ride.

"How long would you say before we reach Frost Falls?" she asked.

"Half an hour, maybe a bit more. That will put us in sight of the town. I'll want to scout the situation, make sure it's safe to go in."

Phoebe appreciated that he had considered that. She had not. "Where do you suppose they are?"

"You mean Shoulders and his men?"

"Yes."

"I wish I knew. You understand I'm trying to avoid them until I get you to Twin Star."

"Yes, but shouldn't you try to avoid them afterward as well?"

"That's not going to happen. The sheriff will put a posse together and Northeast Rail will pay for it. There will be a reward, a substantial one, I'm thinking, because they abducted you. The railroad doesn't like it when someone steals their passengers."

He said this last in ironic tones that made Phoebe smile. "It will all be salacious fodder for the Eastern newspapers, won't it?"

"And the Western dime novels."

"Oh, lord."

"Hmm. Prayers probably won't change a thing, but they can't hurt." When he glanced at her, he saw her shoulders had slumped slightly. "Sit tall."

Phoebe corrected her posture.

Remington said, "I've been wondering about something you said to Shoulders. Or rather, that you told me you said."

"What's that?"

"You led him to believe that a ransom demand would not work, that there'd be no one willing to pay. Do I have that right?"

"I told him that, yes."

"Did you believe it was true or were you lying to explain to him why his plan wouldn't work?"

The moonlight did not help Phoebe see Remington's face clearly when the brim of his hat shadowed his features, but what she heard in his voice made her think he was serious. Patiently, she said, "I explained to him why his plan wouldn't work because what I said was true."

"My father invited you to come to Twin Star. You said so yourself. Do you really think he wouldn't pay a ransom demand?"

"I like your father, and I had an opportunity to spend time with him when he was courting Fiona and she was in rehearsals. I formed the impression that he is a hardworking cattleman with a good sense for business. In New York, he was generous to Fiona but not foolish with his money. Paying ransom would be foolish."

"Because it might not guarantee that you would be released?"

"There is that, of course, but more to the point, your father has no obligation toward me."

"You think so little of yourself?"

"No, not at all. I simply think there is no reason your father should part with money on my behalf."

"You're Fiona's sister."

"That would be a reason for her to consider paying the ransom." She briefly raised a hand to stop the comment she was anticipating. "I know. Fiona has no money in her own right so that brings us around to your father."

"You really don't know him," said Remington. "If Shoulders puts the demand to him, my father will pay, then, regardless of whether you are safe or not, he will hunt them down and take his money back from their cold, dead hands."

Phoebe stared at him. "I did not imagine he was so ruthless."

"Practical, I would say. Not ruthless. A great believer in justice, is my father. As I said, you don't really know him."

Phoebe conceded the point and asked, "How well do you know Fiona?"

Remington recognized dark and dangerous waters. "Not particularly well. It's been six months since—"

"Seven. Seven months since they were married."

"Right. Seven. I travel some for the ranch. Purchases. Sales."

"Your father told me you are a lawyer."

"I am a rancher who went to law school. There's a difference. Ask my professors."

Phoebe didn't believe his professors thought he was anything but brilliant. Thaddeus certainly thought so. She considered saying something to that effect, but he was going on.

"I do the contracts because my father would rather not."

"So you don't have occasion to spend much time in Fiona's company."

"That's right. When I'm around, I'm out of doors. There is a lot of land to cover, always something to do. I often take my meals with the hands in the bunkhouse so the newlyweds can be alone."

"You still think of them as newlyweds?"

"Sometimes. It depends on your sister's mood."

"Mm."

Remington could make nothing of that noncommittal reply, but he thought it probably signaled the end of conversation regarding Fiona. For that, he was grateful.

"What sort of name is Remington? Family name?"

"Someone's family. Not mine. It's the sort of name given to a child whose father was threatened with a shotgun if he did not do right by the child's mother. At least that's the story I've been told. Never changes."

"You don't believe it?"

"There are some holes in it. My mother miscarried twice before she had me."

"But you were the firstborn, if the not the first conceived. Perhaps they were sentimental."

"Uh-huh."

She smiled. "Were they happy, your parents?"

The question did not surprise as much as the wistfulness that accompanied it. "I think so. I was five when my mother died, but I have some memories of her and my father sharing the sofa, talking quietly while I played on the floor. Pa always kissed her on the cheek after dinner, thanked her for the meal. He never said that I should do the same; I just did."

"Fiona said her name was Mary and that she died not long after giving birth."

He nodded. "Childbed fever. There were two more miscarriages after me before she gave birth to a girl. My sister lived for a week. Mother died a few hours later."

"How sad you must have been." When he added nothing to her observation, she said, "It seems a bit odd that Thaddeus didn't remarry until Fiona."

"What's odd about that?"

"Well, he was happy in the marriage. In my experience, men remarry quickly when they've been content with the arrangement."

He smirked. "You have a lot of experience, have you?"

If she did not have to hold on to the saddle, she would have ticked off examples on her fingers. "Mr. Adams, the greengrocer. Mr. Weaver, the stage manager. Mr. Kosterman, my landlord. Mr. Wallace, the man who delivered milk on Mondays and Thursdays. Oh, and Mr. Jakob Meir, the diamond merchant. He was always very good to Fiona, but there was no question but that he would remarry within his faith. Shall I go on?"

"For the love of God, spare me." He heard her chuckle as he was certain she meant him to. In spite of himself, he was curious. "So they all remarried soon after their wives died?"

"Within six months. Mr. Kosterman, within three weeks, but one of the tenants, Katrina Harmon, never tried very hard to hide her interest in him, and there was suspicion that Mrs. Kosterman might have had help falling down the stairs. No one can say for sure."

Remington whistled softly as he tipped back his hat. "You left a colorful neighborhood to come here. Do you think you'll regret it?"

"It seems there are plenty of colorful characters around."

"You are not going to have a confrontation with outlaws every day."

She was not only speaking of outlaws, but she did not tell him that. "Do you think Fiona regrets leaving New York behind? Is that why you asked?"

"She's never said anything like that to me, and I was just making conversation."

"Hmm." Phoebe shifted in the saddle to redistribute the pressure on her bottom and inner thighs. She winced.

"Are you all right? Do you want to stop? Dismount and rest? You could walk for a piece."

"If I get off this horse, I swear to you I will not get back on."

"Then we should keep moving."

She nodded and felt she should explain her lack of equestrian skills. "There was no reason for me to learn how to ride. I walked or hailed a cab. Mostly I walked."

"Sometimes what you learn to do depends on your geography. You can learn to ride at Twin Star if you have a mind to."

"Can I think about that? Later?"

Laughter rumbled quietly in his chest. "Yes. Later."

"Has Fiona learned to ride?"

"No, but she can manage a horse and buggy."

"Really?" Phoebe tried to imagine it and couldn't. "There was always a cab waiting for her at the front of the theater to take her home or to dinner. If she walked anywhere, it was in the park, usually with a gentleman at her elbow."

"I got that impression. Not from your sister. From my father. He told me he competed with a throng of younger men, richer men, and better-educated men for Fiona's attention. It was a coup when she chose him."

"He was young enough, rich enough, and smart enough. And Fiona liked his smile. She told me so."

"His smile," Remington repeated.

"Also, his confidence. She said that's what made her take notice. He stood back, eyes focused, and waited, just as if he knew she would come around to him. Confidence is attractive." Her head swiveled in his direction. "Why didn't you tell me your name?"

The sudden change in subject made Remington feel as if he'd been pushed sideways. Still, he was able to answer without missing a beat. "I wasn't certain about you."

"But you knew who I was."

"Yes, but it doesn't necessarily follow that you were an innocent in this. Even Mrs. Tyler had questioned whether you were taken or went willingly."

"Well, I didn't fight them, that's true. After firing my pistol and missing my target, I didn't see the point. That doesn't mean I was part of some grand scheme to rob the passengers."

"Not only rob the passengers," he said, "but to extort money from my father."

"You know that's something an insane person might say."

"It sounds like it now, but for a while it did not seem so far-fetched."

"How could you even imagine that I had the resources in New York to organize and manage a robbery here?"

He shrugged. "Hadn't gotten around to parsing all the particulars." Which was a lie, but he thought he told it well enough to pass scrutiny. "Let's just say that I came around to another way of thinking, same as you."

"Yes," she agreed. "Let us just say that."

He slanted her a grin. "I can understand why my father enjoyed your company."

"He said that?"

"Several times."

"He was kind to say so. I enjoyed spending time with him as well."

"You're like her, you know, but I suspect you've heard that before."

"I have." No matter how well intentioned, Phoebe did not

find the comparisons flattering. She hoped her curt reply would keep him from waxing on. It did, more or less.

"You're what? A dozen years younger than your sister?"

"Something like that. I am not being coy. For myself, I don't care, but Fiona is sensitive about her age. Most actresses are."

"Twenty-three?" he asked.

"Fiona would be flattered."

"I was asking about you."

She sighed. "Yes. I'm twenty-three."

"I'm twenty-eight."

"I didn't ask."

"Weren't you curious?"

"Actually, no." She bit back a moan as the mare struggled with her footing over rocky ground. "We have to be there soon. Tell me we'll be there soon."

Remington lifted his chin and indicated a landmark up ahead. "See that rise? The break in the trees? That's where we're going. You'll wait there and I'll take a look around."

Phoebe closed her eyes and then opened them abruptly when she felt herself sway in the saddle. Remington must have seen it as well because she felt his hand on her upper arm, steadying her. "Sorry," she said.

"Frankly, I don't know how you've stayed with me this long."

"Nerves, I expect."

"I expect you're right."

Neither of them spoke again until they reached the breach in the trees. Phoebe protested when she realized his intention was to get her off the mare, but she lost the argument. He left her leaning against the brown scaly bark of a spruce while he removed the blanket from under the mare's saddle and spread it on the ground. Although she was nearing collapse, she was also so stiff that he needed to help her down. He pulled on the edges of the blanket and wrapped them around her legs, and then he closed her cape, pulling it tightly about her arms. He took her hands in his, briskly rubbing them to infuse them with heat.

"Do you want my coat?" he asked.

"No. You're riding. You'll need it."

"And you're sitting on the ground. You might need it more."

"If you leave it, I won't wear it."

"Lord, but you're stubborn. All right. I believe you." He released her, stood. "What about the bolster? Would you like me to leave it with you?"

"What would I do with it now? It's too lumpy for a pillow, and there's nothing inside that I need."

Remington nodded. He tethered the mare close by. "If someone comes who isn't me, get on the mare and ride. I know you can do it."

Phoebe was not as confident, but she said she would. He must have trusted her because it was mere moments later that he was gone.

Chapter Seven

Benjamin Madison looked across the wide expanse of the Butterworth's lobby and dining room for Thaddeus Frost. The hotel had opened its doors in the middle of the night to accommodate the passengers who spilled out of No. 486. When the Northeast train had finally arrived, four hours late, the scene was as close to bedlam as Ben thought he'd ever see. That was some thirty minutes ago and it was not much calmer now. People who had been waiting for hours at the station, and he was one of them, were relieved by the arrival and full of piss and vinegar when they heard the explanation for it. The passengers were tired and excited at the same time. It did not take long for them to turn cranky.

Ben saw Thaddeus standing near the kitchen door, his silver-threaded head and sharp profile inclined ever so slightly toward the sheriff. Whatever the sheriff was saying must have been agreeable to Thaddeus because the two showed none of the usual indicators that they were about to be at loggerheads. Ben wended his way through the crowd so he could hear what was being said. He should have been at Thaddeus's side, but one of the passengers, an older gentleman with a broken and bloody nose, needed assistance, and Ben had stopped to help. In the short time it took to find a chair for the man and thrust a clean handkerchief at him, Thaddeus had disappeared, or at least it seemed that he had. Now, when Ben was within ten feet and a cluster of six bodies away, he was stopped again, this time by a tug on his coat sleeve.

He was prepared to jerk away but good manners prevailed. He drew back the step he was about to take and looked down at his sleeve. The hand was small, possibly delicate, but that was hard to tell when it was balled into such a fierce fist that the knuckles were white. At the risk of being swallowed by the press of people around him, Ben hunkered down so he was eye to eye with the little girl who had attached herself to him like a burr.

Ben was confronted by a pair of blue eyes made unnaturally bright by a wash of tears. "I'm Ben," he said. "You're not here alone, are you?" Blond ringlets bounced as she shook her head. A tear dropped, then another. Ben used the pad of his thumb to wipe them away. "What's your name?"

"Madeleine."

He nodded. "Well, Madeleine, as it happens, I'm looking for someone, too. He's gone missing in the crowd. What about you? Who's gone missing?"

She sniffed and wiped her nose with the back of her hand. "Mama."

"Let's find her, shall we?" He looked pointedly at his sleeve then at her. "Let me have your hand."

"No. I want up."

"All right. Makes sense. No one can see us down here." He still had to pry her fingers from his sleeve, but when he did, she practically leapt at his chest. He hoisted her as he stood, giving Madeleine her first opportunity to look around from this new vantage. Her head had barely broken the surface of the sea of black hats, white hats, bowlers, bonnets, and dainty feathered hats when she began squealing and squirming like a piglet rooting for a sow's teat. That meant, he assumed, that Mama was in sight.

"Madeleine!"

Ben rocked back on his heels as Madeleine threw her arms up in the air and leaned toward her approaching mother. He couldn't see the woman, but recognized her advance as people began to step sideways to allow her through. When she finally appeared, Ben saw a blend of exasperation and relief on the woman's face. He knew that blend, having seen it often enough in the handsome features of his own mother. With a chuckle, he gave Madeleine over.

"Thank you," she said. "I called for her, but I don't know how she could have heard me." Awkwardly, she held out a hand. "I'm Mrs. Bancroft. And this is Madeleine."

"We've already introduced ourselves." He took her hand. A reticule dangled from her wrist, swinging like a pendulum. "I'm Ben Madison."

"Are you from around here, Mr. Madison?"

"I am. I wasn't on the train, if that's what you're asking."

"It was, in a way. Maddie, you have to loosen your arms around my neck, dear. Mama can't breathe. Yes, that's better." She smiled apologetically and raised the hand with the dangling reticule. "Could you take this, please, and give it to the sheriff?"

Ben removed the reticule, which was heavily decorated with seed pearls and jet beads, and clutched it in his hand. "This isn't yours?"

"No. I saw it lying on top of the lobby desk when we were filing in from the train. My only excuse for not understanding the significance of it immediately is that I was still brain-addled from our experience."

"Understandable. But what is the significance of it?"

"It belongs to *her*. Mrs. Apple. The woman they took."

Ben's eyebrows, a deeper shade of red than his hair, rose high enough to ladder his forehead. He looked at the reticule and then at Mrs. Bancroft. "You're sure?"

"Yes. I saw them take it from her after she shot the big man. I told Mrs. Tyler that I saw it, described it to her, and she agreed with me. I left Maddie with her while I went to get it. There was no one at the desk to ask if I could have it, so I took it upon myself to carry it off. I intended to give it to the sheriff straightaway, but then Mrs. Tyler found me and said Maddie had disappeared, and"—here she took a deep, steadying breath—"and here I am."

"So you are," said Ben. Madeleine had removed her face from her mother's neck and was staring at him. He smiled at her. "Yes, I'll give it to the sheriff. Of course I will." He looked around. The bodies were pressing in again. "Should I help you find—" He stopped, regarded her questioningly because he could not remember the name.

"Mrs. Tyler. No. Unlike my daughter, she will be precisely where I left her. But thank you."

Ben bounced the reticule in his palm. It had some weight to it. All those seed pearls and jet beads, he supposed. "I'll take this to the sheriff right now. That's my boss with him. He'll be interested, too. He surely will."

Thaddeus Frost made room for Ben when he saw him coming. "Thought I lost you there, son. I want you to hear what Jackson has to say."

"Sheriff," said Ben as he stepped in to make the third leg of a triangle. He raised the hand holding the reticule and unfolded his fingers, presenting the beaded bag on his open palm.

Jackson Brewer looked Ben over. The young man was as lean and ropy as a steer at the end of a cattle drive, and Jackson supposed that no amount of his ma's cooking was going to put meat on the boy's bones. The same could not be said for Thaddeus Frost. Ellie Madison had been setting a fine table for the owner and his hands at Twin Star since before Mary passed, and it was finally beginning to show on Thad just north of his belt. Of course, those extra pounds could have something to do with Thad's relatively recent marriage. His old friend was probably spending more time in bed than he was on the range.

"What do you have there?" asked Jackson. "Someone lose that?"

"A woman gave it to me. She's from the train and she says it belongs to Phoebe Apple. 'Course, she called her Mrs. Apple. I didn't understand that." He addressed Thaddeus. "She's not married, right? You never mentioned it."

"She's not married. Apple's her surname, same as it was my wife's. The woman's just mistaken. Where is she?" Impatient, not waiting for an answer, Thaddeus looked over the crowd. He was half a head taller than either Benjamin or the sheriff, and therefore in a better position to do so. "I want to talk to her."

"She's probably still holding her daughter. Madeleine

will be easier to spot. Yellow hair." He made a curling gesture with his index finger. "Ringlets."

"I see her." He brushed past Ben without excusing
himself.

Jackson looked after Thaddeus, shook his head, and then
turned to Ben. "Man on a mission. Go on. You tell me what
you learned. I've got my deputy getting volunteers for a
search party."

"I volunteer."

"Actually, you've already been volunteered. Thad did
that."

"Good." He nodded for emphasis and handed the reticule
over. "Mrs. Bancroft said the reticule was taken from her.
Mrs. Apple, that is. Or Miss Apple. Whatever."

"Let's agree to call her Phoebe."

"All right. Phoebe. This was hers. She shot the big man.
That's what she called him."

"Mrs. Bancroft."

"Uh-huh. Phoebe shot the big man and the bag was taken
from her."

Jackson Brewer knuckled the salt-and-pepper stubble on his
chin. "That squares with what I heard from two fellas here-
abouts. Similar story. They were in the car, saw what happened,
or mostly saw. They were pretty shook."

Ben screwed his mouth to one side and rubbed the back
of his neck as he considered the presence of the reticule.
"How do you think it got here?"

"Now there's a mystery because she's sure not around."

"You're sure? The Bancroft woman says she saw the bag
just lying there on the lobby desk when she was walking in
with everyone else. Didn't hit her right away, then it did, and
she went back for it. Now you know what I know." His attention turned once more to the beaded reticule. "You think
we should open it?"

"No. I think *I* should open it. You can be my witness."

"All right," Ben said easily.

Jackson loosened the strings, inserted two fingers inside
the bag's throat, and spread the opening wide. "Feel's like

some lady stuff inside." He pulled out a red enameled etui and gave it to Ben. "Needles, thread, and such in that."

"I know what it is."

"Comb. Tortoiseshell. My wife has one like it." He handed it over. "Spectacles." He held them up to eyes. "Looks like they're for reading." He refolded the stems carefully and laid the spectacles on Ben's open palm. "Pencil. He put the stub behind his ear. "Ah. Here's a notepad. Could be she wrote something down."

"Sure. Something like, 'Here I am; come get me.'"

Jackson curled his lip. "Don't let Thad hear you making light of this. He'll cuff you so hard your ass will never find your head." The tips of Ben's ears reddened and the sheriff knew his point had been taken. He opened the slim notepad, wet the pad of his thumb, and used it to riffle the pages. The first six were blank. He stopped on the seventh. "Well, I'll be damned."

Ben leaned in and tried to see what Jackson was looking at. "What is it?"

"Not, 'Here I am; come get me,'" he said. "But close enough." He held up the pad so Ben could read what was scrawled on the paper.

"Two thousand dollars." His blue eyes widened. "They want two thousand dollars?"

"Seems so. Looks like we're seeing a ransom demand." Jackson wet his thumb again and carefully lifted the page. As expected, there was more. "'Cooper's Rock,'" he read. "There's a dollar sign. Guess that's where we're supposed to leave the money."

"That's where we'll find her?"

"You *are* young, Ben Madison. Always thought it was the carroty hair that made you seem so, but I'm thinking now that you just are."

"I'm twenty-three, old man."

"We'll take it up later. I'm just saying, that she's not going to be at Cooper's Rock. That's not the way these things are done. Go get Thaddeus and haul him over here. He needs to be part of this." As soon as Ben began to push his way through the crowd, Jackson turned another page. He read what was written and nodded to himself. Yep, that's how he would have set it up, too.

The Jones and Prescott bank manager was already among the volunteers gathered by Brewer's deputy when he was summoned to open the bank. The two thousand dollars Thaddeus Frost required cleaned out two shelves of the safe, but to his credit, Mr. Pleasance never once hesitated. He bundled the cash, stuffed it into three cloth sacks, and handed it over. He did not ask for a receipt.

There were nine chosen from among twenty-five volunteers. Sheriff Brewer wanted a manageable number and nine was what he settled on. He divided them into three groups of three with instructions to fan out when they were closing in on a mile from Cooper's Rock. The two flanking groups would act as scouting parties, while the head of the spear would ride straight ahead to the rock.

Thaddeus and Sheriff Brewer were at the head of the spear. Thad chose Ben as the third member of their group, which was fine with Jackson. They each carried a sack of money secured behind their saddles.

Jackson insisted that all parties stay quiet and alert, but he allowed himself, as leader, to bend his own rule. Sidling his mount closer to Thad, he asked, "Are you holding out much hope that Remington's tracked her down?"

"I always hold out hope."

"That's some kind of luck that he was on the same train, in the same car, as she was."

"That's why I hold out hope, Jackson. Sometimes we get lucky."

"Hmm."

"You weren't standing there when I introduced myself to Mrs. Bancroft. Her eyes went as wide as silver dollars when I told her my name. Her companion, that Mrs. Jacob C. Tyler, put a hand over her heart, she was that taken back. They told me all about Remington setting out after Phoebe."

Ben moved in on the other side of Thaddeus. "You talking about Remington?"

"We are."

Ben nodded. "Thought I heard his name. Some piece of luck, him being on the train and all. And in the same car."

Jackson gave Thad a significant look that included an eyebrow arched halfway to his hairline. *See?* it said.

Thad ignored his friend. "Jackson was just saying something like that."

"Not something like it," the sheriff said under his breath. "Exactly like it."

Ben leaned forward in his saddle and looked past Thaddeus to Jackson. "What was that, Sheriff?"

"Nothing worth repeating." He backed off, let them ride ahead, while he marked their location and then waved to the other groups to go their separate ways. "Slow and steady," he told Ben and Thad when he caught up. "We don't want to give anyone a reason to shoot us."

They reached Cooper's Rock, a cliff with a broad face that overlooked a waterfall and a swiftly moving stream a dangerous distance below. Moonlight turned the rush of water into a silver ribbon. They tethered the horses a safe distance from the edge of the bluff and removed the money sacks.

"Should have brought a damn lantern," said Thad.

Jackson snorted. "Sure, and make ourselves bigger targets than we already are. Let Ben look around. He's got young eyes."

Ben rolled those young eyes at both of them and went searching for the note that was supposed to be left for them. It did not take him long to find it wedged in a crevice, one white ragged edge sticking out. The piece of paper was the same size as the notepad. Jackson had predicted that when he saw a couple of pages had been torn out. The paper wasn't folded, but Ben didn't glance at it. He handed it to Thaddeus. "Figure it's your right to see it first."

Thaddeus took it, squinted at what was written, and handed it to Jackson. "Don't have my damn spectacles either."

Jackson had to squint as well, but he could make out the writing. "You know that cabin up at Thunder Point? The one that belonged to Old Man McCauley when he was prospecting in these parts?"

"I know it," said Thaddeus.

"Can't say I do," said Ben. He took the note when the sheriff held it out to him.

"That's a map from here to there," said Jackson. "Waterfall. The stream. The cabin. Even drew a little smokehouse, though I would have figured that for having collapsed years ago."

"So that's where we'll find her?"

"Yes. We leave the money here, and that's where they're telling us she'll be."

But she wasn't.

Chapter Eight

Phoebe hit the back of her head against the tree trunk when she snapped awake. She rubbed her scalp and found thin scales of bark in her hair. She picked them out one at a time and flicked them away, wondering all the while how long she had slept. She could not remember nodding off, or even feeling the need to do so. One moment she was wide awake, and then she wasn't. Afraid it would happen again, she stood, biting back a groan as she did. She was not merely stiff; she ached. There were kinks in her joints and knots in her muscles. Stretching cautiously, she turned at the waist until her spine cracked in a most satisfying manner. Something parted the underbrush, disturbed the branches, and she paused, head cocked, waiting. Remington had not told her what sort of animals she could expect to encounter while she waited for his return. Her experience with four-legged creatures was largely limited to the feral cats that managed the rat and mice population in and around the theater.

Phoebe softly cursed her rescuer, but there was no real heat in it. Her lips barely parted around the words. She couldn't fault him for not warning her about wild animals when she had more to fear from the ones who stood upright and carried guns. Phoebe's eyes wandered to the mare, which was still tethered exactly as Remington left her. The horse had not stirred in any significant way in the last several minutes. She took that as a good sign. Whatever had moved between the trees was not a threat. Phoebe breathed out slowly, relaxed.

She stepped out from under the canopy of pine boughs

and stared up into the cloudless night sky. Turning her back on the moon, Phoebe cast her eyes across the deep blue dome that was an unfamiliar heaven. Stars glittered and winked. Some formed shapes that she knew from myth and literature and she marveled at their constancy.

When her neck began to ache, she lowered her gaze from the heavens to the horizon. Here, too, was a view she had never known before. The scale of the mountains had been unimaginable to her until now. She liked to think that she knew something about canyons and passes and trails after years of navigating the streets and alleys of Manhattan, but this, *this*, was something else again. These magnificent mountains, with their snowy slopes and icy peaks glinting in the moonlight, were a revelation, and Phoebe found herself grateful for this moment, no matter how it had come about, that she was witness to this stark, naked beauty.

She shivered, though not entirely because she was cold. The movement was enough to pull her out of her reverie. She returned to the deep shadows under the towering spruce. The blanket tempted her to sit. To avoid that end, she picked it up, drew it tight around her shoulders, and told herself to think about anything besides the cold in her marrow and the ache in her bones.

It was inevitable, then, that she thought about him.

Thaddeus had spoken at some length about his son, in part because he was proud, and in part because Phoebe was interested enough to ask him questions. While Fiona gave Thaddeus her polite attention, which did not involve actual listening, Phoebe hung on every word.

Thaddeus Frost was a natural storyteller, and Phoebe believed he deserved an appreciative audience. She was that. His accounts of his son's accomplishments were not boastful, but they were told in the context of life at Twin Star. Phoebe knew herself to be fascinated by the vastness of the space he described—square miles, not square blocks—and the activities that were utterly foreign to her—roping, mustering, and branding. As Thaddeus told it, Remington was reluctant to head east to school, although "reluctant" was perhaps an understatement since there were arguments that included colorful language and violent threats, and on at least one occasion, a physical altercation that ended only after Thaddeus put his headstrong son in a watering trough.

"He was just a young'un then," Thaddeus had said, smiling crookedly, even a little wistfully. "Needed to get it out of his system. Don't know as I would try to take him down today. Don't know as he would give me a reason."

So Remington had gone off to school, started poorly in the hopes of being called back to Twin Star, but when Thaddeus remained dug in, Remington's pride would not allow him to fail. Thaddeus credited himself for his son's success, but he did so in an ironic way that conveyed the achievement was all Remington's.

Until Phoebe met Remington Frost, she had imagined him in her mind's eye as a younger version of his father, but it was obvious to her now that his mother had been the architect of his finer features. While his height and angular profile were likely passed to him from Thaddeus, his dark eyes and inky hair were not. Thaddeus had blue eyes and salt-and-pepper hair that had once been more brown than black. Remington had a slight slant to his eyebrows even when they were not being lifted in a sardonic manner. That slant was absent in his father. The bridge of Thad's nose was broader than his son's, and only part of that could be blamed on the fact that it had been broken in a bunkhouse brawl. Remington's chin was set more narrowly than his father's, the cheekbones higher and better defined. Their mouths were similarly shaped, each with a fuller lower lip, but Remington's mouth curled slightly at one corner as if he were darkly amused or privy to a secret so profound that a gun to his head could not make him reveal it.

It was a very fine mouth, she thought, pressing her own lips together. Intriguing because of the secret it might be holding back. Maddening because of the amusement it took no pains to hide.

If Thaddeus Frost was a handsome man—and Fiona's presence on his arm was evidence that this was the case—then

Remington Frost was, well, he was just about as beautiful as a man could be and still have his feet firmly in his boots.

Phoebe listened for the sounds of those boots now. Nothing. It never occurred to her that he would not return, only that he might not return before the strength of her shivering shattered her bones. Shifting and resettling the blanket across her shoulders did not help. She stamped the ground, walked around the tree in ever-widening circles before she spiraled toward it again, and briskly rubbed her hands together. When nothing she did helped any longer, she dropped to the ground and huddled against the trunk.

Remington pulled Bullet up hard when he heard the approach of men and horses. The horses were quieter than the men, which he supposed was good in this case because he recognized one of the voices right off. He waited until they passed some fifty yards away and then he followed. If they didn't recognize him immediately, at least his position at their backs would make it more difficult for them to shoot him.

There were three of them. That number alone would have made them suspicious if Remington had not been the cautious sort, but he could not think of a single reason that Sheriff Brewer's deputy would have been involved in the robbery of No. 486, and it was surely Blue Armstrong's Georgia drawl that he'd heard. Neither of the men riding abreast of Blue had the shoulder breadth that Phoebe had described, and certainly the deputy did not.

Even as he thought it, Remington saw Blue raise his hand and halt the three-man search party. The horses shifted, but the men did not. They fell quiet, and it was into that quiet that Remington called out and identified himself.

"Easy," he said as they began to turn. "Don't draw your guns or I might think I'm mistaken."

"Jumpin' Jesus on a griddle! Like to scare us to death, Remington."

Grinning, Remington holstered his Colt and urged

Bullet forward. He spoke quietly when he reached them. "Jumpin' Jesus on a griddle? That's one I haven't heard you use before."

Blue Armstrong, as much a fixture in Frost Falls as the canted sign above the Songbird Saloon, removed his hand from the butt of his weapon and lowered his voice to a whisper as well, or what passed for a whisper if one's throat was full of gravel. "Been saving it for the right occasion. Seemed like it should be now."

Remington nodded at Bob Washburn and Hank Greely. Washburn managed the bank and Greely owned the livery. Neither of them were candidates to carry out a robbery and abduction. "Where are the others?"

Blue used a thickly knuckled forefinger to tip his hat back a notch. "'Course you'd know there'd be others. Stands to reason, don't it? Your pa, the sheriff, and Ben left the ransom for the little gal at Cooper's Rock and then headed northwest. We're the right flank, but except for you, we ain't heard or seen nothin'. Sutherland, Hopewell, and Jeremiah Ripley are the left flank. I expect it's the same for them, else there'd have been a dust up."

"Northwest from Cooper's Rock?"

The deputy nodded. "Saw them go but we're charged with scouting for the robbers, same as the others. Brewer told us there'd be a message waiting for them at the rock telling them where to go next. I figure it's the cabin up on Thunder Point. Our instructions are to stay around here. Keep a look out. Sooner or later, someone's comin' for the money."

"Hmm." Probably later, Remington thought. If he'd heard the deputy talking, then there was good reason to believe the robbers had also. Maybe they would try to make their approach from the left, in which case there was a fair to middling chance that the other search party might spot them, provided, of course, that Sutherland, Hopewell, and Ripley were not also given to noisy speculation.

Remington directed the party to the tree line where there was better cover. "She's not at Thunder Point," Remington told them when they'd settled their horses.

"Of course she ain't," said Armstrong. "Because you ain't. Your pa, once he knew for sure that you were on the train and headin' out to find her, figured you for being her best hope."

Bob Washburn pushed his spectacles up the bridge of his nose. "It seems Thad did not misplace his faith. Where is she? Close by?"

"Not as close as I'd like."

"But she's safe," Greely said, seeking confirmation.

"Yes. When I left her, she was safe."

Blue raised his knobby chin a few degrees so he could scratch the underside. His mouth quirked and he moved it back and forth several times as though swishing a mouthful of water. "Now, see? That's what I'm not understanding. Why ain't she with you? Why did you leave her?"

Trust Blue to get right to the point, Remington thought. He avoided the explanation by asking, "How did anyone know to leave the ransom at Cooper's Rock?"

"Damndest thing, that. Some lady from the train saw Miss Apple's reticule on the lobby desk at the Butterworth and made sure it got handed over to the sheriff. There was a notepad inside that had a message about the money and where to put it. Bob here took it right out of the bank's safe."

Mr. Washburn modestly waved his contribution aside. "Brewer couldn't find anyone who saw it being placed on the front desk, but a number of passengers saw it lying there."

Remington considered the possibilities. "The woman who returned it. Was it Mrs. Jacob C. Tyler?"

"That doesn't sound right," said Washburn. He looked to Blue for help, but the deputy shook his head, helpless to recall the name.

Greely said, "Bancroft. Her name was Bancroft. I heard Ben tell someone."

"My second guess," said Remington. "Miss Apple's reticule was on that lobby desk because one of Miss Apple's abductors put it there."

Greely nodded. He had a long face, eyes that were set a fraction too close to his nose, and a thin slash of a mouth.

He rarely looked anything but grim. "That's what Brewer thinks. Your father also."

"Bold," said Blue Armstrong. "Bold as the painted mouth on a whore. To walk in the hotel like he was one of the others, set the bag down, and disappear again, well, that's bold."

Remington wondered if that were strictly true. "He probably stayed in the hotel long enough to be certain the reticule was found and his message was delivered. He couldn't leave it all to chance. At least I wouldn't."

The deputy once again adopted what passed for his most thoughtful pose, tipping his chin and scratching the underside with his fingertips. "No, you wouldn't, by God, but then you have your daddy's brains and a college education." He pronounced it "edgy-cation." "It's my opinion these fellas aren't that smart."

Remington did not disagree with the deputy. He'd held that same opinion early on. He had only recently begun to revise it. There was more planning than he had originally thought, and much less happenstance. He had even come around to wondering if Mr. Shoulders might have noticed Phoebe's breadcrumbs and let them be, and if that were so, it followed that Shoulders was not concerned that he could be caught. What the man wanted to do was set the odds in favor of Phoebe being found.

"I am going back for Miss Apple," Remington said. "You better stay in the area, continue to scout it out, but I don't think you're going to come across them. Most likely they suspect a trap's been laid. Wherever you are, they are somewhere else."

"Then shouldn't we go with you?" asked Mr. Washburn.

Remington shook his head. "Brewer's expecting you to be here. So is my father. This is where I'll return. Watch for me. For us. And for God's sake, don't shoot. We might be leading the horses, not riding."

"How close do you reckon they are?" Willet Putty, one of the pair now wearing a blue kerchief around his neck, not his face, put the question to his brother.

Doyle Putty squinted hard at the hidey-hole where he'd seen a fortune being tucked away. "Can't say." He was lying flat on the ground with a good view of the bluff as long as he kept his eyes narrowed and his chin tucked. The tucking wasn't difficult. He hardly had a chin to speak of. Willet was on his left; Natty Rahway was on his right but ten feet distant. "You think it's safe to go out there, Natty?"

"You go on," Natty said, shrugging his broad shoulders and wincing only slightly. "Give it a try. If you get shot, then Willet and I will know it's not."

Doyle was up on his haunches before he fully understood the consequences of what Natty was saying. He dropped back down and jabbed Willet with a sharp elbow when he heard his brother chuckle.

"Seems like we've been waiting an age," said Doyle.

Natty pulled himself up on his forearms. "We all saw them split. I said then that one of us should tail each group, but you and Willet wouldn't have any parts of that."

Doyle's lip curled. "Yeah, because you wanted to stay with the money. Me and Willet think it should have been one of us that followed Thaddeus Frost to the rock."

"No point in having that argument again. Here we are. Here we'll wait."

"Should've kept the gal with us," Doyle grumbled. "Insurance. Plus, she was prettier than you."

"You think there is a rock they wouldn't have turned over to find us? I sure don't. We knew how this would go when we agreed to do it. Besides, you and Willet have plenty of spoils to split between you."

"Sure, but we have to find buyers for everything except the cash. That ain't easy."

Natty was not sympathetic. "Your problem. And didn't I offer each of you the opportunity to stay at the cabin?"

"Uh-huh, and like I said, you wanted to stay with the real money."

"She *is* the money, Doyle."

Doyle spit. "The money's the money, and it's right over there."

"So are three men on horseback across the way. Opposite the bluff. Go on. Look. They're riding single file, weaving through the trees. You can just make them out. Can't say for sure which one of them is Jeremiah Ripley, but he's the one I was told about. The sharpshooter. The one that can put a bullet in your skull from sixty yards. He's not quite that far now. You want to chance it?"

"No."

"What about you, Willet? You want to go?"

"No. Never said I did."

"Then the prudent thing is to wait."

Watching the riders position themselves opposite Cooper's Rock, the Putty brothers agreed that what was prudent was best.

Chapter Nine

She was sleeping when Remington came upon her, the blanket wrapped around her like a chrysalis so that he could only see the top of her head. Knowing that she had to be exhausted, it didn't seem right to wake her and so he stood there, waiting to see if she'd sense his presence and come around on her own.

The silver comb that she had left behind on the trail for him to find was lying on the ground near the crown of her head. He wondered if it had finally lost its mooring in her thick hair or if she had taken it out. He bent, picked it up, and turned it over in his hand. He wasn't partial to practicing the kind of law that would put him in a courtroom, but he thought he could make a case that Phoebe Apple was guilty of a crime against nature when she twisted that dark cascade of hair into a knot and stabbed it with the comb. It seemed to him that some kind of penalty should be exacted, and right now, it would have to be the price of the comb. He dropped it in his vest pocket, reckoning that he had as much right to it now as she did, and if she thought differently, he wouldn't mind clarifying his position to her. She'd argue her own points, of course. It would be like law school again, moot court, this time with Phoebe Apple as his worthy adversary.

He remained hunkered beside her, waiting for her to stir. When she did, it was because a shudder went through her. It was no gentle stirring, and still she did not wake. The cocoon that was the blanket changed shape as she drew her knees closer to her chest and burrowed as deeply as she could in the bed of pine needles.

He laid his hand on what he hoped was her shoulder and said her name. She surprised him by bolting upright and doing it with enough force to knock him on his ass and disturb the angle of his Stetson.

"All right, then. You're awake." Watching her closely, he resettled his hat. "But you're not awake, are you?" He waved a hand in front of her face. She blinked but not in a way that made him confident she was aware of him. He pushed to his knees, inched closer, and clapped her lightly on the back. He said her name again, this time insistently, and was rewarded when he felt her spine go rigid. He kept his palm flat against her back and waited.

Phoebe breathed in deeply and then expelled that lungful of air in careful measures. She wrestled her arms free of the blanket and pressed the heels of her hands to her eyes.

"It's time to go," he said, increasing the pressure of his hand at her back.

She nodded. Her hands fell to her lap. "I never meant to fall asleep."

"I believe you." He rose higher on his knees and started to shrug out of his long coat. "I want you to take this." The fact that she did not argue this time was a clear indicator of just how cold she was. He settled the coat around her shoulders, stood, and helped her to her feet. "We get plenty of brisk nights in May. Sometimes we get snow."

Phoebe shivered hard. Remington's coat slipped off her shoulders.

"Sorry. I probably shouldn't have said that." He picked up his coat before she could. "Here. Take off your cape and slip your arms in these sleeves." When Phoebe proved reluctant to part with any source of warmth, Remington did not try to persuade her. He undid the frog at her throat before she could bat his hands away, removed the cape with the flourish of a bullfighter, and then flung it to the side to keep her from reaching for it. His leather duster was ridiculously large for her, but that made it easy to wrap her in it. The shoulder seams hung well below her shoulders and only the tips of her fingers were visible outside of the sleeves.

Phoebe stood taller than many women of Remington's acquaintance, but the hem of his coat brushed the tops of her ankle boots. Although Phoebe did not strike him as a particularly vain woman—unlike her sister—he knew better than to smile at the picture she made. She had managed to make herself smaller by huddling in his coat the way she had huddled under the blanket. He turned up the collar so that it covered her ears and tucked her hair under it.

Phoebe did not stop him, but as soon as he was done, she patted the top and back of her head, clearly searching. "I've lost my comb," she told him and began to look around for it.

Remington glanced around as well. "I don't see it." Which was true on the face of it. "I can come back when there's daylight and look for it." He anticipated that she would harbor some doubts about that, but she merely nodded and thanked him. Awkward explanations aside, he was tempted to pull the comb out of his pocket and give it to her. He didn't, though, because the memory of her silky hair still resided in his fingertips and he had not changed his mind about the comb being an accomplice in the crime against nature.

"We need to go. I came across one of the search parties. They're waiting for us."

Phoebe's eyes sought out the mare. Now her expression was doubtful. "I don't think I can ride. Maybe if someone were chasing me . . ." She shook her head. Her rueful smile wobbled, turned watery. She brushed impatiently at her eyes and sucked in a breath. "I should try. I should do at least that much."

Remington did not attempt to dissuade her. It was a long walk to reach the search party, longer still to reach Frost Falls. The more ground they could cover on horseback, the better. He considered setting her sideways on the saddle, but was not hopeful that she could stay on the mare's back.

"What if you rode with me?" he asked.

Phoebe shifted so she could see past him to where he'd tethered his horse "I don't think Bullet would like that."

"I don't think Bullet would know. I figure that soaking wet you weigh about as much as my little finger."

The absurdity of that made her chuckle. "All right. We'll try that."

Remington mounted first and then pulled Phoebe into the cradle made by the saddle and his thighs. Sitting sideways as she was, he forced himself to remain stoic in the face of all her fidgeting. To keep the saddle horn from digging into her hip, which seemed to be her main concern, he suggested that she put her arms around him. She complied without hesitation. Once she embraced him, it was natural that her head would fall against his shoulder. He had not anticipated that. If he turned his head the slightest degree in her direction, his chin would brush against her hair.

"Is it all right for you?" she asked. "You're probably warmer now."

Warmer? He might have laughed if she had not been so naively sincere. "I'm fine," he said. There was nothing he could do about the slight catch between the words. He cleared his throat, tugged on his collar. "Just fine."

They rode for miles that way, Bullet making the journey in an easy walk, the mare tethered and following close behind. Remington did not know precisely when it happened, but at some point, Phoebe fell sleep again. Her head lolled into the curve of his neck. He did not try to wake her.

Remington counted six men patrolling the general area where he had left only three. He did not make himself known until he had identified all of them, although that did not take long. He recognized his father immediately and then sifted through the other riders until he spotted Jackson Brewer. He saw Ben when the younger man separated himself from Blue Armstrong's side. Mr. Washburn and Hank Greely were slowly circling the group. He threw up an arm and caught Greely's eye. The dour livery owner changed course, heading toward him. Without any kind of observable signal, the others followed.

Remington raised a finger to his lips as they neared and held it there until they nodded their understanding. He waved his father forward and the other riders separated to accommodate Thad's approach. His father's smile was grim as his eyes wandered over Phoebe.

"She's all right?" he asked quietly. "When she wasn't at Thunder Point . . ."

Remington said, "Exhausted, but not injured."

"Then they didn't . . ." Thaddeus left the rest of thought unspoken.

"No. They didn't."

Thaddeus exhaled, turned his attention to Remington. "You, son? You're all right? Mrs. Tyler informed me that you took a hard fall on the train. Cracked your head, she said."

"Of course she did. Mrs. Tyler is a busybody." Sensing that Thaddeus was searching for a lump, Remington touched the side of his head above his temple. "But she isn't wrong. Hurts some. Had worse."

Thaddeus leaned over, set his hand on Remington's shoulder, and gave it a squeeze. "Thank you. What you did, well, it's appreciated."

Remington did not shy away from his father's gratitude. He knew it to be true whether Thaddeus said it aloud or not. His father's next words, though, he wished were left unsaid.

"Fiona will want to thank you as well."

Remington shrugged. It had the effect of removing his father's hand from his shoulder, although that was not his intention. "There's no reason for her to thank me."

"On the contrary." Thaddeus withdrew his hand. "You're bringing Phoebe to her, not Northeast Rail. She'll understand that."

Remington felt Phoebe stir. He wanted to get underway before she woke, but he could not leave before he knew the answer to the question uppermost in his mind. "Is Fiona waiting at the station?"

"No. At the ranch."

Remington did not ask for an explanation. In hindsight, he thought he shouldn't have asked the question. His father's terse response led him to believe Thaddeus was disappointed in Fiona, perhaps embarrassed by her absence. Remington did not want to expose that to the men who had formed a semicircle around them and were waiting patiently for an indication they could leave.

Remington nodded to them. "We can go."

Jackson Brewer elected to stay back to corral the other search party and return to Frost Falls with them. Thaddeus had made it clear, over the strenuous objections of everyone else, that if Phoebe was returned safely, he had no interest in the money. The sheriff was free, of course, even duty bound, to go after the thieves for what they stole from the passengers, but Thaddeus was not interested in pursuing them about Phoebe's abduction.

Remington kicked up an eyebrow when this was explained to him, not by his father as he would have expected, but by Sheriff Brewer. Remington had no response save for silence. He remembered telling Phoebe his father would demand justice; now it seemed her safe return was what mattered. There probably wasn't an argument in his head that the others had not already put forth. The best thing for now was to keep his own counsel. Phoebe might want her pound of flesh, and if she did, he could imagine Thaddeus being persuaded to change his mind. There ought to be a reckoning for Mr. Shoulders and the pair hiding behind blue bandannas. There ought to be, if not justice, then an accounting of the facts. Remington could support that, even if his father could not.

Phoebe woke less abruptly than she had the last time Remington put his hand on her shoulder, but she was no less disoriented. It required several moments for her to understand the hard pillow beneath her cheek was Remington's chest and that what she was gripping so fiercely in her fists was not a sheet but his shirt. Her fingers were stiff, and she unfolded them slowly, removed her hands from beneath his jacket and vest, and then released him entirely.

"Easy," he said, his voice close to her ear. "It's better if you hold on to something."

Phoebe clutched his jacket sleeve and raised her head. Her vision was blurry and her eyelids felt weighted by the depth of her sleep. "Where are we?"

"About three miles from Frost Falls."

That brought her upright. She became aware of two things simultaneously: The saddle horn was digging painfully into her hip again, and they had acquired an escort. Blinking rapidly, she twisted her head around to search for a familiar face. Her gaze settled on Thaddeus Frost and she felt her heart ease and the knot in her stomach uncoil.

Thaddeus had a broad, welcoming smile for her. "Sleeping Beauty," he said. "Is that right? Is she the one?"

"If I look as if I've slept one hundred years, then she's the one."

Remington put up a hand to halt his father's objection. "Come around on my left before she breaks her neck trying to get a good look at you."

Thaddeus slowed, let Remington get ahead, and then came abreast of Phoebe on the other side. He continued as if there had been no interruption. "You look fine, Phoebe. Real fine. My son here treating you like he should?"

"More like he's treating me as I deserve. I have no complaints."

"That's good, then." His cheeks puffed as he blew out a breath. "Not everyone coming to Colorado gets the welcome you do."

"I wondered. Have you found them?"

"No. That's the sheriff's problem now." He introduced her to the others, saving Ben Madison for last. "You remember me telling you about Ben? He's our housekeeper's boy. Been with us about as long as she has and turned himself into a pretty good wrangler."

Phoebe was able to call up the memory of that conversation. She remembered thinking Thaddeus had raised Ben as if he were a second son, though he never described their relationship in that manner. There was affection there, if not a bond as strong as Thaddeus shared with Remington, and Ben had been privileged to have advantages growing up in the Frost household that he could not have had elsewhere. From Thaddeus she also knew that Ben and Remington scrapped as youngsters, tolerated each other in their middle years, and grieved separately when Remington was sent away to school. Older by five years, Remington returned a man full grown and Ben was still doing everything he could to catch up.

"I remember," she said. Her eyes swiveled to Ben. "It's a pleasure to meet you. Forgive me for not greeting you properly." She glanced at her hands and then offered Ben a regretful smile. "I have to hold on."

"You're doing fine, miss. Remington's got you squared away."

He did indeed, Phoebe thought. In spite of his suspicions and his nagging, he had never once given up the mantel of guardian angel. He could have abandoned her and told his father that he'd tried, but his sense of honor would not allow it. Thaddeus must have depended upon Remington's decency, his pride. It said a great deal about the son Thaddeus had raised. It said a great deal about Thaddeus.

"Why did those men take me?" She addressed the question to the group at large, but expected that Thaddeus would answer first. He did not. It was the deputy who filled the silence.

"Most likely they knew you had some connection to Mr. Frost here. Ain't likely you were chosen because they thought your condition was, um, delicate. Remington told us about the package you was carrying. Even miscreants and commandment breakers generally have respect for a woman with child, so it beggars the imagination that they would steal you away on account of that."

"Then there *was* a ransom demand?"

"Oh, sure," Blue said. "Two thousand dollars."

Phoebe gaped. "That can't be right." She looked at Thaddeus. "You did not pay them, did you? Tell me you did not give them a single cent." But she saw that he had. "Oh, Thaddeus. You are too generous."

Blue Armstrong slapped his thigh and chuckled. "No one's faulting Mr. Frost's generosity, miss, but you have to allow that this time it was extortion that moved him to clean out the bank's safe."

"Two shelves," said Bob Washburn. "Just the two shelves."

Phoebe ignored that exchange and said to Thaddeus, "You got it back, isn't that right? We are all heading into town because you got your money back."

Thaddeus said, "We got you back. That's how it works."

Phoebe frowned deeply. "But the passengers. They lost their possessions." As an afterthought, she added in outraged accents, "Those men took my reticule."

Thaddeus chuckled. "We have your reticule. One pair of reading spectacles, a red enameled etui, a tortoiseshell hair comb, one pencil stub, and a notepad. Is that about right?"

"Yes," she said quietly.

Remington said, "I guess Mr. Shoulders wasn't moved to return your derringer."

"So it's true you had a gun," Blue said. "Heard it back at the hotel from some of the passengers, but I wasn't sure I could believe them."

"It was just a palm pistol," she said, feeling heat creep into her cheeks.

"A pea shooter," said Remington.

Ben spoke up. "And you really shot one of them?"

"I *barely* shot one of them."

"Regular Annie Oakley," Remington said. He wasn't able to stop her from jabbing him with an elbow, but she was so close and his coat was so heavy he barely felt it. To give her some satisfaction for having made the gesture, he whispered for her ears alone, "Your aim is improving."

Phoebe swallowed the bubble of laughter that tickled the back of her throat. A shadow crossed her face as a cloud crossed the moon. When her features were exposed once again to the moonlight, her expression was grave and her attention was all for Thaddeus.

"When we get to Frost Falls, I have to face passengers who don't care overmuch that I am returned unharmed. They don't care much at all about your two thousand dollars. What they care about are the things that were stolen from them. Money. Jewelry. Memories. Weapons."

"No one is forgetting that," said Thaddeus.

"Mr. Frost is right, Miss Apple," the deputy said.

Remington said, "It's in the sheriff's hands."

She fell quiet, considering, and then nodded faintly. "There's one other thing," she said at length.

"What's that?" asked Thaddeus.

"Where is Fiona?"

Chapter Ten

Fiona Frost reached out blindly and patted the side of the bed where her husband slept. Thaddeus was not there. He was *always* there, so it took some time for her to reconcile his absence with what she could recall of their last conversation. Her recollection was incomplete. She had pieces of a whole that would never come together without someone showing her how they fit.

She pushed herself upright and leaned back against the iron rails of the headboard and for once did not mind how one of them pressed uncomfortably against her spine. The discomfort helped focus her thoughts. Her eyes were not so bleary from sleep that she couldn't make out the shaft of moonlight stretching across the hardwood floor and spilling onto the rug. The silver-blue light was like a stain, muting the vibrant reds and golds in the rug to shades of gray and dirty mushroom. Turning away, she pinched the slim bridge of her nose between a thumb and forefinger and closed her eyes again.

"Phoebe," she whispered. "We argued about Phoebe."

Fiona let her hand fall away from her face and took a deep breath through her nose. She held the breath until she couldn't, and then she pursed her lips and let the air escape in a long, nearly silent whistle. Throwing back the covers, Fiona swiveled her legs over the side of the bed. Only one of her black velvet slippers was waiting for her. She had a vague memory of throwing the other. She looked around, located it under the padded stool in front of the vanity, and thought it had probably ricocheted off the armoire. She would not have thrown it at the vanity and risked damaging the mirror or breaking any of the little pots of cream and rouge or the atomizers that contained specific blends of fragrances that had been made especially for her.

She'd been angry, but she never lost control of a scene.

Fiona put on the slippers, found her robe draped over the oak chest at the foot of the bed, and shrugged into it. Without looking in the mirror, she gathered her thick auburn hair in one fist, expertly twisted it into a knot at the back of her head, and stabbed it with two ivory picks to keep it in place.

The front room of the house was deserted, as was the kitchen, Thad's study, the dining room, and the formal parlor where they were meant to receive guests but rarely had occasion to do so. Fiona did not open the doors to any of the other bedrooms. Instead, she stood beside the great iron stove in the kitchen, close enough to the housekeeper's quarters to be heard without projecting her voice beyond what would have been the first eight rows in the theater.

"Ellie! Wake up! I need to speak to you." Fiona listened for sounds that Ellie Madison was stirring, and when she heard movement on the other side of the door, she lit a lamp and set it on the kitchen table. She folded her arms and rested one hip against the cold stove. She waited.

When Ellie Madison appeared, Fiona took note that it was unlikely that the housekeeper had been deeply asleep. She was a trifle too clear-eyed and alert to suit Fiona. It occurred to her that Ellie had been keeping vigil while Fiona herself had gone to bed.

She watched Ellie pat down wayward wisps of dark red hair as she stepped into the kitchen. A heavy plait hung over her right shoulder and she brushed it back. Her robe was haphazardly tied and she repaired that now, cinching it tightly around her waist.

Fiona was not impressed. Every gesture was calculated to support the façade that she had been sleeping, but Fiona did not confront Ellie with her suspicions. The housekeeper would never admit it, and it was of too little consequence to haggle over now. And, Fiona thought, there were practical reasons not to antagonize Ellie Madison. She would never get a cup of coffee if she did not sheathe her claws.

"They're not back," said Fiona.

Ellie nodded. "Seems so. The house is quiet. There's a light in the bunkhouse that I can see from my room. Could be some of the hands are still up waiting for them."

"Should I ask someone to ride into town? Ralph Neighbors? Scooter Banks?"

"Late for that now. The train's known to be delayed from time to time."

"It was supposed to arrive around nightfall. Midnight's come and gone. Thad told me that delays mostly happen during the winter months."

"That's true, but . . ." She glanced at the coffeepot on the stove. "How about I make us a pot of coffee, and we'll wait them out right here?"

Fiona appreciated the other woman's predictability. She nodded. "Would you? I'd like that. Truth be told, the company more than the coffee." She continued quickly when Ellie hesitated on her way to the stove. "Oh, but I'd appreciate the coffee as well."

"Hmm."

Fiona thought Ellie added something under her breath, sly boots that she was, but the need for coffee overwhelmed her need to know what she'd said. "The stove's gone cold." She offered this information almost apologetically, although they both knew it was not her job to start a fire or keep one going.

"I'll take care of it."

Fiona felt her hackles rise at the housekeeper's cheerful response. No one could be that pleased about breathing life into the iron behemoth, no one, that is, unless the motive was to prove it could be done to the woman who had never been able to do it. Fiona wanted to spit, but her eyes fell on the coffeepot as Ellie pumped water into it, and she swallowed instead.

She watched Ellie as much for her movement as to take her measure. Fiona had never been able to help herself in that regard. If making comparisons had not been in her nature, it would have come to her eventually. Survival in the theater depended upon it, and she was, above all else, a survivor. When she competed for a role she wanted, she got it, and competition for a man was no different.

There was no denying that Ellie Madison was a handsome woman, a description generally approved for a female maturing gracefully through her forties, and Fiona allowed that perhaps in her youth Ellie had been quite pretty. Her hair had possibly once been a vibrant shade of red, but the years had faded it. Still, although Fiona looked for gray threads that were an inevitability of aging, she never found one. In Fiona's mind, the answer was simple: Ellie plucked them out.

Fiona had known of the existence of the housekeeper before she ever left New York, indeed, before she agreed to marry Thaddeus. It was a comfort, though someone— *Phoebe*—might call it a condition, to know that she would not be responsible for preparing meals or beating rugs or doing laundry. Meeting Ellie Madison, though, had been, if not a revelation, then an eye-opener. Here, then, preparing coffee in the kitchen, laying kindling in the stove, setting out exquisitely painted china cups, was her husband's mistress of the last twenty-plus years.

Thaddeus had failed to mention that when he proposed, nor did it come up in conversation as they traveled more than half the length of the country, and at no time since she had arrived at Twin Star had there been a single reference to the long affair. She did not expect to hear the truth from Ellie, but her husband's silence was insulting. Did he truly believe she didn't know?

Fiona understood why Thaddeus had chosen her over Ellie Madison. Serving as a man's de facto wife as Ellie had these many long years made the housekeeper as intriguing and desirable as the furniture she dusted. She was attractive, like the cabriolet chair at the head of the dining room table; she was familiar, like the oil painting that hung above the mantel in the formal parlor; and she was comfortable, like the brushed velvet sofa in the front room with its slightly worn arms and a depression in one corner of the long cushion that perfectly fit Thaddeus's trim ass.

Fiona was realistic about her own attributes. Ellie Madison could cinch the belt of her robe until she couldn't breathe and Fiona was confident that the housekeeper still would not be able to achieve her classic hourglass silhouette. It was also unfortunate that Ellie spent as much time as she did out of doors without benefit of a parasol or a decent bonnet. Fiona's complexion was fashionably pale. The kindest thing she could say about Ellie's was that it was not.

Fiona was tall but not statuesque or overblown. She commanded attention with a gesture; she could turn her wrist and be certain that eyes would follow its graceful arc. Ellie was short, but not squat. Fiona allowed that a fair description would be that she was petite, and if Ellie garnered a man's attention now, it was because she teased him with a plate of steak and eggs or an apple fritter.

Fiona inhaled deeply as Ellie poured coffee into her cup. "You certainly have my attention," she said on a whisper of sound.

Ellie poured a cup for herself and returned the pot to the stove before she sat. "How's that again?"

"Nothing important. Just finishing a conversation I was having in my head." She raised the cup, holding it in her palms instead of by the delicate stem, and regarded Ellie over the rim. "This is nice. Thank you."

"It *is* nice," Ellie murmured. "Not much occasion to take a moment."

Fiona said nothing. Ellie's observation was true for her, but Fiona had plenty of occasions to take a moment. Lots of moments. Ellie knew it, too. Her comment was meant to get under Fiona's skin, and it did, but not so that the housekeeper would ever know. Fiona had not been the toast of the New York stage because of her face and figure, although they certainly helped. No, she had been celebrated by critics and audiences because she could *act*.

Ellie sipped her coffee. "Your sister might have missed

a connection somewhere. It's possible she had to take a later train. That would explain why Ben and Mr. Frost haven't returned. I bet they're still waiting for her."

It grated on Fiona's nerves every time Ellie called Thaddeus "Mr. Frost," just as if she had never shared his bed. Fiona had asked Thaddeus about it once, thinking they might have an honest dialogue about that relationship, but he had only said that it was Ellie's way, and as many times as he'd told her to call him "Thad" or "Thaddeus," she never had. There was no discussion after that, no room to maneuver the conversation in the direction she wanted to take it.

"Phoebe doesn't miss anything," said Fiona. "That includes trains, I expect." She raised her cup to her lips, drank. It was not so hot that it burned her mouth, but more than warm enough to feel it sliding down her throat. Only a few drops of whiskey would have improved it. Then she would have felt it in the pit of her empty stomach.

"Do you want I should fix you something?" asked Ellie. "I can scramble some eggs. Warm the heel of bread left in the box over there."

Fiona shook her head, chuckled humorlessly. Her eyes, the color of amethysts, slid sideways toward the drinks cabinet in the dining room. "Hair of the dog maybe."

"You don't mean that."

"I do, but I am going to resist. I know when I've had too much to drink. Afterward anyway. Not when I'm drinking."

"Mm."

Fiona looked sharply at the housekeeper. "There's something you want to say? Some judgment you want to pass?"

"No and no. I'm familiar, is all."

"Who? You?"

"No. My husband. He had a taste for it."

"Well, that's where we're different. I don't have a taste for it. I don't even like the taste of it, it's only that sometimes . . ." She stopped, not because she didn't know what she wanted to say, but because when she heard the words in her mind, she knew she did not want Ellie Madison to hear them, too. Ellie, though, was nodding faintly, as if she'd heard them anyway, and that made Fiona want to throw something, if not at the oh, so sympathetic housekeeper pretending to be her friend, then at the wall. Contrary to her instincts, she didn't. She carefully set her cup in its saucer and folded her hands in her lap, where Ellie could not see how tightly they gripped the folds of her robe.

"I'm out of sorts," she said. Her tone captured the nuances of both embarrassment and regret. "I worry about Phoebe. I think it was a mistake for her to accept Thad's invitation. I miss her. Of course I miss her, but I could have gone east, was planning to, in fact, and then Thaddeus informs he's asked her to come here. Can you imagine? Without consulting me, he just extended an invitation."

"Mr. Frost has been making decisions on his own for a lot of years."

"Is that an excuse?"

"No. An explanation."

Fiona did not like having her husband's behavior explained to her, but then she'd opened this particular can of worms.

"If I may speak plainly, Mrs. Frost?"

Fiona could not imagine what she could say that would stop Ellie, so she nodded.

"If you want to be included, then you will have to remind him how to do it. Mary was his partner as much as she was his wife. I know because she was my friend, and she would not have stood for a man who wanted to run this ranch like a renegade. Do you take my meaning?"

Fiona was not sure that she did, but she nodded anyway. "I should have gone with Thaddeus to the station. He wanted me to."

"I know."

In her lap, Fiona's fingers uncurled. She smoothed her robe, lifted her hands, and raised her cup to her lips again. "I was still so . . . so *annoyed* with him that I let him go off on his own. Oh, I know Ben's with him, but it's not the same. I should be with both of them, welcoming her. Thaddeus barely made her acquaintance in New York and Ben doesn't know her at all. They might not even recognize her."

"I believe Mr. Frost has a photograph of Miss Apple. Or at least he did."

"A photograph?"

"Mm-hmm. He showed it to me. She's a lovely young woman, is your sister."

Fiona wondered how she did not know about the photograph. And if she did not know that, how much more was there that she didn't know. Rather than being comforted by the knowledge that her husband could easily identify Phoebe, the realization disturbed her.

She stood, took the pot off the stove, and added coffee to her cup. She offered the same to Ellie, who shook her head. Shrugging, Fiona returned to her seat.

"I still can't imagine why Phoebe agreed to come. There's nothing for her here."

Ellie's eyebrows rose in mild surprise, not disapproval. "You're here."

Fiona was a long time answering. "I am, aren't I?" Her gaze fell on her reflection in the coffee. "Yes, I certainly am."

Chapter Eleven

"Where's Fiona?" asked Thaddeus when Ellie stepped out to greet them on the long front porch.

"Shh. Lower your voice. She's sleeping. Finally. Was up most of the night waiting for you. Drank more coffee than any ten cowpokes sitting around a campfire, and I just tucked her in, thank you very much."

Remington dismounted, took the three steps to the porch in a single leap, and enveloped Ellie Madison in a fierce hug. "Seems like someone else drank their fair share of coffee. You've got the jitters." He looked over his shoulder at Ellie's son. Ben was still sitting beside Phoebe in the buggy they'd used to bring her to Twin Star. "Your ma's got the jitters, Ben!"

"I don't think those are the jitters," Ben said mildly. "Better put her down. I'm not sure she can breathe."

Remington set Ellie on her feet. She promptly slugged him in the shoulder with the heel of her hand. "Idiot child. My Ben was always smarter than you."

"No denying it." He swooped, kissed her cheek, and stepped aside so she could stop ducking and weaving in order to look around him.

Ellie extended her arms in a welcoming gesture. "Come here, young lady, and let us get you inside. Ben, help her down from the buggy. Oh, but what a journey you must have had. Remington, you and Mr. Frost take her bags. Do you have a trunk, dear? Yes? Remington will get that in a moment."

Phoebe took the hand Ben held out, grateful for the support

when her legs wobbled once her feet were on the ground. After Thaddeus formally introduced her to the housekeeper, she was hustled inside while Ellie directed the men around with the authority of a stage manager. Phoebe felt completely at home.

"We've spruced up Ben's room for you," said Ellie. "You're not putting him out. He likes the bunkhouse fine, and come warmer nights, he'll be just as content to sleep out of doors."

"I won't," said Ben in an aside to Phoebe. "But she's right about the bunkhouse."

Ellie cuffed her son on the side of his head. "I heard that. Go on with you; show her to the room. And quietly. Mrs. Frost is sensibly asleep as all of you should be." She herded Phoebe and her escorts down the hall then shooed the men out of the room after they dropped the bags and the trunk.

Phoebe stood beside the bed, hands folded in front of her, waiting for Ellie to shut the door. When she did, the housekeeper was on what Phoebe considered to be the wrong side of it. "You don't have to stay," Phoebe said. "I can manage."

"Of course you can, but that doesn't mean you should. Go on. Sit down before you drop. I'm going to unpack a few things for you, find your nightgown and slippers. Do you have a robe?"

Phoebe nodded dumbly.

"Good. I'll set that out for you as well. There's fresh water in the pitcher. The washstand's in the corner. Soap is beside the basin. Towels and washcloths in the cupboard underneath. Up to you if want to clean up before you crawl under the covers. Piss pot's under the bed. First thing, though, is to get you out of Remington's coat. You must have been chilled to the bone if he gave you that."

There was no resisting her, Phoebe realized, and there was no shame in surrendering to a superior force. In every way it was exactly what she needed to do, and in short order her bags were unpacked with every item disappearing into the wardrobe or the chest of drawers. When directed, she closed her eyes and raised her face for a gentle washing, and with no protest at all, she stripped down to her shift and then allowed a perfect stranger to exchange it for her nightgown.

She was asleep before her head touched the pillow or she would have known Ellie tucked her in.

"Snug as a bug," Ellie said when she entered the kitchen. Thaddeus was slathering sweet cream butter on bread she had baked that morning while Remington was using a knife to get the last bit of strawberry preserves out of a jar. She laid Remington's long coat over the back of his chair. "A spoon would serve you better, Remington. Where's Ben?"

Remington did not stop his excavation work. "Took the horses and the buggy to the barn, then he was going to turn in."

Ellie pulled out a chair and sat. "It wouldn't hurt you to do the same." She looked pointedly at Thaddeus. "You, too, Mr. Frost. I don't know that I've seen you so tired after a week of riding the property and sleeping on the ground. What happened? Because surely this late arrival cannot be because Miss Apple missed a connection somewhere. I cast that line to Mrs. Frost but she wasn't having any of it."

Thaddeus looked up. "No, she wouldn't." He took a bite of bread and washed it down with a gulp of coffee. "I don't think I'm the one that ought to explain. Remington can do it. I have to tell Fiona."

Ellie and Remington exchanged surreptitious glances but neither of them spoke.

Thaddeus looked out the window above the sink. A faint orange glow was just becoming visible on the horizon. "Hardly seems worth going to bed," he said, lifting his chin in that direction. "Day's breaking. Time to get to work."

In the event that his father was serious, Remington quickly finished spreading preserves on his heel of bread and took a bite. He slowed down so he could taste what he put in his mouth when he heard Thaddeus snicker. "Funny," he said, cheeking the bread.

Thaddeus shrugged, stretched his arms wide. "I thought

so." He finished his coffee and stood. "I'm going to bed, to sleep, perchance to dream."

"That's not the kind of sleep Hamlet had in mind."

Thaddeus looked at Ellie. "You ever notice that college knocked the stupid right out of him? Sometimes I think it's a damn shame." He chucked Remington on the shoulder as he skirted the table. "Thank you again for seeing after her," he told his son. "You, too, Ellie. She needed wrangling in the worst way."

When Thaddeus was gone, Ellie's candid gaze fell on Remington. "Are you going to tell me?"

"Are you going to feed me?"

"Fried eggs or flapjacks?"

"Both. It's a long story."

By nature, Phoebe was an early riser. The long nights demanded by the theater had never translated into lingering in bed come morning. Ellie had closed the curtains in her room—Ben's room, she reminded herself—so that contributed to the lateness of the hour when she woke. She knew it was late because somewhere in the house a clock chimed and she counted out nine on her fingertips.

She turned onto her back, pulled the quilted coverlet up to her shoulders, and took inventory of the parts of her that *didn't* hurt. As it happened, it was a short list, and she finished it before she was ready to leave what she determined was an extraordinarily comfortable nest.

The choice was taken from her when the bedroom door opened in a grand manner that could only mean that Fiona was about to make an entrance. In Fiona's hands, the door had such a significant supporting role that Phoebe was always tempted to give it credit in the playbill. Such was Fiona's gift.

"Ah, you're awake. You are, aren't you?"

Phoebe raised herself up on her elbows to prove that she was but did not fool herself into believing that it mattered. Fiona was obviously determined that she should be awake and would have made it happen.

"Good." Fiona closed the door and crossed the room. The hem of her satin robe swept the floor behind her. "Are you comfortable like that? You can't be. Sit up."

Phoebe did, resting against the headboard after she stuffed a pillow behind the small of her back. "Is that better for you?"

Fiona made a moue. "Don't be cross." She sat on the edge of the bed, turned slightly so she could draw up one knee, and set her hands on Phoebe's shoulders. "Let me look at you. Suffer the examination if you must, but I am determined." After several long moments of serious study, Fiona removed her hands from Phoebe's shoulders and placed the back of one of them against her forehead. "You don't have a temperature. You are simply quite fine, aren't you? No ill effects from your ordeal?" She dropped her hand to her lap. "Thaddeus told me all about it. How awful it must have been. Was it awful?"

Phoebe did not expect Fiona to wait for an answer, and she was not proved wrong. Fiona launched into an explanation of her absence at the station and then her absence from the front porch when Phoebe arrived. Further, she explained why she had written so few times and why the invitation to visit had come from Thaddeus and not her. Phoebe listened with half an ear to what was likely only a quarter's worth of truth. She would sort through it later, parse what she thought she could trust. Fiona needed time to settle with the truth as well.

Phoebe waited for the spring inside Fiona to completely unwind before she asked, "What about you? Are you well?"

"Now that you're here, I am. You cannot imagine how I worried."

"Oh, I think I can."

Fiona's amethyst eyes narrowed ever so slightly. "I'm not sure I like your tone." She held up one finger. "No, wait. I *am* sure, and I don't like it."

Phoebe flushed. It was a reminder that Fiona could still make her feel like a child. "I'm sorry. Of course you were worried."

Fiona tilted her head to one side, thoughtful now. "Perhaps you are more overwrought than your appearance suggests. I think a hot bath and a hotter meal are in order." She stood, put out a hand to forestall an argument. "Put your robe on and I'll have a couple of the hands move the tub in here. Once Ellie's heated the water, they can fetch and carry. I have bath salts."

Phoebe admitted it sounded wonderful. "I should help."

"Ellie won't let you," Fiona said. "Doing for others is her domain."

Phoebe thought that the way Fiona said it, it was a matter of fact, not opinion. She wondered, then, about the faint thread of bitterness that stitched the words together. She did not think she imagined it, but it was also difficult to believe that Fiona longed for purpose in her life that included doing for others.

Fiona rose and picked up Phoebe's flannel robe from where it lay over the spindle rail of a rocker. She handed it over. "I'll see that everything's made ready."

Then she was gone.

Phoebe was already wearing her robe but still searching for her slippers when there was a knock at the door. The knock was a sure sign that it was not Fiona returning. She padded to the door and opened it a few inches. When she saw it was Ellie Madison, she stood back and let the housekeeper in.

Ellie wiped her damp hands on her muslin apron. "I was washing up," she said. "Your sister's corralling a couple of the boys to set up a bath."

"I know." Phoebe was apologetic. "I hope it's not too much trouble."

"No such thing. Trouble's trouble. You can't have too much of it. I just came to make sure you had some privacy for personal matters before they came traipsing in here. Outhouse is in the back, about a hundred feet downgrade from the stream, but like I said, there's a pot under the bed."

"I remember. I think I'll use the privy. I need to stretch my legs."

"Suit yourself. I don't know how it is in the city, but there's a bucket of wood ashes inside. Pour a handful down the hole when you're done. Keeps things smelling like the good earth."

"Um. Yes. I'll do that. Do you know where my slippers are?" When Ellie's gaze dropped to the bedside, Phoebe realized Fiona must have accidentally pushed them under the bed. "Never mind," she said. "I know what happened to them."

"You probably want to put on shoes to go out and keep your slippers for indoors."

"You're right. Thank you." Phoebe found her ankle boots on the floor of the wardrobe. She sat in the rocker to put them on, aware that the housekeeper was waiting to provide an escort at least part of the way. "Has everyone else eaten?"

"That's neither here nor there. You haven't."

"I can make breakfast for myself."

"Never thought you couldn't, but it'd give me pleasure to do it just the same. You don't mind that, do you?"

"No," she said. "At least not this morning."

"Good. Come now. Let me point out the way."

By the time Phoebe reached the privy, she had met three of the five hands working the ranch since winter passed. Ralph Neighbors, a bow-legged cowpoke in his early forties, tipped his hat and murmured his name as he sauntered by on his way to the house. Scooter Banks, closer to Phoebe's age, walked like his boots had springs, not spurs, and introduced himself with a firm handshake and a toothy smile. Arnie Wilver's age was indeterminate, but it fell somewhere between Ralph's and Scooter's. He was carrying a coiled length of rope on his shoulder and he merely raised a gloved hand in her direction. It was Scooter who supplied his name.

Working in the close quarters of the theater, rubbing elbows at almost every turn, slipping between actors in various states of dress—or undress—Phoebe allowed that she was on loose terms with modesty. Perhaps it was just as well if she was going to be presented like a debutante every time she walked to the privy.

She smiled around a bubble of laughter, but that faded as she recalled a moment in the cabin at Thunder Point right after Remington had cut her loose. The first thing she had done was rearrange her skirt so that it covered her legs. She wondered that she had felt the urge at all. Was it because she knew that it was expected or because *he* was watching her?

Phoebe also remembered that her reserve, such as it was, was short-lived. How else to explain that she had allowed herself to be fitted against the curve of his saddle and in the cradle of his crotch? And when he suggested that she put her arms around him? Not a second thought; not a moment's hesitation.

She sighed. She could not have given him a good opinion of herself. On the heels of that thought, she wondered if that mattered and whether it should. He had been quiet on the ride from Frost Falls to the ranch. Thaddeus asked him some about his business in Chicago, and Remington responded but kept his answers brief. Ben wanted to know more about the men on the train, and here Remington deferred to her. That was when she realized that she preferred the quiet as well.

She thought he had fallen asleep in the saddle, but then they reached the house and he made the leap to the porch effortlessly. His affection for Ben's mother was real and transparent. It had not occurred to her until that moment that if Thaddeus had come to treat Ben as a second son, then Ellie might feel similarly toward Remington.

It made Phoebe wonder what kind of feelings Remington might harbor for Fiona, but she did not speculate on the subject long. There was a bath waiting for her inside the house and two more hands that she still had to meet.

One of them, Les Brownlee, was shifting his slight weight rather urgently from side to side not above twenty feet from the privy. As soon as he saw her, he blushed red to the tips of his ears, tucked his receding chin against his chest, and mumbled his name as he passed without looking up.

The other, who told her his name was Johnny Sutton, was helping Remington carry pails of water down the hall to her bedroom. He was so young and such a skinny thing, and laboring mightily under the weight of the water, that Phoebe was tempted to take one of the buckets from him. Truly, she was tempted to take both. He was lightening his load by sloshing water each time he took a step.

Phoebe hurried back to the kitchen for a mop, took it over Ellie's protests, and followed the wet trail to the bedroom. She thrust the mop into the young man's hand and pointedly directed him to the door. Remington chuckled until she gestured at him to do the same.

He held up his hands, an empty pail in each. "What did I do?"

"You let that boy make a mess."

Remington lowered the pails. "That boy is seventeen and has to learn to carry more than his weight in water if he's going to last the summer, and since his ma is depending on him to help support the family, he needs to stay motivated. I swear if you had asked him to hand over a bucket, he would have done it."

Phoebe pressed her lips together. "Mm. I came close to telling him to give me the pair. I didn't because I thought it would embarrass him."

"Unlikely." He set the pails down. "I still have to make a couple of trips but the water's heating now." His dark eyes took her measure from head to foot. "How are you?"

"Sore. A little achy. Nothing that won't pass."

"Ellie makes a balm that will put heat under your skin. You rub it in and wait a minute or so. I'll tell her to give you some. It will work best after you take your bath. Oh, and I'm going to ask for a salve for your wrists. They're still chafed."

Phoebe nodded. Of course he would notice what no one else had. She fiddled with the belt of her robe. It was happening again—an odd sensation of shyness was rooting her feet to the floor but making her want to twist in place like a silly schoolgirl. She managed not to do that, but only just. His eyes were not looking anywhere but into hers, and yet

Phoebe felt as if his gaze was wandering over her again, touching the soft hollow of her throat, glancing off her shoulder, lingering just a moment past decency on the curve of her breasts. The sensation that his eyes were moving over her had a tangible quality. There was pressure on her waist, at her wrist, on the curve of her hip. Impossibly, she felt his touch at the backs of her knees.

Phoebe did not blink as much as she slowly and deliberately lowered and then raised her lashes. The effect was owl-like, and when her vision cleared, she saw he was regarding her with both amusement and curiosity. The curiosity faded, leaving only amusement, when she swallowed hard and pointed to the pails.

"Right. More water."

Phoebe swore she heard him chuckling as he exited stage left.

Chapter Twelve

Phoebe found Fiona reading in the parlor. She did not invite herself in but stood in the doorway until Fiona looked up from her book.

"Already finding yourself at sixes and sevens?" asked Fiona. She marked her place with a green grosgrain ribbon before setting the book aside. "Thaddeus has a surprisingly varied selection of books. It cannot compare to the library you frequented in New York, but I believe you will find something to enlighten or entertain, depending on your mood. Shall I show you to his study?"

Phoebe shook her head. She pointed to the fringed shawl that was folded over her forearm. "I thought I would like to go out. It's a beautiful day. I wondered if you would show me around?" She was unsure of Fiona's response, but she thought she should make the overture. Phoebe knew she would not receive an answer of any kind until Fiona had finished inspecting her. Like a good soldier, she stood at attention and waited for the pronouncement.

"I should take you into town," said Fiona, rising from the sofa. She wore a pink-and-white-striped silk day dress with three-quarter-length sleeves that puffed high at her shoulders. There was nothing fussy about the dress, no ruching, no flounces, but none was necessary when she filled the bodice so admirably. "That's what I should do. Take you shopping. Thaddeus established a line of credit for me at the shops I told him I would like to frequent, not that there were so very many choices, you understand. I know he won't mind if I make purchases for you."

Phoebe watched Fiona's complexion bloom pink with excitement and wondered how it was possible that the roses in her cheeks complemented the pink stripes in her dress so precisely. "Fiona," she said gently. "I couldn't possibly. I would be very uncomfortable."

"I mean it. Thaddeus won't mind, but if you like, I will ask him. He'll give it his blessing."

Phoebe shook her head. "No, I'm sure you're right, but I meant that I would not be comfortable riding."

"Oh, we wouldn't be on horseback. That's absurd. We will take the buggy."

"Fiona." Phoebe saw Fiona blink. It was the reaction she had hoped for. "I do not want to go anywhere that my feet won't carry me." To emphasize her point, Phoebe placed one hand on her backside. "I have *bruises*."

"Oh. Well, there's no need to be crude about it. Please remove your hand before someone sees you."

Phoebe did not address the fact that there was no one around since everyone else was engaged with work. To appease Fiona, she let her hand fall to her side. "And to the other point, while I appreciate that you would like to take me shopping, I don't need anything." There was no missing Fiona's skepticism, not when the highest point of her arched eyebrow was halfway to her hairline. "Before you find fault with what I am wearing, perhaps you'll want to remember that you chose it for me. The pattern. The material. The trim."

"Did I?" She sighed. "Was I in a mood?"

"You are always in a mood." To give her hands something to do, Phoebe smoothed her lichen green skirt at the front. The tailored bodice required no attention. The fit was exact, following the line of her shoulders, her arms, the curve of her breasts and waist. Armor would not have protected her so well, she thought, which was why Fiona had suggested it. Phoebe had added a black tie around the high collar and arranged the tails so that they lay flat against the bodice. The knot she had fashioned at her throat was secured with a mother-of-pearl stickpin. The accessories were masculine; the effect was entirely feminine.

"I suppose it's not completely wrong for you," Fiona said. Her eyes narrowed on the stickpin. "Is that the pin that Jonathan Halstead gave me?"

Phoebe put her hand to her throat. "I don't know. It might be, but you gave it to me."

"Did I? I'm sure it's the one I had from Jonathan. I have fond memories of him, you know."

"I'm sure. Do you want it back?"

"No." She waved one hand airily. "You must keep it. I will think of him when I see you." She frowned slightly. "When I see you wearing it, I mean. I don't think of anyone else when I see you."

"Don't you?"

Fiona set her jaw. A muscle jumped in her cheek before the line of her mouth relaxed and her lips parted. "My, *now* who is in a mood? You are entirely disagreeable, Phoebe. I wonder that you are here at all since you are clearly out of sorts with me."

Phoebe spoke quietly, which was always the better course when Fiona was winding herself up. "I came at your husband's invitation, not yours. Remember?"

"So you mean to punish me? That's unfair, Phoebe, and beneath you. I told you this morning that I did not extend an invitation because I had it in my mind to go to New York and escort you here myself. That is not the sort of thing I could do without my husband's permission, and I wasn't confident that Thaddeus would agree. I was still working out the best way to approach him when he told me about the letter he had written to you. Do you see? While I cared enough to seek his approval, he presented me with a fait accompli. That was very wrong of him."

"Are you still angry with him? Don't you have what you wanted? I'm here." Something flickered in Fiona's lovely amethyst eyes and it was then that Phoebe understood the whole of the truth. "Oh, forgive me. I see now that I was a secondary consideration, really nothing more than a convenience you could use to explain your desire to go back to New York. Do you ever miss me at all, Fiona, or is it the city you miss, the theater, the applause?"

Phoebe saw Fiona raise her hand in what was surely going to be an imploring gesture followed by a plea for understanding or a denial of all that had preceded it. That script had been a cliché for a long time. "I think I will explore on my own," she said quietly. Holding tight to the shredded remnants of her dignity, Phoebe turned on her heel and walked away.

So as not to engage Ellie in conversation when the housekeeper was preparing lunch and she herself was feeling particularly brittle, Phoebe left the house by the front door. She stood for a time on the lip of the porch, taking in the broad expanse of land before the distant mountains climbed the sky. She could see now that the road they had taken last night was hardly more than two tracks of dirt rutted by buckboard and buggy wheels. Long shafts of bright green grass were trampled by horses who were deliberately ridden clear of the road. Pink and purple and yellow wildflowers, none whose name she knew, dotted the grass and occasionally formed clusters that dipped and swayed when a breeze stirred close to the ground.

She stepped lightly down the stairs and out from under the shadow of the porch roof and into the sunlight. The warmth on her face was lovely and she basked in it until the crick in her neck forced her to lower her head. She took a path of her own making away from the porch. When she judged she had walked far enough, she turned to face the house. Last night there had been no opportunity to take in more than its silhouette in the moonlight. Now she could see that the porch ran the formidable length of the house. There was a swing she had not noticed when she stood on the porch and two rockers on the left side of it. She would sit there later, she decided, probably on the swing, and read a book from Thaddeus's collection, or then again, she might do nothing at all.

The thought of doing nothing made her smile. It wasn't possible. Doing nothing was hard work, and she didn't have the constitution for it.

Thaddeus came around the house on the swing side. She raised her arm and waved to him. He put up a hand to acknowledge her and then began striding toward her.

"I've been looking for you. Fiona and Ellie didn't know where you'd gone." He took her hands, stood back, and looked her over. "Splendid, Phoebe. You look splendid. You'll see that everything here will agree with you. The air. The sunshine. The . . . company."

"The cows, you mean. You are talking about the cows. I can smell them from here."

Chuckling, he gave her hands a shake before he dropped them. "That particular fragrance is coming from the barn, and we don't keep cows in the barn. That's horse manure and usually the wind's blowing from the other direction and there's no whiff of it here. Young Johnny is supposed to be mucking the stalls, but he's harder to find when there's work to be done than you are."

"Oh, you have work for me?"

"Of a sort. It's not what you think." He turned, held out his elbow. "Will you allow me to show you around?"

"I'd like that." She slipped her arm in his and they started to walk. "I was going to explore on my own, but this is nicer."

"For me also. Ben volunteered early on, but I needed him to go back to town and bring the thoroughbred that Remington purchased in Chicago. There were two, but my son wants to keep Bullet. The horse is a good cutter, so I've decided I can forgive him."

"So the price of me being here was more than two thousand dollars. I cost you a thoroughbred."

Thaddeus stopped dead in his tracks. "Damn me for a clod. Is that what you heard? I wasn't talking about the money. I was talking about my son. Fiona says my sense of humor is impoverished. That's what she says. Impoverished. Always tickles me to hear her say so. She breaks it down to all its syllables. Might even add one that's not supposed to be there."

That made Phoebe laugh. "Where is Remington?"

"Probably trying to scare up Johnny Sutton. Could be anywhere."

"You gave him the photograph I gave you. Why did you do that?"

"The way I remember it, he asked for it. Turns out it was a good thing because he might not have spotted you without it. You don't mind that I wanted to provide you with an escort, do you?"

"It's hard to mind when it turned out to be a good thing as well."

Nodding, Thaddeus steered her around the back of the house, past where the chickens were scratching the ground and the rooster was strutting, past the smokehouse, the woodshed, the pump and troughs, and the pigpen, past the large rectangle of overturned earth and the furrows where tiny green shoots would rise soon and reveal the promise of a garden.

He led her past the bunkhouse to the corral. The three horses inside wandered aimlessly until the smallest one spied them at the rail.

"That's the mare I rode," Phoebe said. "At least I think it is."

"It is."

"Do you think she recognizes me?"

"Maybe your smell."

Phoebe was quite sure that between Fiona's bath salts and Ellie's balm, she smelled nothing at all like she did when the mare was forced to accept her as a rider. She did not explain any of that. "You're probably right," she said.

Thaddeus folded his forearms and placed them on the top rail of the corral and told her about the homestead, some of which she knew from conversations in New York, but had a better appreciation for now. He pointed out the distant grazing pastures in a pocket formed by verdant hillsides. The cattle were already beginning to move there, he told her, and by summer those that weren't clustered around watering holes would spread like the wildflowers she'd been admiring earlier.

Phoebe was loath to interrupt, but in good conscience, she could not allow him to go on as if there was nothing else they needed to discuss. She laid her hand on his forearm and squeezed gently. "Why am I here, Thaddeus? May I still call you that?"

"Of course," he said quietly.

While he stared straight ahead, Phoebe studied his profile. She could not say it was troubled—a profile that stoic did not reveal troubled thoughts—but in the taut set of his bluntly carved features, Phoebe saw evidence of his grit and his reticence.

"Do you want to know what I think?" she asked.

"Honestly? I'm not sure. You scare me, Phoebe."

"I do not."

He glanced at her, an eyebrow cocked. "No? Believe that if you like." He returned to staring straight ahead. "All right. Tell me. What do you think?"

"It's Fiona. I'm here because of Fiona. What has she done, Thaddeus? What is it that I'm expected to make right?"

He pressed his lips together, shook his head. "No expectations. Just hoping."

"I see. Then what is it that you hope I'll make right?"

"She wants to leave. Me. Twin Star. It's not one or the other. They're one and the same."

"I know."

"Do you think she understands that? Would it matter if she did?"

"I can't answer either of those things." She watched him nod as if her answer did not surprise him. She said carefully, "What makes you think Fiona wants to leave? Did she tell you that?"

"She wanted to go back to New York, allegedly—there's a lawyer's word for you—to bring you here."

"Remington told you this?"

"Because he overheard Fiona practicing her lines."

Phoebe did not require an explanation. Fiona's approach to managing or manipulating difficult situations was to compose the script in her head and find the right tone by engaging in a conversation with an imaginary partner. Sometimes she would speak in front of her vanity mirror to find complementary expressions, but just as often, she spoke aloud as she paced the floor or soaked in her bath.

"You said 'allegedly.' Is that because you don't believe her? The part about bringing me here, I mean."

"That's right. That's my judgment, not my son's. He encouraged me to confront her, hear it from her. It was one of the few times I did not take his advice. I chose to head her off at the pass, so to speak."

"I understand. You invited me and told her afterward."

"Yes. God help me, Phoebe, I couldn't let her go and just pray that she'd come back. In the first place, I'm not much for praying. Haven't been since my Mary died. In the second place, they say God helps those who help themselves."

"I see."

"Do you? I can't lose her, Phoebe. Sure, I know she's a stick of dynamite, knew that right off. She has so many airs that it's a wonder she doesn't float herself back to New York. I knew that and plenty more about her when I proposed, and if I hadn't figured it out for myself, you had a way of dropping hints that I couldn't ignore."

"Breadcrumbs," she said. "Apparently I drop breadcrumbs." When she saw his confusion, she shook her head. "Not important. What is it you'd like me to do?"

"Well, you being here is a good start. By accepting my invitation, you took away her excuse to go back to the city."

"You're not keeping her prisoner, are you?"

"Hell no."

Phoebe gave a start when he slapped the heel of his hand on the rail to emphasize his denial, but then she caught his sidelong glance and definitely saw guilt there. "Thaddeus?"

"This is why you scare me, Phoebe. I have a feeling you've always seen too damn much, pardon the language."

"I don't care about the language. Tell me what else you've done."

He pushed away from the rail, turned around, and settled his back against it. He crossed his arms. "I keep a tight rein on the household accounts. When I started getting an inkling that she was thinking in that particular way—and that was before Remington told me what he heard—I stopped giving her an allowance. I opened up store credit for her instead. Always had it at the mercantile, the feed store, leather goods, and such, but I set up credit at the dressmaker's, the milliner's, and the drugstore because Fiona does like her bath salts, soaps, and specially made fragrances. She has everything she needs but not the one thing she wants."

"And you think that's a ticket in her hand?"

"The money to buy a ticket. Yes."

Phoebe said, "Is there more?"

"I don't let her go to town alone any longer. There's always a reason to send someone with her. Usually Ben goes along. She tolerates him better than the others."

"Really? I thought it would be Remington."

Thaddeus shrugged. "They're a little like oil and water. They can be together for a while, but they prefer to be separate. It's all right. Better than gun powder and a lighted match."

Phoebe supposed that was true enough. "She wanted to take me shopping today. Would you have permitted that?"

"Of course. That's even better."

"I have a little money. You're not worried that I'll buy her a ticket?"

"I am depending on you to spend your money more wisely."

Phoebe said nothing.

"You will, won't you?"

"I'm not answering, and if I discover my money's missing and you are the culprit, you will not like what I will do to get it back. I will promise you, though, I will not tell Fiona that I have it, nor will I put it anywhere she's likely to find it. You'll have to be satisfied with that. Besides, I think you hold enough sway in Frost Falls that you could persuade the station agent not to sell her a ticket."

"Oh, I've already done that, but if she had the means, she could always get someone else to purchase one for her."

Phoebe regarded him steadily until he was the one who looked away.

"I'm not proud of what I've done, or what I'm doing, but I am a proud man, and I love her, Phoebe. I *love* her."

"Do you think I never came to know that?" she asked. "But Fiona can be careless with a man's heart, and I worried on your account because I liked you so well. She's never said 'yes' before. Not to a proposal. Did you know that?"

"She told me."

"You probably didn't believe her but it's the truth. You need to do more than remember that. You need to embrace it. She had reasons for saying 'yes' to you. There were practical considerations, I'm sure, because Fiona is nothing if not practical, but she is also a romantic and in your case I believe love did not merely rule her heart. It ruled her head."

Frowning, Thaddeus used his thumb and middle finger to smooth his eyebrows. He closed his eyes briefly. "What are you saying?"

"Look at me, Thaddeus." When he did, she lifted her chin and regarded him frankly. "I am saying, quite plainly I thought, that Fiona married for love, and if she wants to leave, it is because you have been careless with her heart."

Chapter Thirteen

"May I join you?" Remington stood beside the porch swing, one hand on the chain. Phoebe was either ignoring him or so deep in her own thoughts that she didn't hear. He decided he'd go with the latter and put the question to her again. When her head came up suddenly, he knew he had chosen correctly.

She inched closer to the far arm of the swing to give him plenty of room. The swing bounced a bit when he sat, but the movement stopped once he stretched his legs and used his boot heels to keep it steady.

"Have I thanked you?" she asked without looking at him. It was late in the day and dusk was settling over the ranch, muting the colors that been so vibrant this afternoon. "I can't remember if I thanked you."

"I don't recall if you said it outright, but it's never crossed my mind that you weren't grateful. Let's just leave it at that."

"I've never been good at leaving a thing. It niggles."

"That doesn't sound restful."

"It's not, so thank you."

"My pleasure." He grinned when her laughter mocked the idea. "What? You don't believe me?"

"No, it couldn't have been a pleasure, and you're a liar to say so."

He chuckled under his breath.

Their silence was easy. Remington gave the swing a small push every once in a while and let it sway until it stopped on its own. He removed his hat, dropped it beside him on the porch, and pushed a hand through his hair. He turned so that he was angled in the corner of the swing and thought about closing his eyes until he realized she was watching him. He merely lifted an eyebrow.

Phoebe shrugged and looked away.

"Oh, no," he said. "Tell me. I don't like the niggles either."

That made her smile. "If you must know, I was thinking that you aren't without your hat often. There was the train, of course, after you were knocked senseless, but I couldn't truly pay attention then. Tonight, though, you weren't wearing your hat at dinner, and it was the first I've seen you without it for longer than it takes you to plow furrows in your hair. Until now."

Remington's hand went straight to his head, only this time he didn't rake his hair. Instead he feigned a deeply thoughtful expression as he rubbed behind his ear. "Yes, well, Ellie won't cuff you for wearing a hat at the table."

"That explains dinner. What explains now?"

He dropped his hand to the arm of the swing. "End of the day, I suppose. I don't sleep in it."

"I wondered." Her gaze drifted past him as she tried to get a look at the hat.

"You want to try it on?" he asked.

"I do. Could I?"

In answer, Remington scooped it up and presented it to her.

Phoebe did not put it on immediately. Holding the brim in both hands, she turned it slowly, studying it. "Shoulders wore a black hat like this. So did the others."

"A hat like that is common around here."

"This isn't." She fingered the silver band. "I don't remember anything like this on their hats."

"That's a good observation. I'll take it off if I decide to rob a train."

She smirked and lifted the hat above her head. "Are you certain you don't mind?"

"I wouldn't give it to another man to put on, but you're not going to stretch it."

"God forbid."

He looked pointedly at her feet. "Would you allow Fiona to put on your shoes?"

"Not if I wanted to wear them comfortably again."

"Exactly. Go. Put it on."

Phoebe lowered the hat carefully. It would have slipped to her eyebrows if not for the thick twist of hair at the back of her head. She did not try to force it past the combs. "Well?" she asked, raising her head as carefully as if she were balancing a stack of books.

"Fetching." He leaned over. "Here. Let me." He adjusted the tilt and reshaped the brim then sat back and critically regarded his work. "I stand corrected. *Very* fetching."

"Fool." But that pronouncement did not keep her from leaving the swing to go to the front room window. She angled her head from side to side trying to catch her reflection in the glass. "I believe you are right. It *is* very fetching." She turned to him. "Oh, you needn't be smug about it. I'm sure you've been right before."

"Once. Maybe twice."

Shaking her head, amused, Phoebe returned his hat on her way back to the swing. When she sat this time, she swiveled sideways and rested her back against the arm. She lifted her feet onto the seat, hugged her knees to her chest, and made certain her skirt remained a modest cover.

Remington set the hat in his lap, fingered the brim. "Do you think you'd like one?"

"Do women wear them?"

"Sure. Some. If a woman's working the ranch, she'll wear one." He saw her clear skepticism. "I'll introduce you to Willa Pancake. Willa McKenna now. She and her husband go to the same horse auctions I do. This will pin back your ears." He lowered his voice to a whisper and leaned in. "She wears trousers, too."

Phoebe touched one of her ears. "I do believe it's pinned back." She resumed hugging her knees. "Trousers. Really?"

"Hmm."

"I suppose it's a practical choice. Like the hat."

"That's right."

She nodded, thoughtful. "Why don't you and Fiona get along?"

Remington blinked. "What?"

"Practical," she said. "As soon as I heard myself say it, I remembered something I said to your father this afternoon, that Fiona is nothing if not practical, and then I recalled that he told me you and Fiona are like oil and water, though he didn't say who is water and who is oil. I'm wondering what makes you that way."

"Your thoughts do that often? Hop like a frog from lily pad to lily pad?"

"They do. You have to learn to follow because I generally don't take time to explain. I made an exception." Before he could comment, she said, "So what is the answer?"

He shrugged. "Oil and water, like my father said."

"That is not an answer."

"It is, but I can appreciate that from where you're sitting, it's not a satisfactory one."

"Is there somewhere else I should be sitting?"

Had she posed that question with any hint of flirtation, he would have lifted his hat and invited her onto his lap. Flippancy had no place here because the bent of her mind was serious. "Beside Fiona," he said. "You should be sitting beside Fiona. Opposite might be better."

"So I can see her face when I ask her? I can understand why you'd think that, but Fiona's had years of practice schooling her features. If you believe you know what she's thinking or feeling, it's because she wants you to know."

Remington thought that was probably true. "Just the same, you'll have to put your question to her." He thought that would end it, but Phoebe immediately reminded him that she did not give up the bone easily when it was between her teeth.

"You said I was like her."

"Did I?"

"You did. I remember because I don't favor the comparison and it's rare that I favor the person who says it."

"Another exception for me? I am encouraged."

"Don't make me regret it. My point is—"

He held up a hand, cutting her off. "I know your point. You're going to say that we get along and ask me why that is."

"I was going to say we get along *reasonably* well and ask you to identify the particulars that make the difference."

He gave her a long, steady look. Dusk was a deeper shade of gray now, cloaking her in shadow, making her features more difficult to read. Still, the lack of inflection in her voice and that butter-wouldn't-melt tone told him all he needed to know. "You weren't going to say that. Nobody would say that."

Phoebe was not entirely successful swallowing her laughter.

"There's a difference," he said. "You think I'm amusing."

"I think you're a fool, but all right, I'll allow that a fool can be amusing."

"And there's another. You give it right back."

"You must not know Fiona very well if you think we are different there. I've never known her not to give it back."

"Not the same. Not the same at all."

She was quiet, then, "Sometimes Fiona can be a bit mean-spirited."

"A bit? Mean-spirited?" Remington drew back, took a moment to modulate his response. "She's your sister, which is why I did not want to have this conversation, but you pushed and here we are." He wasn't sure Phoebe was breathing any longer so he said it quick and matter-of-fact. "Fiona is cruel."

Phoebe's lips parted. She stared him. "Not always," she said on a thread of sound. "Not even very often."

"I hope you are trying to convince yourself because I'm unlikely to change my mind."

"Do you mean that?"

"Afraid so."

"What did she do to you?"

Remington returned his hat to his head and adjusted the brim. "Well, she didn't hurt my feelings, if that's what you're thinking. As for what she did, what she continues to do, you'll have to hear it from her."

"We are not talking about oil and water any longer, are we?"

"No. And we are not only talking about me." Because he'd said more than he meant to, Remington started to rise. He was halfway to his feet when he saw her put out a hand. He stopped. "What is it?"

"Don't go. It was nice. Before."

He sat down slowly. "It was nice." He caught her opening her mouth to speak. "Don't you dare apologize."

"Why not?"

"Because I'll never know for sure if you're apologizing for her or for poking the bear."

"Oh."

"Uh-huh."

They were quiet then. Occasionally the swing creaked. A horse whinnied. A cow lowed. But they did not speak. It was deep into that silence that Phoebe stopped hugging her knees and straightened her legs. She used the toe of one of her soft leather ankle boots to poke him gently in the thigh.

Remington gave a small start, looked down at her foot, and then at her. He had no difficulty making out her absurdly wide smile in the deepening shadows. "Full of yourself, aren't you?"

"Half full." She poked him with the other toe. "All full now." She laughed, trying to pull back when he made a grab for her foot.

"Not so fast," he said, circling her ankle with his hand. He didn't try to pull her close, didn't try to make the moment into something neither of them was ready for. Instead, he lifted her foot and placed it on his thigh and then did the same with the other. "Just leave them there," he said, resting his hand over both. "Like that."

So she did. And fell asleep while he slowly rocked the swing.

Not long after that, the bear returned to hibernation.

Chapter Fourteen

"Don't be absurd," said Fiona. "If you won't choose a proper hat, then we are going to leave here without one."

"That's fine." Phoebe's tone held no rancor. "Haven't I been saying we should?" She looked to the milliner, inviting her into the argument, but saw she'd get no help from that quarter. And why should Mrs. Palmer support her? The woman not only wanted to make a sale, but also wanted to keep Fiona Frost as a satisfied customer. Seeing that she had little choice, Phoebe pointed to the red velvet cocked hat that was perched at a roguish angle on a faceless head. The underside was lined in black velvet, and bunches of osprey feathers spilled over the brim. "I like that one."

Fiona followed the direction of Phoebe's finger. "That hat? I hope you are not serious. You would look like a pirate." She turned to Mrs. Palmer. "Don't you agree?"

Phoebe smiled apologetically at Mrs. Palmer, whose doorknob of a chin was already quivering. The poor woman looked as if she might begin wringing her hands. "She did not mean that the way it must have sounded. It was no slight against your talent, which is considerable. She means that she could carry it off and look quite stunning in it, but if I wore it, someone would try to run me through." She extended her arm as if she were holding a sword and slashed the air in a large X. "Arrgh."

"Phoebe! Whatever has gotten into you?" Fiona forcibly lowered Phoebe's arm as she addressed the milliner. "I hope you will excuse us, Mrs. Palmer, and not judge my sister too harshly. I fear she is not yet recovered." Her voice dropped to a stage whisper meant not only for Mrs. Palmer but also for the two women loitering in the corner who were hanging on every word. "The *abduction*, you understand."

"*The Pirates of Penzance*," Phoebe said, adopting Fiona's whispered aside.

Fiona grasped Phoebe firmly by the arm. "We are leaving." She hustled Phoebe toward the door but paused just before they exited. "I'll have that darling red hat for myself, Mrs. Palmer, and trust you to choose something appropriate for my sister."

"Yes, Mrs. Frost. Yes, of course."

Afraid Mrs. Palmer might actually bow and scrape, Phoebe pulled away from Fiona and hurried out the door on her own steam. She waited on the boardwalk for Fiona to catch up to her.

"You embarrassed me in there," said Fiona. "Did you even notice we had an audience?"

"The two women in the corner fussing over the fancy straw hat? Yes, I noticed them. I believe they will find no fault with your performance. You handled me admirably. And purchasing two hats from Mrs. Palmer before you left? You have a particular genius for improvisation."

"I will not be flattered into forgetting I am put out with you, but just the same, I happen to agree."

Phoebe laughed because she could not help herself. "Oh, Fiona, I do love you, you know." She took three more steps before she realized Fiona was no longer walking with her. She stopped, turned, and was confronted by Fiona's unreadable stare and colorless face. "What is it? Are you all right?" She stepped in, took her hand. "Fiona?"

Fiona blinked. "Did you mean it?"

Phoebe frowned. "Mean what?"

"Hmm. I thought so." She removed her hand from Phoebe's. "Sometimes you can be so cruel."

Now it was Phoebe who blinked. Fiona's stare was no longer unreadable. It was implacable. Phoebe quickly stepped aside when Fiona made to brush past her. "Fiona! Wait!" Her words had the opposite effect. Fiona increased her pace so that Phoebe was forced to lengthen her stride to catch up.

They passed the feed store, the mercantile, and the land office without exchanging a word. Their kid boots lay down a soft and steady tattoo on the boardwalk. Fiona stared straight ahead, her chin bobbing occasionally to acknowledge the greeting of a passerby, while Phoebe cast her eyes all around. It did not escape her notice that no one seemed to be in expectation of engaging Fiona in conversation; they simply nodded and moved on. What Phoebe could not divine was whether this was the usual course of things, or whether it was a consequence of Fiona's high dudgeon.

"That was the apothecary that we just walked by," said Phoebe. "Didn't you say you wanted to go there?"

"I'm not talking to you yet."

"I understand. I still don't know why."

"And you are accounted to be so clever." She stopped without warning and looked up and down the wide dusty street. "Where is Remington? I don't see him, his horse, or the buggy. I don't understand why Ben could not have accompanied us. In fact, I don't understand why we needed anyone along." The considering look she gave Phoebe was not a complimentary one. "It must be because of you. You draw trouble, Phoebe. You know you do."

"Would you prefer that I walk on the other side of the street?"

"Hah! That is precisely what you want, isn't it? To cut loose from me so you can meet up with Remington. I'm sure you know exactly where he is."

"I think he's at the wheelwright," Phoebe said with credible calm. "Something about one of the buggy wheels wobbling."

"Well, you would know that. You hang on his every word. *There* is something I have noticed. And I'm not the only one. Ellie's remarked on it. So has Thaddeus. If I wanted to pretend it wasn't happening, I would not be allowed that luxury."

"Maybe you would like to say these things when we're

alone?" When Fiona drew a breath as if she meant to continue, Phoebe suggested, "Or at least say them while we're walking?"

Fiona nodded stiffly, stepped down to the street from the sidewalk, and indicated Phoebe should follow. "How could you, Phoebe? How could you let yourself be seduced by him?"

Phoebe might have stopped in her tracks if it was not for the buckboard bearing down on her.

"Lord, watch where you're going," Fiona said. "And step lively. One would think you had no experience crossing Fifth Avenue at midday."

Phoebe was still trying to get her bearings so she did not mind when Fiona took her by the sleeve and pulled her across the street as if she were a child. When they were once again safely on the boardwalk, Phoebe hissed, "He has not seduced me."

"Then it's because you went willingly. Really, Phoebe, what possessed you to share the swing with him and put your feet on his lap? As if that behavior was not egregious enough, you made it worse by falling asleep. Falling asleep!"

"Fiona. By my calculation, that occurred nearly four weeks ago."

"It occurred on the second night you were here."

"I understand, and I do not disagree with your estimation of my behavior, but why are you only calling it to my attention now?"

"Because I had no words before. None. But now I want to throttle you so I'm speaking my mind instead."

Phoebe thought she would prefer being throttled. "Nothing's happened. Nothing. As for hanging on his words, he's instructive, Fiona. When he has the time, which is not often in spite of what you think, he is teaching me about Twin Star, about the land, about the business of ranching. I am going to learn to ride."

"Thaddeus can teach you all of that."

"Yes, he can, and I've asked, but he's the one who pointed me to Remington. First, there is the matter of his time. He wants to spend it with you. Also, he believes that his son is the better teacher."

"Hogwash."

Phoebe chuckled. "I've noticed you've acquired the local vernacular."

Fiona sniffed. "Here's a word from the old neighborhood: yenta."

Phoebe spared a fond thought for Mrs. Jacob C. Tyler. "You're saying he's a busybody?"

"Meddler," said Fiona. "He's meddling."

"Remington?"

"No. Really, Phoebe, could you be more obtuse? I'm talking about my husband. Thaddeus is the meddler. Do you remember Mrs. Meir?"

"The diamond merchant's wife?"

"The *shadkhnte*," said Fiona. "The matchmaker. She brokered seventeen marriages before she died. I think Thaddeus would be happy to broker one." Her mouth flattened as she shook her head. "The *shadkhn*."

Phoebe did not try not to laugh. She pictured Thaddeus Frost wearing Mrs. Meir's black woolen shawl, eating kosher, and kibitzing with the other yentas. Alternatively, she saw Mrs. Meir in a Stetson and chaps. She had to stop walking to catch her breath.

"What is wrong with you?"

"I'm not going to even try to explain," she said. She opened her beaded reticule, which Thaddeus had returned to her, and took out a handkerchief to dab at her eyes. "Anyway, there really isn't time." She lifted her chin to indicate a point farther down the sidewalk. "You asked about Remington. There he is."

"I see him. He came out of the leather goods store. He has packages, Phoebe, and we are empty-handed." She sighed. "Topsy-turvy."

"It's not the end of the world."

"So say you."

"Why don't we help with his packages?" Phoebe suggested. "And no one who sees us will be the wiser. Besides, we have hats waiting for us at Mrs. Palmer's."

Fiona brightened. "That's right. We do."

Together, they barred Remington's path and plucked the parcels from his arms. He offered a few protests, but they would have their way, and he finally gave up everything save for the box with the carrying string.

Phoebe was only interested in the contents of the box he would not surrender. "What's in there?"

"Something I've been set on buying for a while now."

"And that would be . . ."

"None of your business."

Fiona said, "Don't wheedle him."

Phoebe looked askance at Remington. He was grinning. Phoebe couldn't really blame him. It must be a relief for him to be out of Fiona's sights. There had been quite a few barbs directed his way as they rode to town, and she doubted that he had been able to deflect all of them.

"I want to go to the apothecary," Fiona said in a tone that brooked no argument. "Phoebe, you should have said something. You know I wanted scented bath salts. And it occurs to me now that I am in need of headache powders."

Phoebe smiled weakly. She could use a packet of the powder herself. "Are we having lunch at the Butterworth?"

"After we visit the dressmaker's. You should have at least two new day dresses. I swear I recognize castoffs from the theater among your things. That cuirass bodice, that mossy thing I've seen you in, I believe I wore that when I played Nora in *The Doll House*."

"I told you that you chose the pattern, the color, and the trim. I added the tie and took it in, of course."

Full comprehension struck Fiona as she was preparing to step down to the street. She faltered on the lip of the walk and would have fallen if Remington had not caught her by the elbow and steadied her.

"Are you all right, Fiona?" he asked. "Here. Let me take those parcels back."

Except to wave Remington away, she ignored him and turned her narrowed eyes on Phoebe. "Why, you little cat."

Phoebe stared back. Her green eyes, very much like a cat's with their flecks of gold, projected only innocence in

the face of Fiona's heat. It was then that Phoebe thought
Remington truly saved her, saved them both really. He
stepped between them.

"Here's how we will proceed, ladies. Fiona, you will go
to the apothecary while I escort Phoebe to the dressmaker's.
I'm assuming you're using Mrs. Fish. Is that right?" When
Fiona nodded shortly, he said, "We will meet at the Butterworth for lunch and neither of you will put a paw in the
cream or claws in each other. Understood?" He waited for
them to nod in turn before he blew out a long breath. "All
right, then." He assisted Fiona's step to the street, turned,
and held out a hand to Phoebe.

"For God's sake," Fiona said when Phoebe hesitated.
"Don't be churlish because I'm standing here. Take it."

Phoebe did. Her fear that Remington might allow the
handclasp to linger came to nothing. He released her hand
and gestured to her to proceed. Fiona was already marching
ahead. They followed her to the apothecary. Remington
opened the door for her but did not step inside.

"What is she carrying?" Phoebe asked when he joined
her again.

"Your trousers, a blue chambray shirt, two neck cloths—
one blue, one red—and a brown leather vest. The neck cloths
will not be a problem, but the rest . . ." He shrugged. "I can't
be sure anything will fit. I bought the smallest I could find."
He added wryly, "But you might have to take things in."

"If you think that's amusing, it's not. I envy Fiona her
figure, and she knows it. No matter what she believes, I did
not say that to get under her skin. I didn't know I could, and
I don't know why it worked, but when she turned those ac-
cusing eyes on me and called me a cat, I decided right then
that I would let her believe what she wanted to, and that it
would serve her right."

"I'm never accompanying the two of you to town again.
I'm sending Johnny Sutton, and I'll muck stalls."

Phoebe smiled a little at that. "Are we so bad together?"

"Maybe I just don't understand women." He gestured
ahead to the door on his left. "That's Mrs. Fish's shop."

Phoebe's shoulders sagged and her steps slowed. "Do we have to?"

"You have what you came to Frost Falls for, even if you haven't seen it yet, and Fiona is right about you needing a couple of sensible day dresses."

"I don't recall her mentioning sensible."

"My adjective. Things suitable for summer. You'll thank her."

"Maybe." She waited while he opened the door for her, but before she stepped over the threshold, she held up the large parcel she held. "What's in here?"

"Boots."

"Ah. And in your box?"

"Your hat."

"Black?"

"Pearl gray. Silver band, though."

Phoebe wondered if her smile was as wide as it felt. "Thank you."

"Wait," he said, "until we can see if you can keep it on your head when you fall off your horse. Then we'll know if it's a good fit."

Chapter Fifteen

A week later, Phoebe was back in Frost Falls with Fiona, and this time it was Ben who accompanied them. Phoebe found the arrangement satisfactory when comparing it to the prospect of having gangly Johnny Sutton riding post. From the outset, it put Fiona in a much better mood.

There had been a mild thaw in the past seven days, but Phoebe imagined that Remington, who had been there when the freeze set in, was likely the only one who observed it. The cold shoulder that Fiona pressed in her direction was made more noticeable because she was warmhearted to everyone else. Even Thaddeus, with whom she was piqued but had not yet confronted, and Remington, whom she had marked from the first as disagreeable, received her kind regard.

Phoebe was delighted for Thaddeus, who reveled in the attention, although she lived in some dread of the moment Fiona would drop the hammer. As for Remington, he made being out of Fiona's reach his priority. That meant he was also outside Phoebe's. She had hoped for one riding lesson, but a week gone, all she had been able to do was try on the clothes he bought for her—using money she gave him—and make minor alterations.

If Fiona was correct, and Thaddeus meant to push Remington in her direction, then Fiona was equally committed to pushing him the other way. Phoebe considered herself well out of it, except that she rather missed Remington being around.

All the hands offered their company when they weren't

working, which meant she saw a lot of Johnny Sutton. It was Ben who most often rescued her, gently leading her away and showing an interest in what she was reading or asking her about New York. He would stay with her until someone barked at him to get moving, and he always begged her pardon before he took off, usually at a run.

Phoebe liked all of them, but she was especially fond of Ben. She watched him around Ellie, how gentle he was, how he looked out for her. He would remove a heavy stew pot from the stove and just grin when she tapped him on the wrist with a wooden spoon. He let her fuss over him in front of the other men after he took a nasty spill from the back of a horse. He just sat there grinning, the only visible sign that he was embarrassed the scarlet tips of his ears. Phoebe thought that had less to do with his mother's attentions and more to do with the ribbing he was getting for taking the tumble.

Phoebe thought that Fiona would insist on coming to the dressmaker's with her if for no other reason than to criticize her choices, so it was a pleasant surprise when she snapped open her parasol and announced she was simply going to walk and see what, if anything, struck her fancy. Phoebe's second surprise was less pleasant.

Fiona insisted that Ben accompany her.

Remington balanced himself on the top rail of the corral and watched Scooter Banks gentle one of the mares before he climbed into the saddle. "Scooter's got a way about him. The animals respond."

"I've noticed. Puts me in mind of you." Thaddeus climbed the rails to sit beside his son. "I thought you'd come looking for me as soon as you got back."

"Haven't been back that long. Here I am. Here you are. There's not much to tell you."

"Tell me first, did you run into them on your return?"

"No. Saw them, but they didn't see me. I stayed clear of the road, and none of them knew I was out anyway."

Thaddeus nodded. "Good. So what did you hear from Jackson?"

"You're going to be disappointed. There wasn't much he could tell me." He cupped his hands around his mouth and called to Scooter. "Watch you don't pull the reins tight. She has a tender mouth." When Scooter acknowledged him, Remington went on. "There's been a search, a thorough one from Sheriff Brewer's description, and he can't find any evidence that the robbers were local men. He's been working with a detective hired by Northeast Rail to investigate the robbery and Phoebe's abduction."

"Well, that's something, isn't it?"

"It is, but Brewer is not hopeful the investigation will continue beyond a few more weeks. Not without a lead. There's precious little evidence."

"Hmm. What's the man's name? The detective. Would it help if I had a word with him?"

"His name is Smith. Michael Smith. I don't know if you could influence him to stay on longer or not. He was not around when I was talking to Brewer, so I don't have a good sense about him. The sheriff seems to think he's competent and motivated, but he takes his marching orders from the company."

"I understand."

"All the passengers have been interviewed. Smith tracked them down and spoke to them."

"Really? Then why didn't he come here? Speak to Phoebe and you?"

"I asked the same question. Brewer said it was because he already had our statements. You can imagine he gave me a good ribbing about the fact that I was unconscious during the entire robbery."

"I'm sure Jackson would have been sympathetic if Mr. Shoulders had clobbered you senseless, but you—"

"Tripped over my own feet. Yes, I know."

"That isn't what I was going to say. Phoebe never once said you tripped. That is Jackson's invention, and shame on you for letting him get away with it. Phoebe told him you were on your feet because you were trying to reach that little girl. The train lurched and you went down."

"That's Phoebe's invention. I don't have a clear memory, but I'm fairly certain I was on my feet to reach her, not Madeleine."

"Well, if you were, that's my fault. I asked you to look out for her and you did."

"Mm." He called out another direction to Scooter to test the mare's agility. "I'm thinking I want to go back to Thunder Point. Have a look around."

"The place has been trampled. I was there that night, don't forget. Brewer and Ben were with me. I imagine the Smith fellow asked to see it as well. What do you think you'll find?"

"Probably nothing, but I want to look. You have objections?"

"None that are going to stop you."

"I'm taking Phoebe."

Thaddeus whistled softly but said nothing.

"What are you thinking?"

"I'm wondering if you're asking her or abducting her."

"Something in between. I'm telling her."

"Huh. Do you know anything about women?"

"I've been asking myself that a lot lately, and I'm convinced I know all the wrong things."

"I'm inclined to agree," he said dryly. "It's widely accepted that telling a woman what she's going to do is ill-advised."

"We'll see."

"Oh, we certainly will. I'm pulling up a chair to watch."

Remington looked over at Thaddeus to judge how real that threat was. He glimpsed a hint of humor in his father's fading smile. "What is it?" he asked. "There's something else."

"Not that I think it will matter to you, but Fiona's not going to like it."

"You're half right. It doesn't matter and she'll *hate* it."

Thaddeus's sigh was inaudible. "I wish . . ." He did not finish his thought. "Never mind. We've been over that ground before."

Relieved that they would not have to walk it again, Remington said, "Appreciate that, Thaddeus. I guess if you want to pull up a chair when I talk to Phoebe, I'll let you."

Phoebe unwrapped her two new dresses and placed them in the wardrobe before she went hunting for Remington. She was careful not to draw attention to her search by rushing. She kept her steps slow of a purpose, stopping to chat with Ellie and stealing a sand tart from the cooling rack before she went out the back door.

She found Remington in the barn rubbing down the mare everyone called Buttercup. The name suited the horse's golden coat but not her temperament. Phoebe hung back.

"You have an apple on your head?" asked Remington. "I think she wants a bite of you."

Since he hadn't yet turned around, Phoebe asked, "How did you know I was here?"

He shrugged. "She told me."

Phoebe did not ask him to explain that or even suppose it was true. She'd noticed before that Remington seemed possessed of eyes at the back of his head. His awareness of his surroundings was uncanny, and he'd caught her out more than once watching him when she meant to be unobtrusive. Her excuse on those occasions was that she was merely daydreaming, not observing him, and how like a narcissist he was to think that was where her interest lay. She didn't think she was entirely convincing, but she liked him for pretending to be convinced.

It was hard not to watch him now, when his every crisp move drew her eye to the muscles bunching under his shirt, but she purposefully turned her head aside and began walking the length of the barn. Aware that Buttercup was watching her, Phoebe gave the animal a wide berth as she passed.

"What are you doing?" asked Remington. He swept a brush across Buttercup's shoulder and back. "Not you, Miss B. I know you're preening." He rooted around in a sack on the bench behind him and found what he wanted. "Here, this is for you." He held two dried apple slices in the flat of his palm. They disappeared at once.

Phoebe warily eyed the empty hand that he was still holding out to Buttercup. "Aren't you afraid she'll bite you?"

"No." He stroked the mare's nose. "So tell me what you're doing."

"In a moment." She looked into the last four stalls. Horses only. She pointed to the loft, a question in her eyes that she did not have to voice.

Remington followed the direction of her finger and shook his head.

"All right," she said, approaching cautiously. "I need to speak with you."

"Yes?"

"Alone. I was making sure we're alone."

"Ah. You might have just asked."

She gave him the disdainful look he deserved. "And if we weren't alone? Don't you think the question might have raised an eyebrow?"

"I concede to your superior logic. We can talk over there." He cocked his head to indicate the buggy that Ben had recently brought inside and unhitched. "I know you're skittish around Buttercup, and God knows, she's jealous of you. I'll just put her in the stall."

Phoebe waited until Remington joined her before she asked, "You were pulling my leg about Buttercup, weren't you?"

Straight-faced, he said, "Ask her yourself."

Phoebe waved his answer away and came to the purpose of her visit. "I think I saw him. Mr. Shoulders, I mean. I can't be sure, not completely, and yet if it didn't feel as if I were, I wouldn't be telling you now." She doubted that Remington was aware that his easy way of standing, loose and limber, had vanished. He was alert in a manner he had not been before; his dark eyes had sharpened and narrowed their focus, and his finely molded features were set in a fashion that made them impenetrable.

"Where?" he asked.

"In town."

"*Where* in town?"

His tone was not merely impatient, but mildly belittling, as if she should have known to tell him that at the outset. Her nostrils pinched as she sucked in a breath and prepared to match his tenor, but at the last moment, an element of common sense prevailed and she answered evenly and with dignity. "He was walking out of the saloon. The Songbird, I think."

"That's it. There's only the one saloon."

"Oh, I didn't realize. I didn't see his face, but I don't think that would have helped identify him just then. He turned toward the depot end of town, which put his back to me. He paused, and I confess, I stopped as well. It just struck me suddenly, the way he stood there, and all I could do was stare."

"So you didn't call attention to yourself?"

"No, but I reached for my gun before I remembered that it's likely still in his possession." When his face darkened, she smirked. "You are an easy mark, Remington Frost, and that you believed me for even a single moment is not flattering."

"This is serious, Phoebe."

"I know it is, but he's not suddenly going to appear on Twin Star land, and there's every chance that he left town since he eventually began walking in the direction of the station. There's nothing to be done right now."

He rolled right over her explanation. "Tell me what you saw that made you think he was Mr. Shoulders."

"I don't know if I can describe it. He wasn't wearing the duster, so it wasn't that. There was something about the way he hunched his shoulders, I think. It stretched his vest across his back. This isn't something I could have seen when I was with him, yet I was put in mind of how he sat in the saddle, his shoulders pushed forward. It was not even something of which I was aware at the time, but then I saw it and it touched a memory. He turned, only briefly, but just enough for me to glimpse a quarter profile. First, there was the angle of his hat. It was so familiar. The hand that I could see had its thumb hooked in the waistband of his trousers, but more importantly, it rested above his gun and holster. Deputy Armstrong asked me that night if I recalled the gun, but I didn't, and there was nothing I could tell him. I still don't know what type of gun he was carrying, but I know now it had an ivory handle. I *know* it."

She fell silent, waiting for him to challenge her. When he didn't, she forgave him for his earlier misstep. "It sounds fantastical, I know. I can't explain it. I think there must be tiny seeds in my brain that began to sprout images when I saw him. Do you think that's possible?"

"Do you believe Mr. Shoulders is sunlight and water?"

"Hardly."

"Then you probably don't have seeds."

"I didn't mean it quite so literal."

His smile was gentle. "I know."

She flushed. "Oh, you were having me on."

"A little." He let that rest for a moment and then said, "I was in here when Ben came back with the buggy and took care of the horses. He didn't say anything. Did you ask him not to?"

"I didn't tell him."

"I don't think I understand. Wasn't he with you when this happened? He would have noticed something was wrong; furthermore, he would have asked you about it."

Phoebe had hoped she could avoid this part, but there was no point in prevaricating. "He was with Fiona, and she had it in her mind that she wanted to walk, so I can't say precisely where they were at that time."

"With Fiona," Remington said under his breath. "Of course he was. Thaddeus would have put that in his head."

"I thought so, too. He told me that he thinks she means to leave him."

"Did he? I wasn't sure that he would."

"Yes. I know why I'm here."

"Oh? And why's that?"

"You know. Incentive to keep Fiona here, or at least remove an excuse for her to leave."

"Really? You keep thinking that. I have to say, the two of you don't strike me as that close."

"Put that in the drawer where you keep all the things you don't understand about women." Phoebe appreciated his rumbling laughter and the fact that it accompanied the return of his relaxed posture.

"My father commented in that same vein earlier."

"Oh?"

"I'm going to Thunder Point tomorrow and you're coming with me. Call it your first real riding lesson. I'll get Ellie to put together a meal for us to take. No jerky and day-old biscuits, I promise. I figure with what you told me about seeing Mr. Shoulders, the time is right for you to go back. It would not astonish me if another seed or two sprouts when you look around."

Phoebe's answer was immediate. "Of course. What time should I be ready?" A small vertical crease appeared between her eyebrows. "You look smug. Why is that?"

"Because I'm going to enjoy telling my father there's a thing or two he needs to put in his own drawer." When she continued to regard him oddly, he added, "You know, the one where he keeps all the things he doesn't understand about women."

Chapter Sixteen

They prepared to leave at first light. It was agreed that it was better if Fiona found out after the fact. Ellie filled a sack with cold ham, wedges of sharp cheese, hard-boiled eggs, and a thick heel of bread. It fit snugly into Remington's saddlebags. Phoebe filled two canteens with cool fresh water.

Only Thaddeus knew their destination. Ellie asked once, but when neither of them was forthcoming, she let it drop. None of the ranch hands showed any particular interest when they headed out except for Arnie Wilver, who commented good-naturedly that from where he stood, Remington's saddle looked a lot more like the catbird seat, and Johnny Sutton, who leaned against his shovel, wistfully envious that Remington was getting out of real work for the day.

"Did you see Johnny's face?" asked Phoebe when the ranch was finally at their backs. "I thought he might cry. He doesn't realize how hard you're going to have to work to keep me on this horse."

Remington looked over at her. She was sitting tall and not fighting the mare's rhythm, although the look of fierce concentration on her face told him she was still thinking about every aspect of what she was doing. There was nothing natural about her riding yet. "You're doing all right. The stirrups feel a good length for you?"

She nodded.

"You think you want to take the reins up yourself?"

She glanced at him doubtfully. "Um, maybe in a little while."

"Sure. Have you named her yet?"

"Named her? Oh, you mean the horse. Doesn't she already have a name? I don't want to confuse her."

Remington grinned. "I think she can get used to a new name. And maybe Mr. Shoulders never thought enough of her to call her anything. She's a gentle animal." He caught Phoebe's skeptical expression, and remembered the wild ride, at least from Phoebe's perspective, when the mare bolted. He amended his last statement. "Gentle, that is, when she hasn't been startled."

Phoebe dared to lean forward and lightly rub the mare's neck. "That does not exactly inspire confidence, Remington."

"Sit up," he said. "What are you doing?"

"Soothing her."

"More like confusing her. Just keep your hands where they are."

"Yes, sir. I'd salute you, but I'm keeping my hands where they are."

"That's sass, isn't it? You're full of sass this morning." She shrugged, but her superior smile told him all he needed to know. "Yeah. Full of sass."

"Truth?" she asked. "I am so happy to be out that I don't even mind that you didn't ask me if I wanted to go to Thunder Point."

"Oh, you noticed that."

"I always notice when someone tells me what I'm going to be doing. I just didn't care."

"Huh."

She laughed. "Something to think about, isn't it?"

"What I'm thinking about is that we need to stop talking." When she didn't reply, he looked over and realized the tight-lipped placement of her mouth meant she had already started. She spared him a look that was just long enough for him to see her green eyes sparkle and dance. She really was full of sass.

She was also beautiful. It crossed his mind to tell her, but he could imagine her animated features going perfectly still and the light in her eyes disappearing. She would think of Fiona, make comparisons that she did not like anyone else to make, and find herself wanting. How had that come to pass when in his mind she was so clearly wanting for nothing? Remington could only imagine the answer lay somewhere in her complicated relationship with Fiona.

When it came to verbal sparring, he knew firsthand that Phoebe could hold her own. She had driven him to the corner more than once and he had seen her do the same with Fiona, and yet he had also observed that the matches with Fiona left her bruised. She wouldn't back down, but she did not walk away unscathed.

He judged Phoebe to have a fairly realistic grasp of Fiona's character in that she acknowledged Fiona's considerable talent but was not unaware of her flaws. It was in her nature to protect Fiona but not defend her.

Remington wondered if Phoebe was able to see herself as he did when she stood outside Fiona's shadow. She was certainly outside it this morning. He had no doubt that Fiona would have taken one look at Phoebe's manner of dress and pronounced it vulgar. Phoebe would not have changed her clothes, or left her hat behind, but she would not be as comfortable in her boots as she was now.

She wore the unfamiliar clothes, not as a costume, but as someone born to them, and perhaps she had been since he could detect some of the fine alterations she had done in private to make the fit her own. The trousers were not tight, but they hugged her slim hips and long legs when she saddled up, and the blue chambray shirt, a common enough garment for anyone at Twin Star, looked decidedly uncommon when it was taken in to suit her tapered figure. The brown leather vest fit her tolerably well when she buttoned it. Today she wore her hair in a single braid that fell halfway down her spine, and the pearl gray Stetson sat squarely on her head without slipping over her brow. Her trousers disappeared into her boots, and he had noticed earlier when he helped her mount that the tops and sides of the boots were gently scuffed and the soles showed signs of wear. It made him smile to think that she had been breaking them in from the first, probably hiding them under her skirts and petticoats while she walked around very pleased with her deception.

In many ways, Phoebe was a pared version of Fiona, and while Phoebe had come to accept the notion that it made her less, in Remington's eyes, it was a case of less being more. Considerably more.

Phoebe and Fiona were of equal height, able to look most men in the eye, but it was Fiona who so often commanded the high ground and Phoebe who stepped to one side. Had Fiona ever recognized how gracefully Phoebe did it?

Phoebe's splendid hair was a deep shade of cocoa brown, thick and lustrous, often with unruly strands framing her face in spite of the anchoring combs. In the sun, the wayward threads became a halo of light that paradoxically complemented her dangerous, devilish smile. The irony intrigued him.

Fiona knew nothing of irony. She coifed and groomed her auburn hair into twists and curls that never once danced in the wind or stepped out of line. The effect was as haughty as the cool and considered placement of her lips.

While the amethyst color of Fiona's eyes was unusual and therefore likely to be remarked upon, it was Phoebe's gold-flecked green gaze that settled levelly and calmly on her surroundings and invariably drew his attention. Fiona was watchful, but rarely curious, marking her territory with the same regard a predator has for prey. In contrast, Phoebe observed people, their activity, her surroundings, and all of it was grist for the mill. She asked more questions than any three people and listened with real interest to the answers. She wanted to engage conversation. It seemed to Remington that Fiona still preferred soliloquies.

Remington held out the mare's reins for Phoebe to take. "You have to take them sometime. It's not much of a riding lesson if you don't."

"Then we are talking again?" she asked, staring at the reins, undecided.

"We are."

"Very well. But stay close."

"Like butter on bread."

She took the reins. The mare kept on walking. "She doesn't seem to notice."

"Give her time. She'll come to know you're in charge."

"I don't think I am."

"Give yourself time. Relax. You don't have to hold your hands up like a puppy begging for a treat."

Phoebe lowered her hands but not before giving him a reproving look.

"Better. Find your balance." He looked over the alignment of her body. Without any instruction from him, the willow-slim length of her was set perfectly: ear, shoulder, point of hip, and heel perpendicular to the horizon. "Unlock your lower back," he told her. "You're too stiff again."

"Because you gave me the reins."

He ignored that, showing her instead how to use her center of gravity to achieve balance and how to follow the movement of the horse's back. "We'll go through the gaits when we're closer to the ranch. No trotting. No cantering. No galloping. For now it's all walking."

"What if she has other ideas?"

"Butter on bread," he said. "Remember? I'm here."

Her eyes shifted sideways. "Yes."

"Use your legs to control her. Your hands to guide her." He demonstrated bringing Bullet to a halt and starting up again and then helped Phoebe do the same by applying the right pressure of heels and knees and using the reins with authority. He was not surprised that she showed relative competence from the first, but he kept that observation to himself. There were plenty of nuances that would require hours in the saddle for her to master, and overconfidence would be her enemy.

They rode five miles before he judged he could safely encourage her. "Not bad," he said.

"Don't dress it up. You wouldn't want to turn my head."

"Precisely."

She sighed. "It will take a long time to learn to do this well, won't it?"

"Define 'long.'"

"The remainder of my life."

He considered that. "If you learn to enjoy riding, the remainder of your life will seem too short."

Phoebe nodded, thoughtful. "You're something of a philosopher, aren't you? Have you ever had a sweetheart or maybe a fiancée?"

He considered stopping Bullet so he could get a good look at Phoebe's face. From his present angle, her smile, if there was one, eluded him. "Are those two things somehow connected in your mind?"

"What? Oh. No, they're not. The first was more of an observation. It's the second thing I've been wondering about for a while now. I thought I might as well blurt it out as keep it in."

"Hmm. I'm surprised you didn't ask someone."

"Why? It's about you, but if you sidestep it again, I will probably change my mind."

Remington took her at her word. "Yes," he said. "Several sweethearts beginning with Miss Addie Packer. She was the schoolteacher in Frost Falls for three years before she married Jackson Brewer. He wasn't sheriff then. Even now I think about not voting for him come election time."

Phoebe laughed softly. "So she broke your heart."

"Mine and just about every other boy's in the classroom." The memory made him smile. "Then there was Mary Ellen Farnsworth. She was first girl I asked to dance, and we were sweet on each other for a time, but mostly we liked kissing under the stairs at the back of the hotel."

"I think I should stop you now if the sweetheart list is more than seven." When he didn't say anything, she said, "I see. All right. Maybe you could jump to the fiancée. Were there many of those?"

"Just the one. Alexandra Kingery. I met her when I was in law school. Her father was one of my professors. I proposed to her after I finished my first year. We were going to be married when I graduated. The engagement had her father's blessing. Thaddeus met her twice, making the trip east both times. Alexandra charmed him because she was charming. She did not know how to be any other way, or if she did, she never showed it. In hindsight, I think Thaddeus had reservations that he wasn't able to put into words.

"I'm not sure when I understood that she and I had very different expectations about our lives after the wedding. I always knew I was returning to Twin Star. I never hid that from her. The problem was she didn't believe me. She was planning our life around remaining close to the university so she could be near her family. There was to be a law practice for me, something modest in the beginning, but she envisioned that changing over time so I could run for elected office. At the very least, she thought I would secure a teaching position at the university as her father had and make my mark there. These were not plans that she shared with me. I learned them from her father when he mentioned that a friend of his, also a lawyer, had been making inquiries about me joining his firm.

"I spoke to Alexandra later, and for all intents and purposes, our engagement ended that night. It merely required three painful weeks for us to realize it."

Phoebe nodded slowly, saying nothing for several long moments, then, "I'm sorry."

Remington was struck by her sincerity. "It's been years, Phoebe, and it was better that it ended before it began. We were both fortunate there."

"Yes, you're right. Of course you're right, but . . ."

When she did not finish her thought, he said, "Are you sad for me?" Her rueful smile was answer enough. "Why, you're a romantic, aren't you?"

"You sound surprised."

"I thought you were a realist."

A shade defensively, she said, "Sometimes I am. Mostly I want to be."

"Why?"

She shrugged. "It's safer, isn't it?"

He thought she might explain, but she didn't, and he did not pursue it. A heavy raindrop had just hit his sleeve. He looked up at the sky and felt another splatter his shoulder.

He reached over and took the reins from Phoebe's hands before she startled. "Do you feel that? I think we're in for a soaker. We are not far from the cabin, but we need to pick up the pace."

They did, but it didn't matter. By the time they reached the old prospector's abandoned lodging, the dark clouds had all rolled in and opened up. They were wet through and through and wretchedly cold.

Remington stamped his feet as he entered the cabin while Phoebe stood in one place, hugging herself as she shivered. "I'm sorry, Phoebe. If I'd had any hint this storm was coming, we would not have set out." He thought she nodded, but it could have been she was only shaking with cold. "Look, there's a lean-to around the back where I can shelter the horses, and an old smokehouse where I might find some wood for the stove. If there's nothing inside, the smokehouse is so close to collapse I'll knock it down, and we'll use that wood to start a fire."

"All right."

"I won't be long. You should walk around some, maybe take off your shirt and wring it out." He was out the door without waiting to see what she thought of this last suggestion, but he was a romantic as well, and he lived in hope.

Chapter Seventeen

Remington's hopes were dashed when he entered the smoke-house and found Phoebe standing there with an armload of wood.

"What?" she asked, feigning innocence. "You told me to walk around."

"I also told you to take off your shirt."

Phoebe smirked. "Uh-huh."

Remington bent, picked up another piece of wormy wood, and dropped it on top of the pile in her arms. "Take that." And then, because her arms were occupied and the best she could do was dropping the wood on his feet, he leaned over and kissed that splendidly sassy mouth. "And that, too," he said, when he straightened.

There was nothing about Phoebe that was disingenuous. She tilted her head and gave him a long, considering look. "You're a dangerous man." Then she shoved her armload of wood against his flat belly, forcing him to take it. "You go on inside now, Romeo. I'll follow directly." Because he let her, she was able to maneuver him out the door and into the driving rain, but as soon as he was gone, she pressed her knuckles against her mouth and held them to the lingering imprint of his lips.

Remington was stripping bark off some of the wood to serve as kindling when Phoebe returned. He stopped to help her unload. "Where are you going?" he asked when she headed for the door. "Oh, no. Not outside again. Do this and I'll get more wood. Besides, I still have to get the saddlebags, canteens, and horse blankets."

Phoebe returned to his side, hunkered down, and relieved him of the log in his hand. "Do we have matches?"

"In an oilcloth in my saddlebag."

"Hurry, please." She applied herself to stripping bark and tried not to think about how long he would be gone, or that he should have thought about the saddlebags, canteens, and blankets before he thought about getting the wood—or about kissing her. He was obviously addled.

Phoebe kept at her task for two reasons: She had an overwhelming urge to be warm again, and as long as she worked, her back was to the bed where she had been tied. As soon as she walked into the cabin, she had glimpsed a short length of rope on the floor at the foot of the bed. She had shivered then, and it shook her bones. Remington was not the only one who was addled, she decided, although she doubted their reasons were the same.

She gave a small start when the door banged open. Remington was carrying the blankets under one arm, the canteens under the other, and the saddlebags from both horses over a shoulder. The door got away from him.

"Sorry," he said, closing the door with the heel of his boot. "I didn't mean to scare you."

"I thought for a moment it might be Fiona. She knows how to use a door to great effect as well."

"Indeed," he said dryly. He tossed one of the blankets, both canteens, and a saddlebag on the bed, and carried the rest to her. He snapped the blanket open and handed it over. "Wrap yourself in that. It's drier than the other one and a modest enough cover if you want to get out of your shirt."

"You are relentless."

"Persistently optimistic."

Phoebe sat cross-legged on the floor and huddled in the blanket. "Mm. Aren't you cold?"

"For all but a minute back there in the smokehouse."

"I suppose you mean the kiss."

"You'd be wrong," he said, unwrapping the matches. "I was referring to uncovering a yellow-bellied racer in the woodpile."

She wrinkled her nose. "What is that exactly?"

"A snake."

"Is it venomous?"

"No. Harmless. Doesn't matter, though. I don't like snakes." When that provoked a spark of laughter from her, he felt warm again, but also curious. He cocked an eyebrow at her as he struck a match. A whiff of sulfur and a yellow glow accompanied the strike.

"Goodness," she said. "Light the kindling. You look positively satanic."

The matchstick was burning down, but he gave the flame a little shake in Phoebe's direction before he held it against a dry strip of bark in the stove. He blew gently on the fire, making sure it was well caught before he closed the door. "Why did you laugh?" he asked, choosing a log from the pile that he could add to the stove.

"Oh. The idea of you being afraid of snakes struck my funny bone. I don't think it occurred to me that you might be afraid of anything." She tilted her head to one side and gave him her full regard. "Maybe Fiona." As soon as she said it, she realized that she had given him the opening to point out that, as he saw it, Fiona *was* a snake. The urge was there, she saw it in his face, but he resisted and swallowed what he would have liked to say. "Thank you," she said quietly.

"Mm." He opened the door to the stove and carefully added the log. "It will be warm enough soon for you to feel it. You can come closer."

Without releasing the blanket or unfolding her legs, Phoebe inched closer to the fire. She leaned her face toward the grate and closed her eyes. That was how she missed the lightning strike that stretched jaggedly across the sky and was unprepared for the roll of thunder that shuddered the cabin. She felt as if she jumped high enough to clear the floor, but when the thunder passed, she was still sitting solidly on it.

Phoebe looked around uneasily and then focused on the cabin's only window. "I suppose I know why it's called Thunder Point."

"Which one is your yellow-bellied racer?" he asked. "The thunder or the lightning?"

"It's all a bag of snakes to me. I don't think there's ever been a time I didn't cower in a storm. When I was young and small enough, I would crawl into a trunk in one of the dressing rooms and close the lid."

"Dressing rooms. You're talking about in the theater. Did you live there?"

"It felt as if I did."

"What about your parents, Phoebe? Fiona mentions them, but not often. You never speak of them."

"And I won't now."

Remington was more disappointed than surprised. He knew from Fiona that her parents both worked in the theater, although not as players, and while she never said it outright, he had the impression that Mr. Apple was a failed playwright and a successful drunk, and his wife did mending, laundry, and cleaning for the troupe. Mrs. Apple may have performed other duties outside of her marriage but on this count, Fiona was understandably vague.

Remington shoved another log into the fire. "I'm going to get the other blanket and join you, unless you want me to use it to cover the window so you can't see the lightning."

"No. Get warm. There's nothing you can do about the thunder, and the lightning prepares me for it." The words were barely out of her mouth when there was another close strike. The cabin creaked and rumbled. In the far corner, water began to drip from the ceiling. Recalling there was a pot under the bed, she quelled the ridiculous urge to place it beneath the leak.

Remington sat down, folding his legs in the same tailor fashion as Phoebe. His knee bumped hers. Neither moved away.

"How are you doing?" he asked.

"How do you mean?"

"Any way you like."

"I'm warmer, and I'm not sore from riding, so that's something."

"It is."

She stared into the fire for a long time before she spoke. "I saw pieces of the rope when we came in the first time. I haven't looked back since."

"I wondered if you'd seen them."

She used the thumb and forefinger of one hand to circle the wrist of the other. "I had the oddest sensation I could feel the rope here." She released her wrist, examined it, and slipped her hand under the blanket when she couldn't see anything. "It still tingles."

Remington held out a hand. "Let me."

She didn't, not right away. "What are you going to do?"

In answer, he reached under the part in the blanket and took it. Using both hands, he rubbed her wrist between his palms. "Better?"

Phoebe nodded and didn't question him when he tucked her hand away and reached for the other. The tingling was certainly gone, but that was because he had replaced it with heat that went all the way to her marrow. This time she withdrew her hand while he was still holding it. "Mm. Thank you." She felt heat creep into her face and would have blamed her proximity to the stove if he had said something. He didn't, though, and she was glad for not having to tell a lie that he would have seen through anyway.

Remington pitched another piece of wood into the stove and brushed his hands on his knees. "I could bring the mattress over and we could sit on it. Bound to be more comfortable than this floor."

Because the damp and cold seemed to be seeping up through the floorboards, Phoebe agreed. She didn't offer to help him and he didn't ask. Her contribution was moving out of the way to give him enough space to throw down the mattress. She had already claimed her place on top of it when he returned with the canteens and the other saddlebag.

"Something to drink?" he asked, holding out a canteen.

She shook her head. "I'm fine."

"Something stronger?" He reached into the same saddlebag that had held the matches and came out with a silver flask. "Whiskey."

"Yes, please."

He opened the flask. The cap hung from the neck by a thin silver chain. "Ellie and Ben gave me this when I graduated." He held it out to her. "It's engraved."

Phoebe tipped the flask to her lips and swallowed a generous mouthful before she examined the engraving. The flourishes were elegant and quite elaborate. "RFL." She returned the flask. "What does the L stand for?"

"Lawrence. My mother's maiden name."

"Was she a city transplant like Fiona?"

"No. Born and raised in Frost Falls."

"So this is what she knew, what she always knew."

"This?" he asked. "You mean growing up in a small town that was barely settled when she was young, living on a ranch with no neighbors within shouting distance?"

"Yes."

"Then, yes, it's what she knew. In the case of Twin Star, it's what she chose when she agreed to marry my father."

Phoebe nodded slowly, faintly, and pulled the blanket tighter around her shoulders. "Do you ever wonder why Thaddeus married Fiona?"

"Never have." He saw surprise flicker across her face. "Oh. You think it's because I haven't been curious, but that's not quite right. I haven't been curious because I've always known the answer. He loves her. Now, the why of *that* puzzles me some, but I'm in no hurry to work it out. It isn't necessarily a bad thing when a man as steady and considering as Thaddeus can lose his mind and surprise everyone who's known him."

"Is that what you thought? That he lost his mind?"

"Didn't you?"

Phoebe's smile was rueful. "I did, yes. I thought exactly that in the very beginning. I had some experience, you know, observing men abandon their good judgment where Fiona was concerned. Sometimes I thought they deserved what they got, which was to be led about by the nose and then dismissed, but there were some true gentlemen, and your father was one of them, men who were genuinely kind, mostly clear-headed, and would not allow Fiona to lead them anywhere they did not want to go. The men she could not control fascinated her, but they also frightened her. She did not so much dismiss them as make it intolerable for them to stay. Those men packed their own bags and left."

Phoebe unfolded her legs and drew her knees toward her chest. Hunching, she hugged them. "You know why she married Thaddeus, don't you?"

"Well, it wasn't because she lost her mind."

"Oh, I see. You think it was a consequence of careful calculation. Thaddeus has money, and Fiona rarely does, so that must be it. He's not merely fine-looking, he's distinguished, and that would have been a factor for someone like Fiona who finds pleasure in being accompanied by a handsome gentleman. He rarely drinks and never to excess—another point in his favor—and he has an even temperament, never once demonstrating the urge to raise his hand even when provoked. You probably assume Fiona's time in the theater was nearing an end, that she recognized she would have to take secondary roles or remove herself entirely. That assumption would be wrong. She had years of work ahead of her, and she walked away from all the offers to be with Thaddeus. *Now* do you know why she married him?"

"For love? Is that what you want me to believe?"

"You don't have to believe it, but it's true."

Remington extended his hands toward the warmth of the stove. "I want to think about it. You're right about some of the assumptions I made, but I don't know that it matters. You saw the matchstick when I struck it. The flame was hot and bright and brief. It burned itself out."

Phoebe presented no counterpoint. She fell silent, and when he offered her another drink from the flask, she refused it. Rain beat relentlessly against the roof. Sometimes the wind shifted and raindrops splattered the window, falling heavily against the glass like batter on a hot griddle. Remington got up twice, once to look out the window, and the second time to open the door and peer up at the sky. He had no commentary on what he saw, but Phoebe had the impression that he was not encouraged.

"Why did you come, Phoebe?"

She gave a small start when he spoke after so long a silence. Maybe if she had not been mesmerized by the fire and the rain's steady tattoo, she would have understood what he really was asking and answered differently. What she did, though, was regard him with some confusion and said, "You know why. You told me to come."

He shook his head. "I didn't mean *here*. I mean why come west?"

"Sorry. My mind was elsewhere and nowhere. Hmm. Why did I come? Well, there was the invitation, of course, and I was curious about Twin Star. Until my train left the station, I'd never been very far outside the city, so there was the prospect of adventure. I wanted to see Fiona. She never had occasion to write many letters, and it's difficult for her, so I wasn't surprised that her correspondence was sporadic, but that she had so little to tell me was concerning. Your father wrote to me more often than she did."

"Why is it difficult?"

"What?"

"You said writing letters is difficult for her. Why? It's something more than lack of practice and opportunity."

"I shouldn't have said that. She wouldn't like you knowing." She saw it on his face, then. The understanding. "Fiona's never had schooling beyond what she was able to acquire in the theater. She learned to read because there was always a script lying around and someone who cared enough to help her. It was not as important, I suppose, that she learn to write. That came later, much later, and it still frustrates her."

"But not you."

"No. I attended a parochial school. Fiona insisted, and she paid for it."

"Fiona?"

"Hmm. She had regular roles by the time I was ready for school. She supported us." She shrugged. The blanket slipped off one shoulder and she drew it back. "So that's why I came. There were lots of reasons, but only one of them put me on that train. I needed to see her, to know that she was well. I understand why Thaddeus invited me, and I understand now why she didn't, but that's not important to why I came."

"You love her."

"You say that as if it surprises you. She's maddening and critical, impulsive and selfish, but she's also frightened and vulnerable and has to protect a heart that's as soft as pudding. Of course I love her."

Phoebe blinked, sat up straight. "That's it! That's what I said to her that put her in a snit." She saw Remington preparing to ask a question, and she shook her head quickly to forestall him. "She and I had just left the milliner's. We couldn't come to consensus on a hat that she thought was appropriate for me. I'm afraid I was entirely disagreeable. I was trying to make amends for my behavior when she said something that struck me as so absurd and so very like her that I realized it was hopeless. I said something like, 'Oh, Fiona, I do love you, you know,' and she stopped right there and asked me if I meant it."

"And you told her . . ."

"That's just it. I'd said the words so offhandedly that I didn't know what she was asking about. I swear I didn't. No wonder she was in such a mood. She accused me of being cruel." Phoebe rubbed the furrow in her brow with her fingertips. "Do you recall that afternoon?" she asked. "We came across you not long after, relieved you of your parcels."

"I do remember," he said. "She called you a cat."

Phoebe nodded. She closed her eyes and used a thumb and forefinger to smooth her eyebrows. "I have to speak to her. She doesn't believe me. Somehow I have to make her believe I meant it." She dropped her hand, opened her eyes, and stared at Remington. "She makes it so difficult to like her sometimes that I probably don't tell her nearly often enough that I love her."

Remington listened, nodded, and then pointed to the window. "I understand you feel some urgency to set things right, but it's not going to happen today. Old Man McCauley built this place close to the stream. Most of the time that was a convenience, but right now that stream's on a rapid rise and will be spilling over its banks in an hour or so if this rain keeps up. The cabin rests off the ground, so that's good, but the stone pillars that support it are not as fixed as they used to be."

"And that would not be good," she said.

"No." He regarded her candidly. "That would be an understatement."

Chapter Eighteen

Phoebe rose and went to the window. She set her hands on either side of her eyes, pressed her forehead to the glass, and peered out. The sky was dark, ominous, but it was hours yet to nightfall and she could clearly see the stream and hear the rushing water. She looked over her shoulder at Remington. "Should we leave?"

Before he could answer, another bolt of lighting struck the ground somewhere nearby. Phoebe jumped back from the window and clamped her hands over her ears. It dulled the crash of thunder but did nothing to blunt the rumble that went through the cabin. She had just lowered her hands when there was a second crack, markedly different from the first. The floor shuddered this time, but not the walls. "What was that?"

"Tree. Lightning must have hit one."

"So maybe we shouldn't leave."

"Come here." He patted the space beside him, the one she had left when he told her about the rising water. "We're not going anywhere. Do you recall that shallow river we waded through on our way here?" When she nodded, he went on. "That will be running too deep and fast for the horses to cross safely. They'll lose their footing. We're better off here."

"What about the foundation? What if it buckles?"

"I'll keep an eye on the water's approach. We'll have enough warning to get out and climb to higher ground." He indicated the space beside him again. "I wouldn't take you out in that storm now. Bullet might manage, but your mare would spook, same as you. We're safer here."

Phoebe joined him. "Turn around," she said. "Or look some-where else, anywhere else, but not at me." She threw off the blanket and began to unbutton her vest. "I mean it, Remington."

"Let me add a log before you get any further." She paused, and he tossed more wood into the stove. When the fire blazed, he shut the grate and lowered the brim of his hat until it effectively covered his eyes. "Let me know where you're done."

Phoebe slipped out of her vest, folded it, and set it aside. The sleeves and collar of the chambray shirt were uncomfortably wet, while the part of it that had been mostly protected by the vest was merely damp. Still, it clung to her like a second skin and she had to peel it off. The camisole she wore under it was damp as well. While she debated whether to remove it, her skin prickled and the decision was made for her. She removed the camisole and placed it beside the shirt as close to the stove as she dared, then she fit the blanket under her arms and tied a knot above her breasts. Her shoulders were bare but warmer now with firelight glancing off her skin than they had been when she was wearing the shirt and vest.

She took off her hat, placed it beside her, and unwound her plait. She used her fingers to sift through her hair and arranged the cascade of soft waves so they covered her shoulders.

"Done?" he asked.

"Just. How did you know?"

"I heard you sigh." He raised the brim of his hat with a forefinger and looked her over. "I'm thinking you're warmer already." He could have said the same for himself, but she was already as skittish as a kicked kitten so he kept quiet. "I have some rope. I can rig a line to dry our clothes. I wouldn't mind getting out of my shirt."

Phoebe didn't know how she felt about him taking off his shirt, or rather she did know, and was not as against it as she thought she should be. "All right." When he started to rise, she caught his hand and pulled him back. "Wait. Where's the rope?"

"Still hanging from Bullet's saddle. I wasn't thinking I

might need it. Look, Phoebe, I have to check on the horses anyway, make sure they haven't bolted, and I should bring in more wood while I can. The smokehouse is the structure most likely to float away and take our wood with it."

Everything he said made sense, but she did not want to be left alone, not in this place, not during this storm. "Let me get dressed again and help you."

He shook his head but cupped the side of her face to gentle the refusal. "Watch me from the window. You can't see the lean-to, but you'll be able to follow me back and forth from the smokehouse. I'll drop the wood right inside the door, and if you still want to help, you can start stacking."

It was not a satisfactory answer as far as Phoebe was concerned, but she knew she had to be satisfied. She nodded. Her cheek rubbed against his palm. It was oddly comforting, and she missed it when he lowered his hand and got to his feet.

"I won't be long," he said. He pointed to the window as he crossed the room to the door. "Go on. Watch."

Phoebe waited until the door closed behind him before she swept the tail of the blanket over one arm and scrambled to her feet. She was at the window in time to glimpse him hurrying toward the rear of the cabin and the lean-to. In her anxious mind, he seemed to be gone a long time, but it was probably less than two minutes before he reappeared with a coil of rope hanging off his shoulder. He veered right to the smokehouse and was in and out between two quick lightning strikes. She was at the door to scoop the armload of wood from him before he dropped it on the floor.

They repeated that pattern three more times until she begged him to come inside. Rivulets of water poured from his hat brim when he bent over the stacked wood to add the last load. Without asking permission, she swept the Stetson off his head and beat it twice against her thigh. Beads of water sprayed the stove and sizzled. She tossed his hat beside hers and then got behind him, set her hands flat against his back, and pushed him in the direction of the bed. The frame that had supported the mattress was solid and she jabbed a finger at it.

"Sit. Take off your vest, your shirt, and whatever you're wearing under it." She did not wait for him to comply because any reasonable person would, and she judged him to be reasonable more often than he was not. She was kneeling at his feet when he sat. "Boots."

"I can take them off," he said.

"You're supposed to be taking off other things. Slide the left one over here."

He did. "They're muddy. Your hands, they'll get—"

She stopped him with a jaundiced look. "The one thing we have plenty of is water for washing." She grabbed the boot by the heel and worked it off. She noticed the knife sheathed inside but didn't comment. He'd been out so long that even his sock was damp, and that was concerning. She stripped it off without giving him a chance to argue. "Other one." She lifted his foot. "I notice you're not doing much about that vest. I'll do it for you if you can't."

"I don't think I noticed before how bossy you are."

"And single-minded. Go on. The button goes through the hole."

Chuckling, he began to undress. "Do you want to know that your knot is coming undone? The view from up here is like looking down into the Valley of Elah. I've read that's fertile ground."

"Not for you, it's not. And so you know, referencing the Bible will not assist your cause. Look the other way or close your eyes. You don't need to see to take off your clothes."

He did neither. "What's my cause?" he asked, keeping a close eye on the knot. There was definite slippage as she unrolled his sock and tossed it toward the stove. When she looked up and caught his blatant stare, she mocked him with a smile that scolded.

"I don't think I'm flattering myself when I say you'd like to get me out of my clothes."

"Huh. What gave me away?"

"It would be easier to tell you what didn't."

He laughed appreciatively at that.

Phoebe took his vest when he handed it to her and waited

for his shirt. "Isn't there a woman in Frost Falls in want of your attention?"

"There is, but I have to leave a dollar on her night table when I go."

She batted his leg. "I believe you, but isn't there anyone else?"

Remington peeled off his damp shirt as she had done and gave it over. "Why do you think there must be?" Under it he was wearing a long-sleeved cotton shirt that fit him closely when it wasn't wet, and since it was, he wore it like a glove. He pulled it over his head when she held out her hand for it.

Phoebe stared at his naked chest. It was not the first one she had ever seen, but it was easily the most appealing. In the theater, she was used to men with pasty complexions managing their figures with corsets and braces. Remington required no such artifice, and for reasons she could not clearly define, that put her out of sorts with him.

Somewhat impatiently, she said, "You have to know that you possess qualities attractive to women."

"A man doesn't get tired of hearing them, you know. Start with the A's. Admirable. Amusing. Articulate. Attorney-at-law."

And as quick as that, her irritation faded. "Ass. Go on. Go over there and get the blanket around you. Warm yourself before you rig the line."

He rose, stepped past her kneeling figure, and went to the stove. It was Phoebe who thrust the blanket at him. He pulled it around his shoulders and held it in one fist while she used the time to adjust the knot at her breasts. They stood side by side for a long time. She felt him shiver and found his hand under the blanket. She threaded her fingers in his. Except to gently squeeze her hand in acknowledgment, he didn't stir again.

It did not happen suddenly, or even by thoughtful design. Phoebe leaned into him, rested her head on his shoulder, and that was fine until it wasn't. He opened his blanket and she stepped into the curve of his arm. He closed around her, embraced her. It was a light touch, an easy one, full of warmth. There was security, too, and comfort.

Phoebe knew he would not turn her away if she came to him. Did she want to come to him? She had never gone willingly to any man, but that had not necessarily mattered.

Fiona had taught her early that it might not always be her choice, and she had learned the truth of that when she was sixteen, between acts one and two of *Much Ado About Nothing*. It was a small blessing, she supposed, that she was three years older than Fiona had been when it happened to her. It was Fiona who drove him out when she surprised him in her dressing room. She stuck him with a hatpin to make him leap away and then raised welts on his back and buttocks with his ebony walking stick, the one with the silver-plated lion's head. He had limped out of the theater by the back door, his shirt in shreds, his back bloody, calling Fiona every vile name he knew. Phoebe recalled quite clearly that Fiona had bested him there as well.

Fiona had been her champion, but it was left to others to comfort her. After all, there were four acts remaining and Fiona had the role of Beatrice. That evening, when they had retired to their rooms, Fiona gave her a revolting concoction to drink saying only that it would prevent the most serious of consequences. Phoebe understood precisely what that meant, and for eight days following the rape, Fiona asked her if she had begun her monthly courses. When she was finally able to say that she had, nothing about that night was ever mentioned again.

It happened a second time, and a third, both with the same man, a suitor of Fiona's, but Phoebe never told anyone. She couldn't. Montgomery Hobart the Third, heir to a textile fortune, showed her the diamond-encrusted stickpin in his ascot and promised—not threatened—to permanently scar Fiona's face if she spoke a word. So she hadn't. On both occasions she visited the gypsy witch who had given Fiona the drink that had seemed to be efficacious the first time. She was so sick with cramps that a physician was sent for. He asked her some pointed questions and she lied without the least compunction.

Phoebe made plans to kill Monty Hobart, plans she was

certain she could carry out, and there was still some part of her that regretted never having the opportunity to test her resolve, but Monty robbed her of that, too. Two weeks before he was supposed to visit New York again, he died in a factory fire.

Without preamble, she said, "I am not a virgin. Is that something you want to know?"

Remington blinked. "How *does* your mind work, Phoebe?"

"In leaps and bounds apparently. Are you sorry I told you? Does it make a difference?"

"You should be able to say what you like even if I can't always—hardly ever—follow the path that got you there. As for it making a difference, it'd be hypocritical for me to say so, don't you think? Not only am I not a virgin, but I've been standing here contemplating a path of my own, the one where I'll encounter the least resistance getting you on that mattress again, preferably on your back and under me."

Her throat felt very thick and there was a weight on her chest that made it difficult to breathe. She said, "Oh."

"Uh-huh. So if you were a virgin, it wouldn't be for long anyway—if I ever work out the path, that is."

"Down."

"How's that?"

"Down. The path is down."

"The shortest route, then."

"Yes. The shortest route."

Chapter Nineteen

First there was the kiss. Remington opened the other side of his blanket and Phoebe turned, stepped in, and then she was enveloped in his arms, cocooned. His head lowered, hers lifted. Their mouths touched.

Phoebe had little experience with kissing. When Remington had surprised her in the shed, planting that hard, brief kiss on her mouth, she counted it as her first true kiss. It was all she had to compare with what he was doing to her now.

He nudged her lips with his, parting them. She caught just a sip of air before he began to explore the shape of her mouth, and it was warm and musky on her tongue. She realized she had stolen that breath from him. That made her smile.

He felt the change in the slant of her mouth, thought he could actually taste the sweet bubble of laughter that hovered on her lips. He brushed her mouth. Once. Twice. Their lips clung. He touched the tip of his tongue to her upper lip. She shivered. A moment later so did he.

Neither of them was cold.

Her mouth opened under the pressure of his. Her lips were damp, soft, and sensitive, and what he did with his mouth and tongue kept them that way. She moaned because it was not possible to keep that sound trapped in the back of her throat. *He* made it impossible. It was all right, though, because she meant to give him everything.

The kiss deepened. Every thread of tension that supported Phoebe's legs snapped. She sagged against Remington, and whatever space existed between them vanished. Her arms were caught at her sides. She wriggled, slid her palms up his chest, over his shoulders, and then folded her hands behind his neck. She kept his mouth to hers. Why had she never known hunger for this until she was starving?

The shortest route was indeed down. With Phoebe's arms locked around him, Remington only had to lower himself to the mattress. The blanket unfolded as he stretched out and Phoebe stretched out over him. It was not the position he had imagined when calculating his path, but it was a very good one. He was grinning when she lifted her head, and he surrendered that smile when she lowered it again.

She kissed the corner of his mouth, brushed her lips against his jaw. She teased him with tiny tasting kisses along the cord in his neck. He brought her back to his mouth and kept her there with the heat and the hunger.

Without quite knowing how it happened, Phoebe found herself under Remington, not completely, not so his weight was pressing down on her, but covered by enough of him to feel all of his warmth. That was important right now because he was tugging at the knot that kept her blanket closed. This knot did not require the use of his knife. He raised himself on an elbow, watching her, not what he was doing.

The blanket did not fall open at once, but that was because Phoebe was not in charge of this curtain. Remington was. And he damn well was going to take his time. He studied the narrow part in the blanket; or rather he studied the slim line of milky flesh that it revealed. He rested his hand on the flat of her abdomen and then walked his fingers up the part, through the Valley of Elah, and on to the hollow of her throat. He could feel her faint pulse against his fingertips.

Remington bent, kissed her lightly, and then retraced his trail to where the knot had been. He nudged one side of the blanket. Under his fingers, the edge of it climbed up her breast, caught on the stiff bud of her nipple, and then made a rapid descent when he flicked it aside.

He cupped the underside of her breast and passed his thumb across the pink aureole. The little rosebud stood at attention so he gave it his, covering it with the gentle suck of his mouth.

Phoebe's spine arched as if he had pulled hard on a thread. She found support by driving the heels of her hands between lumps in the mattress. She pressed her head back and felt the line of her neck stretch taut. It drew him there. He left her breast and set his lips against her throat, her neck, and when he came to the hollow just behind her collarbone, he used his teeth to make his mark and his tongue to lave it.

She wanted to weep with the pleasure of it. She whimpered instead.

He followed the same path he had walked with his fingers but used his mouth this time. The blanket no longer covered her—the lift of her arching spine had taken care of that—and Remington now gave attention to the breast he had ignored. She did not react as if she were going to come out of her skin, but she did clutch his shoulders and make small crescents in his skin with her nails. Remington took that as a sign of her approval and stayed where he was until she reversed the pressure and pushed him away.

Raising his head, he searched her face. Her eyelids were heavy, but her eyes were alert. She had pressed her lips together and was breathing shallowly through her nose. "Too much?" he asked. His voice was rough, like gravel, but the whisper softened it.

"Mm. A little." She whispered as well and was barely able to hear herself above the sound of the rain hitting the roof. "And not quite enough."

The corners of his mouth turned up in a shadow of a smile that was equal parts regret and empathy. "I understand. Perhaps I should return the reins."

She didn't know what he meant until he was once again on his back and she was stretched along his length. He slipped a hand under her upper leg and lifted it across both of his. It was natural for her to rise up on one elbow and set her gaze on him. She ran the back of her hand along his jaw. The brush of his stubble was a pleasant sensation against her knuckles. She tapped his chin once with her forefinger before she slid it up to his mouth and rested it against his lips.

"I'm not shushing you," she said. "I'm letting you keep your secrets."

Because she did not raise her finger, he said, "Mm."

"You have the kind of mouth they hide behind, the kind that rests easy on your face, seems open, friendly, but then it twists slightly, reveals the wryness and says there's something you know that I don't, that maybe no one does. I like it." She raised her finger but not so he could comment. She kissed him on that beautiful mouth and whispered, "Perfect," against it.

She moved her hand to his chest, rested her palm over his heartbeat, and felt its thrum. Much as he had done, and because he had shown her how to do it, Phoebe walked her fingers to the flat of his belly and then spread them across it. His skin retracted under her touch, and she felt a sense of, if not quite power, then control. Somehow he had known she needed that before she recognized the same, and he gave it to her without hesitation, never risking the possibility that she would not ask for it. Where she was concerned, his instincts were flawless.

It was the same with the horses.

She was able to swallow her chuckle but was unsuccessful biting back her smile. It was not the thought that tickled her, not exactly. It was because she had thought of it *now*.

"What is it?" he asked.

She sighed. "Of course you would notice."

"Phoebe. You are lying beside me in what anyone would say is a provocative state of undress, and you—"

"Half-naked," she said. "That's what anyone except you would say, although it was nice of you to add 'provocative.'"

"And you," he went on as if she had not interrupted, "are smiling as widely as the Cheshire cat. It's disturbing."

She did laugh, then, and showered him with the sound of joy.

Remington let her fumble with the buttons on his fly until she asked for help between gulps of air. She surprised him by not trying to work his trousers over his hips. Instead, she attended to the fly on her trousers. She began to wriggle out of them, which made her breasts bounce in a most appealing way. She stopped, though not, it seemed, because he was ogling her.

It was a matter of her boots. She took back the leg he had pulled over his and sat up. "I forgot about these," she said. "There's an order, isn't there, when you want to get out of your trousers?" She bent one knee, pulled up her calf crossways, and wrestled the boot off.

Remington watched her toss aside the boot and then begin to contemplate her sock. It would have been amusing if his cock were not as hard as an iron bar and pressing with some urgency against his drawers. He almost groaned with relief when she decided to keep the sock on and turned her attention to the other boot.

The boot thumped to the floor. This sock also stayed on, although for a long, painful moment it appeared she was reconsidering her decision. Remington was tempted to thump his head against the mattress. He could make at least as much noise as the boot had and probably feel better for it.

"Are you all right?" she asked, turning her head to look at me.

"Fine." He wondered if his voice sounded as strangled as his throat felt. "Fine," he repeated and it was marginally better this time. "Are you going to take those off?"

"My socks?"

"No. God, no. The pants."

"Oh, I thought I'd let you."

He had to roll out of the way when she flopped backward. The mattress was narrow and he spilled right over the edge. It was only a few inches to the floor but he landed with a satisfying thump. He rolled right back on, sat up and straddled Phoebe, and then worked the trousers over her hips. He inched lower as he tugged the pants past her thighs, her knees, and finally pulled them away.

"The flourish was nice," she said. She imitated it, raising her arm and rotating her wrist, then letting the invisible pants in her hand fly. "Very theatrical."

Remington hadn't given any thought to what she might

be wearing under her trousers. If he had, he would have supposed she had on a pair of long flannel drawers similar to his—and he would have supposed wrong.

She wore a pair of split-crotch, white cotton knickers with three fussy tiers of ruffles where they ended just below her knee. He had seen fancier. Dance hall girls wore knickers with ruffles over their backsides and all the way down to the hem, and sometimes there were cascades of delicate lace, but this was the first time he'd seen feminine wear exposed after the removal of a pair of men's trousers.

When he realized those little ruffles had been hiding there all day, it was nearly his undoing. Now when she wore trousers, he would always wonder.

He bent his head, put his mouth close to her ear, and whispered, "Witch."

There was no way Phoebe could hear that as anything but a compliment. She turned her head, lifted it to find his mouth, and kissed him for a deliciously long time.

He ended up removing his own trousers because they were both impatient by then. There was no repeat of the theatrical flourish; he simply shoved them out of the way. They rearranged the blankets, tugging and yanking until one mostly covered the mattress and the other covered them. Their bedding was musty, smelled of horses and sweat and wood smoke, but that was of no account when their senses were teased by the fragrances of musk and sex.

Remington nudged her knees until they made a V for him. She raised them on either side of his hips; he levered between them and supported himself on his forearms. He brushed her lips, gently pushing them apart to tease her with his tongue. "Do you want to help me?" he asked against her mouth.

Phoebe took a shallow breath and whispered, "Tell me how."

Her answer surprised him, but he didn't reveal it in any way. What he did was tell her in terms both plain and temperate what he wanted her to do, and if he surprised her, she also did not reveal it.

Phoebe reached between their bodies, found the opening

in his drawers, and slipped her hand inside. She closed her hand around his erection and felt his blood surge. She remembered the thrum of his heart against her palm. This was like that, only stronger, more insistent, and Phoebe's fingers began to uncurl.

"No," he said.

Her fist tightened reflexively. When he groaned, she understood that it was pleasure that pushed the sound past his throat. She lifted her hips and guided him to her. She expected there to be pain, had prepared herself to accept it as the natural consequence of the intimacy she wanted with this man, but then he was inside her and she realized that she had never known intimacy with any man. In every way that mattered, he, Remington Frost, was her first.

His hips fell as he settled in her. He could have prepared her better, he thought, taken more time to make certain she was ready. She was tight, tight as her fist had been, and he wanted to drive into her as deeply as he could. He held back because the pleasure he felt was not shared. Not yet.

"All right?" he asked.

She nodded because she believed it was true, and she continued to believe it right up until the moment he proved to her that it wasn't.

"Come here," he said. "Another riding lesson, I think."

She didn't understand, didn't pretend to; she simply followed his lead. With some adjustment, some awkwardness, he turned them so she was straddling him and very much riding tall in the saddle. "I suppose you should let me have the reins again," she said.

And he did, letting her establish the rhythm. She leaned forward, made her breasts available to his lips and tongue. His hand slid between her legs, parted her lips with his fingertips, and stroked that other rosebud until it was wet with her dew.

He watched her pupils darken, grow larger, until her gold-flecked green irises were only thin rings of color. Sometimes the tip of her pink tongue would appear at the corner of her mouth. She unlocked her back, rose and fell with him, swayed.

Her cadence matched his and she began to take increasing short and shallow breaths as the rise and fall of her body quickened.

Remington recognized her rising pleasure. He felt it, too. He grabbed her thick mane of hair when it fell over her shoulder and hung on until she came. The shudder that rocked her, rocked him, and he bucked sideways, toppling but not dislodging her, and finally drove into her as deeply as he'd wanted to from the first. Four hard strokes and he came to the same noisy end that she had.

They were no better than half on the mattress. Remington's head and shoulders rested against the rough wooden planks of the floor while the small of his back was curved uncomfortably at the mattress's edge. Phoebe had it better because she lay on Remington, and while he was smoother than the floor and less lumpy than the mattress, he was only marginally softer than either.

Phoebe's cheek was pressed to his shoulder. She raised her head, regarded him through eyes that were vaguely unfocused, and immediately dropped back to his shoulder. "I'll move," she said. "Soon. I promise."

"Don't. Not yet. I can't."

She smiled because it required too much effort to laugh. She closed her eyes. "Neither can I."

In the corner of the cabin, the roof continued to leak. The steady drip had the excellent timing of a metronome. In minutes they were both sleeping.

Chapter Twenty

"I'm worried about her, Thaddeus." Fiona made full use of the front room, pacing the length of it from the upright piano at one end to the gun rack at the other. Sometimes she circled, but mostly it was a straight line back and forth.

"Fiona." Saying her name had no impact. She did not turn in his direction and she did not slow. Thaddeus watched her from his perch on the wide velvet arm of the sofa. He was sitting hipshot, one leg stretched out for balance, the other slightly bent. She disliked it when he sat on the arm of any piece of furniture instead of the seat cushion, so he had chosen to roost here hoping it would distract her long enough to get her to listen to reason. Thus far, it had not worked. "I understand you're worried, but you have no foundation for it. I swear to you Phoebe is safe and she will return no worse off than when she left."

"You don't know that. You can't know that."

"I know my son. He will see it as his duty to keep her out of harm's way. You have evidence to prove that he has done it before and no reason to think he will not do it again. Besides, Fiona, it is *rain*, not robbers."

She turned her head to glower at him, but there was no pause in her step. "It is a *storm*, Thad. Phoebe is afraid of storms. She used to hide in a trunk when she was a child. A trunk. She hasn't outgrown the fear, only the trunks."

Thaddeus admitted he didn't know about Phoebe's fear, but rather than mollify Fiona with the modest apology, it froze her anger. The glare from her amethyst eyes was glacial. He faced it head on. "She has good instincts. So does Remington. They'll seek shelter."

"Where?" she demanded. "Where will they find that? I don't understand why they left at all. Why couldn't he give her a riding lesson right here? Taking her away from Twin Star on horseback is not my idea of keeping her safe."

"I believe Phoebe had the impression you would not approve of her learning to ride."

Fiona stopped, set her hands on her hips. "That is not an impression. That is a fact. Learning to ride serves no purpose. It is an unnecessary risk for her to take and for the rest of you to support. She'll have no use for it in New York."

Thaddeus tilted his head, regarded her as he had not done before, and saw what he had only suspected. "Is that why you've never wanted to learn?"

Fiona's hands fell to her sides. "I don't know why you would say that. I am talking about Phoebe."

"I thought we were," he said. "Now I'm not so sure."

Fiona resumed walking but without the anxious edge. Her steps were slower, more deliberate. "And I'm sure I don't know what you mean."

"Hmm."

Fiona changed course and went to the window. She drew back the curtain and looked out. Rain cascaded from the porch roof and made a second curtain that was almost impenetrable. When the storm stopped, there would be a moat around the house, and that struck her as oddly perfect for her husband's purposes. Without the requisite drawbridge, she was effectively his prisoner.

She let the curtain fall and turned her back on the window. "Where did he take her? You must have some idea." Before he could answer, she added, "Please don't tell me they went into town. I know Ellie prepared food for them. That suggests your son had something else in mind."

"I wasn't going to lie to you," he said. "I don't know if they got there, but they were headed to Thunder Point."

Fiona leaned backward, pressed her hands flat to the

roughly plastered wall. "No," she said, although the word was hardly given sound. "Why? Why would he take her there? Isn't that where . . . I don't understand. Why would she agree?"

"Remington wanted to have another look around; he thought Phoebe could help. Neither of them has been back there since that night. It was time."

"It was time? Time for what? For Phoebe to be reminded of every awful thing that happened to her? There is no sense in that. She needs to put it behind her; that's what you do when terrible things happen. You put it behind you and walk on."

"Has that been your experience?" he asked quietly.

Fiona gave a small start. She pushed away from the wall and took a step forward. "I don't know what you mean."

"Putting bad things behind you and walking on. It sounded as if you were speaking from experience."

"Did it? I was speaking from common sense. What is the point of dwelling when nothing can come of it? What kind of life can Phoebe make for herself if she is forced to confront the consequences of her past?"

"She wasn't forced, Fiona. She wanted to go."

"You have that from Remington, I suppose."

"I do, and I have no reason to doubt him. I want to hear about these consequences. What is it that you think Phoebe is confronting out there?"

"She's confronting what happened."

"I understand, but what is it that you think happened?"

"What do you mean? She was held against her will in that cabin. Tied like an animal. Bound to a *bed*. What do *you* think happened?"

"Not what you're thinking. Did she say something to you that she did not say to anyone else? Do you know she was raped?" He observed Fiona flinch, but he did not call the word back, did not try to soften it. "Do you have reason to suspect? Remington did not."

She threw up her hands. "How would he know? If he asked her if they violated her, she would deny it, but I know these things. I *know* them, Thaddeus, and I know Phoebe. She could drink hemlock and would only admit to a mild case of dyspepsia."

Thaddeus stood and went to her. She did not pull away when he gently took her by the wrists and lowered them. He held her hands loosely. She cast her eyes downward and watched the sweep of his thumbs across the pale blue veins. Her breathing slowed.

"Will you say it now?" he asked, his voice calm, barely a whisper.

She shook her head, unable to look at him.

"There should be at least this much trust between us," he said. It was the wrong thing to say, but Thaddeus didn't know that until it was said. She wrested her hands from him and stepped away, and now that she was looking at him again, he wished she weren't. The icy rage was gone. Her eyes burned hot. Angry tears hovered but did not spill, and he was helpless in the face of them, not because a woman's tears had ever undone him, but because he did not understand what he had done to provoke them.

"You should never speak of what you don't understand."

Thaddeus did not try to call Fiona back as she walked away, and he harbored no hope that she would return. He was not even sure she would hear him. He stood just as he was, hands at his sides, lips pressed into a grim line, until he heard Ellie bang a pot in the kitchen. The sound jerked him out of his stillness. Turning on his heel, he went to seek her out. After more than a score of years living in each other's pockets, he could depend on her to have something to say. He might even listen.

Remington opened the saddlebag that Ellie had filled for him and began to unpack it. "Come away from there," he told Phoebe. She was standing at the door poking her head through the small opening she'd made. "It's finally decently warm in here and you are letting in both the cold and the damp."

She was reluctant to step away and it showed in how long it took her to close the door. "I think the rain is slowing."

Remington cocked an ear toward the roof. "I can hear."

"I needed to see it with my eyes." Phoebe crossed her ankles, folded her legs, and gracefully lowered herself to the mattress so she was sitting opposite Remington. "The stream's still rising, though."

"And it will continue to rise for a while after the rain's stopped."

"You don't seem to be concerned. Water is lapping at the smokehouse."

"We're going to be fine, Phoebe." He held out a chunk of bread to her and a slice of ham. "I couldn't find any plates. Old Man McCauley took everything his pack mules could carry when he left."

Phoebe took Remington's offering, tore off a smaller portion of the bread, and put it in her mouth. "Did you know him?" she asked around that bite of food.

"No, not so I could call him a friend. He was hardly an acquaintance. We crossed paths in town, but out here I gave him a wide berth. Everyone did."

"So this place is known. If people avoided it, it's because they knew it was here."

"Yes." He rolled his slice of ham and bit off the end as if it were a cigar.

"It follows, doesn't it, that Mr. Shoulders is likely from the area, not from Frost Falls specifically, but from somewhere close by."

"It's possible. Northeast Rail's detective is working from that assumption."

She nodded. "I don't think you are, though."

"How's that?"

When Phoebe shrugged, her unbound hair fell over her shoulder and she swung her head to toss it back. "I'm not sure. I think you have other ideas that you don't want to share." She watched him take a second large bite from his ham cigar and knew he had no intention of responding. "That's what I thought."

Remington slid one of the canteens toward her. "There's cheese in the bag, if you'd like that."

"Not just now, thank you. In the event we could be here for days, I think rationing is in order."

Laughing, he shook his head. "If you don't eat it, I'm sure the mice will. We're leaving tomorrow morning. First light. I promise." He used his chin to point to the window. "I don't anticipate the rain letting up completely until dark, maybe not then. Better if we wait."

Phoebe set the ham and bread on her knee and tightened the knot at her breasts. Remington's dark eyes had been following its slow descent. He actually sighed when she secured it. "Uh-huh," she said. "I know when you have ideas."

"I don't mind sharing this one."

She waved him off and picked up her food. "We are done with that."

"You sound definite."

"Oh, I am." He probably didn't believe her, she thought, because she had already shown him that she had the spine of a slug where he was concerned. She needed to keep that rather unpleasant image in her mind when she felt herself being drawn to him. And she was drawn. There was no accusation she could lay at his feet, not when the attraction was so clearly mutual that no seduction was required.

After they had lain together, they had slept deeply but not for long. They were still drowsy as they roused, he first, and then she after a few nudges. It was the act of settling themselves on the narrow mattress that roused them again, this time in a different way.

"My leg won't go there," she had said.

"Yes, it will. Here, give me the blanket."

"No. I want to keep it."

"It's tangled. That's why you don't fit."

Phoebe felt her cheeks growing warm as she remembered how he had yanked the blanket from her fist and pulled her bottom hard into the cradle of his groin. She was still wearing her knickers. He, his drawers. Except to call attention to a barrier that was flimsy at best, their clothing was of no significance.

"That's better," he had said.

She pushed deeper into the cradle he'd made for her. "You think so?"

"I do." His voice was strangled.

She reached behind her, found his arm, and pulled it across her body.

"Comfortable now?" he asked.

"Hardly. But I'm warm." He, on the other hand, was like a furnace. "I still want the blanket."

He'd spread it over them. His fingers brushed her breast and they didn't move on. She had turned slightly, then, just enough for his hand to cover her. The rough pad of his thumb moved over her nipple. She felt a sweet ache between her thighs and the sensation that he was there, inside her, moving slowly, deliberately, and she was contracting, holding him, holding on, because this was what she wanted.

It was perhaps inevitable that it became the reality.

Phoebe was aware that Remington was watching her. His mouth was tipped in a manner that told her he was amused, but set in that way that meant he would not tell her why. She ignored him.

That hadn't been possible earlier. He'd held her still, slipped into her from behind. She had moaned, and he had rubbed his chin against the crown of her head. "Phoebe," he'd whispered. Just that. "Phoebe." He'd said it as if it were important, as if she were important.

And right then she felt as if she were.

"There," one of them had said. "I want you to touch me there."

"Hold me." Had that been her? "Yes. Like that."

His hand went between her thighs. She was tender there and the sensation of pleasure was so sharp it was almost painful. Her mouth, too, was swollen, and she had run her tongue along her upper lip to trace the new line. A sound escaped, a whimper as he moved in her, and she closed her eyes and allowed herself to feel.

"You can shout if you like," he'd said. His mouth was close to her ear again. "No one will hear you."

"You will."

"Hmm. I know."

She reached behind her, palmed his buttock. It clenched under her hand. He held himself still. "That's good," she'd said. "A moment. I need . . ." And her voice had trailed off because what she needed was more. His thumb flicked her nipple. She drew in a sharp breath. He rocked her with his next thrust. Her head went back and knocked him on the chin.

There was a hasty, husky apology. Low, wicked laughter. And then he was pushing into her again and she was taking all of him.

Phoebe held out her hand for a wedge of cheese when she saw that Remington had taken it out of the bag. "No sense giving it to the mice," she said. Thanking him, she bit off half and chewed. He was rooting in the bag again and no longer curious about what she was thinking. That suited her.

It was afterward that they'd slept again, this time for much longer than the first. It was the rain, she decided. Lightning and thunder had already moved into the distance, but the rain and the gloom remained. There was also that devilish drip in the corner. It had finally stopped keeping good time, but then, when she had curled against him, her head on his shoulder, it had lulled her to sleep.

Phoebe's eyes shifted to the line where their clothes were hanging. Remington had used the hook supporting the lantern to secure one end and attached the other to a knob at the head of the bed. The line sagged in the middle under the weight of their clothes but none of them swept the floor.

"The sleeves of my shirt aren't dripping any longer," she said.

Remington glanced in that direction, nodded, and returned to rooting in the saddlebag. He came away with a hard-boiled egg. When she declined his offer to share, he cracked it on the floor and began to peel it. "Is that what you want to talk about?" he asked. "Our clothes?"

"What then? I haven't remembered anything." She pressed a finger to her temple. "No seeds. No sprouts." She turned to look at the bed. "Maybe if I—" She rose and walked over to the bed, dragging the blanket behind her.

Remington made a grab for her, then the blanket, and missed both. The egg fell out of his hand and wobbled on the floor. "Phoebe. Stop. You don't have to do that." But she was already beginning to sit. He forgot about the egg, his appetite, and went to her. "It will come to you or it won't. You don't have to force it."

"Isn't this why I'm here? You didn't plan the other, did you?"

He blew out a breath and raked his hair with his fingers. "No! Jesus. Why would you ask me that? You damn well know better."

Phoebe's face flamed but she held her head up and did not look away. He deserved at least that after what she'd said. "I'm sorry. That was thoughtless. You're right. I know better."

"Jesus," he said again, this time on a thread of sound. He backed off and went to the window. Hunching his shoulders, he stared out. Phoebe was right about the water; it was lapping at the smokehouse. He thought he should go out and check on the horses again. They'd sense the water coming toward them. Also, he had to piss. Phoebe probably wanted some time to herself. "I'm going outside," he told her. "Horses. Nature call."

"But it's still raining." As an objection, it was inadequate. She watched him dress in clothes that were only moderately drier than when he had taken them off, and then followed him to the door. He stood there, his fingers curled around the handle, not moving, his head slightly bowed. His hat was not sitting at its usual angle but tilted forward, and she could see that his hair was once again long enough to brush his collar.

Mr. Shoulders had worn his hat like that, tipped down in

the front, higher in the back, but the black scarf that was wound twice around the lower half of his face also hid his hair. She knew it was dark because she had seen his eyebrows, but she couldn't tell if it was overlong or trimmed short.

He was arguing with his men, trying to convince one of them to stay behind. No one was willing. The scarf was brushed wool. She saw that now. It would have been warm against his face. Too warm for comfort. That's why in his agitation he had tugged on it, pulled it away from his mouth and neck, and lifted his chin above it for a second, maybe two, before he ducked behind it again.

Phoebe blinked. Then, softly, because she needed to hear it first and know it was truth, she said, "He has a mustache."

Chapter Twenty-one

Remington's head came up and he turned. "What?"

"He has a mustache." She laughed suddenly, delighted, and held her forefinger above the curve of her upper lip and wiggled it. "It's thick. Like a . . . like a plump, wooly caterpillar."

"A caterpillar," he said slowly. He released the door handle but didn't approach.

"A plump, wooly, and dark, dark brown caterpillar. That's why I didn't see it clearly. It was almost the same color as the scarf around his face. And his chin, Remington. I saw his chin." She removed her mustache and used the same finger to poke at the center of her chin. "Dimple. He has a dimple right here."

He rolled his lips in to keep from smiling. "You probably should cease hammering your chin."

She stopped, withdrew her finger, and examined the tip. "Oh. Probably so."

Remington closed the gap between them and hunkered in front of Phoebe. "I'm sorry to have to ask, but are—"

"Sure? Yes. I'm sure. It was you this time, standing there at the door, and it put me in mind of Shoulders standing in the same place, only he was mostly facing me, not turned away. I never mistook you for him, if that's what you're thinking. You just helped me conjure a picture of him." She touched her upper lip again. "His mustache brushes the top of his lip. It's uneven, not groomed as your father's is. I had a better image of his hair, thick and dark brown like his mustache, but I couldn't tell if it was long or short at the back. The scarf hid it even when he pulled it away from his face."

"Are you all right?" he asked. "I can tell you're pleased that you've remembered something, but I don't imagine it's a pleasant memory."

The faint smile tugging at her lips faded. "No, you're right. It isn't pleasant. I was afraid. Perhaps I should have been relieved when none of them would agree to stay behind with me, but escaping on my own was hardly a consideration when I imagined all the calamities that might occur if I couldn't. I developed a rather lengthy list of unfortunate ways to die if no one came for me." Her eyes moved past Remington to the window behind him where rain continued to spatter the glass. "And yes, drowning in a flash flood was one of them." She managed a weak smile in what was a gravely set face. "I never stopped trying to get away, but I was ever so glad to see you."

"Oh, Phoebe." He cupped her cheek. "I wish I could have spared you this."

She laid her hand over his and shook her head. "I wanted to come, remember? No matter what you think, I wouldn't be here if I hadn't wanted to be. It was a good idea, Remington, and I'm not unhappy that you thought of it."

He nodded and withdrew his hand when she removed hers. He leaned in, kissed her lightly on the mouth, and then stood. "I still have to go out," he said. "The horses? That call of nature?"

"Oh. Yes. I suppose you do."

Still, he hesitated. "It seems wrong to leave you alone. I didn't understand so well before."

"Remington, you have to. I know that. Go on. It's better now than when you were going to walk out angry with me."

"I wasn't angry," he said.

"Disappointed, then."

"Frustrated," he told her. One corner of his mouth lifted. As a smile, it was self-mocking. "And all right, a little angry."

Phoebe waved him away, but she was smiling, too. "Go."

As soon as the door closed behind him, Phoebe dragged the pot out from under the bed and used it, thanking Old Man McCauley for leaving it behind. She stepped outside long enough to empty the contents and let the rain rinse it out. She didn't notice that the tail of her blanket was wet until she came back in. After toeing the pot under the bed, she checked her clothes. The thin camisole was the only article that was completely dry. She dropped the blanket and put on the camisole. She was standing in front of the stove drying the blanket when Remington reappeared.

Phoebe looked him over, saw he was almost as wet as he'd been when they arrived at the cabin, and jerked her thumb in the direction of the clothesline. "You're going to have to remove your boots yourself."

"I think I can manage," he said dryly, "but I suppose it means you're done courting me. That's disheartening . . . and inconvenient."

She laughed, shaking her head. "I didn't realize that helping you out of your wet boots could be mistaken for courtship. You have me at a disadvantage. I don't know the native customs."

Remington laid his vest over the line, tossed his hat on the bed, and began unbuttoning his shirt. "Do you want to hear them?"

She gave him a wry, over-the-shoulder glance. "Oh, yes. Entertain me."

"Well, there's sharing a horse, for instance. Riding double with a fella generally means the gal has her toe in the water."

"Fella? Gal? You *are* giving me the local color, aren't you?"

"Aim to please, ma'am."

"Go on."

Remington shrugged out of his shirt and then peeled his undershirt off over his head. He tossed both on the line without straightening the wet, wadded fabric. "Then, there's sharing a porch swing in the moonlight. A fella and gal that do that are reckoned to be sweet on each other, but when the gal rests her pretty little ankle boots in the fella's lap, most folks would consider them betrothed."

"Is that right?"

"Hmm." He sat down on the bed and shucked his boots and socks. He set the boots beside the bed and slapped the socks over the clothesline. "When a gal asks a fella to buy clothes for her, it's—"

She interrupted. "I gave you money for those clothes."

He put up a hand. "Do you think I'm talking about you? I am explaining the commonly held opinions regarding courtship." He added a distinctive drawl as he went on. "Anyway, I'm comin' around to that. So, like I was sayin', the gal askin' is one thing, the fella agreein' to do it is another, and the fact that there was money passed from the gal to the fella, well, that is acknowledged to be an intimate exchange no matter how it's sliced."

"Huh. There is so much to learn."

"It's like walkin' in the grasslands after the herd's moved on. You have to watch where you're going every step of the way."

Phoebe's laughter came in short bursts. She knuckled tears away from the corner of both eyes. "Of all the things I've heard so far, that might be the one worth remembering."

"It'd be a risk to ignore the others."

"I appreciate the caution." Phoebe stepped away from the stove, turned, and regarded the untidy clothesline. It was not that she wanted to do it; it was more that she could not help herself. She had organized the precious space of too many theater dressing rooms to allow Remington's chaos to stand here. She lifted his socks off the line, wrung and smoothed them out, and then rehung them. "Is that everything?" she asked, removing his wadded shirt.

"Almost. There would be folks who'd point to a gal accepting an invitation to go riding out alone with a fella and say that she's thinkin' real hard about her weddin' dress. Probably about the cake, too."

"Fiona would say that," she said, snapping out his shirt. Droplets of water sprayed the floor. "Would Thaddeus?"

"Hard to say. Ellie would. Maybe it's a woman's view."

Phoebe arched a brow. "I need to be clear, then, that never once during our ride did I think about a dress or a cake."

"Probably because you were trying so hard to stay in the saddle." He threw up his hands to ward off her glare. "That's not me saying that. That's what they'd say."

She balled up the shirt she had taken such pains to smooth and threw it at his head. He caught it easily and pitched it back underhand. "That was not at all as satisfactory as I'd hoped," she said, unfolding the shirt again. She placed it carefully over the line. "That has to be the last of it."

"Not quite. It would be accepted as fact that a gal who is fussin' with her fella's wet clothes is already hitched in her own mind, whether or not there's been a proper exchange of vows."

Phoebe snorted. "Now that is plain ridiculous."

"Maybe. But that's the customary thinking. You asked."

"So I did." She finished straightening the clothes and looked back to see if he intended to give her his pants. "Are you going to take those off?"

"They're not so wet. They'll dry quickly once I'm sitting in front of the stove again." He looked her over, head to toe. "Do you have anything you can put on over what you're wearing?"

Phoebe looked down at herself. She was modestly covered in her camisole and knickers, and was still wearing her socks. It occurred to her that Remington had never seen her toes. For some reason that made her grin. She wiggled them. "This is no more revealing than a bathing costume," she said. "They are all the rage at Gravesend."

Remington's mouth took on a wry twist. "I've been to Coney Island. Just once, but it was only a year ago in July. No woman on the beach or in the water was wearing anything comparable to what you have on."

She plucked at her camisole until it hung more loosely. "The costumes have sleeves," she said. "I'll give you that. And some have a skirt, but you must have observed that many women leave off the skirt and swim in bloomers."

"Bloomers. Yes. I saw those. Bladders attached to a woman's hips."

Phoebe laughed. He wasn't entirely wrong, although she might have called them balloons.

"Those women also wore stockings," he said. "Dark stockings."

She wiggled her toes again, drawing his attention to her feet.

"Very nice," he said, "but I'm noticing a fair amount of bare skin between the ruffle at your knees and the top of your socks."

"Then don't look there."

"You would not say that if you knew how difficult it is to look anywhere else."

"Surely not a Herculean task."

"Just about." Remington tore his eyes away from her finely curved calves and met her amused gaze. "Have pity, Phoebe. Wrap yourself in that blanket."

She shrugged. "All right. But what do folks say about courtship when the gal's closing the barn door after she's let the horse out?"

"Nothing about courtship, I can tell you. They'd say the gal's feeding that horse from a bucketful of sass." He pointed to the blanket on the mattress. "Go."

Phoebe picked up the blanket and wrapped herself in it. It had absorbed heat from the stove and was pleasantly warm around her shoulders. She settled in, facing the fire, then drew up her knees and hugged them.

Remington added two logs to the stove then took up the other blanket and joined her. Neither of them spoke. He did not know what she was thinking as they slipped into silence, but he doubted her thoughts were very different from his. He let her dwell on them, while he came to terms with his.

An ember popped, startling them both. Remington resisted the urge to use the break in the quiet as an excuse to talk. He waited for a more propitious sign and had it when Phoebe leaned into him and set her head on his shoulder.

"We should talk," he said. He did not add that it would be a serious discussion. She would know that.

"Yes." Her temple rubbed his shoulder as she nodded. "Will you begin, or shall I?"

"In almost any other circumstance, I would defer to you, but I want to go first this time."

"All right. If you're sure."

Remington plunged in. "I didn't plan on sleeping with you, Phoebe, but it would be a damn lie if I told you I hadn't thought about it. A lot. But coming out here with you today was never about more than what I thought you might remember and what I thought I might find. Do you believe that?"

"I do."

"Because you think I'm decent, I suppose."

"No, not at all. That isn't to say you aren't decent, because you are, but you're a bit more dangerous than decent, and that's why I think if you'd planned this, you would have chosen somewhere less . . ."

"Dilapidated?"

"Rustic. I was thinking rustic."

"That is without a doubt the kindest word ever applied to Old Man McCauley's cabin, but you're right to suppose I would have chosen differently. God knows, the barn loft would have been better, but I had something like a room at the Butterworth in mind."

"Because no one would have known us there or what we were about. Yes, that's a much better plan."

He nudged her head with his shoulder. "Something *like* a room at the Butterworth."

"Another hotel in another town. That might have been worked if you could have gotten me there."

"When I was thinking about it, you have to understand I had the end in mind, not the getting there."

"Yes." She tilted her head and looked up at him; the smile that lifted the corners of her mouth a mere fraction was settled more firmly in her eyes. "I see that now."

He turned his head and kissed her high on her brow. "So there you have it. It wasn't planned, but somehow it was right. Or almost right."

"Remington."

He ignored the note of caution she used when she said his name. "I want to make it right, Phoebe. And wanting to make it that way is not an afterthought. I wanted to make it right before I made it wrong."

"You've been thinking about this, then."

"For a while. Maybe since I saw you on the train. Maybe before."

"There was no before, Remington."

"There was the photograph."

"You don't mean that. Even you are not that romantic."

"Jumpin' Jesus on a griddle," he said under his breath. "Maybe I am."

She gently poked him with her elbow. "I won't say a word."

He didn't believe her, but he wasn't sure whom she would tell. Not Fiona. Probably not Thaddeus. Maybe Ellie. Could be she'd tell one of the men; that way everyone in Frost Falls would know inside of a week.

"It was probably not the photograph."

"See? You are already backing away from it nicely."

"It was the photograph *and* all the things Thaddeus told me about you."

"Thaddeus. The *shadkhn*."

"The what?"

"Matchmaker. It's Yiddish. Fiona called him that. She also said he was a yente. A busybody."

"Like Mrs. Jacob C. Tyler?"

"Exactly like her."

"I'll be darned."

"Don't pretend you're surprised. I think you've always known about your father's matchmaking. But me? I didn't believe Fiona."

"Maybe you did. A bit. But maybe it was more difficult to believe that Thaddeus would try his hand in it."

She laughed a little jerkily. "True. I held your father in higher esteem."

"The mighty have fallen. Is that it?"

"Mm. I think so."

"That will hurt him some—he values your good opinion—but probably not as much as failure."

"I can see that. He likes to do everything well."

Remington slipped a finger under Phoebe's chin and

raised it so she was looking at him again. "You are not making this easy."

"Is it supposed to be? You're the one with experience. You've proposed before. I've never heard one."

"Alexandra said 'yes' before I finished."

"That's because she'd already chosen her dress. Silk, I imagine. Muttonchop-shaped sleeves. Perhaps a pouter pigeon bosom. Yards and yards of material for the train and veil. Oh, and a stiff lace collar around her throat to show off her swan-like neck."

Remington stared at her.

Phoebe smiled. "Would you like to know about the cake you didn't get to eat?"

"That's it, Phoebe. You're going to marry me."

"It doesn't sound as if you're asking."

"I'm not. There are some words a man can't risk saying if he has to punctuate them with a question mark."

Her smile widened. "You make a compelling argument for telling a woman what to do, but you're still wrong if you think it works on me. I'm going to marry you, Remington Frost, but only because I want to."

Chapter Twenty-two

Fiona did not speak, did not look up, when Thaddeus entered their bedroom. She continued to read, although mostly it was a pretense. She had not turned a page in quite some time, but it didn't matter because he didn't know that. She thought he would say something, cajole her into conversation, but he went straight to their small dressing room and closed the door. It was not long before she heard water splashing in the basin and the sound of him rooting in the cupboard to find his shaving things.

Her stomach rumbled uncomfortably and she pressed a hand to her abdomen to quell the hunger pangs or at least silence them. She had stubbornly refused to leave the bedroom for lunch or dinner and suspected that because she was absent from the dining room, Thaddeus ate in the kitchen with Ellie and Ben. Thaddeus had carried a tray in at lunch, but Fiona had denied she had an appetite. Ben brought a dinner tray. When she refused it, he left it on the small round table just inside the door. She hadn't touched it. The temptation to eat something, no matter how cold or stale, kept drawing her eyes to the table, but the thought that Thaddeus would surprise her stuffing a honey-soaked biscuit in her mouth kept her seated firmly in the rocker.

Fiona rearranged her dressing gown so it spilled attractively around her curled legs. She went back and forth as to whether she should show a bare knee, trying it both ways before she settled on revealing a slim slice of a knee and calf. She purposely did not tighten the sash so the gown could remain casually open from her breasts to her throat.

One slippery sleeve drooped over her shoulder. The narrow strap and lace-edged neckline of her sleeping shift were thus displayed.

The oil lamp on the table beside her had provided sufficient light for her to read. Now she moved it closer so the pool of light fell more on her than the book. If she had learned anything from her years in the theater, it was the importance of staging.

She waited.

And waited.

She could hear him moving around, imagined him removing his clothes, but what was taking so long when his habit was to leave things where they lay was a mystery. It was worse when she couldn't hear him at all. There was a stool in the dressing room. Sometimes he sat on it and watched her while she dressed or undressed as though it were both fascinating and formative. He would sit there, leaning back against the wall, his long legs stretched out in front of him and mostly in her way, and follow her movements from under a heavy-lidded gaze. He would talk to her, too. Because he was almost always up and working hours before she got out of bed, he would tell her what he'd been doing and what he planned to do. At the end of the day, he'd talk quietly about the calf that needed to be rescued from a thicket or describe how a stallion everyone called Beelzebub had thrown two ranch hands to the ground and almost trampled a third.

Fiona didn't particularly care what he talked about. She loved his voice, loved the rumble in the back of his throat when he laughed. When he spoke, she was put in mind of whiskey washing over sand, his voice at once smooth and gritty. She did not know how that was even possible, but it was a fact that it had the power to make her shiver.

Still.

Fiona wished he would say something now. Call to her, perhaps, if he needed help, or rail at her if she had finally put him into a temper. His continued silence disturbed her. That's why, after all her careful staging, she was rising awkwardly from the rocker when Thaddeus stepped out of the dressing room. She caught the book as it was sliding off her lap but knocked the table with her elbow when she made the grab. The oil lamp wobbled dangerously until the table settled and the pool of light that was supposed to highlight her best features flickered unflatteringly across her startled countenance.

Thaddeus took the book from her hands as she dropped back in her seat and he used the toes of one bare foot to steady the rocker. He closed the book with his forefinger marking her place and regarded her from the advantage of his greater height. Several moments passed before she raised her face and met his eyes.

"All right?" he asked.

"Mm." She wanted to be annoyed with him for spoiling her scene but had no energy to expend on that emotion. What she felt after her initial surprise was nothing but relief. She searched his face much as he was searching hers. "You?" she asked. "You were in there so long . . ."

"Was I? I didn't realize. I was thinking, I suppose."

Fiona pressed a hand to her stomach but not because it rumbled. She knew what question she should ask and knew herself to be a coward for not asking it. She did want to know what he had been thinking. Instead, she asked, "They haven't come back, have they? I've been listening. I haven't heard them."

Thaddeus held out the book to her. When she shook her head, he removed the finger he had been using as a marker and set it on the table. "No, they're not back. I would have come for you right away. I think, now that it's dark, it's safe to say that they're hunkered down wherever they found shelter."

"But you believe that's Thunder Point."

"Yes. It makes sense that Remington would have tried to get them there. They might have reached it before the storm."

"It's still raining."

"A drizzle." Thaddeus removed his foot from the rocker runner. "They'll be back tomorrow." He went to the bed, turned back the covers, but did not climb in. Instead, he sat on the edge facing Fiona. He leaned forward and rested his forearms on his knees. He folded his hands together. "You are so goddamn beautiful."

Fiona blinked. She heard nothing complimentary about his observation; he said it merely as a statement of fact, one that did not seem to particularly please him. She had no idea if he meant for her to respond so she remained silent.

"Sometimes I wonder if that's why you think I asked you to marry me, as though I believed your beauty were the sum total of your worth and you accepted that because you think it's true."

Fiona's fingers curled around the arms of the rocker. Her nail beds whitened with the strength of her grip. Still, she spoke evenly and without rancor. "You are wrong, Thaddeus. I do not accept it. Or I didn't. Not when we were in New York. I had a place in the city, a role on and off the stage. I knew what I was about. What am I about here?" She raised her chin a fraction. The movement helped her keep it from wobbling. "Tell me, Thaddeus, what am I about here?"

She did not know how he might answer her question or even if he would. She held his dark, impenetrable stare until the aching pressure of tears she refused to shed made her blink.

"What did Ellie say when you spoke to her?" she asked. "I know you did. It's what you always do after we've argued. You might have sought out Phoebe if she'd been here—I've noticed that, too—but she isn't, so it would have been Ellie."

Thaddeus finger-raked his hair, lifting salt-and–pepper strands at his temple. He sat up and settled his hand on his knee. "She heard us, Fiona. She could hardly help but hear since she was in the kitchen."

"I heard her rattling around."

"So did I. That should have been our cue to take our discussion to another part of the house, which I believe was her intention in making noise in the first place."

"Why are you telling me this? It's not an answer to what I asked."

"I'm telling you because I think you're under the misapprehension that I share our private conversations with her, or at least my side of them. I don't. There's nothing private when she's heard everything. She told me in my effort to allay your fears, I dismissed them, and that when I tried to understand, I cornered you. That's why you fled as soon as you had the chance. It probably explains why you holed up in here the rest of the day. Does that sound as if it might be right?"

Fiona found a curlicue in the pattern of the rug where she could cast her eyes. She tugged on her earlobe. "It might be right," she mumbled.

"How's that again?" he asked, cupping an ear.

She raised her head and gave him a haughty look. "You heard me. And if Ellie just had, she'd say you were cornering me again."

The shadow of a crooked, self-effacing smile crossed his face as he acknowledged the truth. "She would. And I was."

"Well, stop it. You see what happens when I feel trapped."

"I do," he said quietly, "I should have seen it before now."

Fiona had no use for the look of resignation that suddenly defined his features. It frightened her. "I think I'm hungry now," she said for want of anything better to say and started to rise from the rocker for the second time.

Thaddeus was having none of it. "You're a changeling, Fiona. It's never been clearer to me than it has been today. Sit down. I'll bring the tray." He got up and retrieved it and then made room on the table beside her. "I see you're reading *The Count of Monte Cristo*. How many times is that now?"

"Three."

"Do you want the biscuit? Honey?"

"Yes. Both."

He prepared it for her, slicing the biscuit in half and drizzling each open face with a honey spiral. He gave her one half and left the other on the plate within easy reach before he returned to the bed. "Is it the city you miss, Fiona? Or the activity? The stage? Or the purpose?"

She said nothing.

"I ask because I haven't been aware that you have an interest in learning about Twin Star. You don't come to the corral when we're breaking horses or ask after a mare when I've told you about a difficult birth. I think you know the names of the hands but not how many head of cattle we're raising or the boundaries of the property. You know the road back and forth to town well enough, but I don't think you could find Boxer's Ridge with a map. It's less than three miles from here. You could walk. See a lot from up there."

Fiona waited to hear if there was more. There wasn't. Not at the moment. "It's only now beginning to feel like any spring I've ever known. It was snowing the day we arrived. Remember? It was beautiful. And then it went on. And on. There were breaks in the weather. I learned to drive a buggy during one of those thaws, not that there were many opportunities to go anywhere. You didn't seem to like me out of your sight. You didn't seem to want me out of your bed."

"Our bed."

She smiled a bit ruefully. "Yes. Our bed. My activity and purpose."

"That's not true. That's not how I see it."

Fiona set the biscuit aside. She had not taken a bite. "Then fix it, Thaddeus, because that's how I see it."

Remington's head rested in the cradle of his palms. He had been awake for a while with nothing to do except stare at the cabin's rough ceiling. It had stopped raining sometime during the night, and the roof had stopped leaking sometime after that. He thought the silence was probably what had awakened him. The fire was gone except for embers. He could reach the short stack of logs but not add one to the stove without sitting up. Movement like that would have disturbed Phoebe, and he was loath to wake her.

She was lying flush to him, one knee drawn up and resting over his thighs. Her breath came softly and easily. When she stirred, her chin rubbed pleasantly against his chest. He wanted to sift through her hair with his fingertips, but he would have to lift his head and unclasp his hands. He did not want to do that either. He wanted to stay just this way. It was perfect.

Phoebe Apple was going to be his wife. He had it from her own lips that she wanted to be. There had been no declaration of love by either of them. Was it understood, then? Or had she no expectation of it existing? That disturbed him some. Alexandra had harbored no doubts that she was loved. He wasn't sure that was true of Phoebe. He wasn't entirely sure that she loved him.

There were realities in the light of day that he wished could be shadowed by an overcast sky, maybe some thunder to roar over his thoughts.

"You're awake," she said. She did not lift her head or raise her eyelids, but she did use the arm lying across his chest to give him a small squeeze. "You know how I know?"

"How?"

"You think louder than any man I know." She felt the rumble of his laughter against the soft underside of her arm. "Do you want to tell me?"

"No."

"All right. I've been thinking, too. I bet you couldn't tell."

"I couldn't."

"That's because I whisper-think."

"Uh-huh."

"I like kissing you, and I like you kissing me. It's all right to think about that, isn't it?"

"Why wouldn't it be?"

"Well, do you think about it?"

"I wasn't just then, but I'm thinking about it now." He felt her nod but sensed more distraction in it than encouragement. There was more she wanted to say, and he waited to hear it.

"I don't have much experience with kissing, not any really, except with you. You probably find that odd, since I told you I wasn't a virgin, and now you know I was telling the truth."

"I knew it was truth because you told me it was."

"You are the first man who's ever kissed me on the mouth. Do you believe that?"

"If you say so, I do."

"It's true. It will be a shame if I look out the window this morning and see that the smokehouse has been washed away. I had begun to think of it as a monument to my first kiss."

That made him smile. "Sentimental, are you?"

"Yes. This cabin, too. I hope it stands for a long, long time. This is where you made me clean in a way all the scrubbing could never do."

Remington sucked in a breath and he knew Phoebe felt it because she lifted her head and looked at him.

"I was raped," she said. "Is that something you want to know?"

Chapter Twenty-three

Remington stopped cradling his head and used his hands to take Phoebe by the shoulders. He pushed her back while he sat up. "Why didn't you tell me, Phoebe?"

She did not shrink from him but her voice was hardly more than whisper. "I was afraid it would make a difference. It was selfish, I suppose, but I wanted to be with you. I never thought I would want to be with anyone, and then there was you, and it felt right to want something for myself."

"It is right. Of course, it is." He circled her with his arms, drew her close. "You should want something for yourself. Always." He held her that way, one hand at the small of her back, the other at the back of her head. His fingers slipped into her hair.

Phoebe rested against him, supported and reassured by his embrace. She laughed softly, a bit unevenly around the lump in her throat. There was an ache behind her eyes. "I think I'm going to cry, Remington. In fact, I'm sure of it."

"That's all right, then. You don't have to announce it."

"I was w-warning m-myself. I-I'm n-not the w-wee-pi-pi-ing s-sort."

"I know." She did not cry long or hard, although he would have understood if she had. She wept silently; tears that she didn't knuckle away fell on his shoulder. Once, she lifted her head and began to apologize for them. He settled her head back where he thought it belonged just then and would not let her wipe them away.

Neither of them carried a handkerchief, so after Phoebe swallowed the last sob and sniffed, she tore one of the ruffles off the bottom of her knickers and blew her nose loudly and inelegantly into that. When she was done, she ripped a ruffle off the other leg and used it to wipe her eyes and clean her face, then she balled up both ruffles and tossed them into the stove. They flared briefly as they caught on the embers. She took advantage of the fire and shoved one of their few remaining logs into the flames.

She turned to Remington. "My face is splotchy, isn't it? Puffy eyes? Red nose?" When he nodded in answer to all of those things, she sighed. "Fiona cries quite beautifully. Have her seen her?"

"No." He added firmly, "And I will count it as one of God's little favors if I am able to avoid it." The smile Phoebe turned on him was a little watery. He said, "I don't think I would believe Fiona's tears."

"I know," she said. "Sometimes it is all artifice, for effect, but there are those times when it is so real that she's liable to break your heart."

"She's broken yours?"

"Too often to count."

Remington acknowledged Phoebe's frank gaze. "Not only because she's wept real tears, I bet."

"That's right."

He considered that, considered that her expressive eyes remained candid in their regard, and considered that she was waiting for him to throw open the door that she had left ajar. He said, "Does Fiona know, Phoebe?"

"Yes and no."

Her answer confused him, but it was also the sort of response that raised his slightly slanted smile. "You'll have to explain."

"Mm. She knows about the first time. I never told her about the other two."

Remington had no words. It was all right, though, because she accepted his silence as an invitation and told him everything, and when she was done, he had words, none of which adequately expressed his empathy or his rage.

"You don't have to say anything," she said. "You wanted

to know, and I told you. You listened. I can't properly explain how important that was to me, and if I hadn't thought you could, I would have cut you out."

"Is that what you did to Fiona? Cut her out?"

"I think so, yes. I believed Monty when he said he would permanently scar Fiona if I said a word to anyone. It occurred to me at the time that he'd heard how Fiona had attacked Alistair Warren, perhaps that he even knew why she had attacked him, and therefore had some reason to be afraid of her. Revenge could have also been his motive. That occurred to me, too. Monty and Alistair were acquainted outside of their association with Fiona, so an exchange could have taken place regarding the events of that night."

"I understand," said Remington. "But later, after Montgomery died in that fire, you still didn't tell Fiona. Don't you think she would have wanted to know?"

"No. That's the one thing I never thought."

"Even now?"

"Especially now. Oh, perhaps if I wanted to be deliberately cruel, I would tell her all of it, but there's no good reason to do so."

"She would blame herself?"

"Yes, that's part of it, but there would also be accusations leveled at my head, and my younger self would always wonder if they were true. It's hard to defend against charges of any kind when you harbor even a small notion that you might be guilty." She gave him a significant look, raising her eyebrows and smiling ever so slightly. "If I were to tell her, I would require the services of a very good lawyer."

"I might know someone," he said.

Phoebe's look became suspicious. "Are you being modest?"

"No," he said, straight-faced. "I was going to refer you to Henry Abrams over in Jupiter."

She knocked him backward and kissed him soundly on the mouth. "See? You *do* know what to say. You may only be an adequate lawyer, but I think you are very, very good for me."

"I'm better than adequate," he said between kisses.

"Mm."

Just when he thought they might be heading in a decidedly carnal direction, Phoebe broke the kiss and sat up. He knew what she was going to say before she said it, and oh, how he wished he was wrong.

"It's past first light," she said. "We need to leave. You said we would."

He had, though he hated to be reminded of it now. "All right. Get dressed. There are two eggs left. Do you want one?"

"Aren't you getting dressed?"

"Eventually. Breakfast first."

Shaking her head, Phoebe said she would have an egg and then went to take her clothes off the line. She was buttoning the fly of her trousers when Remington held out a peeled egg to her. She ate it in three polite bites. He cheeked both halves like a squirrel and choked them down while he was gathering his clothes.

Phoebe finished dressing first and began gathering their things. She snapped and folded the blankets, repacked the saddlebags, and dragged the mattress back to the bed. Remington took down the rope, coiled it, and slung it over his shoulder, then closed the grate in the stove to extinguish the fire.

"The smokehouse is still there," Phoebe said, looking out the window. "Listing dangerously, but standing. The stream is back in its banks."

"Good. Then we should have no trouble crossing when we have to. You ready?" He watched Phoebe take a last long look around Old Man McCauley's cabin before she announced that she was. He wondered if she believed it, because he certainly didn't.

Phoebe expected that Remington would resume instructing her on the ride back to Twin Star, but except for a few corrections regarding her posture and the pressure she was exerting with her knees, he said very little. It would have been encouraging to believe that she was doing that much better—if it were true—but it seemed more likely that his lack of attention had to do with his thoughts being elsewhere. He stayed close to her. Butter on bread, she recalled, and she had no doubt that if she were to find herself in trouble, he would be quick to respond, but his quiet did not make her easy.

Rather than ask him what was occupying his mind, she decided to tell him what was on hers. "I've been thinking about the wedding, Remington. Not my dress or the cake. I've been thinking I don't want to tell anyone. Not yet." She felt him slow beside her because her horse did the same. There was no better sign that she had his full attention.

"I am compelled to remind you that there's been no wedding. There's nothing to tell. Are you saying you want to elope?"

"Hmm. I've started badly, I think. I don't want to tell anyone that there's been a proposal and an acceptance and a marriage to follow. The wedding is the very least of it. Why? Were you thinking about the cake?"

"I was not."

Phoebe heard the edge in his tone. Her comment had not amused him. "Remington?"

"Have you changed your mind, Phoebe? Is that what you're telling me? Very badly, as it happens."

"No! I am *not* telling you that. The idea that you will be my husband is precious to me, and I want to keep it close to my heart awhile longer, savor it, if you will, before I shout it from the rafters."

"You would do that? Shout it from the rafters?"

"That, and put a full page announcement in the *Rocky* and maybe in the *Times* for my friends in New York. I don't want to keep it a secret because I have doubts."

"Others will, though, won't they?"

He was finally getting to the heart of the matter, she thought. "Not your father, certainly, but Fiona? Yes. Fiona will have doubts. More than that, she will have objections, and she will not keep them to herself. Do you want to hear them? Because I don't. Not when there are so many things still undecided."

"For instance?"

"Where we will live. That is at the top of my list. You've thought about that, surely."

"I don't have a list."

"Then you should probably start one."

"Hmm." Remington held the horses up when they reached the stream and watched the flow of the water, the force of it against the rocks. "Stay close," he said. He did not offer to take her reins. "Mind your step and hers."

"I'm calling her Thundercloud," she told him as they started across.

"No. You're not."

"Lightning?"

He lifted an eyebrow in a truly skeptical arch.

"McCauley, then. You can't talk me out of it."

"She's a mare," he said dryly.

"Mrs. McCauley. You don't know, perhaps the old man was married once upon a time."

"All right. Mrs. McCauley." He looked at the mare, whose preferred gait was less like walking and more like moseying, and said, "Hard to believe, but I think it suits her." When they were safely on the other side, he urged Bullet to increase his pace. Mrs. McCauley came along, but reluctantly. "Is it New York?" he asked.

Phoebe frowned. "What? I don't follow."

"Where we will live. Is it New York?"

Her frown merely deepened. "Do you want to live there?"

"No."

"Well, neither do I. Sometimes, Remington, you astonish me with the odd turn your mind takes."

"Me? Have you heard the one about the pot and the kettle?"

She pursed her lips. "I know it."

"What was I supposed to think?" he asked.

"You are supposed to think that maybe we should have a house of our own, a place where Fiona and your father do not sleep down the hall. A place where we are not under their thumbs and they are not under our feet. I, for one, would like to be able to lift a pot in my own kitchen or set a table without getting rapped on the knuckles with a spoon."

"Ah. You're talking about Ellie."

"I am. Don't think that means I want to live in the kitchen or at the washboard or beside the fireplace darning your socks."

"Trying to imagine it," he said. "Can't."

"Good, because I will want help doing those things and I know you can afford it. I will also want to ride with you and sleep under the stars and drink coffee from a pot that's been heated over a fire. And don't tell me I've read too many dime novels and romanticized my vision. I know the riding will be hard, the ground will be cold, and the coffee will be vile, but I'll be with you, sharing something you love, and that's what I want."

For a time he said nothing, then quietly, a little roughly, he told her, "I don't think you can imagine how much I want to drag you off Mrs. McCauley right now."

Phoebe laughed, not because she couldn't imagine it, but because he'd used Mrs. McCauley's name. It just was the brake she needed to apply before she dismounted the mare without his help and pulled him out of his saddle.

"Just a thought."

She nodded. "Practically indecent."

"Can you lean a little this way?" he asked.

"I think so."

He leaned, too, and they shared an awkward, yet somehow satisfying, kiss that left them both smiling a shade regretfully when they parted. "Moments like that will take some planning," he said.

"Moments like that probably shouldn't happen once we've returned. All those courtship customs, remember? Besides, it won't be forever. We'll tell them . . . eventually."

Remington looked askance at her and spoke out of the side of his mouth. "If it helps to hurry things along, you should know I've started a list."

* * *

Thaddeus was the first to see them coming. He didn't rush to greet them. He immediately took off for the house. The back door swung hard behind him and he saw Fiona give a little start. She was drinking tea at the kitchen table and some of the hot liquid splashed the back of her hand. She didn't seem to notice; her beautiful amethyst eyes were all for him.

Ellie turned away from the stove, where she was stirring a pot of ham and beans. "What is it, Mr. Frost?" she asked. "What's happened?"

Thaddeus put out a hand to stop her and spoke to Fiona. "They're coming now. Do you want to step outside with me? We can wait on the front porch."

"Yes," she said, pushing away her cup and saucer. "I do."

He skirted the table and took her arm as she stood. It was a good thing he did, he thought, because she challenged his long stride by double-timing it to the door and then teetered on the lip of the porch until he pulled her back. "It's all right, Fiona. They see us. Go on. Give them a wave."

She did, raising her arm high over head and swinging it back and forth as if she were hailing a ship in New York harbor. "Oh, I hope she doesn't try to wave back. What if she falls? Does it look to you as if she has a good seat? I can't tell."

"She's doing fine. And see how close Remington is? He's not going to let her fall. There. Did you see that? She gave you a little finger wave. I think you can put your arm down."

Fiona dropped it with an alacrity that made Thaddeus chuckle. "I don't know why that amused you," she said.

"And I couldn't tell you." But he could have. He could have told her that she was always a delight when she behaved as if her corset was not so tight, or better yet, when she behaved as if she were not confined by one at all. "They're coming this way first, not going to the barn."

"She looks so small on that beast."

"That mare is hardly a beast. She's probably the gentlest

animal stabled here." He did not mention that it was the mare that Mr. Shoulders had provided for Phoebe. If Fiona had forgotten that, she would not want to be reminded. Out of the corner of his eye he was aware that Fiona was poised to set her hands on her hips. He circled the wrist closest to him and gave her arm a gentle tug. "Not like that, Fiona."

"Are you my director now?"

"If I have to be, yes."

She let him draw her arm down and slid the other over the curve of her hip as though smoothing the fabric.

"Nicely done," he said. "Now smile. Can you do that?"

She could and she did. There was nothing about it that was forced.

Thaddeus felt her fingers brush his in a way that made him believe it was no accident. He took her hand, and when she didn't pull away, he squeezed it. He was confident enough in the moment to let Fiona speak without feeding her the lines.

"Oh, aren't you just a sight," Fiona said. There were ways she could have spoken those words that would have made them a criticism, but there was not the slightest nuance of censure in her tone. "How I worried; but look at you. There are roses in your cheeks, Phoebe Apple. It's been an adventure, is that it?"

"Yes." Phoebe's smile was tentative, a little wary. This was not the welcome she would have predicted if Remington had asked. He hadn't, though, most likely because he anticipated something quite different himself.

"Did it rain where you were?" asked Fiona, her brow creasing. "Cats and dogs here."

"There, too. Thunder and lightning."

Fiona nodded. Her eyes were moist. She asked, "Did you find a trunk?"

Quite without warning, Phoebe felt a hot, hard ache in her throat and the pressure of tears at the back of her eyes. She answered Fiona's question with a nod and a watery smile because it was all she could manage.

Fiona held out her free arm to Phoebe. "Will you come

in now?" Her eyes darted to Remington. "She doesn't have to take care of the horse, does she?"

"No, ma'am. She doesn't have to do that. I'll see to it."

"Good. See, Phoebe, you can come inside now. Remington will take care of the horses." She curled her fingers in invitation. "Do you need help dismounting? Help her, Thaddeus. Please?"

He released her hand and dropped down the steps. "Come here, Phoebe."

She gave Remington Mrs. McCauley's reins and levered herself off the mare, dropping easily into Thaddeus's waiting arms. His hands tightened briefly on her waist and he dropped a kiss on her brow before he turned her over to Fiona.

"I'll go with Remington," Thaddeus said. "She's yours."

Fiona nodded. "Yes. She is."

Chapter Twenty-four

"Did you tell him?" asked Phoebe. Hot water lapped at her breasts and curling ribbons of steam rose from the tub. She waved them away and slid deeper until the water almost touched her shoulders. Fiona sat on a padded stool beside the tub. Her fingers dangled in the water. Sometimes she made ripples. The soap floated toward Phoebe but she didn't reach for it.

"No," said Fiona. "I didn't. I think he knows. Maybe he has all along, but it's for me to say, isn't it? Thaddeus is a good man that way. He waits for me. When I'm ready, I'll tell him." She slowly made a spiral in the water with her fingertip. "This is how he drizzles honey on a biscuit." She made the spiral again. "He's so particular about it. Very careful. He leaves his clothes all over the floor in the dressing room. How do you understand a man like that?"

Phoebe smiled, thinking of Remington's wadded clothes on the line. "I don't know. Who wrote 'Woman's at best a contradiction still'?"

"I think it was Pope."

"Yes, that's right. Well, he should not have been pointing fingers at our sex."

"True," said Fiona. "'What a piece of work is man.' That's something worth pondering."

Phoebe smiled wryly. "Especially when it's so easily taken out of context."

Fiona shrugged. "When it serves, it serves." She glanced at the floor near the foot of the tub, where Phoebe's clothes lay in a heap. Leaning over, she used a thumb and forefinger to pick up the chambray shirt. "Shall I burn this?"

Phoebe merely raised an eyebrow.

Fiona dropped it. "All right. I'd put it all away if it didn't need a thorough washing. Everything smells like wood smoke. Your hair, too. I suppose that means you were able to keep warm."

"Yes." She did not elaborate.

"Where did you get these clothes?" She glanced at the pile again. "And the hat."

"You know.'

"*He* bought them for you, didn't he?" When Phoebe was quiet, she said, "I suppose I did know. These were in the parcels and boxes we took right out of his hands, weren't they? How you must have laughed when I helped you carry them. I recall adamantly opposing the purchase of items such as these."

"I didn't laugh, Fiona. Neither of us did."

"Didn't you? Well, you got what you wanted over my objections. It's hard to believe he did not take special delight in it."

Phoebe felt as if their fragile peace was fraying at the edges. She ducked under the water and stayed there until her hair was thoroughly wet. When she came up, she held out her hand for the soap, and Fiona obliged her by slapping the slippery bar in her palm. She worked up a lather and applied it to her hair.

"Why do you dislike him so?" she asked.

"He is rude. Arrogant. Unpleasant. Is that enough for you?"

"More than enough, I think." Phoebe scrubbed her scalp and then soaped the rest of her hair. She twisted her hair into a rope, wound it on top of her head, and left the soapy crown there while she began to wash. "Will you tell me what you did to provoke him?" She gave a little start when Fiona slapped the water and sent competing waves in every direction. "Why did you do that?"

"Why? Why do you think? You put that ridiculous

question to me, that's why. It is offensive, Phoebe, that you believe I must have done something to goad him into behaving badly. I've known him a great deal longer than you, and while Thaddeus thinks his son can do no wrong, my view of his base nature is decidedly different."

"You don't even like to say his name," said Phoebe.

"Remington. There. I've said it. I don't know what you imagine is changed by it."

Phoebe searched Fiona's stubbornly set features and recognized that they were at an impasse. She could only offer a contrite smile to ease the tension in the moment. "Will you help me rinse my hair?" she asked.

"Of course."

And just like that they closed the door on the subject of Remington Frost.

Thaddeus tossed a brush to Remington after they removed the tack from the animals. He picked up another one and began grooming the mare. "How did this one do?" he asked.

"Fine. She led Phoebe around a little, but Phoebe doesn't know that. They're both feeling their way." Remington paused and looked over at his father. "You know what Phoebe named her? Mrs. McCauley."

Thaddeus gave a bark of laughter that made both horses stir. He quieted the mare. "I'll be damned," he said, applying the brush again. "Suits her, though, doesn't it?"

"I thought the same thing."

"So tell me. Did you treat her right?"

"I wondered when you were going to get around to asking. I think it's safe to assume you're talking about Phoebe."

"I am."

"You probably should ask her, then."

"I might do that, but I'd feel better hearing it from you. Fiona says that Phoebe could drink hemlock and would only admit to a mild case of dyspepsia. That's about verbatim."

Remington chuckled. "And it sounds accurate. As to your question, yes, I treated her right." He told his father most of what had transpired at Thunder Point, and if Thaddeus suspected there was a great deal left unsaid, he did not press to hear more. Remington was grateful for that. He had no illusions that Fiona would let Phoebe off so easily.

Thaddeus said, "Tell me again what she said about Shoulders."

Remington repeated the description that Phoebe was able to give him. "She thinks she has seeds in her brain. Maybe she does. She can recall the odd detail now and again. I don't think her memory is playing her false, but I don't suppose we'll know for sure until we find Mr. Shoulders."

"We?"

"Me. Sheriff Brewer. Blue Armstrong. The detective from Northeast Rail."

"You're not going to leave it alone, are you?"

"I know what you said the night we found her, but is that what you really want?"

Thaddeus said nothing for a time. He brushed Mrs. McCauley's coat with increasingly harder strokes until Remington laid a hand over his and stopped him. "I don't care about the money—you know that—but I don't imagine that's your motivation. I won't ask you to let it go."

Remington held his father's gaze. For all that Thaddeus's eyes were a clear shade of blue, they could still be as impenetrable as his own darker ones. But that was not the case now. "You know something," he said, and watched his father's eyes dart sideways before returning to him. As a lapse, Thaddeus's shifting gaze was infinitesimally brief, so brief, in fact, that Remington might have been convinced he had imagined it if his father had tried to explain it away. He did not, though, and Remington amended his thinking to an earlier notion he'd had when his father had announced that there would be no pursuing Shoulders and the others on Phoebe's account. "You suspect something."

Thaddeus shook his head.

"You do," said Remington. "What is it?"

"It's nothing, is what it is. Phoebe's safe. I can be content with that. Jackson will do what his job requires. So will that detective. I'd like to see the passengers have returned to them what was stolen, but after all this time, I suspect there's nothing left. As for Phoebe's abduction, that's a stone I'd rather not overturn. I won't put her through the unpleasantness of a trial."

"Supposing Shoulders and his men are eventually found, surely that would be her choice."

"Hmm. Has she said that she wants her day in court?"

"We never talked about it."

"And maybe there's a reason. Are you confident that she's told you everything that happened when they took her to Thunder Point?"

Remington's first inclination was to say that he was, but he hesitated, and then held back his answer entirely.

"Precisely," said Thaddeus. "You don't know. You'll want to think about that when you're going after Shoulders. Could be that things happened there that she doesn't want anyone to know."

Frustrated, Remington lifted his hat, plowed his hair with his fingers, and then reset the hat. "Is that something you've been chewing on for a while, or did someone, say, your wife, spoon-feed that to you?"

"Why do you dislike her so much?"

"She's selfish. Bad-mannered. And she acts as if she's entitled."

"Entitled? To what?"

"To everything."

"She is my wife, Remington. There are entitlements; however, you are my heir and that is made clear in my will. But if something happens to me, I expect that you will take care of her."

Remington sighed heavily, shook his head. "How did we arrive here? Let's finish. I want a bath and breakfast, and not necessarily in that order."

And just like that, Fiona Apple Frost was no longer a bone of contention.

* * *

Natty Rahway fingered his mustache. The dark tips brushed his upper lip. He was aware of Doyle Putty's narrow-eyed stare and ignored it. Willet was ignoring his brother as well, tucking into his scrambled eggs with the ferocity of a man who hadn't eaten in days. Natty could barely look at him.

He lifted his cup, finished his coffee, and gestured to the waitress to bring more. "I noticed you fellas are still trying to unload certain . . . um, *articles*, shall we say. Seems like Denver would be the place for that. Wouldn't attract attention."

"You hear something?" asked Willet. He spoke with his mouth full. Bits of egg coated his tongue.

"Jesus, Willet. Swallow your food and drink some coffee. You have the manners of . . ." He was at a loss to find an appropriate comparison until he glanced at Doyle. "Of your brother."

"Hey," said Doyle. "No call for that."

Natty sat back while the waitress filled his cup. "Thanks." He watched her walk away, liked the gentle sway of her hips. Her daddy owned the place and Natty liked the rooms and the food well enough not to risk eviction by making a pass at the daughter.

"Did you hear me, Natty?" Willet asked. He coughed weakly when he aspirated coffee because he tried to talk and drink at the same time. Doyle slapped him hard on the back. Natty just shook his head.

Doyle took up his brother's question. "Is there something you want to tell us, Natty? Maybe you heard someone say something about one of the pieces?"

"Didn't hear a thing. Saw a woman, though, showing off a ring to a couple of her friends. Sure looked like something I'd seen before. I thought you were going to melt that gold."

"Now what do we know about that? And what else was I supposed to say when those women on the train objected? Where did you see this anyway? We never sold no rings to a woman."

"Do you know Sylvia Vance?"

"The whore?"

"The madam. It was at her place."

"You go all the way to Collier to fuck a whore?"

Natty looked around to see if Doyle had drawn the notice of any of the other diners. It did not appear that he had. "I was never one for fishing in my own pond."

Willet shrugged. "Here suits me just fine. Always did like Harmony gals best. Those bitches in Frost Falls? Not one of them will let you dip your wick for less than a dollar."

Natty said, "You should stay away from Frost Falls."

"Now, didn't I just say I didn't like the gals there? But even if I did, where's the harm? No one knows it was us."

"Just the same, better you don't go." He cut a triangle into his small stack of pancakes and lifted his fork to his mouth. Syrup dripped on his plate and he waited for the last drop to fall before he ate. "About the ring," he said. "I guess you still want to hear about that." When they looked at him expectantly, he went on. "One of the girls—doesn't matter who— was showing off the sparkler she got from the man she swore was going to marry her and take her out of the life. Why she hadn't run off with him already was a question in my mind, but I didn't want to show interest in the bauble or in their conversation. I figured she didn't trust her man all that much. Probably thought that diamond was paste. I could have told her different. You two remember the woman that Phoebe Apple got all bothered about when you tried to take her ring?"

Willet and Doyle exchanged questioning looks and then nodded in unison.

"It was hers. Can't recall her name if I ever heard it, but it was her ring, the one she tried to hide by wringing her hands together like a Nervous Nellie. Now, do you think that little pear shape diamond was paste?" He didn't wait for them to respond. "Because I sure don't, and now some gal's showing it off to her friends in an establishment frequented by men from all over. There is no tellin' who might see it, might recognize it. Do either of you know where Nervous Nellie was going?"

They shook their heads.

"Yeah, well, neither do I. Maybe she was on her way to here. Why not? People come here. And maybe she is no longer the apple of her husband's eye, and he visits Sylvia Vance's house from time to time. You see how this goes? He sees the ring and tugs on that thread and pretty soon that spool's completely unwound." He stared the Putty brothers down to make sure they understood. "Whatever you have left, fellas, get rid of it in Denver. It'd be a needle in a much bigger haystack."

Blue Armstrong pulled up his suspenders and gave them a satisfying snap. Behind him he heard Caroline Carolina, she of the improbably musical name, give up a giggle just as improbably musical.

"One of these days, Blue, you're going to leave a bruise snapping your suspenders that way. It'll hurt so bad, you'll probably drop your britches, too."

"And wouldn't you just like to see that?" He leaned across the bed and bussed her cheek when she offered it. Caroline didn't like lip kissing and he'd settled with that a long time ago. She was his favorite girl at Miss Sylvia's place, so he was willing to compromise.

Coming to Collier was also a compromise. Once he'd become a deputy, he started taking his carnal pleasures outside of Frost Falls. It just seemed that he should; a matter of principle, he called it, although he'd never taken the time to suss out the particulars.

"Next week?" he asked, headed for the door.

"Sure. If I'm here."

That stopped him. He turned around. "What do you mean? Where would you be?"

Caroline Carolina had a triangular face and a deeply dimpled smile. She gave her bright yellow hair a toss to make sure Blue saw her best feature clearly. "There's a fella been seeing me regular that might have other plans for me. Wanna see?" When Blue nodded, Caroline reached for the drawer in the bedside table and opened it. She did not have to root long before she found what she wanted. She slid the diamond ring on her finger and held up her hand for him to see.

Blue's eyebrows lifted. "I do believe my eyes have seen the glory. I want to look at that up close." He returned to the bed and took her hand, turning it this way and that in the lamplight. He whistled softly. "Who's this fella that has a mind to remove me from your affections?"

"I'm not saying," she said saucily, removing her hand from his grasp. "Besides, I'm not counting my chickens just yet. The smart thing to do is have it appraised, leastways that's what Sylvia says I ought to do. Who knows, if it's as real as it looks, maybe I won't wait for my knight. Maybe I'll just sell it and go off on my own. Buy a nice house, have girls working for me for a change."

"Good to know you're not overreaching. Maybe I can still visit you."

"Sure."

Blue studied the ring. Could be nothing. Could be something. "How are you going to find someone to give you a fair evaluation? I would hate to see someone telling you that diamond's paste if it's real."

"I haven't worked that out yet. Sylvia's asking around for me."

"You trust her?"

Caroline hesitated. "Yes?"

"You askin'? Because you don't sound certain to me."

"Well, I trust her some. She's been no worse than any other madam I've worked for and better than most."

Blue nodded. "Fair enough. What about me? Do you trust me more than Sylvia or less?"

There was no hesitation this time. "More. And it's not on account of you being the law; it's on account of you being you."

"Well, that's real nice of you to say. I've got a thought about that ring and who might know its true value."

"I'm listening."

"There's a fella I'm acquainted with over in Liberty Junction. You know where that is?"

She nodded. "Straight down the line from Frost Falls."

"That's right. Now, this man I'm talking about isn't any kind of jeweler, but he's managing the hotel and gambling house over there, and if there's anybody shrewder than a man operating a hotel and gambling establishment, I haven't met him. He's used to making trades for chips. He has to make sure the games run fair and smooth and he doesn't want to cheat his players any more than he wants to cheat himself."

"And you think he'll be fair and honest?"

"I have no reason to think otherwise. Name's Tyler. Jacob C. Tyler, Junior. Before you go running off with this fella, you see about Sylvia giving you a day for yourself. Any Sunday would be good. I'd be pleased to escort you."

Chapter Twenty-five

Phoebe used her lower legs to gently squeeze Mrs. McCauley and push the mare forward from a walk to a trot. During the transition, when Mrs. McCauley was most likely to balk, she pressed her heels lightly into the animal's sides. Phoebe adjusted the swing of her hips until she had the horse's rhythm and then sat heavy in the saddle to keep from bouncing out of it. She had been practicing almost every day for two weeks, sometimes circling the corral without her feet in the stirrups to help her strengthen her seat. Early on, it was exhausting. She would bounce high out of the saddle because she was gripping too hard with her thighs, and without her weight on Mrs. McCauley's back, the mare would stop because she didn't know what to do.

There wasn't a ranch hand around who didn't have some piece of advice for her. None of them were shy about hollering it out. Sometimes the suggestions were contradictory. She tried everything at least once and used what worked for her. If Thaddeus was nearby and heard them shouting instructions at her, he growled at them to put their two cents away and get back to work.

"She's coming along," said Ben to Remington.

The pair stepped out of the barn together and into the bright sunshine. Ben lifted his hat, beat it once against his thigh, and returned it to his head. In that brief hatless moment, sunlight glanced off his hair, turning it flame orange, and highlighting every one of the freckles sprayed across his nose and cheeks.

"Mm-hmm." Remington's eyes followed Phoebe as she circled the inside of the corral.

Ben set his shoulder against the barn and folded his arms across his chest. "She's not going to be satisfied staying inside the rails much longer."

"Why do you say that?"

Ben shrugged. "I don't know. I guess because she asked me yesterday if the trail to Boxer's Ridge would be easy for her to follow."

"Christ," Remington said under his breath. He looked over at Ben. "What did you tell her?"

"What you'd expect. Told her about the snakes and the loose rocks and the steep climb and the switchback that makes it seem like you and your horse are going to fall off the edge of the earth."

"She believed you?"

"Why wouldn't she?"

"Because she's not . . . never mind. I'll take care of it." He shook his head. "Boxer's Ridge. Wonder how she heard of it."

"I'm recollecting hearing Fiona's name in our conversation."

"Hmm."

"Speaking of . . ." Ben jerked his chin toward the house. "Where is Mrs. Frost today? I saw the buggy's gone. She take it out?"

"Thaddeus drove her into town. He's rounding up help for branding the calves so we can get them out to pasture. She's probably shopping."

"Ralph and I rode out early to count head around Baker's Knob. Guess that's how I didn't see them leave."

"What's the count?"

"Four hundred, give or take. We chased off some cattle from the Double H. We can expect Hank Henry's men to direct some of our cows back this way. Always a tangle after a long winter."

Remington nodded. He continued to watch Phoebe. Her concentration was all for what she was doing. He didn't think she was aware of his interest. Or Ben's.

Ben said, "My mother mentioned she sent you to town a couple of days ago with a list as long as her arm."

"I was already intending to go, so I got the list. And it was every bit that long."

"Huh. She usually sends me."

Remington looked crossways at Ben. "You have a particular interest in everyone's comings and goings, or are you just making conversation?"

"Just making conversation, I expect. Why?"

"Jeez, Ben, you're not exactly a stranger to me. I've known you all your life, or near to. It occurs to me that you have a niggling question you can't figure how to ask. If that's the case, just ask it."

"All right." He lifted his chin to indicate Phoebe. "I was wondering if you maybe spoke to Brewer about her. About the investigation, really. Haven't heard anything in a while, not that it's my business, not directly, but I was there that night, waiting, same as everyone else, and I set out to find her with your father and the sheriff."

"I remember."

"Yeah, well, I've got an interest."

Remington arched one dark eyebrow. "You do?"

"Sure." He saw Remington's gaze return to Phoebe. "Oh, no. You got it wrong. I like her just fine, *like* her, you understand, but my interest is in getting justice for her."

"Has she talked to you about that?"

"No. And I don't bring it up. Figure it's a tender spot, and I'm not one for poking at it the way you do."

"Me?"

"You're the one that took her back to Thunder Point. If that's not poking at what's tender, then I don't know what is."

"What makes you think we went there?"

"If you're saying you didn't, I'm going to have to call you a liar. My mother overheard Thaddeus and Fiona arguing about it. Maybe she shouldn't have told me, but she did, probably because she knew I was concerned. I haven't repeated it. I can't say whether Phoebe might have said something to anyone, but if she has, it never reached my ears that way."

Remington said nothing for a time, rolling the potential responses over in his mind. "I've been talking to Sheriff

Brewer. I've had concerns, same as you. I want justice for her, same as you."

Ben nodded. "Good to know we're of like minds and on the same side. Her side." He straightened and dug his thumbs into the pockets of his jeans. "So what have you heard? Brewer must know something by now. Lord, it's been what, better than eight weeks?"

"About that."

"So?"

"You know Northeast Rail sent one of their detectives to investigate. Michael Smith."

"Yes. Thaddeus told me that. It was expected."

"Brewer informed me the other day that Smith left the Butterworth a week or so ago. Cleared out. He—Smith—could no longer justify his stay to the company. Nothing he learned led anywhere."

"Nothing?"

Remington shook his head. "Lots of information from the passengers but nothing to give him a trail to follow. In the meantime, there have been no other robberies."

"So that's it. He's gone and Brewer's done."

"It'd seem that way."

Frowning, Ben knuckled the bridge of his nose. "What else? There's something else. I know you, too, and I can tell when you've got more to say and are still thinking about whether you want to say it."

Remington slanted a wry grin Ben's way. "Seems that Blue might have stumbled onto something significant."

"Blue? Our Blue Armstrong?"

"You know another Blue?"

"I thought maybe one moved to town. Jumpin' Jesus on a griddle. Blue Armstrong. I'll be damned."

"Brewer says that his deputy's biggest advantage is that people underestimate him."

"That's fair. What's the significant something he stumbled on?"

"A piece of jewelry taken from one of passengers during the robbery. Blue was able to match it against the description he was given from the owner, but to be certain, they want to have it authenticated. They're working out the details of that now. It's taking longer to make the arrangements than Blue thought it would."

"What's the piece?"

Remington put a hand to his throat as if he were choking himself. "A seed pearl collar. I guess it shows off a woman's neck to a particular advantage."

"Huh. Don't see how. Not if the thing covers up her neck."

Remington lowered his hand. "I asked Phoebe about it. She says it favors the length of a woman's neck. Draws a man's eye to it."

"You told her about the necklace?"

"Uh-huh. I wondered if she remembered anyone wearing it."

"Did she?"

"No. She said whoever owned it wouldn't have been wearing it on the train. It's for fancy dress. Evening wear, she called it. She thought it was probably kept in a case."

"But you said you had the owner's description. You know who it belongs to."

"The sheriff wanted to see if Phoebe could verify ownership. He wants to make sure he gets it back to the right hands."

"Makes sense. Must be worth something big, a necklace like that."

"Collar," Remington said. "I guess that's the proper term for it. Phoebe called it a dog collar."

"That's probably what's referred to as a woman's prerogative. I wouldn't dare call it that." He dropped his shoulder against the barn again and crossed his legs at the ankle. "Unless the woman's a bitch. Then I might reconsider."

Remington said nothing; he didn't smile, didn't raise an eyebrow. For all of Ben's casual way of dropping the comment, Remington thought about it long after Ben was gone.

Chapter Twenty-six

Branding was not for the faint of heart, Phoebe decided, so when Fiona arrived at the site where the calves were penned so they could be dropped, heeled, sometimes castrated, and finally branded, it was not merely a surprise; it was shocking. That Fiona was wearing jeans tucked into a pair of embossed leather boots, a pale yellow cotton shirt, a tan leather vest, and a flat-crowned black hat, caused mouths to gape as she alighted from the buckboard. The only person who did not gape was Thaddeus, and Phoebe suspected that was because he had had a private showing of this very outfit.

"Close your mouth, Les," Thaddeus called out above the bawling of the cattle. "Unless you like the taste of cow shit."

Les Brownlee spit. "Developing a taste, sure enough." But he closed his mouth.

Thaddeus passed the hot branding iron he was holding to Ralph Neighbors and hopped the pen to get to Fiona. He removed his gloves and took her hand. "You certain about this?"

"I must be. I'm here."

He turned her hands over to examine her palms. "Where are your gloves?"

"I put them on the kitchen table while I was packing the baskets, and then I forgot them."

Thaddeus looked past her shoulder to where five hampers rested in the bed of the buckboard. "You packed them?"

"It's insulting that you're asking," she said, although there was no scold in her tone. "I've spent a lifetime packing trunks."

Phoebe was close enough now to hear Fiona. She tried to recall the last time Fiona had packed her own trunks. She couldn't. Still, she did not offer a contradiction. If she took the long view, then she counted it as a very good thing that Fiona wanted to impress Thaddeus.

"Fiona! You look striking." Phoebe meant it. Her smile split the lower half of her face. "Come. I'll help you with the baskets. The men put together a table for the spread." She pointed to the rough planks supported by sawhorses thirty yards from the pen. "We'll set things out like a grand buffet and they can eat as they're able."

Fiona looked over the setting doubtfully. "There is no place for them to sit."

Thaddeus chuckled. "Do you think any of these men are going to object to the ground? They've been wrestling calves, Fiona. They'll be grateful just because they don't have to wrestle their supper."

Phoebe waved him away and took Fiona by the elbow to lead her to the rear of the wagon. "Where's Ellie?" she asked. "You didn't murder her, did you?"

Fiona pursed her lips disapprovingly. "You should not say things like that." Then she qualified her disapproval. "Where people might hear."

"I can barely hear myself," Phoebe said, gesturing toward the pen where men were shouting, calves were bawling, and the cows, separated from their unweaned babies, were crying as if it were all happening to them. "But I take your point."

"She was still in the kitchen when I left," said Fiona. "She's bringing jugs of beer and fresh water."

"The men will appreciate that." She slid one of the baskets toward her and thrust it at Fiona. She lifted another and hugged it to her. "Heavy."

Fiona nodded and stepped aside to let Phoebe lead the way. "What is that stench?" she asked, wrinkling her nose.

"Burnt hair and flesh. You understand what branding is, don't you?"

"Thaddeus told me. He failed to mention the stink."

Phoebe set down her basket. "I have a couple of scented handkerchiefs. I haven't pulled one out yet. I didn't want the men to snicker. Would you like one?"

"And have them snicker at me? I don't think so. How did you know to bring a scented handkerchief?"

"Remington suggested it."

"Mm. Thoughtful, but it appears he neglected to account for your pride."

Phoebe grinned. "Let's finish this and go and watch. You've never seen anything like it."

Fiona was sure that was true.

In addition to the men who worked for Twin Star, there were a dozen volunteers from neighboring ranches and a few young men from town who wanted to try their hand at roping and wrestling. The experienced hands enjoyed ribbing the greenhorns, but it was all good-natured jibing since every one of them had started out barely knowing a head from a hoof.

No one was immune to the stench, but some bore it better than others. Young Johnny Sutton excused himself twice from the gathering to go off alone to puke. The stink got him once, but watching a calf lose its balls to a Bowie knife took him out the second time. A couple of men burned themselves wielding the hot iron and a couple more got kicked by understandably disgruntled two-hundred-pound calves, but no one complained. The shared sentiment was grin and bear it and don't get careless again.

Pairs of men grabbed a calf, one by the head, the other by a rear leg or tail, and if they knew what they were doing, they could drop the calf in seconds. Once the animal was pinned, the red-hot Twin Star branding iron was applied for three seconds to the calf's left shoulder. If the calf was male, Thaddeus performed the castration. Johnny Sutton, once his stomach settled, was charged with collecting the testicles.

The greenhorns chased the calves, whooping and hollering, tiring themselves out before they mostly scared one into submission. The seasoned ranch hands knew how to conserve their energy, but when they broke for supper, Phoebe watched them stretch, bend, shake out their joints, and check themselves somewhat surreptitiously for injuries.

Ellie's arrival was greeted enthusiastically because she was well liked but mostly because she brought the beer. Phoebe expected her to claim the territory around the long tables as her own, but she allowed Fiona to help without any noticeable balking.

Women and girls and children arrived from ranches and town soon after, bringing more food, more beer, and more in the way of that good-natured ribbing. Phoebe had not understood until then what a social event this was, one that would be repeated in the days ahead as the branding chores moved from one ranch to another until all the calves were sent to graze in open pastures. It was like an after-opening-night theater party without the trepidation of critical reviews.

Phoebe shared this perspective with Remington when he joined her at the buckboard. She made room for him to sit with her on the bed of the wagon and eyed his heaping plate of food with appreciation for the hard work he'd been doing.

"I saw one of the calves kick you," she said. "I don't know how you're walking without a limp."

"And draw more attention to my carelessness? No. Anyway, it's not so bad. I've been kicked worse." He used a thumb to point over his shoulder in the direction of the table. "Did you know Fiona was going to show up dressed like that?"

Phoebe turned her head and saw Fiona was passing one of the town boys a plate of food. He thanked her, she beamed, and Phoebe thought the boy actually staggered backward. Another conquest. Phoebe was helpless to do anything but smile and shake her head. "I had no idea," she told Remington. "But then she's always known how to make an entrance." She stole a cold medallion of roast beef from Remington's plate before he could slap her hand away. "That's not fair to her," she said, reconsidering. "I think your father has already seen her in those clothes, so if there was a grand entrance, it was also a private one."

"The same occurred to me."

"Something's different between them. Have you noticed, or is it wishful thinking?"

"I've noticed, and it's not because I've had any wishful thinking about it."

"What does that mean? Don't you want them to get along?"

Remington forked a small boiled potato. "I shouldn't have said that." He opened his mouth and closed it around the potato.

Phoebe watched him. "You did say it, and you can't shovel food in your mouth forever to keep from explaining yourself."

Remington chewed, swallowed. "All right. The truth is I don't trust her, Phoebe. I can't see far enough into the future to a time when that will be different."

Phoebe pressed her lips together, nodded. It was not an unexpected response, but she had needed to hear it from him. "I asked her, you know, what she did to make you dislike her so much."

"Did you? I didn't know. What did she say?" He stopped her from answering by raising his fork hand and waggling the utensil. "No. Let me guess. I figure she threw it back at you, probably with some self-righteous irritation to deflect your question. She'd wonder how you could ask her. She would be hurt."

Phoebe's eyes dropped to her hands.

"Am I close?" asked Remington.

Phoebe thought she might know what it felt like to be kicked by a two-hundred-pound calf. "Dead center," she whispered.

"Then I'm sorry. For your sake, I wish I'd been wrong."

She nodded because she believed him. "So what did she do?"

"Do you really want to know? Here? Now? That doesn't sound like a good idea to me."

Behind them someone hollered as if he were the one losing his balls to a Bowie knife. They both turned to make certain no one was dead on the ground, but it was only one of the greenhorns being dragged by a calf he was too stubborn to release.

"That's one way to do it," said Remington, unconcerned. He renewed his interest in his food.

"Maybe now isn't the right time," said Phoebe. "But I still want to know. And I still want to—" She stopped because she saw a familiar figure approaching. "Isn't that Blue Armstrong?"

Remington looked up. "Sure is."

"Is he here to help?"

"Unlikely. Maybe he's come for the food." He passed his plate to Phoebe and hopped off the buckboard. "I'll be right back after I see what he wants. Hey, Blue!" He waved once and hurried away to head him off.

Blue veered sideways, following Remington's diagonal path until they met. "I saw her," Blue said, pulling up his horse. "I wasn't going to say anything in front of her."

"Didn't think you would, Blue, but business first. All right? Then you can socialize and eat your fill. I hope you'll do that."

"Sure. I had to arm-wrestle Jackson for the right to come out here. He likes Ellie's apple pie."

"Whereas you like Ellie."

Blue scratched behind a red-tipped ear. "Now, 'whereas.' That'd be a smart-ass lawyer word, wouldn't it?"

"Damn right. Tell me what you know."

"Miss Carolina finally has a day to herself. That'd be this Sunday. Two days from now. We are going to take the train to Liberty Junction and talk to Junior about what I'm pretty sure is going to turn out to be his mama's ring. Like I told you when you came 'round the office, I don't know if his mama is still visiting or if she's gone back to Saint Louis, but Liberty Junction is a mite easier place to start."

"I don't disagree. So why are telling me now?"

"Besides coming out for the food and the company, the sheriff and I figured you might want to tag along. Miss Apple, too, if she's of a like mind and you think there's no harm in it. If Mrs. Tyler's still there, we thought she'd like to reacquaint herself."

"And she's also familiar with the ring," Remington said flatly. "I'm sure you and the sheriff thought of that, too."

"Crossed our minds. Doesn't hurt to get a second confirmation, and I can't exactly bring Miss Carolina out here to show off the ring. She trusts me, but I can see that she runs to suspicion when she thinks too hard or too long."

"I'll go, but I want to think about Phoebe."

"Fine. Now about that tagging along . . . it's better if you get there ahead of us. Miss Carolina is in Collier, so that's where we will be boarding the train. If you're already in Liberty Junction, there's no chance she'll spy you getting on at Frost Falls and wonder why you're going to a gaming establishment in the Junction. You know folks from here don't do that."

"I understand, and I appreciate your caution and the invitation. I'll be there." He gestured toward the table. "Looks like Ellie's free at the moment."

"I see her." He dismounted, gave Remington the reins, and headed for Ellie Madison, the feast laid out on the table, and a slice of cinnamon apple pie the size of his hand.

Remington tethered Blue's horse with the other animals and then returned to Phoebe. She gave him back his plate, but she looked as if she wanted to stab him with the fork. She laid it down carefully, deliberately, in his open palm, which merely felt as if she'd stabbed him. "Business," he said, sitting hipshot on the wagon bed.

"Hmm."

"May I eat first? I'm going to tell you." When she nodded, he tucked in before she changed her mind and made him reverse the order. He set the plate and fork aside when he was done and repeated what Blue had told him.

"Mrs. Tyler's ring?" she said, puzzled. "I thought it was a seed pearl collar that had been found."

"You did? Where did you hear that?" But he knew, and he was not happy about it.

"Ben mentioned it. For some reason, he thought you had asked me about the collar. The only conversation I could recall was the one we had about your fiancée's wedding dress, but I thought I said it was lace, not seed pearls."

"So what did you tell him?"

"What you'd expect. That a dog collar like that shows off a woman's neck, but it's the kind of accessory a woman wears in the evening for a special occasion, not for traveling."

"That's what I told him you said."

"But I hadn't said it. Not to you."

"I know." He didn't explain. "Can you leave it for now? Trust me?"

"I don't like leaving it, but I trust you."

"Thank you." He raised a questioning eyebrow. "Do you want to go to Liberty Junction?"

"Is that truly a question in your mind?"

He chuckled. "All right. I'll make the arrangements. You know what you'll say to Fiona?"

"Yes. I'll tell her I want to see Mrs. Tyler before she returns to Saint Louis. It's true. I will be disappointed if I learn that she's already gone. I suppose you're acting as my escort."

"That's the reason I'm giving for going there. It's the only one that will stand scrutiny."

"You're not going to tell Thaddeus the truth?"

"No. Not yet. He doesn't want to know."

Phoebe smiled a little at that. "Not so different than Fiona, then."

"Not so different," he agreed. He might have said more, but someone shouted for him. He picked up his plate and fork and shoved away from the wagon. "Sounds as if the calf wrestling has come back around to me."

Phoebe watched him go and then went to see if Ellie was in want of rescuing from Blue Armstrong or pleased with the deputy's attentions.

Chapter Twenty-seven

"Did one of you do an inventory of what you collected from the passengers?" Natty Rahway asked. He set three glasses of beer on a corner table near the window in the Sweet Clementine Saloon and pushed two of them toward the Putty brothers.

"Inventory?" asked Willet. "You mean like make a list? Why the hell would we do that?"

"You might if you wanted to split the spoils fairly." Natty sat. "Listen, I don't care if you wrote it down, but do you remember what you took and what you pawned, fenced, or buried?"

"Didn't bury a goddamn thing," said Doyle. "Squirreled some things away, thank you very much. Why? You need money? Took yours all in cash as I recall."

"I'm fine." Natty picked up his beer, sipped, but didn't return the glass to the table. His eyes darted back and forth between the brothers. "I'm wondering about a choker. Heard it called a dog collar. Something a real lady might wear for a fancy dress occasion. She'd come from money, I expect, since this collar was made of seed pearls."

Doyle used his forearm to wipe beer foam from his upper lip. "A dog collar, you say. And the bitch is well heeled?" He slapped the table, enjoying his joke. He heard Willet snicker, but Natty did not join in. Doyle dropped his hand to his lap and cleared his throat. "Don't recollect I saw one of those. Willet? You holding out on me?"

"I wouldn't, and I ain't. What's this about, Natty?"

Natty wasn't sure he believed either one of them, but he

went on to explain in spite of that. "Seems someone saw a collar like the one I just told you about and thinks it's connected to the robbery."

"Where'd they see it?" asked Willet.

"I don't know. The sheriff, his deputy, and few other folks wrote down what the passengers reported was stolen. Descriptions, amounts, the approximate value if it was known. That Jackson Brewer was thorough."

"Somebody's lying." Doyle took another swallow of his beer and set the glass down hard. "I'm telling you, Natty, one of those passengers is a damn liar. There was nothing like that."

"Nothing," Willet said, an echo of his brother.

Doyle was staring at his beer. "Could be something like that turned up missing, but it isn't because we stole it."

"Insurance," said Willet. "If it's as expensive as you say, then maybe it was reported as missing to collect something for it."

Doyle turned his bent head, sneered at his brother. "Then how is it that it's been seen? You sure you didn't hold something back? You fingered just about everything."

"I didn't."

"Fellas," said Natty. "All will be revealed. Seems there's a plan to put it in the owner's pretty little hands."

Doyle looked up. "So the deputy has this collar in his possession?"

"It would appear so."

"Then I think we need to keep an eye on him."

"One of us should." Natty picked up his beer. "We don't need to cluster around him like iron filings on a magnet."

Willet's recessed chin made it impossible for him to effectively jut it forward in a challenging manner, but it also never stopped him from trying. He made the reflexive gesture now. "Who, then?"

"Yeah," said Doyle. "Who's it going to be?"

Natty sat back in his chair and regarded them from under a hooded glance. "I think you boys know the answer to that."

* * *

Phoebe and Remington left Saturday afternoon over Fiona's strenuous objections and Thaddeus's milder ones. Fiona offered to invite Mrs. Jacob C. Tyler to Twin Star, and that was an alternative for which Phoebe was unprepared. She bald-faced lied and said that Mrs. Tyler was visiting her son and daughter-in-law because the birth of her grandchild was imminent. "She won't want to be away from the baby until she has to return to Saint Louis. You understand, don't you?"

Fiona's mouth had snapped shut, and she kept it that way, although Phoebe would have rather argued with her than have to listen to her thunderous silence. It was tempting to see if she could find a trunk to crawl into.

Thaddeus had wondered about the suddenness of the trip, and this time it was Remington who offered the bald-faced lie. "Blue delivered the invitation when he came out to the branding. Stationmaster asked him to bring it out. It was the only mail he had for the ranch, so Blue obliged him."

Phoebe sat back on the wooden bench seat as the train pulled away from the Frost Falls station. "Do you think they believed us?"

"About what in particular?" asked Remington. He slung his long legs into the aisle.

"About all of it. I can't remember what I even told Fiona now. We should have considered what they might say and been better prepared."

He shrugged. "Fiona cannot dislike me any more than she already does, so I—"

"Don't be so sure," she said.

"So I am fine with it. And my father? He'll forgive me."

Phoebe lowered her voice. "That's because he thinks you are planning to compromise me."

"He's late to that conclusion."

She jabbed him in the ribs. "If anyone is thinking about my dress and our cake, it's your father."

Remington laughed. "Damn, that's probably true."

"You shouldn't swear so often. I won't tolerate it around the children."

He sat up a little straighter. "What children?"

"Ours. Aren't they on your list of things we have to discuss?"

"Putting it on there now."

"Really, Remington, you should find someone to help you."

He fell silent as he gave it due consideration, then he slid down in the bench seat again and tipped his hat forward. "What do you think about Mrs. Jacob C. Tyler?"

"I think she would be an excellent choice." Phoebe was smiling to herself as she turned to face the window. Her stomach quieted. Her satisfied smile stayed exactly as it was.

The Boxwood Hotel was modeled after the Hotel de Paris over in Clear Creek County and prided itself on being able to offer amenities rarely available to the transient populations of mining communities. The hotel's restaurant boasted fine china for dining, spotless linen tablecloths, and silverware so highly polished one's reflection was visible in the soupspoons. Guests spending the night slept on thick mattresses in solid cherry wood beds. Sheets were changed daily, and the washstands were topped with granite and boasted hot and cold taps. The Boxwood had three suites, each with a claw-footed tub and a water closet, that were often reserved for the discerning gambler who made his living at the card table and tended to stay in Liberty Junction for weeks at a time.

Phoebe and Remington registered separately. He took a room on the third floor. Phoebe was given one of the available suites on the second. They each had a bag, which they were made to surrender to the boy eagerly waiting to show them to their rooms. It was to this young man—who could have not been more than twelve and introduced himself as Handy "I can get you anything" McKenzie—that they asked for information about Mrs. Jacob C. Tyler.

Not surprisingly, Handy embodied his moniker, and they

learned that not only was Mrs. Jacob C. still in residence, but that she was in the dining room at that very minute overseeing the placement of flowers and candlesticks on the tables.

"And really," said Phoebe in an aside to Remington, "why would she be doing anything else?"

Remington hung outside Phoebe's door while Handy showed off the room and the amenities, and then he followed the boy up another flight of stairs to his room. Handy, both clever and observant, pointed Remington to a door at the end of the hall and explained there was another, seldom used, stairwell for moving between floors without notice. Remington did not thank Handy for this information or even acknowledge that he'd heard it, but he did share it later with Phoebe, who very prettily feigned shock and alarm.

Mrs. Jacob C. Tyler was no longer in the elegant dining room when Remington and Phoebe went looking for her. They found her holding court at one of the tables in the large gaming room. She was not only dealing, but she also had more chips in front of her than any of the four men at her table.

"I stand corrected," said Phoebe. "Why would she be doing anything else?"

Remington's laughter turned heads, Mrs. Tyler's among them. She saw them before she recognized them, and when full awareness came to her, she quickly finished the deal and folded, and then she was on her feet hurrying toward them.

She folded Phoebe in a fierce embrace. "Oh, my dear, how lovely it is to see you." And then, before Phoebe could greet her in turn, Mrs. Tyler took her by the shoulders, held her at arm's length, and gave her a thorough looking over. Her features softened and her eyes expressed apprehension. "The child?"

"My lumpy child?" Phoebe asked. "You are so good to inquire, but I think you suspected something was not quite right. I did not set out to deceive you. The pregnancy was supposed to offer protection for a woman traveling alone. We all witnessed the failure of that plan."

Remington reintroduced himself, although it was not necessary according to Mrs. Tyler. She remembered him very well, and how could she not, she asked, when he was so kind to little Madeleine Bancroft and so attentive to the child's mother and herself. And then, she announced in an aside to Phoebe, there was the undeniable fact that he was as tempting as sin.

"Come," she said, looping an arm under one of Phoebe's. "We'll go to the dining room. They are setting it up for dinner, which will not be for another hour or so. We can talk. You must tell me everything that has happened since we parted."

Phoebe hesitated, pointing to the table that Mrs. Tyler had vacated. "Your game?"

"That?" She waved aside Phoebe's concern. "They were humoring me. My son denies it, but I think he pays them to play with me and let me win just often enough to keep it interesting for me and not break his bank. His motive is pure. For as long as the game lasts, I don't have my fingers in his business."

They took a table in one of the dining room cozy alcoves. Although neither Remington nor Phoebe asked for privacy to be a consideration, they were pleased that their table was set away from others by the nook and the tall potted greenery better suited to a hothouse.

Remington sat back while Phoebe and Mrs. Tyler, who now insisted on being addressed exclusively as Amanda, exchanged pleasantries, finished each other's sentences, and shared questions in equal number and provided answers in excruciating detail.

Remington knew when it was finally his turn to speak because they swiveled slightly in their chairs and regarded him expectantly. He said, "I believe your ring has been found."

Mrs. Tyler immediately grasped her ring finger, twisting it as though she could feel phantom pressure of the missing piece. "Oh, my. Can it be true?"

"We won't know until you identify it for us, and no, we don't have it here, but you should be able to see it tomorrow." He explained how the discovery had come to pass and how the ring would be available for her viewing. "We have your description of the ring, and Phoebe is here to provide confirmation."

She nodded. "Yes. Yes, of course. So this woman, the one who will be wearing it, or at least carrying it, she's a . . . a . . ." She leaned in and mouthed the words. "A bride of the multitude?"

Remington blinked at the expression. "Um, yes. She is that."

Mrs. Tyler sat up and pressed her palms together in an attitude of prayer; the tips of her steepled fingers touched her lips. Her smile began to spread wide behind her hands. "That's extraordinary, isn't it? Yes, I really think it is extraordinary. I will write to my husband immediately, well, after I see the ring and can be sure it's mine. Jacob has a wicked sense of humor, you know, and this will tickle him. It tickles me. A soiled dove. Tell me her name again."

"Caroline Carolina."

"Could it be more delightful?"

Phoebe was struck by Mrs. Tyler's composure, and when she looked sideways at Remington, she observed that he was not so much struck as amused. "I confess, I did not anticipate that you would take it so well in stride."

"What? That a young woman no better than she ought to be is in possession of my wedding ring? Did I give you the impression that I was a moralist? Because I can assure you, the moral high ground is largely occupied by people living close to the edge."

Phoebe's laughter was quiet, but Remington did not hold back.

Mrs. Tyler's gaze darted from one to the other. "You look very well together. I am glad to see it. I had an inkling on the train that something was in the wind. Have you already registered?"

Remington nodded. "Before we came in search of you."

"Good. The Boxwood is a lovely hotel and my son is doing a fine job. One room or two?"

They stared at her.

"I should have the grace to blush," she said, "but I don't. Never mind. I was in no anticipation of hearing the answer to something I can learn easily enough."

"By checking the register?" asked Remington. "You have access, I suppose."

"The register? Heaven's no. I am not allowed near it after the unfortunate business with Mr. and Mrs. Sawyer." When neither of them inquired for further information, she sighed. "From now on, I simply ask Handy McKenzie. He knows everything."

Remington's mouth twisted wryly. "And can get it for you, too."

It was late when Remington finally let himself into Phoebe's room. He was concerned that she might already be sleeping, and as reluctant as he was to wake her, he had every intention of doing so. If she had any sense, she'd have barred the door to him, because now that the opportunity to have her again was upon him, he was hardly in his right mind.

A lamp was burning low on the bedside table and provided sufficient light for Remington to see that Phoebe was not only not in bed, but not in the room. He picked up the lamp, wandered into the small sitting area, and then saw a sliver of light under the closed door of the bathing room. When he paused, he heard the faint splash of water.

Remington knocked. "Phoebe?" Without waiting for a reply, he pushed the door open and poked his head inside. Phoebe was reclining in the great claw-foot tub, water almost to her shoulders, a towel wrapped turban-like on her head. She was using her big toe in a lazy attempt to regulate the hot water tap, and she spared him scant attention when he came forward.

"Was there a question in your mind that I was not the occupant of this room?"

There was a hint of something caustic in her tone that gave Remington pause. "You're upset," he said.

"I didn't think you were coming. It's made me testy."

"Ah." He used the toe of his boot to push a footstool close to the tub. When she did not object, he sat.

"I had it in my mind to present you with a vision of Botticelli's Venus on the half shell—hoping I was not flattering myself overmuch—and your tardiness has made me as wrinkled as an old crone in a watering trough."

"A vision of the future, then."

Without looking in his direction, Phoebe scooped a handful of water and threw it at him.

"Feel better?" he asked, picking up a towel. He mopped his face.

"Marginally. You will be made to answer for your lapse."

"I hope so. I am counting on it, in fact." He leaned over, brushed her toe aside, and turned on the hot water. He let it run for a minute before he turned it off. "I like the turban."

Phoebe put one hand to her head as if she'd forgotten it was there. She patted and straightened it and then let her arm slip under the water again. "Compliments will not mollify me, although it's good of you to try." She faced him, then, and gave him the full benefit of her narrow-eyed stare. "Better you should start with where you've been and why you smell of whiskey and women."

Chapter Twenty-eight

Remington held up three fingers. "Three shots." He folded two fingers so only his index finger was standing. "One woman."

"If that is your defense, I believe I understand why you do contracts and not trial law. Who was the woman?"

"Mrs. Tyler."

"Now you have disappointed me with your very poor lie. That is not her perfume. The scent is too cloying."

"*Molly* Tyler," said Remington. "The daughter-in-law. After we returned from our walk and you went to your room, I went to the gaming parlor and bar for a drink. I told you I wanted to make Jacob Junior's acquaintance before tomorrow and the arrival of Miss Carolina on Blue's arm. In the event that he recognizes a—what did his mother call her?"

"Several things," Phoebe said dryly, "but a 'bride of the multitude' stands out in my memory."

"Yes, there was that. In the event he recognizes a bride of the multitude when he sees one, I did not want him barring her from the hotel before she got as far as the front desk."

"I recall that was your intention. I also recall that was two hours ago."

"Yes, well, Junior is as loquacious as his mother, and his wife provided a steady echo of everything he had to say. Neither of them shares Amanda Tyler's ticklish sense of humor."

"The moral high ground, I suppose," she said. "That explains the three whiskeys. What explains the perfume?"

"Molly Tyler might have stumbled into me when I excused myself."

"Might have?"

"Hmm. I don't want to think that she tried to hug me, so let's leave it at that. She has a taste for good whiskey and no head to hold it."

"I wish I had gone with you." She closed her eyes. "More hot water, please."

Remington obliged her, pulling the plug first to let some of the water drain before he added more. When he shut off the tap, he asked, "Are you stubborn enough to sleep there?"

"I might be."

"All right." He stood and began to undress.

Phoebe opened one eye the narrowest of fractions. "Are you entertaining the notion of joining me?"

"I am."

"Hmm."

Because a murmur was hardly an objection, Remington continued to unbutton his jacket. He hung it on a peg by the door, added his vest, his shirt, and then turned his attention to the belt and fly of his trousers. He was lowering himself to the stool to remove his boots when Phoebe rose abruptly from the tub. She whipped the turban towel off her head and wrapped it around her in a single, fluid motion. Remington stared at her as she tightly secured the towel just above her breasts and carefully stepped out of the tub.

"It's all yours," she said.

"But—"

Phoebe pointed to the tub. "Yours," she repeated. Her comb was lying on the granite-topped sink basin and she walked past Remington to retrieve it. She turned to him as she began working it through her hair. "I don't care if the woman was Mrs. Tyler Junior or Mrs. Tyler Senior, I am not sharing a bath or a bed with any man who stinks of another woman's perfume."

"Oh."

"Mm-hmm."

Remington dropped like a stone to the stool and yanked off his boots, his socks, and then pulled his light cotton undershirt over his head. He tossed the shirt at another wall peg, grinning when it hit its mark and hung there. Phoebe, he noticed, was not as impressed with the feat as he was.

Her mouth had flattened and she was shaking her head in a mildly reproving fashion. For some reason her withering look deepened his grin.

"Did your father teach you how to do that?" she asked. "I don't see how. Fiona says he leaves his clothes where he drops them."

"That was never an option for Ben and me. We had to get them off the floor. Ellie insisted. So we made a game of it."

Phoebe leaned against the basin as a tangle in her hair thwarted her comb. She held the knot against one palm and carefully used the comb's teeth to tug at it. "You and Ben are close."

"Is that a question?"

"No. An observation." When Remington said nothing, she asked, "Why do you suppose Ellie and Thaddeus never married?"

Remington was standing again, this time on one leg, as he shucked his trousers. He gave them a toss toward the peg, but they missed and slid down the wall. "I used to think they were married," he said, retrieving the trousers and hanging them up. He dropped his drawers, hooked them on a peg, and walked to the tub with no concern for modesty. He tested the water with his hand before he stepped in it. "She was the housekeeper before my mother died, and she helped us, my father and me, just by being there. I don't recall that she ever said much." He shrugged a little, helpless to explain it better, and lowered himself into the water.

"She did all the things my mother did, at least as I understood it then. She cooked and cleaned and washed and mended. She tended the garden. She ate with us, went to church with us, and attended social functions with us. Ben came along. We were family. We still are." He rested his spine against the back slope of the tub and closed his eyes. "Mostly," he said quietly. "Differently."

Phoebe ran the comb through her hair twice more and then plaited it. When she was done, she sat on the stool he had occupied. "How did you come to realize that they weren't married?"

Remington gave a small start when Phoebe spoke. He hadn't heard her approach or known she was sitting next to him. He settled back when she touched his shoulder with her fingertips. She said nothing to encourage him to speak; it was in the caress, in the finger sweep that was both casual and deliberate.

"It was the lack of affection, I suppose." He thought about that, tried to recall what he had seen as a young boy, and shook his head. "That's not quite right. There was affection, but they did not touch the way my parents did. I never witnessed a hug or a kiss. No fanny pats when one of them slipped past the other. They didn't share a bedroom, but back then I didn't fully appreciate why that would have been important. I guess I eventually figured it out because I don't remember ever asking my father or anyone else. I don't know what Ben thought when he was growing up; he never said a word, so I imagine he came around to understanding it, too."

"Did you ever wish Ellie was your mother?"

"She was. Is. It seems an unimportant detail that she is not my father's wife."

Phoebe nodded. "Of course."

"But I think you want to know something else. I think you want to know if I ever wished they had married."

"And?"

Remington watched her out of the corner of his eye. "Do you really want me to answer the question you couldn't bring yourself to ask?"

Phoebe's smiled thinly, regretfully. "You just have. It must have crossed your mind after Thaddeus returned to Twin Star with Fiona."

Remington reached for Phoebe's hand resting on his shoulder. He took it, folded it in his palm, and raised it to his lips. He kissed her knuckles. "It crossed my mind," he told her. "I didn't dwell on it. There's a difference." He gave her back her hand, put the floating bar of soap in it, and gave her a hopeful look.

"You are shameless," she said. "Lean forward."

He did. He almost sighed when she began to soap his

back. He did close his eyes again. "Is there some reason you're thinking about this now?"

"I'm only asking about it now. I've been thinking about it for a long time."

"You have?"

"Mm. Sometimes I put myself in Ellie's shoes. Sometimes in Fiona's." She cupped a handful of water and sluiced his back. "I can tell you, I prefer my own. I have some sense of place, of belonging. I'm not so certain that either of them does any longer." She laughed a bit unsteadily, tapped him on the shoulder with the bar of soap. "This is what happens when you leave me soaking in a tub. My waterlogged mind wanders. I can hardly be held responsible."

Remington recognized Phoebe's retreat. He let her go. It was easy to do when she manipulated the soap with a magician's sleight of hand, touching him unexpectedly on the knee, running it up the inside of his upper thigh. She drained some of the water when it cooled and added hot from the tap as he had done for her. He could have slept there, but she had other ideas, and she made them clear when she abandoned the soap and cupped his balls in her slippery palm.

She laughed, low and wicked. "I have your full attention, I think."

"Maybe," he said. "And maybe it's that I have yours."

She released him, but only after she scored the length of his penis with her thumbnail. "It's very bold, isn't it?" she said when it practically jumped out of her hand.

His wry smile mocked her. "I know I've referenced the one about the pot and the kettle before, but I'm not certain you understand the gist of it."

Phoebe's arm dipped deep into the water near his knee and came up with a washcloth. She tossed it at him, and when he was distracted by the pitch, she planted a bold kiss on his perfect mouth and danced out of his reach before he could pull her in to join him.

She paused at the door, gave him a come-hither glance over one bare shoulder, and simultaneously warned him, "Not a *hint* of that perfume." And then she was gone.

Amused, entranced, Remington stared at the door she closed behind her for all of three seconds before he got busy. He scoured with a purpose, dunking his head and lathering his hair, taking the precaution to wash behind his ears in the event there was an inspection, and scrubbing his chest where he thought the generous fragrance of Junior's tipsy wife might have leaked through his clothes.

When he was finished, he pulled the plug, hoisted himself out of the tub, and searched for a towel. He found two, one he used mostly to dry and then slung around his neck; the other he hitched around his hips. His erection was no longer at a full stand, but neither was he hiding what was behind the curtain. He finger-combed his damp hair without glancing at the mirror and rinsed his mouth with warm water and baking soda paste that Phoebe had left on the basin top. It had to be good enough, he thought, because he could not wait any longer.

Phoebe was sitting up at the head of the bed when Remington stepped past the threshold. She looked over; saw the damp gleam of water at his throat, on his arms, and across his chest. Beads of water dripped on the floor near his bare feet. Wide runnels separated his thick hair where he had plowed it with his fingers. The towel around his waist was riding low. She could make out the intriguing arrow of dark hair and followed it to where it disappeared under the towel's edge.

He had not taken much time to dry. That made her smile. *He* made her smile. It was one of the moments she held close to her heart.

Phoebe patted the space beside her and threw back the covers to make the invitation clear. She watched him approach, watched his easy walk, the way his hips moved and how the towel shifted, threatened to fall but somehow never did. When he sat on the edge of the bed, she stole the towel from around his neck and dried his back and shoulders. She didn't touch his hair. She liked the furrows and the curls that lay against his nape like thick black commas.

Remington turned his head, found Phoebe's mouth waiting for him. She kissed him, parting her lips, touching him with the tip of her tongue. He followed where she led him, which was flat on his back with her hovering above him.

She looked down, searched his face, and imagined she could see her reflection in his unfathomable eyes. Her voice was a husky whisper. "What do you think of this mattress?"

"Very fine."

"I miss our old place."

That made him laugh. "Uh-huh."

She nudged the tip of his nose then his lips. She spoke against his mouth. "I am going to be very bold now."

"Mm. I hope so."

She was. He made it easy for her. Nothing she did or wanted to do seemed out of the ordinary because he was so comfortable in his own skin. She called on the memory of lying with him at McCauley's cabin to guide her when she felt herself faltering. She remembered all the ways he had touched her, all the sensations his touch had provoked, and began there, setting her mouth in the curve of his neck and sipping his skin. The branding was still fresh in her mind, and what she did to him there did not seem so very different.

Phoebe told him that when she lifted her head to examine the mark she'd left on his flesh. Between applications of hot branding kisses, he begged her not to castrate him. She showered him with her laughter instead and left him the weaker for it.

Phoebe set her mouth at the corner of his, teased him with the tip of her tongue, and when he responded, she moved on, tracing the line of his jaw and using her teeth to tug on his earlobe. She whispered against his skin, sometimes telling him what he could expect, sometimes giving him direction.

She led the exploration of his chest with her fingertips and followed it with her lips. She laid her palm against his heart, felt the strong steady beat, and the change of that rhythm when her free hand slipped under his towel. Watching him, she delicately walked her fingers up his inner thigh and brushed his thickening erection with her knuckles. She saw it in his face, his need for something more substantial than the fleeting touch of her flesh against his. Lifting her eyebrows, she posed the silent question, and when he nodded, she used her teeth to pluck open his towel and found him with her mouth.

Chapter Twenty-nine

Phoebe put his cock to the hot suck of her mouth. Her tongue laved the tip, circled, and drew him in. Her damp hair fell forward over her shoulders, draped the sides of her face, and swept his skin as she moved. She felt his fingers sift through her hair, brush it away from her cheek. His hand drifted to her shoulder, and his touch was both firm and gentle. The cadence of his breathing changed. She altered the slant of her mouth, manipulated his sac with her fingers, and then made a fist around the length of his penis below her lips. Her palm was almost as warm as her mouth, and it was as if she had taken all of him. She knew that because he told her so, but not all at once. What he said came in fits and starts between harshly indrawn breaths and sips of air. His fingers found her hair again, wrapped a thick coil around his hand, and he held her like that until his body jerked and jerked away.

It was his turn, then, and in movements both fluid and fierce, Remington released the rope of her hair, caught her under her arms, and wrestled her onto her back. Phoebe's knees came up, her neck arched, and the breath she had been inhaling lodged in her throat. It did not seem at all strange to her that her body welcomed him outside of her consciousness. She wanted him, wanted him inside her, and her arms and legs and mouth all acted in concert to make that happen as though directed by a force outside her.

She was unaware of losing her towel until he flung it over the side of the bed, and she did not have a sense of her own nakedness until his mouth closed over her nipple. She hugged him with her thighs; her fingers slipped into his damp hair. Her hips rose and fell, at first in response to the rhythm he set, and then to one that was hers. He followed her lead. Time seemed to slow. When he lifted his head, she searched his face, saw the evidence of self-denial in his taut features and in his clear, steady gaze. He did not hide his need from her but neither would he allow it to overcome him, and this was his gift to her, would always be his gift.

She was safe.

"Don't wait," she whispered. "Come. I want you to come."

It was her words as much as the contractions of her body that forced his surrender. The slow, measured thrust of his hips became quick and shallow. He arched his back, pushed himself up and in, and gave up a guttural cry as he shuddered with violent pleasure. He collapsed and lay heavily against her for a time, unable to move. It felt like an act of will to breathe just then.

His face was buried in the curve of her neck, and when he spoke, his moist breath shifted a few strands of her cocoa-colored hair. "Sorry," he said, and started to rise.

"No. Not yet," she said. "Please, not yet."

He stayed.

It struck Phoebe that she had never known her body until she had known his. Somehow, lying under him in just this way, Remington's long, hard frame, his tight belly and broad shoulders, the slim hips, and firm thighs, all of it defined the shape of hers. She was aware of the hollow of her throat, the delicate underside of her wrists, the way her breasts flattened against his chest, and the contrast of her pale complexion against the sun-beaten color of his. He made her understand how her body was meant to accommodate the presence of a man—this man—and that there could be pleasure in the accommodation. What had been largely a mystery to her was now revealed, and that it had been revealed to her with real reverence for her woman's body, with passion and compassion, made her want to weep.

"Phoebe?" When Remington lifted himself away this time, she did not stop him. He yanked on the covers tangled at their feet and then stretched beside her, levering himself on one elbow so he could see her face. "Are you all right?" She nodded, but in a way that he found unconvincing. "What is it?"

She shrugged, though not in a careless manner.

Remington used a forefinger to nudge her chin his way. Her eyes shifted from the ceiling to him. "Did I hurt you?"

Shocked that he even thought it might be a possibility, Phoebe found her voice. "No!"

Her vehemence was reassuring, but it did not help him understand the bent of her mind. "I'm not good at this," he said. "You have to tell me."

She shook her head but did not dislodge his finger. "I can't," she whispered. "I don't have the words, not the right ones, but what you make me feel about myself, what you make me know, all of that is so much more than fine. You are good, Remington. Very good." A faint smile lifted the corners of her mouth. "You're blushing."

He did not attempt to deny it. There was no point when he could feel the warmth rising under his skin. "Those words you said you didn't have? They were nice."

She took his hand and raised it to her mouth. She kissed the fingertip that had been holding her chin hostage. "I need to excuse myself." Her eyes darted in the direction of the bathing room. "I won't be long."

Remington nodded. He lifted the covers so she could slide out. Somehow she managed to find the towel he had been wearing and wrapped herself in it before she rolled out of bed. Watching her walk away, he said, "You can't imagine how much I regret not tossing that one aside when I had the chance."

"You never had the chance," she reminded him, but then, just as she reached the doorway, she turned, gave him her sauciest smile, and while his eyes were riveted on her mouth, she dropped the towel.

Remington groaned and flopped onto his back when she disappeared from view. "You have no concept of fair play," he called out. He heard her offer some kind of reply but could not make it out through the closed door. He stretched toward the bedside table and turned back the lamp, then rolled back to the middle of the bed and folded a pillow under his head. He had managed to erase the odor of whiskey from this breath but not its effect on his brain. He was tired. It was not a decision to close his eyes; it was more that he had no choice.

When Phoebe returned to bed, she found Remington deeply asleep. She crawled naked into bed beside him and used his body like a bolster at her back. She arranged one of his arms so that it hugged her waist and pushed her bottom snug against his groin. She smiled to herself when his penis stirred and he did not. He would probably add it to his regrets when she told him about it later. It was her last thought before she fell asleep.

And it was gone from her mind when she woke. Remington was deep under the covers, his face buried between her parted thighs, his tongue darting in a way that brought a sharp rise of pleasure each time it flicked over her skin. She had a drowsy memory of desire unfulfilled when she had left his side earlier, and he was laying that to rest now. Her fingers curled in the covers; her heels dug into the mattress. She inhaled in jagged little gasps that marked the steep climb of pleasure.

Phoebe closed her eyes, finding that even the deep shadows of the room were distracting to what she was feeling. He was tugging on a single thread of pleasure and she was unraveling. It did not frighten her, this feeling of abandon; she welcomed it, welcomed the anticipation, and embraced every nuance of the sensations that followed.

When his head appeared from under the covers, he regarded her with what she deemed was indecent satisfaction. She forgave him because she, too, was indecently satisfied, and reproaching him required infinitely more energy than she had now or in the immediate future.

Her perfect exhaustion was the same reason she did not try to stop Remington when he rolled out of bed. She did not even turn her head to follow his shadowed movements as he padded to the bathing room, and she was barely recovered enough to hold up the covers for him when he returned to the bedside.

He got in, and with no word passing between them, they inched together until they found the sweet spot where two bodies could lie as easily as one.

"When are you going to marry me?" he asked, nudging the crown of her head with his chin.

"Soon, I think."

"There's a judge here right now who would do it."

"How do you know that?"

"I asked him. He was one of the men playing cards with Mrs. Tyler this afternoon. I saw him again at another table when I was talking to Junior and his wife."

"Oh, of course, you would know him."

"He wasn't particularly pleased to see me outside of his courtroom," said Remington. "Mostly because he was losing badly." He waited for Phoebe to respond to his overture. When she didn't, he prompted her. "So?"

"I don't know. I'm not sure it's the right thing to do. If we did, would you want to tell everyone when we get back?"

Treacherous waters, Remington thought, and stepped in them anyway. "Yes, wouldn't you?" She didn't answer, which was answer enough. "I see."

Phoebe closed her eyes. His throat sounded tight.

"I think I need to ask you again, Phoebe. Are you going to marry me?"

"Yes."

"But not tomorrow."

"Not tomorrow," she repeated.

"And not the day after that," he said.

"Probably not."

"But soon, you said. You think."

"Yes. I'm sorry."

Remington said nothing for a time. The silence was not a particularly comfortable one, but neither of them sought physical distance. "I think there is something more to this than holding these moments close to your heart or Fiona's objections or even the fact that I've barely started my goddamn list of things we need to discuss. What is it, Phoebe? What is it that you're not telling me?"

She shook her head. "It's not for me to say. It's never been my secret to tell."

"All right," he said flatly. "You want to know what I did that put me in Fiona's bad graces?"

"I never accused you of—"

Remington interrupted her without apology. "I turned her away, Phoebe. She tried to get me into her bed—my *father's* bed—and when I would not oblige her, she came to my room, to my bed, and I came as close as I ever hope to striking a woman."

Phoebe pressed a fist against her mouth to keep from howling. She felt as if her heart were being squeezed. Tears sprang to her eyes; she blinked them back.

He went on relentlessly. "I don't pretend to understand her motives. I don't believe for a moment that she wanted me in any real way except as she could use me. Her overtures were so bold, so likely to be discovered, that I thought she wanted to make Thaddeus jealous, or make him send her away, or make him send me away. Maybe she was driven to do it by something in her that I can never comprehend. Maybe she was simply bored. I pity her, and I told her so, and she will not forget nor forgive that as long as she's drawing breath."

Now Remington drew a breath and waited for his heart to settle into its natural rhythm. "That's all of it," he said. Urgency was absent from his voice. "What I did. What she did. It's done."

Phoebe lifted her hand from her mouth but only a fraction. "I think I am going to—" She did not finish the sentence, couldn't finish it. She kicked at the blankets, found a way out, and leapt out of bed before there was any chance that he might stop her. Her hands trembled, the one that covered her mouth, and the one that fumbled with the door to the bathing room. She barely reached the sink before she began to retch.

Remington left the bed more slowly than she did, but he also had the presence of mind to take a quilt with him. He stood beside her at the sink, held back her hair, and laid the quilt across her shoulders and kept it there. When she stopped shuddering and heaving and could hold the blanket closed herself, he poured her a glass of water and tilted it against her mouth. She gulped, rinsed, and spit, and did it two more times before she was ready to swallow. Afterward, he made to lead her back to the bedroom, but she stopped at an overstuffed chair in the sitting area and curled there instead. Remington left her long enough to put on his trousers, and when he returned, she hadn't moved.

He found her shift in the wardrobe and gave it to her. "You can keep the quilt," he said, "but you'll be warmer with this." She did not object, but neither did she do anything with it once she had it in her hands. It was left to Remington to help her into it. When he was done, he laid the quilt over her and tucked on all sides. The sitting room had a rocker, an upright chair at the writing desk, and an ottoman large enough to seat two. He pushed it toward Phoebe and sat facing her.

"Give me your feet," he said. "Like on the porch swing." When she didn't, he reached over, slid them out from under her, and placed them on his lap. He warmed his hands by rubbing his palms together before he laid them over her toes and the balls of her feet. He was satisfied when she closed her eyes and sighed.

"I don't think you were surprised," he said. The shake of her head was almost infinitesimal, but because he was looking for some reaction, he saw it. "But I don't know if you allowed yourself to suspect."

"I couldn't," she whispered. She stole a glance at him. "Ben?"

He knew what she was asking. "I don't know if she approached him. He's never said, but he took to sleeping in the bunkhouse a lot. Then again, he's willing to escort her into town."

"You never said anything to Thaddeus."

"No."

"He would have believed you. Even now, after all this time, he would believe you."

He shrugged. "It doesn't matter. He'll never hear it from me." He pressed his thumbs along the arch of her feet. "Too much?" he asked when she squirmed just a bit.

"Almost."

Remington resisted applying more pressure. He worked his thumbs up and down her soles and watched her sink more heavily into the chair as she relaxed.

Phoebe watched him from under the sweep of dark lashes. "Why do you want to be with me, Remington? Knowing her the way you do, why in the world would you ever want to be with me?"

"You are not her."

"But she's . . ." Phoebe stopped, shook her head, helpless to continue in that vein. "You said I was like her."

"I know what I said, and I know what I meant. I don't think you ever did. You are nothing like her and exactly like her, but you are *not* her. There's never been once that I thought so."

"Marriage to me will tie you to her. Forever."

"So? It will be a long leash. Your list, remember? I have an idea about building our home in the valley beyond the first pasture. That's Frost land but well away from the ranch house. It's green and lush in the spring and summer and has a fast running spring that even a harsh winter has not been able to freeze. I would have taken you there, made sure you agreed about the location, but I didn't think you were ready to ride out with me when there was no good excuse for going."

"Beyond the first pasture?" she asked. "How far is that?"

"About five miles."

"So a very long leash."

"Yes. Fiona and Thaddeus can tug on it, but we will be able to see them coming."

"It would be our home?"

"Mm-hmm. I drew plans. I'm better at that than lists. Right now we can easily accommodate four young ruffians and add on if we have to."

"Four?"

He nodded. "It seemed right, give or take a ruffian."

"All boys?"

He chuckled. "You surprise me, Phoebe Apple. Little girls can be ruffians, too. I had it in my mind that ours would be."

She dug one of her heels into his thigh because she couldn't quite kick him. "Stop it." She swiped impatiently at her eyes. "You are going to make me cry. I swear I am not a weeper. At least I never used to be."

He lifted her foot so it was no longer pressing into him and continued massaging. "We'll find someone to help you once we've moved in. Someone who can live there and keep you company when I have to travel."

"Then we will have to find someone to keep her company because I will be with you."

"Oh."

"See? This is why we should have discussions."

"What about the young ruffians?"

"Thaddeus will just have to find someone else to send on trips. You will want to stay close. I will *want* you to stay close."

"Uh-huh. You've given this some thought."

"I have names picked out."

"And still haven't thought about your wedding dress. You continue to put the cart before the horse."

She nodded. Her smile was vaguely sly. "Don't you see? If we go on as we have been . . ." Here she glanced toward the bedroom. "There is every chance a child will present itself sooner rather than later. I was thinking we might continue a Frost tradition."

A crease appeared between Remington's eyebrows. "And what tradition is that?"

"Why, naming our child after the shotgun at our wedding, of course. Colt. Winchester. Henry. Sharp. Spencer. Springfield."

Remington let her rattle on as he pulled her out of the chair and carried her back to bed. Really, she was very good with lists.

Chapter Thirty

Mrs. Jacob C. Tyler did not try to hide her disappointment when she clapped eyes on Caroline Carolina. The younger woman looked nothing like the vision of a bride of the multitude that Amanda Tyler had in her head.

First, there was the undeniable fact that Miss Carolina was not a recently plucked flower, which put her age somewhere north of Phoebe's and well south of Amanda's own. Second, there was the matter of her attire, all of which was perfectly suitable for traveling or a stroll in the park. She would hardly bring notice to herself for what she wearing except that she was wearing it very well. The walking dress was soft wool in a brightly colored plaid of a yellow, orange, red, and black. Under her skirt she wore the firmer, shelf-like bustle that added inches to her posterior and made her waist seem impossibly small. Her flat crown straw hat had a projecting brim that shaded her heart-shaped face. The hat was trimmed with roses the same shade of yellow as appeared in her dress, and a black lace frill enhanced the brim.

Mrs. Tyler and Phoebe were once again seated in an alcove in the Boxwood's large dining room. This time, though, they were alone, as Remington was sitting with Junior at a round table closer to the kitchen. Both men rose as Miss Carolina approached their table on the arm of Deputy Blue Armstrong. Amanda leaned heavily toward Phoebe and whispered out of the side of her mouth. "Not what I was expecting, and I must say, I am a tad disappointed."

Phoebe gave the woman a gentle push to center her back

into her chair. "Don't stare. We don't want to attract notice or put notice on them."

Mrs. Tyler glanced around the dining room. The usual Sunday-after-church crowd was in attendance to partake in the hotel's fine brunch. The gaming room was quiet and largely empty, but come two o'clock when the brunch was no longer being served, a fair number of men, most of them dedicated churchgoers, would leave their wives and sweethearts at the door and give in to the temptation of cards, dice, and drink.

"No one is paying us the least attention," she said, raising her teacup to her lips. She continued to speak behind the delicately painted china cup. "Can you see if she is wearing a ring?"

Phoebe refused to look. "No, I can't see. We will have our chance soon enough." She broke a crisp strip of bacon in half, took a bite, and surveyed the dining room much as Mrs. Tyler had. "They are making introductions now," she said. "And a girl has just approached their table to take their orders." Her eyes moved on. "Where is your daughter-in-law this morning?"

Mrs. Tyler momentarily pursed her lips. "Molly is indisposed."

"Oh. I am sorry she doesn't feel well. I was looking forward to meeting her."

"Hangover," Amanda Tyler said bluntly. "No head for drink. I sent Handy up to her apartment with the cure. With any luck it will persuade her not to imbibe anytime soon. She is a dear, and I like her very much, but she can be rather full of herself, and in my view, alcohol is the great leveler of puffery. It's why I never criticize her drinking." She smiled shrewdly, a little full of herself as well. "And the opportunity to give her cure is frankly irresistible."

Amused, Phoebe simply shook her head as she did another casual inspection of the room. "Are most of the diners familiar to you?"

"Most, yes, and 'familiar' is the correct word. I don't

know them. I am better acquainted with the hotel guests, some of whom were here before I came and will be here after I leave. It astonishes me still that there are men who make a comfortable living at the card table."

Phoebe's gaze did not linger on any one diner, and she was only listening to Amanda with half an ear. Out of the corner of her eye, she had seen Miss Carolina open her reticule and produce a small black velvet pouch.

"I think your son is about to have his first look at the ring," she said. She quickly placed one hand on Amanda's forearm and cautioned her again. "Don't stare."

"Whatcha lookin' at?" Handy McKenzie pulled out the empty chair at the table and flopped into it. He grinned toothily as both women stared at him, and because his back was to the other diners, he had to go through several contortions to get the same view they had before he joined them. "Oh, her. You like her dress, Mrs. T.? Puts me in mind of the sun." He swiveled around in his chair. "Probably good for one's disposition to wear all that yellow."

Mrs. Tyler ceased looking put upon and waggled a strip of bacon at him. "Don't you have somewhere to be?"

"Of course I do." With all the cheek of a young hooligan, Handy plucked the bacon strip from Mrs. Tyler's fingers and bit down on it. "I'm here, aren't I? So this must be the somewhere I have to be."

"Impudent rascal," she said, picking up her fork. "Did you deliver the cure?"

"Certainly." He eyed her scrambled eggs. "Are you going to eat those or wave your fork over them?"

"Here." It was Phoebe who passed her plate, not Mrs. Tyler.

Handy hesitated. "Oh, I couldn't, ma'am." But his eyes darted to Mrs. T. for permission. When she nodded indulgently, he seized the plate in both hands before Phoebe could change her mind. There was an extra setting of silverware on the table. He chose the correct fork but not before he carefully spread a napkin over his lap. "I stayed with Mrs.

Molly until she drank it all down, just like you said. I think you're right, Mrs. T., she drinks it a mite quicker when she knows I won't leave. She says, 'Thank you very much.'"

"I'm sure she did," Mrs. Tyler said.

Handy jerked his head backward to indicate the table that had interested the women. "So what's the law doing here?"

Phoebe blinked. "Mr. Frost is not the law."

"Not him. The other fellow. The one I don't know. He's the law."

Mrs. Tyler returned to staring at young Handy. "How could you possibly know that?"

Handy shrugged his bony shoulders. "I been scrappin' with the law since I was a young'un. You get a feelin' for it. Where's he from?"

"A little town north of here called None of Your Business."

He laughed appreciatively. "You tickle me, Mrs. T. That's a good one. And I suppose that woman with him works at the Never-You-Mind cathouse." He cast an apologetic smile at Phoebe. "Sorry, Miss Apple. Probably shoulda said 'brothel' instead of the other. I got a feelin' for those places, too."

Mrs. Tyler spoke before Phoebe could. "Not the time for your life story, Handy. Take your plate, napkin, and silverware to the kitchen and don't let Mrs. Anderson put you to work before you've finished eating. If it's a problem, send her to me."

"Yes, ma'am. Sorry to you, too, about the cathouse comment. I figure my tongue outruns my manners most every time."

Mrs. Tyler nodded. "We will keep working on that."

Phoebe noticed that Handy did not seem at all displeased to hear it. He jumped up from the table, caught his napkin before it fell, and cleared his place. He wended his way through the dining room with the agility of a little monkey until he came to the table occupied by Remington, Junior, the law, and the whore, and then didn't he just manage to knock everyone about so that he had a good look at what they were inspecting. He retreated quickly when Junior threatened to cuff him and backed through the swinging kitchen door. In spite of his rushing, he still had time to catch Mrs. T.'s eye and gave her a crafty, face-splitting grin.

Mrs. Tyler sighed and sat back. "Isn't he a one? What can I do but have a soft spot for him? God help us all if he pinched the ring."

"He wouldn't."

"No, not so he'd keep it, but—" She stopped because there was a scramble at the other table as the men ducked and Miss Carolina rose and it was obvious from their postures that everyone was looking for something. "That's what I mean," she said with considerable composure. "Give them a moment. Someone will find it."

It was Blue who came up with the prize. Pleased with himself, he held the ring aloft and showed it off. It was only when the diamond sparkled in a ray of sunlight that he realized that the attention he had called to himself was not solely from his table companions. He sat slowly, took the velvet pouch that Miss Caroline held out to him, and dropped the ring inside.

Phoebe breathed more easily once the ring was confined to the little drawstring bag. "Is it yours?" she asked Mrs. Tyler. "Could you tell?"

"Not from here, but I am confident my son knows. I am less confident that Miss Carolina intends to give it up. I had not considered a reward, but there should be one. I will offer it myself if he does not have the good sense to do so."

As it happened, Junior showed good sense and made his mother proud. It was he who escorted Miss Carolina to his mother's table and pulled out a chair for her after making introductions. Remington and Blue remained at their table, but Phoebe saw they were watchful.

Junior stood behind and slightly to one side of Miss Carolina. Except for his eyes, which were like silver coins, he possessed a less rounded countenance than his mother. He was also more severe in his dress, his posture, and his presentation.

Miss Carolina's demeanor was polite, but she did not engage

in pleasantries. "I understand this may well belong to you." She passed the pouch to Mrs. Tyler without opening it. "I am disappointed, of course, but your son has offered me a handsome sum for its return and I am not in a position to refuse it."

"Yes," said Mrs. Tyler. "Yes, of course." She opened the drawstring and turned over the pouch so what was inside fell into her palm. The pear shape diamond winked at her before her fingers folded around it. She nodded. "It's mine." There were tears in her eyes when she looked at Miss Carolina. "Thank you. It's not merely the diamond that makes me know it." She opened her fist and allowed the other woman to look at it again. "Do you see the deep scratch in the gold band? Yes? I did that slicing onions with a very sharp knife. The tears, you know. I could not see properly. My knife hand slipped and this ring saved my finger." She slipped it on. "This finger." She reached for her son's hand and took it in hers. "He's heard the story, haven't you?"

"Too many times," he said dryly.

"Yes. Probably." She smiled at Miss Carolina. "But that's how he could identify the ring. There's no doubt." She released her son's hand and showed off the ring to Phoebe. "You didn't know about the cut."

"No. This is the diamond I remember, but I didn't know about the other."

Mrs. Tyler took Miss Carolina's hand in both of hers. "You are very good to do this."

"Not that good," she said candidly. "I really had no other choice."

"There are always choices. You made the right one."

Miss Carolina nodded faintly. She took back her hand, stood, and raised her hand to bring Blue Armstrong to his feet. "My escort is waiting for me."

"Oh, but don't you want to—"

"It's better if we leave."

Mrs. Tyler nodded. "Jake, you'll be a dear, won't you? See that she has her reward before she leaves the hotel."

"Right away," he said, holding out his elbow. "Come with me, Miss Carolina."

Phoebe watched them walk toward the entrance to the dining room. Deputy Armstrong cut a diagonal route to meet them. Remington rose, and in movements that mirrored Handy McKenzie's earlier ones, took his plate, napkin, and utensils and followed a meandering path among the tables to reach her side.

"May I?" he asked, indicating Miss Carolina's vacant chair.

"Of course."

Mrs. Tyler's greeting was more effusive, and she got the attention of a girl who was pouring coffee to bring the pot around to the table.

Phoebe noticed that Remington took the fussing in stride. She smirked, communicating clearly that he should not ever expect the same of her. She might fuss from time to time, but he should not expect it.

"What happened to your plate?" asked Remington.

It was Mrs. Tyler who answered. "She gave it to that young scamp Handy. He pleaded hunger and she believed him. He's probably eaten three times already."

Remington grinned. "Soft touch, is she?"

"The softest."

Phoebe pointed a finger at each of them in turn. "I'm right here." The girl with the coffeepot arrived, and Phoebe ordered another breakfast for herself. "It seems to have gone quite smoothly," she said when the girl was gone. "What did you learn about the man who gave Miss Carolina the ring?"

"John Manypenny. He's a whiskey drummer. Takes orders from saloons and certain private individuals. Collier is on his regular route and she generally knows when he'll be coming through. She thinks he lives in Denver. He won't be hard to find. If the ring did not pass through too many hands before it got to his, we should have a good description of the seller soon, perhaps even a name to go with it."

"You're confident," said Mrs. Tyler. It was not a question. "I approve of that. It's an attractive quality as long as it does not drift sideways into arrogance. I do not approve of that at all."

"Good to know," said Remington. He drizzled honey on the open face of a sliced biscuit and noticed that Phoebe seemed oddly fascinated. He replaced the honey wand in the jar and held out the biscuit to her. "Would you like it?"

Phoebe shook her head. "You applied the honey in a spiral. I don't believe I ever noticed that before. You are truly your father's son."

Remington corrected her. "My mother's son. It was her way. Thaddeus and I adopted it."

"Then I won't mention it to Fiona."

"Better you don't."

Mrs. Tyler was at a loss to understand the conversation but that did not stop her from inserting herself into it. "If there is a question before you, why not let the judge decide? He is coming toward us now." She cast a mischievous glance at Remington. "Shall I be witness to a marriage today?"

Remington turned to Phoebe. "Will she?"

Phoebe stared at him. Shock left her cold.

"Phoebe?" Remington set the biscuit on his plate. "I thought last night . . . you said . . . you said it wasn't your secret to tell, so I told it to you. I thought it was settled then."

Phoebe rose to her feet stiffly. "You thought wrong," she said tonelessly. "It was not your secret to tell either."

Chapter Thirty-one

Two days after Remington and Phoebe returned to Twin Star, there was still nothing settled between them. There were apologies, politely accepted, but they changed very little. Phoebe was ashamed that she had left the table so abruptly that she failed to make the acquaintance of the judge and had left Remington and Mrs. Tyler to offer excuses for her. Remington deeply regretted that he had misunderstood their conversation and believed that with his secret revealed, Phoebe meant to marry him before they left Liberty Junction. He was no closer to understanding what it was that she needed to hear before she would marry him, but he was clear that whatever it was, she was not expecting to hear it from him.

Perhaps he should have been relieved to know it, but what he was, was frustrated, and he did not take any particular pains to hide it.

"He's showing himself," Fiona told Phoebe.

"What?" Distracted, Phoebe looked up from her book and saw Fiona was intending to join her in the parlor. She managed to keep from sighing and closed *A Tale of Two Cities* around her finger. "I'm sorry, Fiona. I didn't hear you."

Fiona chose to perch in the middle of the sofa. Out of habit, she smoothed her gown and set her hands in her lap. "He's showing himself. That's what I said."

"Who?"

"Remington, of course. Really, Phoebe, you can be obtuse at times. Or is it simply that you do not wish to see?"

"Oh, I think it must be that I'm obtuse."

"And now you are being perfectly disagreeable."

Now Phoebe did sigh. She removed her spectacles, carefully folded the stems, and placed them on the table at her side. "Is there something in particular you want to say? Perhaps explain what you mean by Remington showing himself?"

"Why, he's positively surly. I've seen the like before, of course, but not since you arrived. It is quite an achievement that he maintained that façade of cheerfulness for as long as he did."

"Cheerfulness? I believe that is overstating his general disposition."

Fiona waved aside the objection. "You know what I'm saying. He is unpleasant to everyone. I am rather more immune than others, but he set Ben back on his heels this morning, pinned that young Johnny Scooter fellow to the—"

"Johnny Sutton," Phoebe said. "Or Scooter Banks."

"Does it matter? It was one of them pinned to the corral by Remington's abusive language. He has barely spoken to Thaddeus in spite of several overtures, and last night he went straight to the bunkhouse after dinner and slept there."

Puzzled, Phoebe frowned. "Are you pleased? Satisfied? Concerned? Or simply the harbinger of doom?"

"There is no need to wax dramatic. I want you to know him for what he is, Phoebe. I could see you were developing an attachment. I can't say what I thought he was doing because it would not be polite, but I believe your feelings were becoming fixed. If something happened on your trip to Liberty Junction that changed that, then I, for one, am glad of it."

Phoebe did not respond immediately. Her quiet had a purpose. She needed it to preface what she wanted to say to Fiona, and she needed Fiona to hear her. When she saw Fiona lean slightly forward in anticipation of her reply, Phoebe judged she could speak. "Nothing happened on our trip," she said. "My feelings for Remington have not changed; they are as fixed now as they were before we left. As to the composition of those feelings, it is not for me to say to you before I have said the same to him. You should leave it at that, Fiona."

Phoebe watched with jaded amusement as Fiona flung

herself backward on the sofa. She stopped short of placing her wrist against her forehead and a hand over her heart, but otherwise was the embodiment of waxing dramatic. Phoebe was tempted to applaud, but that would have been giving the performance approbation it did not deserve.

"You are in love with him," said Fiona.

It was no mere statement Fiona flung at her. It was an accusation and it was all Phoebe could do not to recoil. "Am I?"

"Do not play coy with me." Agitated, Fiona sat up. It was not enough, so she stood, and when that failed to quiet her jangling nerves, she began to pace. "You will have to leave, Phoebe. I forbid you to be in love with him. Distance will help you see him more clearly, and you will be gratified that I stepped in to save you from yourself."

Phoebe set the book aside and folded her hands in her lap. Her eyes, not her head, tracked Fiona's movements. She did not respond directly to what was said; instead she advanced her terms. "You need to tell me what happened between you and Remington to make you revile him. I will not leave without hearing it from you. Tell me what he did."

Fiona made a small huffing noise at the back of her throat. "The last time you put that question to me, you asked what I had done to him. It is small gratification that you recognize the shoe is on the other foot."

"I am not asking a question now," said Phoebe. "Tell me."

Fiona stopped pacing so suddenly that she seemed to vibrate before she went completely still. "You will not like it."

"That is the one thing of which I am certain, and it does not matter. Tell me."

Fiona's bosom rose with the fullness of the breath she took. She spoke as that same breath rushed out of her. "He propositioned me."

"Propositioned?"

"He wanted me in his bed. Is that plain enough for you? I am his father's wife and he wanted to fuck me."

Without inflection, Phoebe said, "That certainly is plain speaking."

"You're a cool one, aren't you, Phoebe?"

"I don't know what you mean. It's rather a lot to take in. I don't want to make hasty judgments."

"What are you saying? You wanted to know what happened, and I told you. I sincerely hope you are not judging me. I am the wronged party."

Phoebe nodded, though not in response to what Fiona said. "Why do you suppose he did it? Proposition you, I mean."

"Why did he—" Fiona could not finish, not just then. She took a steadying breath and went on as evenly as she was able. "Why did he want me in his bed? Could you possibly be more insulting? Why wouldn't he want me?"

Phoebe stared at her. "Of course that was a slight against you, Fiona. How could I have meant anything else by it? You are offended if a man doesn't show interest in you." Fiona opened her mouth to speak, but Phoebe cut her off. "Let us say I believe you—because I don't doubt that you believe yourself—can you not imagine another reason besides your devastatingly fine face and figure that a man like Remington might want to compromise you?"

Fiona's eyes widened fractionally. She said nothing.

"Perhaps he hoped the two of you would be found out and Thaddeus would send you packing. Or perhaps it was Remington who wanted to go and couldn't find the courage to say as much. Maybe he hoped his father would send him on his way. Could you consider either of those possibilities? No? Then I'm certain you are right. He must have wanted to fuck you because he is a man and that is what men do because they are helpless when confronted by their baser needs. You told me that, remember?"

Fiona shook her head. She clasped her hands together because they were trembling. Her denial was barely audible. "I never."

"You did, but I have always believed it was in aid of arming me with knowledge meant to protect me. You still don't remember? Think back to Alistair Warren. You beat him bloody with his cane, drove him out of the theater. You explained the facts of what happened to me later. Mr. Warren was acting according to his nature; therefore, it would always fall to me to seize control. That is what I've observed you doing, Fiona, so it is difficult for me to imagine that in any encounter you had with Remington, you were not the one with the upper hand."

"You have a knack for twisting my words, Phoebe. You twist everything to suit your perspective."

"That's interesting," said Phoebe. "Do you know the one about the pot calling the kettle black?"

Fiona curled her upper lip, not amused. "Go back to New York, Phoebe. I cannot abide you remaining here while Remington poisons you against me. We are better friends, you and I, when we are not breathing the same air."

"And there, in a nutshell, is the fundamental difference in our perspectives. It has always been you who insisted that we be friends. I don't think we are. I don't think we can be. I blame myself for that. I know now that I held out too long hoping you would want to be anything else." Phoebe stood and squarely met Fiona's gaze. "But then, you always said I was stubborn. I intend to remain so. I am not leaving, Fiona. I want to stay here even if it means we must breathe the same air."

Phoebe smiled. The effort was faint and forced, and she wished she had not tried. "Excuse me."

Fiona reached out but was too far away to stop her. "Wait, Phoebe. Please."

Phoebe's step faltered. She shook her head and kept going.

It was Remington who ruined her exit, not that she had intended a stagy departure, but she had hoped for a dignified one. He caught her by the upper arms and steadied her before she walked straight into his chest. It was indicative of the state of his mind when he did not apologize. She looked up at him. His dark eyes were not implacable now. She saw very well that he was troubled.

"What is it?" she asked. "What's happened?"

He didn't answer her. Instead, he looked past her to Fiona. "Would you mind leaving us?"

"Leave you? With no explanation?"

Remington did not argue. "Phoebe, will you come with

me?" His hands dropped to his sides so there would be no question that she was forced.

"Of course."

Fiona's cheeks puffed with the strength of her exasperated sigh. "Please. Don't give me a thought. I'm leaving." She brushed past them before they could properly step aside and marched down the hall.

Phoebe was reminded again of Remington's state of mind when he did not comment. She took him by the hand and led him into the parlor. She stopped in front of the sofa but not because she had any wish to sit. "What's happened?" she asked again. "Is it Thaddeus? Is that why you asked Fiona to leave?"

He shook his head quickly. "No. Not Thaddeus. In fact, he's out on the porch speaking to the sheriff. It's Blue Armstrong, Phoebe. He's dead. Murdered."

Phoebe thought he could tell her anything and she would remain standing. She was wrong. Her knees folded and she sank to the sofa. "Murdered? I don't understand."

Remington joined her on the sofa. He spoke carefully, evenly, repeating what Jackson Brewer had come to Twin Star to tell them. "He never left Collier after escorting Miss Carolina home. In fact, he never left her room. Miss Carolina was with him. Also murdered. The madam found them the morning after they returned. Brewer was notified late last night. He went to Collier, spoke to their sheriff, and arranged for Blue to be brought back. He's here now because of what he thinks Blue's murder means."

Phoebe closed her eyes and pressed fingertips against one eyebrow. Her stomach was roiling and she could taste bile at the back of her throat. "Miss Carolina," she whispered. "And Blue. Jumpin' Jesus on a griddle." She tried to choke back the nervous laughter that bubbled inappropriately on her lips. "I'm sorry. Sorry. I don't—" She stopped, opened her eyes, and stared at Remington. "I am so sorry."

He took her hands in his, pressed his thumbs lightly against the backs of them. "I know you are. I am, too."

She nodded, kept her eyes focused on his. "How?" she asked. "Were they shot? Does anyone know who did it?"

"Only because you asked," said Remington. "I hoped you wouldn't. No shots. No sounds. Blue was strangled. Miss Carolina suffocated under her pillow. You don't want to know more."

He was right. She didn't. "This is about the ring, about the robbery. That's what Sheriff Brewer thinks, isn't it?"

"Yes. Blue's been a regular at Sylvia Vance's house for years, and Miss Carolina was his preference, but Sylvia says he never behaved as if he thought she were exclusive to him. In other words, no fighting other patrons for her favors. Everyone who was in the house around the time the murders are suspected to have occurred has been accounted for. All the girls. All the customers. Names all around. Most cooperated. Brewer will follow up their sheriff's interviews. He will not let this rest, but there were more immediate concerns to address."

"Like coming here. To warn us."

"Yes. A precaution. He can't be sure their murders are related to the ring, but it would be foolish to ignore the possibility. Apparently Miss Carolina had shown it off even before she showed it to Blue. Someone wanted it or someone wanted it back."

"What about the man who gave it to her? Couldn't he have done it?"

"I asked Brewer about him. He didn't have the name on his list of men who were there. Remember, Blue hadn't had an opportunity to speak to him about what we learned at the Boxwood. If Blue and Miss Carolina were murdered to get John Manypenny's name, then the whiskey drummer could well be in danger. Perhaps he's already met the same end. He is the first link between the ring and men who took it. If I had committed that robbery, I would surely want to find and dispose of Mr. Manypenny."

"Then Sheriff Brewer must find him first."

"I had the same thought. That's why I am leaving with him. I volunteered, but he swore me in as his deputy anyway."

"Because you know the law."

"Because I can shoot."

"Oh." She worried her bottom lip. "It seems an unlikely coincidence that they were murdered so soon after they returned from Liberty Junction. Why not before? She had the ring then. It doesn't make sense. And wouldn't the men who stole it know who they sold it to?"

"Not necessarily, especially if it traded hands, but they might never have asked in the first place. Now they know they made a mistake and have to backtrack."

"Were they followed? Blue and Miss Carolina. Is that what happened?"

"I don't know."

She spoke as if he had not. "Mrs. Tyler could be in danger. Her son. We all heard the same information. What if the robbers were there in the dining room? All three of them, eating Sunday brunch, and observing everything, just as if they had a right to sit among decent folk."

"We don't know that they were there. There is more we don't know than we do. It's not helpful to get ahead of ourselves."

"I understand." She said nothing more. It was the wrong time to tell him she had been thinking about her wedding dress.

Chapter Thirty-two

"What about Ben?" asked Jackson Brewer. "He want to come along?"

Remington shook his head and turned his horse to come abreast of the sheriff. "I asked him when I was saddling Bullet. He thinks it's better if he stays here with Phoebe. She's more worried about people in Liberty Junction than she is about herself, so I agree with him. It's probably best." Remington had other reasons for thinking so, but he did not share these now. "Thaddeus needs the help around the ranch as well."

"Your father was ready to join us. I had to talk him out of it. I did that while you were speaking to Phoebe. Fiona helped me there. She did not favor the idea of him leaving."

"It's not often that she and I are of a like mind. In fact, I don't know that it's ever happened, but I can stomach it this time."

Brewer knuckled the coarse salt-and-pepper stubble on his jaw. "No love lost there. I see Thad's right about that."

"I don't suppose I've hidden it well. It's mutual."

"He told me that, too. Pains him some."

Remington merely nodded.

Brewer said, "I get the impression that maybe you feel different about her sister."

"Your impression, huh?"

"Thad might've given me reason to think so."

"Phoebe's special." He looked over at the sheriff. "And I like her just fine."

"Subject's closed, then."

"That's right. Subject's closed."

"I got another one. Subject, that is. How do you think Ellie's going to take hearing about Blue's murder?"

"You don't know? You didn't tell her?"

He shook his head, shrugged a little helplessly. "She didn't come out on the porch while I was there. Thought it was odd, her generally being so welcoming and all."

Remington found it odd, too. Ellie greeted all comers, not only because she was friendly, but also because she was curious. She was the person at Twin Star most likely to know something about everything. "Maybe she heard you talking to Thaddeus from inside the house and retreated to her room."

"Could be. Thad said he'd talk to her. Preferred it that way, in fact. I know Blue had feelings for her, but I can't say that I ever thought they were returned in the same way."

"You're right, but she showed him some special attention when he was out here last. I think she enjoyed his company, and God knows, he enjoyed hers." He sighed inaudibly. "The branding. That was not a week ago yet."

"I know. Hard to believe."

They rode ahead in silence, Blue a presence for each of them. Jackson Brewer was grieving. Remington Frost was grim.

Fiona sat at the piano in the front room and ran her fingertips up and down the keys. Occasionally she depressed one enough to make a sound, but that was by accident, not by intent. She did not know how to play. No one at Twin Star did. The piano had been Mary's, and Thaddeus could not bring himself to part with it. She understood his attachment to the instrument, to the memories it invoked. She did not fault him for wanting to keep it, but his refusal to have it tuned bothered her. Jackson Brewer's wife gave lessons, and Fiona had expressed an interest in learning, but Thaddeus showed no inclination to support it. He never said that he could not bear to hear it played again; that was her interpretation.

She moved down the bench and patted the space beside her when Phoebe approached. "It is terribly sad about Deputy Armstrong," she said. "I keep thinking about him at the branding. I believe he ate an entire apple pie." Her smile was pensive. "And talked to Ellie almost exclusively. I don't think she minded. Was that your impression?"

"Yes. Yes, it was. I went to her once, thinking she might need rescuing, but that wasn't the case at all. Where is she? I don't hear her in the kitchen."

"She was in her room for a while. Thaddeus spoke to her, and she retired there, but then he went outside and she went out soon after."

Phoebe's eyes narrowed. There was something more that Fiona was not saying. "She probably went in search of Ben."

"Yes. That's probably what she did. They're close."

Phoebe found Fiona's agreement unconvincing. She laid one hand over Fiona's, stilling the movement of her fingers over the keys. "Since she's out, and very likely grieving, we should make dinner. What do you think about that?"

"Together? The two of us in the kitchen?"

"I know there are knives in there. I've seen them. I shall endeavor to control myself. Can you?"

"Oh, I think I can manage."

Phoebe stood and waited for Fiona to join her. They walked into the kitchen together and looked over what Ellie had begun preparing. Phoebe checked the oven. There were six potatoes inside, none close to being fork ready. The chicken stock on the stove had not yet begun to simmer. She handed Fiona a long wooden spoon and pointed to the pot. "Give it a stir."

Fiona did. "What are we having?"

"I think she had baked potato soup in mind. We can manage that." She checked the bread drawer. "There's plenty here that we can warm."

"The men will want meat."

"You're right. The smokehouse. I'll be right back." She returned minutes later with a three-pound fillet that Les Brownlee cut down for her. She laid it on a dishtowel on the table and wiped it down, then trimmed it and removed the fat. "Les will be bringing in more vegetables from the root cellar."

"Les? Which one is he?" When Phoebe gave her a reproachful look, Fiona removed the spoon from the stock and used it to emphasize her point. "They all look alike. Same hats. Same shirts. Same boots. It's worse in the winter. Same scarves. Same coats."

"Les Brownlee is the one with the narrow face and the weak chin."

"Oh. Well, I know him. The chin is an unfortunate distinguishing feature."

Shaking her head, Phoebe put butter into a skillet and set it on the iron stove. The butter hadn't started to melt when Les appeared at the back door with a sack of vegetables from the cellar. Phoebe relieved him of his bounty and thanked him before he left. "Do you want to clean and cut these?" she asked as she placed carrots and onions on the cutting board.

"I've got my hand full stirring the stock," said Fiona.

Phoebe chose a lethal-looking chef's knife with a six-inch blade and placed the hilt solidly in the hand Fiona wasn't using for stirring. "I'll take the spoon. You should put on an apron. They're hanging in the pantry. Get one for me."

"Have you always been this bossy?" asked Fiona.

"Yes." Phoebe thought Fiona accepted the answer with surprising equanimity. Maybe they could breathe the same air for short periods of time. She hoped so because Fiona was now in possession of the knife. When Fiona returned with the aprons, Phoebe put one on before she placed the meat into the skillet. The butter hissed and spat at her.

Fiona scrubbed the carrots and then sat at the table to peel and cut them. "What if I went back to New York with you?"

Phoebe turned away from the stove and stared at Fiona. For a long time the only sounds in the kitchen were the sizzle from the frying pan and Fiona's rhythmic chopping. When Phoebe finally found her voice, it was a harsh whisper. She pointed to the back door. "Anyone could walk in. Why are you bringing it up again? We settled this."

"Do you think so? The conclusion seemed one-sided to me."

"Only because you didn't get your way."

Fiona gave no indication whether or not she thought this was true. She said quietly, "It occurred to me that you would not want to make the trip by yourself, not after what happened to you on the journey here. And now that we've had this terrible thing happen to Blue, it makes more sense for you to have an escort. Why not me?"

"Why not you?" Phoebe could only shake her head. "I truly do not know where to begin answering that."

Fiona finished chopping a carrot and scraped the medallions to one side of the cutting board. She chose another. "You must see that the men cannot escort you. They have responsibilities here. Remington was the only one who might have been spared because Thaddeus often sends him to auctions or away on some bit of legal business, but we all know how Remington failed to protect you, and given your feelings for him, it would hardly be seemly for him to accompany you."

This was so much for Phoebe to absorb that she lost sight of Fiona's point and fixed her argument on what pricked the most. "You don't know what my feelings are for Remington."

"You think so? It hardly requires a leap of imagination to see that you fancy yourself in love with him. Say what you like, Phoebe, but I will remain firm in my views."

"Then I won't waste my breath denying or confirming. Let us consider practicalities for a moment. How would we arrange going back to New York?" Phoebe held her gaze steady. "I have no money to purchase tickets or to set myself up in New York once I return. I gave up my lodgings. I have no job to go back to and no promise that one would be made for me."

Fiona dismissed that with an airy wave, careless that she was holding the chef's knife in that hand. "None of that should be a consideration. I have money."

"You? You never have money."

Fiona shrugged. "I do now."

"But . . . but how?"

"What do you mean how? I have it. That should be enough for you."

Phoebe jumped away from the stove when sizzling meat and butter spat at her again. She turned back to the skillet, grateful for the distraction, and dealt with browning the fillet. "Did you sell your jewelry?"

"Lord, no. All but a few pieces are paste anyway. I thought you knew."

"How would I know that?"

"You went to that private school, didn't you? How do you think I paid for that? How do you think I paid for any of the privileges we enjoyed? You cannot be so naïve, Phoebe. My wages as a performer would have barely kept us fed and clothed, so I accepted gifts. Why wouldn't I? I had many generous admirers who could well afford to part with tokens of affection. And some of those tokens were worth a great deal. I sold pieces bit by bit as I needed the money. I had paste copies made—Mr. Meir was an excellent artisan and could keep a secret—and I used the excess of funds for incidentals."

"Incidentals," Phoebe repeated. She set down the fork she'd been using to turn the beef and pulled out a chair to sit beside Fiona. "My education was no incidental."

Fiona shrugged again and did not look up from the cutting board. "Well, perhaps there was occasion to use the money for more than trifling things."

"Fiona."

"You are not going to become maudlin, are you? It's done, and you know as well as I do that it was the very least I could do."

"Does it seem to you that I have been ungrateful? I'm not, and I should have expressed it more often. I did. To others. I should have said it to you." She laid a hand over Fiona's to stop the rhythmic chopping. She waited until Fiona set down the knife and looked at her before she spoke. "And you were right that I knew about the jewelry, or at least that I suspected. I shouldn't have lied. You caught me unawares." She lightly squeezed Fiona's hand. "I *am* grateful, Fiona, and I am sorry that I ever gave you reason to doubt it."

Fiona's response was a faint, watery smile. Her amethyst eyes glistened. "Onions," she said in way of explanation for her weepy response, although she had yet to cut into a single one.

"If you like." Phoebe removed her hand. "Tell me about this money you have. If not jewelry, then how?"

"Ellie."

"What?"

"You should not frown so deeply, Phoebe. You will en-grave your brow with creases and age well before your time."

"Yes, because that is what is most important right now." Still, she schooled her features because she knew Fiona would otherwise remain distracted. "Ellie. Tell me about that."

"There is nothing to tell. Not really. She offered me money. I swear to you, I never asked her for it. Even if I suspected she had funds sufficient for my needs—which I absolutely did not—I would not have approached her."

"But you took money from her."

"Not exactly. I don't *have* it. She does, but it is mine if I want it. It will pain me some to tell her that I will accept her offer. I made it clear that if the time came, I would only take it on condition of a loan. I have every intention of repaying her. I will not be beholding to Ellie Madison."

"How much money are we talking about?"

"Very nearly one thousand dollars."

Phoebe found the amount unfathomable. "You must have misunderstood her."

"I assure you, I did not. She showed me her savings book. She has the money in the bank; it is a matter of withdrawing it, which Ben can do without raising the least suspicion because they share the account." She put up a hand to fore-stall Phoebe's next question. "Her husband," she said. "I knew he was a faithless drunk, but even faithless drunks can get lucky. He was a partner in a silver mine. When he died, the partners bought her out. She wanted the bird in hand, so she accepted their offer. She tells me that if she had stayed in, her housekeeper would have a housekeeper. She would be that well situated."

"It seems to me that she was thinking of Ben's future back then. Why would she want to give you any part of that?"

"Isn't it obvious? She wants me gone. She has from the first. I have often wondered why she has not poisoned me already, and I can only imagine that it is because she does not have the stomach for murder. It certainly has crossed my mind to attempt the same with her, but then she doesn't allow me in the kitchen long enough to see it through."

"Fiona!"

"I am not serious, Phoebe. Truly. Besides, I have no idea where she keeps the arsenic."

Phoebe slumped in her chair. "Lord, Fiona, if I age before my time, it will all be on your head."

Chuckling, Fiona got up and took over at the stove. "If you trust yourself with the knife, finish the vegetables."

Phoebe pulled the cutting board toward her and began to work. "I realize that you think I should know the answer to this, but I don't. Why does Ellie want you gone?"

"As a rule, women do not like to share a man. Neither Ellie nor I are exceptions to the rule. She wants Thaddeus back in her bed and I have him in mine. I acquit them of carrying on behind my back, but I do not acquit them of being tempted."

"You're wrong," said Phoebe. "Thaddeus loves you, Fiona. He *adores* you. I am certain I can speak for him on that count. I don't know what Ellie thinks because she keeps her own counsel, but I believe you are wrong there as well. It is your lack of confidence that has made you suspicious of them. I have never observed anything between them that leads me to suppose they are tempted in the manner you are suggesting."

"I have never lacked confidence. You would know that if you stood in my shoes. You would know everything if you stood in my shoes."

"I am trying," Phoebe said. "Except for your own imaginings, which are hardly evidence, what is there to suggest that they ever shared a bed?"

Now it was Fiona who turned away from the stove and stared at Phoebe. "What is there?" she asked. "There's Ben."

"Ben?" But even as Phoebe said it aloud, she knew, and wondered why she hadn't known it before.

"Yes. Ben. Thaddeus's bastard son."

Chapter Thirty-three

Natty Rahway managed not to put his fist squarely in the middle of Doyle Putty's face, or jam it into the underside of his weaker brother's even weaker chin, but it was a narrow thing. What he did was pound his fist against the table hard enough to make it jump and shudder and push the Putty brothers back in their chairs.

The Sweet Clementine Saloon was far less crowded than the last time he'd shared a table with Doyle and Willet, but Natty understood the consequences of drawing even a single customer's attention to them. He regretted his loss of temper before the table stopped juddering. He leaned forward and spoke quietly, harshly. His narrowed eyes darted but when they lingered, they lingered on Doyle.

"We agreed I would follow them," he said. "We sat right here and agreed that I would handle the situation."

"There was no agreement," said Doyle. "There was only you saying what you would do. Willet and I talked about it and decided that wasn't good enough. We brought you along. You joined us, not the other way around." He nudged his brother with his elbow. "Tell him, Willet. Remind him who it was that set this in motion. Remind him how we came to answer the call."

Willet pulled his chair back to the table and picked up his beer. "Doyle's right, Natty. We did invite you to come along. Seemed fair as you'd done right by us in the past. Of course, nothin' we ever done together was like this. More risk. More reward. I know you see that. It's on account of our cousin that we heard tell of this in the first place. There's no gettin' around that."

Doyle nodded. "Les is a good'un. All the Brownlees are. Hard, honest folk, and we Puttys pity 'em for it. All the same, it was Les who put us on to this, even if he doesn't know it, and we aim to see that he never finds out. Let him live in ignorance, I say. Willet agrees."

Willet nodded. "I do. No sense in the families never speakin' to each other because of something like this."

"What *this* are you talking about?" asked Natty. He pushed his beer aside, too angry to drink. "The robbery? The abduction? The goddamn murders?"

Willet shrugged. "All of it, I expect. Les doesn't put his fingers in any of those pies."

"Jesus," Natty said under his breath. "No one was supposed to get hurt. Do either of you recall that?"

"On the train," said Doyle. "And afterward, with the Apple girl. But things have changed since then. That job's done, and we have an obligation to cut ourselves from connections to it."

"Certainly," said Natty. "But murdering a lawman?"

"And a whore," said Willet.

Natty swore softly. He looked around. There was a tall fellow at the bar, pale yellow hair, mustache, looking their way. Natty stared him down and he turned back to the bar and ordered a whiskey. "We should take this up to my room, boys. Better to talk privately."

Doyle almost blew out a mouthful of beer. He choked it down and accepted Willet pounding twice on his back. "Not a chance in hell."

"Not a chance," Willet echoed. "We'll stay here."

Natty kept his fury in check, in large part because he was mostly furious with himself. The Putty brothers had duped him, and he was having difficulty believing they had even tried, let alone succeeded. He was supposed to have been on the train to Liberty Junction when it left Collier, but he got held up by two of Miss Sylvie's girls just as the deputy and Caroline Carolina were leaving the cathouse. He knew now it was no accident that they waylaid him, but it was his fault that he underestimated the time it would take him to reach the station and purchase his ticket. The girls couldn't have known the consequences of keeping him from the train would be the eventual murder of their friend, but he could draw a straight line, and this one led from the Putty brothers to Liberty Junction and right back to the brothel. Even worse, Doyle and Willet wouldn't have known about the whore's intention to go to the Junction if he hadn't told them. He was the one who had overheard her talking about her plans. Maybe he had gotten a little too full of himself thinking that they were a slow pair, always a half step behind.

They often were, but not always. Lesson learned. He would not forget it.

Not raising his voice above a whisper, he asked, "What was the point of killing them?"

"Information," said Willet. He rubbed the underside of his feeble chin with the back of his hand. "You were wrong about it being a seed pearl dog collar that turned up. It was that ring you first mentioned to us. The one Doyle got from that old woman on the train. That's what the whore had."

Doyle tapped his brother's beer glass. "Don't know where you came by that other story. We told you we didn't have a piece that like, but you always have your own ideas about such things. It's no never mind now. It was the ring. We saw it plain as day when this rough little rascal knocked into the table where it was being examined. I was sitting close enough that I could have scooped it up, but that would have been wrong . . . and stupid. The deputy got it and eventually it was returned to the old woman."

Willet nodded. "Doyle and me pondered long and hard trying to come up with the name of the fellow we sold the ring to. Don't know that he ever said, and it wasn't important at the time, but we figure that's information that the deputy heard straight from Miss Carolina. That didn't leave us much choice, did it?"

"And?"

"And we got it. Name's James Cashdollar. Whiskey drummer out of Denver. The deputy wasn't giving him up, but the whore came around when she saw how serious we were. I guess she didn't realize that we'd have to kill her no matter what, seein' how she saw us real good."

Doyle pointed to himself. "I got a face folks trust. I guess she believed me when I said we'd help her get out of town, set her up someplace else."

Natty closed his eyes briefly. "Yes, Doyle, trust is what comes to mind when I look at you. I heard there have been questions being asked. Anyone come to you?"

"We weren't there," said Doyle. "Least not so anybody knows. Lots of ways in and out of a whorehouse where nobody really sees you."

"So it's done."

"More or less. There's Cashdollar. Still need to take care of him."

Willet finished his beer. "And the Apple girl. She was there when the old woman got her ring back. And you recall that fellow that was lying in the aisle on the train? Turns out he's Remington Frost. He was there."

"Are you planning on killing everyone?"

Doyle said, "Not if we get to Cashdollar first. I'm just being practical here. If the law finds him before we do, then we might have another situation on our hands."

"So the two of you could be identified and connected to the robbery, but I'm in the clear."

"That's right," said Willet. "Nothing to connect you to anything."

"Except the two of you." Natty thought Willet and Doyle looked surprised to hear it, just as if they hadn't already considered it and what it could mean to them. Natty slid his beer in front of him again and raised his glass as if he intended to toast the Putty brothers. "Something to think about, isn't it, boys?"

Phoebe did not know why she had expected that Remington would return before nightfall, but she had. Several times after dinner, while Fiona and Thaddeus cleared the table and cleaned up so Ellie could rest, Phoebe found herself drifting to the front porch in anticipation of his arrival. It was there that Thaddeus found her sitting on the swing and gently explained to her how it was going to be.

"Days?" she asked. "Where will he stay?"

"I suppose that depends on where the trail takes them. Could be he'll spend some nights in Collier. Jackson might send him to Denver. He'll be fine."

"Will he?"

"Yes." The swing rocked as he sat beside her. "What about you? Will you be fine?"

"I'm not the one chasing murderers."

"I've found that is rarely significant. You're waiting and you're worried. That takes a toll like nothing else."

Phoebe nodded. She said nothing for a time, working up the courage to talk to him about the other matter on her mind. "You and Fiona were together for a long time in the kitchen."

He chuckled. "There was a lot of food to clear. I think the two of you emptied the larder. No matter. It was delicious. Fiona said that was because of you, so thank you."

"She did her share."

"Of stirring and chopping, she says. Fiona never misled me that she was a cook." When Phoebe fell silent again, Thaddeus gently prompted her. "What is it? I think there's something more you want to say."

"Fiona wants me to leave, Thaddeus. She's pressed me several times. Twice today. While we were preparing dinner, she suggested that she accompany me back to New York. She presented her idea as though returning with me was for my benefit in the event I was afraid to travel alone." Phoebe stole a sideways glance at Thaddeus. He was staring straight ahead, his granite profile without expression. She could not begin to guess what he was thinking. She waited.

"I thought . . ." His voice trailed away as soon as he began. Eventually he cleared his throat and asked, "What did you say?"

"It is disappointing that you feel the need to ask, but I understand. I informed her that under no circumstances was

I going back, which is why we never seem to close the door on the subject. She did not explicitly say that she would not leave New York after escorting me there, but I suspect she plans to stay."

Thaddeus nodded slowly. "I see."

"I don't know if you do, Thaddeus. I don't know if I do, but I take heart when I consider that while she plans to stay, it is not her desire to do so." Phoebe let the words sit there and knew the impact of them when Thaddeus turned his head in her direction and two vertical creases appeared between his eyebrows. "Yes," she said. "You heard me correctly. I truly believe she wants to remain with you. I've never known Fiona not to fight for what she wants, but then she has never had to fight to keep a man. If there was competition, there was always someone waiting for her quite literally in the wings. This is outside her experience. She's afraid and she wants to run."

"Keep a man?" Thaddeus quietly echoed the words, adding the disbelieving inflection that made them a question. "You're talking about me? I'm the man she has to fight to keep?" When Phoebe nodded to all of it, he asked, "Who the hell does she think she has to fight? Who is her competition?" His eyes widened fractionally as he stared at Phoebe. "You! Jumpin' Jesus. Of course it's you. That I should have to be led like a horse to water is humiliating. When I think back on how I enjoyed your company in New York, and then invited you to come here, it's clear that Fiona must have misinterpreted my interest. And you, merely a young woman and one she calls sister, it never occurred to me once that she would embrace such a cock-eyed notion. No wonder she is pressing you to leave. And apparently she's taken it in her head that she has to stay behind to make certain you stay away."

Thaddeus shook his head. "There is no greater mystery than the bent of a woman's mind."

Unsure whether she wanted to laugh or cry, Phoebe bit down on her bottom lip so she could do neither. "It is perhaps premature for you to think you understand the bent of this particular woman's mind."

"What do you mean?"

"Only that I am not the other woman."

"But—"

She put up a hand. "You need to speak to Fiona. Make her tell you. I think if you take her away from here, it will be easier for her to talk. The Butterworth perhaps. Or the very nice hotel in Liberty Junction. You could go there. There is nothing so critical to be done here that you cannot be gone for a day and a night or even two. You were weeks away when you visited New York."

"Remington was here then."

Phoebe watched Thaddeus closely as she said, "And I am certain that set your mind at ease, but shouldn't Ben have an opportunity to take responsibility? He must be ready."

"He is. You're right. And this is important. *Fiona's* important."

"Yes."

"You recommend the Boxwood?"

"I do." She smiled, reached for his hand, and gave it an encouraging shake. "Be sure to make the acquaintance of one Handy McKenzie, although for the life of me, I can't imagine how you could avoid it."

Ellie Madison sat at the kitchen table, her hands wrapped around a mug of black coffee, and allowed herself these few quiet moments to simply breathe in the aroma without thinking once of what she needed to do next. She closed her eyes and raised the mug to her lips. Her slight smile was one of regret, of infinite sadness, but it vanished as though it had never been when the back door opened behind her.

Without turning around, she asked, "What do you need, Ben?"

He did not bother asking her how she knew he was the one at the door. Even when he tried to disguise his footfalls, she was never wrong. Sometimes she confused Thaddeus and Remington, especially when Remington got older, but she never mistook him for anyone but himself. "Don't need a thing," he said. "Came to see how you are doing."

He bent, kissed her cheek, and took a seat in the chair at a right angle to her. Almost immediately he bounced back up to fetch a mug of coffee. "Les burnt the coffee this morning. Scooter and Ralph drank it, but Arnie and I couldn't stomach it. Don't worry, I won't tell them you have good, fresh brew in here." He returned to his seat. "Did you see Thaddeus and Fiona leave?"

Ellie nodded. "I made breakfast for them." She had stood at the window to watch the buggy pass the house and roll on down the road. She did not mention this to Ben. It sounded wretched when she thought of it and too unbearably pathetic to speak aloud. "Do you think you have it all in hand? I heard Thaddeus tell Phoebe he had quite a list of responsibilities for you."

"He went over everything last night. Twice. But that's his way. He still does it with Remington. There is nothing to do that I haven't done before. It's being in charge that's different. He expressed his confidence in me."

"He should. You've earned it."

"Have I?" It was an earnest question. His mouth twisted to one side as he scratched behind his ear. "I wonder."

Ellie firmly set down her mug. "You shouldn't question yourself. Not only have you earned his confidence, you deserve it."

Ben regarded his mother candidly. "I know you think so. You've always thought so . . . but at least one of us has to admit that our situation is different than it was."

"I don't want to hear it. Did you eat breakfast? Or did Les burn that, too?"

"I'm good."

In spite of that not being an answer to her question, Ellie stayed where she was. She said, "Phoebe's still abed. I don't think she slept a wink last night. I heard her get up several times. Once she stepped outside. I think she's worried about him."

"And why shouldn't she be? I am. After what happened to Blue, we should all be worried."

Ellie's fingertips whitened where she pressed them against her mug. She cast her eyes down. "When I think about Blue . . ." Her voice trailed off and she shook her head.

"I know," said Ben.

"I never, *never*, imagined this. His duties . . . perhaps I should have realized . . . but I didn't. I never did, Ben. I wish I had been kinder to him, more attentive. Did you know he liked my apple pie?"

"I think everyone knew that."

She laughed softly, ruefully. "Probably so."

"He understood you did not return his feelings, not in equal measure."

Ellie still did not look at her son. "I suppose I can tell you now that once upon a time he proposed."

Ben's dark red eyebrows climbed his forehead. "He did?"

"You were in your middle years. Eleven or twelve, I think. Blue saw us every Sunday back then because he went to church regularly in those days. Do you recall that he sometimes invited us to dinner at the Butterworth afterward? It's all right if you don't, but it was on one of those occasions that he asked me to marry him."

"Where was I?"

She looked up. "You had wandered off to sit with Thaddeus and Remington. I could see where your affections were attached."

Ben's eyes widened. "Did that influence you to turn Blue down?"

"No . . . well, perhaps a bit . . . but mostly it was because of me. I couldn't marry him. I loved your father. I know you don't understand. I've told you things, and perhaps I should not have. He was not perfect, far from it, but the love I bore that man . . . that was perfect."

Chapter Thirty-four

John Manypenny carefully closed his suitcase so the small bottles of sample liquors inside were not thrown together. He tipped his bowler and thanked the owner of the Angel's Rest Saloon for placing an order for two cases of rye, a case of gin, and three cases of whiskey blends, and then removed his wares from the polished surface of the long mahogany bar. The suitcase was heavy and he was not a large man, but experience had taught him how to shift his shoulders and heft the case so it did feel less of a burden to carry than it was. He was not a drinking man himself, but on occasion he liked to take a chair at a table and sip a sarsaparilla while he observed others enjoy the fruits of his labor, so to speak.

The owner had invited him to sit a spell, and John had declined, but he changed his mind before he got to the swinging doors. Collier was the next stop on his route, and for the first time in recent memory, he was not eager to go there.

The *Rocky Mountain News* had reported on the gruesome murders of Deputy Buford "Blue" Armstrong, late of Frost Falls, and Miss Caroline Carolina, born in Monroe, Louisiana, and now laid to rest in Collier, Colorado. The *Rocky* had treaded carefully around the profession that called Miss Carolina to any man's bed, but John Manypenny believed that was in deference to Deputy Armstrong and not indicative of the newspaper's respect for Miss Carolina. He had been on the train between Denver and Jupiter when he read the account, and he had a clear recollection of neatly folding the paper and placing it on the empty seat beside him. He'd reached for his suitcase, then, and without thinking twice, or thinking at all, he had opened it and quickly downed four sample bottles of his finest Kentucky bourbon and one bottle of gin. The recollections that followed were hazy at best, but he knew he missed the stop in Jupiter and ended up in a hotel in Lansing nursing a sore head the morning after.

With that in mind, John Manypenny carried his case to the nearest table, which happened to be a few feet from the door, and called to the barkeep that he would have his usual.

He was close enough to the window that his view of the street was unimpeded by patrons at neighboring tables. When his drink came, he cupped it in his hands but didn't raise it. Occupied as he was with watching passersby and his own mawkish thoughts, he failed to notice the arrival of the pair of men who walked right past his table and went straight to the bar, and he failed to hear the barkeep call out his name or see the man point in his direction. It was only when they were standing so close to his table that their shadows darkened his vision that they finally had his attention.

"Mind if we join you?"

John Manypenny blinked owlishly behind his gold-rimmed spectacles. The lenses magnified his rheumy blue eyes. He looked from one man to the other, vaguely aware of familiarity with one but not able to place him in a particular situation or in a particular moment in time. He dragged his case from the seat of one of the chairs and set it on the floor. He turned over a hand, inviting them to sit.

"John Manypenny," he said as they each took a chair. He noticed that neither was drinking. Not troubling himself to hide his puzzlement, he addressed the man who had spoken. "Do we know each other?"

"Haven't had the pleasure, Mr. Manypenny. Remington Frost."

John shook the hand Remington Frost extended and then he rose slightly from his chair as he held out his hand to the other man. "Now, you and I, I think we've met. I'm good with faces."

"Jackson Brewer." He released John's hand and opened

his jacket to reveal the tin star on his vest. "Sheriff Brewer. Frost Falls."

John Manypenny's gaze narrowed a fraction. He lifted his spectacles and resettled the stems on his ears and the crosspiece on the hooked bridge of his nose. His face cleared as the occasion of their meeting came to him. "On the sidewalk outside the Songbird Saloon. I believe I caught you in the knee with the corner of my case as I was hurrying out. Had a train to catch. I didn't know you were the sheriff or I expect I would have been more mortified."

Brewer dropped a hand to his knee and rubbed it absently. "I recall it now. You walloped me good with that thing. Wish we had exchanged names. That might have helped some."

"Helped? How?"

Remington said, "We have a matter to discuss with you, Mr. Manypenny."

"John. What sort of matter? Have I done something?"

The sheriff shook his head. "Not at all, or at least not that I'm aware. We've been trying to cross your path the last couple of days. We missed you in Jupiter and again in Collier. I wasn't confident we'd run you to ground here, but I don't mind being wrong. We have a few questions for you. You're under no obligation to tell us anything, but Remington will empty every bottle in that suitcase if you don't. One. By. One."

Manypenny did not react to what the sheriff said. He reacted to the sheriff. "You're Jackson Brewer," he said. Even to his ears, the revelation sounded more like an accusation. "Buford Armstrong was your deputy."

"Blue," said Brewer. "He hated Buford."

Aware that Remington Frost had fixed his dark gaze on him, Manypenny shifted his attention. He resisted the urge to take a handkerchief from his pocket and wipe his brow. His stomach clenched under the deputy's implacable stare. "What is it?"

"I'm thinking you might have some idea," said Remington. "The connection you made between Jackson and Blue is telling."

"I read the *Rocky* same as a lot of folks. It just came to my mind."

"Uh-huh."

Jackson removed his hat and set it on the table. He raked his mostly graying hair with his fingers, slouched casually in his chair, and then folded his arms across his chest. "Seems to me you might be coming around to the notion that we're here because my deputy is not. Miss Carolina, too, is likewise gone. Murdered. You read that."

Manypenny did not deny it.

Remington said, "Tell us about the ring you gave her."

He couldn't help himself. He stuttered. "The r-ring?" He saw Remington's eyes dart to the suitcase at his feet. He tried to push it under the table, but the deputy pushed his foot forward and stopped him. He inhaled and the breath whistled softly through his teeth. "What do you want to know about it?"

"A good place to begin is where you got it."

"Do you know the Sweet Clementine Saloon?"

Remington shook his head, but Jackson nodded and said, "Harmony, right?"

"Yes. Harmony's on my regular route, but usually I'm there early in the day and I move on. It's rare that I spend the night. I took a lot of orders that day and I missed a train in the morning and another in the afternoon. That's how I ended up staying at the Harmony House. Sweet Clementine has nicer rooms, but it was full up, so after I made my sales there, I went over to the Harmony House and settled in." He stopped abruptly, seized his glass, and took a deep swallow of the sarsaparilla.

"And?" asked Remington.

"And I had dinner in the restaurant. I sat alone and ate and observed. I do that frequently. Observe." He pushed his glasses up his nose. "It passes the time."

Jackson said, "Go on. If you tell us what you had to eat, I swear I'll start drinking out of your case myself."

Manypenny decided it was better to ignore the threat. "I observed money and goods exchanging hands and my curiosity got me noticed. I was approached, much as the two of you approached me. Only one question, though. Was I interested in buying a bauble or two? I thought of Caroline so I said I was. I looked over earbobs, hair combs, stickpins, brooches, and rings."

Remington asked, "What did you think you were seeing? Did it occur to you the items might be stolen?"

"Stolen? No. As a matter of fact, that never occurred to me. I figured the gems for paste and the rest for cheap metals. I had no reason to think otherwise, not for the asking price. Are you telling me different?" When neither the sheriff nor his deputy answered, he went on. "I fancied the ring. Pear shape cut. Thought I could see a hint of blue in the facets, like smoke. It was probably a trick of the lamplight and the smoke in the restaurant, but I wasn't really thinking about that. I knew I wanted it. I paid fourteen dollars." His mouth was dry. He took another large swallow of his drink. "That's it."

Remington shook his head. "Not quite. Not even close. Who sold it to you?"

"Oh, I should have supposed you'd want to know that. Afraid I can't help you there. We didn't exchange names."

"You said you're good with faces," said Remington. He removed a small notepad and pencil from his vest pocket. "Prove it."

Phoebe saw him coming when he was still more than a mile away. It was the height advantage at the top of Boxer's Ridge that gave her the splendid view, not only of the verdant expanse of Twin Star Ranch, but also of Remington's rapid approach. It looked as if horse and rider were flying, and she thought it suited them, all speed and power unleashed like great mythic creatures of another time. Perseus, perhaps, and Pegasus coming to the mountaintop.

Boxer's Ridge was not nearly a mountaintop, and Bullet and Remington were hardly mythic creatures, but all the same, Phoebe soared above the ground on a flight of fancy that made her laugh aloud. She hoped her voice carried down the ridge and over the sound of Bullet's pounding hooves. She hoped Remington heard it above the beating of his heart because it was in his heart that she wanted her laughter to live.

Phoebe moved side to side, ducked and weaved, trying not to lose sight of him as he began to climb. It was not possible to follow his route. Fir trees and limber pine, rocky outcroppings and hairpin curves, thwarted her again and again. She grabbed Mrs. McCauley's bridle and urged the mare to a flat patch of grass where she could be tethered to a scrub pine so she wouldn't wander off. "He's coming, girl," she told the mare. "Your friend, too. They're coming back to us."

Remington did not so much dismount as throw himself from the saddle. He let Bullet find his own way to Mrs. McCauley; he wanted Phoebe and made no apologies for it.

He caught her by the waist, pulled her close, and kissed her hard, kissed her breathless, kissed her quiet. What movements she made were those meant to keep him locked in the embrace. At first, surprise kept her arms loose and limp at her sides, but then she raised them, folded her hands behind his neck, and rose against him instead of leaning away. Her breasts flattened against his chest. Her fingers flicked his hair where it lay against his nape. It was when she removed his hat and flung it sideways that she realized he had already done the same to hers. His fist was wrapped around the rope of her braid. He controlled the lift of her head by tugging on it. She controlled the slant of his mouth by cupping his face in her hands.

He opened her vest and his fingers scrabbled to pull the tails of her shirt out of her trousers. She relieved him of his jacket and vest and then went for his fly. His sudden whoop of laughter startled her and she paused, raising her head to look at him. She followed the line of his gaze and saw he was looking at the blanket she had unfolded on the grass.

"Just saw that, did you?" she asked, rising on her toes to kiss him on the mouth.

"Picnic?"

She shook her head. "Not unless you brought food. I ate before I rode out here."

He bent his head, nuzzled her neck, and whispered against her skin. "I am very glad to hear it." He thrust his hips forward and she resumed releasing the buttons on his fly. He attended to the matter of her shirt.

At some point there was mutual, if silent, agreement that they would be better served by managing their own clothes. They shucked articles until they were satisfied with the state of their undress and then Remington scooped Phoebe into his arms and bore her down to the blanket.

Hunger could not quite mask discomfort and there were awkward moments between kisses as Phoebe tried to remove a sharp stone from under her shoulder and Remington jammed his knee into another. They winced, but their urgency also made them laugh, and it was just as Phoebe hoped it would be with the laughter residing in their hearts.

Her body had been preparing for him from the moment she saw him flying toward her. Given the state of his readiness, she believed it had been the same for him. She welcomed him into the cradle of her thighs and wrapped her legs around him. He thrust deep, pushing hard, and it was not a wince that changed her features this time, it was a whimper.

"God, Phoebe." He strained to reach her mouth, nudged her lips open, and used his tongue to match the carnal rhythm of their bodies. She held him close, and there, in that place between her thighs where he fit so snugly, she held him closer still.

Her smile was vaguely wicked and a bit secretive when he raised his head. She did not look away. Her palm ran up his arm, across his shoulder, and rested against the curve of his neck. He rocked her back. She gasped, sucked a deep breath, and then her body was trembling and he felt every one of her intimate contractions. She tripped the single nerve that was holding him taut and together. Remington arched, tensed, and finally embraced release.

Chapter Thirty-five

They lay side by side as their hearts returned to normal rhythms and their breathing eased into silence. Phoebe found his hand and laid hers lightly on top of it. She stroked the backs of his fingers and then threaded hers between them. The sun was behind them and it was possible to stare at the endless blue sky without being blinded. The clouds were high and thin and trailed one another like wisps of smoke until they simply dissolved into the ether.

"It's been very hard for me to say the words," Phoebe said. "I don't exactly know why except that I've had so little cause to use them that I suppose I needed to be sure I wouldn't choke on them." She turned her head sideways and regarded him in profile. It was probably better for what she wanted to say that he was not looking at her, but it had not occurred to her that he might have fallen asleep. His eyes were closed. That was disappointing.

"Remington?"

"Hmm?"

"Oh, you're awake."

"Mm-hmm."

"Then you heard me."

"I heard a lot of words. You didn't choke on any of them."

"That's because . . . well, never mind. I should just say them."

"Probably best to get it done. One of us has to go first."

That made her smile. She spoke quietly, solemnly, giving the moment the importance it deserved. "I do love you, you know."

He opened his eyes and turned his head. "I had a suspicion, but mostly I had hope." His fingers tightened against hers. "I love you, Phoebe Apple. Early on, I fought it some. The idea of it, you understand. Wrestled with it, I'd guess you'd say."

She rolled on her side toward him, lifted her head, and kissed him lightly on the mouth. "I wouldn't say that. No one would say that. You surrendered, same as me, but sometimes you have to wave the white flag to know for sure."

Chuckling, Remington lifted their clasped hands a few inches off the ground and gave them a little shake. "Waving the white flag now," he said. "Now and forever."

Phoebe's smile deepened. "That was nice."

"Mm." He lowered their hands. "I have my moments."

"You do. I like it when I'm in them."

"It's hard for me to think of a time these last few months when you weren't. I mean it, Phoebe. It was hard being away."

She nodded. "For me, too. Before you left, I wanted to tell you that I had been thinking about my wedding dress, but it was not—"

He released her hand, sat up, and leaned over her, trapping her with a stiff arm on either side of her shoulders. "Tell me when you're going to be wearing it and surprise me with the rest. I promise I'll be there."

Phoebe laughed. "I think the *when* is something we need to decide to together. There are considerations, I believe, unless you tell me that Sheriff Brewer no longer needs you. Is that true?"

"No."

"I didn't think so. I'm disappointed, not surprised."

Nodding, Remington sat up and began straightening his clothes. Items that belonged to Phoebe and were in easy reach, he passed along, not because he felt any urgency to see her dressed, but because she distracted him when she wasn't. "We found John Manypenny," he told her, pulling on his shirt. "That took longer than either of us thought it would, but the good news is that no one else found him first.

He'd read about Blue and Miss Carolina in the *Rocky*, but the details and the consequences had to be explained to him. When we left him, he was planning on exchanging his ticket and heading back to Denver to resign from his job with Reynolds Liquors. I believe he intends to visit his sister in Jefferson City. After what he heard, it's likely he is considering permanent residency."

"You must have put the fear of God into him."

"Something like that."

"Was he helpful?"

"He was." Remington rose to his knees to fasten his trousers. "Jackson and I are fairly confident that Manypenny purchased the ring directly from the men who stole it. He told us that he was shown a variety of pieces, and based on when he was shown them, it was early days yet. The thieves were just beginning to get rid of the property. It's unlikely they found anyone so quickly to do it for them."

Remington reached for his vest but didn't put it on. Instead, he patted it down and found the small notepad and pencil in the inside pocket. He showed them to Phoebe. "Thank you for these. They came in handy."

"And you thought you only needed a gun. The pen is mightier . . ." She pointed to the notepad as he opened it. "Don't keep me in suspense. Tell me."

"Manypenny didn't have names for us, but he claimed to be good with faces."

"You made sketches?"

Remington arched an eyebrow. "No. No talent for it. But I did write down what he described. Only two men approached him, Phoebe."

"Not Mr. Shoulders, then."

"What makes you say that?"

She shrugged. "The pair hiding behind the blue bandannas worked together. They collected the jewelry, the guns, the reticules. Mr. Shoulders was a presence, a constant threat, and he directed them while they were on the train, but later, it was less clear to me that he was in charge. They were not afraid to argue with him, and one was comfortable speaking for the other, as if they had a long-standing connection. He was the odd man out."

Remington glanced at his notes then at her. "From what Manypenny said, they could be kin. Brothers, but probably not twins. Cousins at least." He read to her from what he had written. "Brown hair cropped close at the neck. Brown eyes, set wide. Narrow face." He shrugged. "I guess that's why the eyes seemed wide-set." He looked back at his notes. "No obvious missing teeth but all of them on the yellow side. No chin. Fair skinned. No facial hair. Oh, and here's something to distinguish the pair. One of them had a flat bridge. Manypenny guessed a broken nose that was never properly set. They were wearing what you'd expect. I don't see anything different here from what you described them wearing on the train."

Phoebe nodded. "Fiona says the hands at Twin Star look alike to her because they all wear the same thing. She's not far wrong. She didn't know who Les Brownlee was until I told her he was the one with the weak chin. An unfortunate distinguishing feature is what she called it."

Remington closed the notepad. "When she's right, she's—"

"No chin," said Phoebe.

"What?"

"Les Brownlee doesn't have a chin. Well, he does, but it sits so far back in his face that it might as well not be there."

"That's true, but I've known Les for years. If you're thinking that—"

She interrupted him again. "I wasn't. Just picturing him, getting it straight in my mind. If you could draw what you wrote down, you'd have a near perfect image of Les Brownlee. That's odd, don't you think? Brown hair. Brown, wide-set eyes in a narrow face. Ruddy complexion, though, but that's because he spends almost every waking hour out of doors. Clean shaven, at least most of the time, and I'd say he takes better care of his teeth, but there you have it. Oh, and his nose is straight, so I suppose he better resembles the one whose nose was never broken."

Remington put the notepad and pencil away. "It's not much to go on, is it?"

"Not if it means you're going to arrest Les Brownlee or every other man who looks like him."

"That'd mean taking in a lot of the Brownlees and fair number of their kin. It's a big family, and among the ones I know, that no chin feature makes a regular appearance."

"It's like a brand, isn't it?" she said, grinning. "Little wonder they hid behind those bandannas. Maybe you should round them all up. Cut them from the herd the way you do the unweaned calves." She finished yanking on a boot and looked up at him. He was not smiling. On the contrary, his face had no expression. He was a man struck dumb. "What? You know I'm not—"

Remington bent, grabbed her by elbows, and hauled her to her feet. "It doesn't matter what you're not." He kissed her hard on the mouth. "It matters what you *are*, and what you are is exceptionally clever."

"But I—"

He kissed her again.

Phoebe had trouble catching her breath when he finally lifted his head. She could feel the heat of a deep flush in her cheeks. Her eyes felt wide and vaguely unfocused. She pressed fingertips against her lips and spoke from behind them. "Oh, my. Perhaps you are a mythic creature." It wasn't important that he didn't understand so Phoebe did not try to explain. "You have an idea, I take it."

"I have your idea," he said. "And I'm taking it. Brewer is coming out this evening. I told him I wouldn't stay in town if I could be here. He said he'd come to me after he stopped in his office. Charlie Hopewell was left to hold down the fort while we were gone. That's Charlie from the land office. Good with paperwork, not so good with a gun." Remington picked up his gun belt and strapped it on. "You can sit with us if you like."

"I wasn't going to wait for an invitation."

Because he was expecting a response along those lines, he grinned as he looked her over. "Your shirt's buttoned wrong." He brushed her hands aside and did her up correctly, taking more time than was strictly necessary just because she was letting him. "I asked after you first thing when I got back. Funny, but it was Les who told me you were out here. I didn't ask after Thaddeus or Fiona, but I saw the buggy was gone so I figured they were somewhere together."

"They left the morning after you did. You should probably be sitting down, but they went to Liberty Junction. They're staying at the Boxwood. I thought they'd be back by now, but there might be several good reasons why they're not."

"I think I'd like to hear those."

Phoebe picked up her vest and put it on. "It's possible Thaddeus is still trying to wrangle the truth out of Fiona, or that she's told him the truth already and they are either engaged in further argument or taking their time about making up. It's all likely. One can never tell with Fiona."

"And the truth according to Fiona? Do I want to know?" He walked over to where the horses were grazing and untethered Mrs. McCauley. "Well?" he asked when Phoebe didn't say anything.

"I don't know if I want to tell you," Phoebe said. "It seems as if you've already closed your mind. Probably your ears, too."

"I'm listening. Promise." He walked the horses back to where she was standing and gave her the mare's reins. "Leg up?" When she nodded, he gave her a boost and then looked around to see if they had collected everything. All that was left was the blanket. He folded and rolled it and attached it to Mrs. McCauley.

Phoebe said, "Fiona has it in her mind that Thaddeus and Ellie have been lovers for years. She acquits your father of being an adulterer, but not of not being tempted."

Remington mounted. "But not of not being tempted," he said more to himself than to her. "Yes, I think I understand."

"Good." Phoebe urged the mare forward and waited for Remington to come abreast. "I asked her what evidence she had to support her thinking, and she did not hesitate."

"Ben," said Remington. "She told you Ben was Thaddeus's son."

Phoebe almost lost her seat.

"Careful," he said when she wobbled and shifted.

She recovered and stared at him. "How did you know?"

He shrugged. "Fiona's not the first person to think it. People have been saying it as long as Ben's been alive. Maybe before he was born. It's not surprising. I told you Ellie came to work for us when my mother was confined to bed with her last pregnancy. She did not arrive with Ben in arms; he was born later. People will think what they will. There's no changing that."

"What do you think?"

"I don't," he said. "Think about it, I mean. There's only one person who knows, and that's Ellie. If Ben is my father's son, then Ellie never told Thaddeus. I know she didn't because he's never claimed Ben as his own. He would do that. He wouldn't raise him *like* a son. He'd raise him *as* his son. There would be no rumor. There would be fact."

"If Thaddeus never slept with Ellie, then he also knows the truth."

"That's right."

"But you think he may have."

"I think it's possible," he said. "My mother died. He was grieving. He might have sought comfort in Ellie's bed. Once. Twice. I don't know. I was a child. If it happened at all, I don't believe it was an affair of long standing."

Phoebe lowered the brim of her hat as they began to descend the ridge. "I wonder what he'll say to Fiona. She talked to me about leaving; this might be his only chance to convince her to stay."

"She doesn't have the means to purchase a ticket."

"Two tickets," said Phoebe. "She wants me to go with her, or rather she wants me to leave and will go along as my escort. And she does have the means, or so she says. Not in hand, but she's had the offer." She saw that surprised him. "Ellie. Ellie offered her money. Just around a thousand dollars. I know, it seemed strange to me, but Fiona says it's because Ellie wants her gone that badly. Fiona swears she didn't ask for it. The money wouldn't only be for the tickets;

it would pay for an apartment and essentials until Fiona and I could find work. In the event that there is any doubt in your mind, I told her no."

"No doubt," he said. "But still good to know. It's not impossible to believe that Ellie wants Fiona gone. She's been a burr under Ellie's saddle since she arrived, and only part of that can be explained by Ellie being in love with my father."

"So you think Fiona's right about that?"

"I think Fiona is likely to be more aware of it than any of the rest of us."

"She said something like that to me. Told me to stand in her shoes and I would know. When she said Ben was Thaddeus's son, I believed it and wondered how I hadn't seen it for myself." Out of the corner of her eye, Phoebe saw him nod and realized he was not at all disturbed by her confession. "What are you thinking?" she asked.

"Mm. Thinking about the money. Wondering how Ellie came by it."

"I thought you'd know, but I can explain. It's from the mine. Her husband's partners bought her out after he died. She's saved it for Ben, but apparently she's willing to part with it to see the last of Fiona."

"What mine? What partners?"

"Um, I don't know. Don't you?"

"This is the first I'm hearing of it."

"Thaddeus must know. It was so long ago, and as you said, you were a child. No reason that anyone would have talked to you about it. She showed Fiona a savings book from the bank. The money is there."

"Huh. I'm a little surprised Ben never said a word. You'd think it would be something he'd know."

"That seems likely. According to Fiona, his name's on the savings book."

Remington said nothing, but his expression was thoughtful.

Phoebe said, "I'm hoping Fiona will tell it all to your father. He can sort it out."

"He probably can." He started to reach over to take Phoebe's reins when the descent steepened, but he stopped

and withdrew his arm when he saw how well she was han-
dling the mare. She was good on her own. "When you say
you hope she'll tell it *all*, is there something more than we've
discussed that she should be saying?"

"You know there is."

"So this secret that isn't yours to reveal and isn't mine to
say actually belongs to Fiona. Is that right?"

Phoebe nodded. "Yes. It's hers."

"Can we assume that she's already told Thaddeus and
that you're free to tell me?"

"I suppose we can assume anything, but that doesn't
make it true."

"Let's call it a premise."

"Dress it up, you mean."

"Sure. Let's dress it up, take it out, and see how it does
at a social." He pointed to her and then to himself. "You and
me. We are the social."

Phoebe did not answer immediately and Remington did
not press, which in the end was what tipped the scales in
favor of speaking. "I won't be shocked if you've known all
along, or at least suspected for some time, but it really hasn't
been for me to say. You asked not long after I met you about
the difference in our ages, mine and Fiona's. I never say
exactly. Fiona's sensitive, you understand. It's because of
her work, and she thinks it is more important to be young
than old. The truth is that she is young, and I make her feel
old. There were fourteen years between us when I was born,
which means she was thirteen when she conceived me. Do
you understand?" Phoebe did not wait for him to answer.
"Fiona is my mother I've never had."

Chapter Thirty-six

Remington turned Phoebe's words over in his mind. She had said them with precision and she meant for them to be taken precisely. *Fiona is my mother I've never had.* Not *the* mother, but *my* mother.

"I don't know what to say, Phoebe."

"It's all right." Her smile was rueful. "I don't know myself. She doesn't forbid me to say so. At least she's never made me take a blood oath."

"Phoebe." He said her name as a gentle admonishment, but then he imagined that flippancy guarded her heart. "Never mind. Say whatever you like."

"No, you're right to reproach me. I'm too hard on her; I think I always have been."

"I did *not* say that."

Phoebe went on as if she hadn't heard. "I follow her lead. That's more or less what she expects. When the mood suits her, I am her daughter. And when there are other considerations, such as a new suitor, especially one with deep pockets, then I am her sister. My task is to keep it straight in my mind."

"What about the people around you? Members of your company? They must know the truth."

"They do. Many of them helped raise me, especially after my grandmother died. I was still an infant when she passed, and by everyone's account, she had as little interest in raising me as Fiona. To her I was an inconvenience. To Fiona I was a doll."

"People told you that?"

"No, not to my face. No one was that heartless. I learned it just the same. A conversation overheard here and there, and as I got older, I saw things that confirmed it." She shrugged carelessly. "But to your question . . . yes, they knew, and they went along. It was practical. Fiona was younger than I am now the first time she told someone I was her sister, and she was already a lead performer, much admired and sought after. The troupe supported her story by remaining quiet, and in return, she showed her generous appreciation."

"But you always knew you were her daughter?"

"Yes. It was more difficult to understand what that meant. When I look back on the years before she began introducing me as her sister, I think I was not as much a daughter to her as an afterthought."

"What about your grandfather? Was he still alive when you were born?"

"Yes, but I never met him, at least not that I remember. Fiona says he was there when she buried her mother, but he had moved on, found work elsewhere. He left when he learned Fiona was pregnant. She says he was deeply ashamed." Phoebe's slim smile was both ironic and rueful. "I know, given that he was hardly a father to her, it seems hypocritical, but I suppose everyone draws a line for themselves somewhere. That was my grandfather's."

Remington glanced Phoebe's way again. She was gripping the reins too tightly. Her knuckles were white. He did not comment or correct her. Mrs. McCauley would eventually do that. "There's no way to ask this, Phoebe, except straight out. May I do that?"

"He's not my father, Remington."

He was caught off guard when she answered the question he hadn't asked. "What?"

"That was what you wanted to know, wasn't it? Is my grandfather my father? He's not. I asked Fiona once." She touched the left side of her face. "She slapped me. Right here. I swear to you I can still feel the imprint of her palm on my cheek." She lowered her hand and took up the reins, holding them more loosely this time. "Fiona won't tell me my father's name. I think that's because he still works in the theater district. A director perhaps. Possibly a producer."

"It was rape?"

"I think so, but she's never said. You might expect that when it happened to me, she would have confided, but she never did. She was only thirteen, so even if she was an outrageous flirt, or an ingénue with her eye out for a better chance, someone took advantage. A *man* took advantage."

"Jesus," he said under his breath. "Fiona."

"Don't pity her, Remington. She'll sniff it out and dislike you the more for it."

"Compassion. Not pity."

"I know. It's hard to spend time in the shoes she lives in. She was tired, Remington. I know that now. Fiona wanted out. She wanted away. She may not have realized it until she met Thaddeus, but once met, he became her whole world. I'm sure of it. I was there. I watched it happen. She loves him, Remington, but she's lost here, and if a few days and nights in Liberty Junction aren't enough to help her find her place, she'll go back to what is familiar. It will be without me. She doesn't need me to do what's best for her. She never has."

"Pity, Phoebe?"

She laughed a little unevenly. "Self-pity."

"Good to know you're not above it."

This time when she laughed, it was with genuine amusement. "This is why you're good for me, Remington Frost. You have a gift for not allowing me to take myself too seriously."

"Maybe," he said. "But it doesn't mean that I don't take you seriously. You have a way of getting me to see things differently, and I appreciate the view even if I don't always agree with it. I'd say we're good for each other, but to be honest, I'd feel a mite better if you'd seriously nail down that wedding date."

* * *

Jackson Brewer carried his coffee to the parlor's wide armchair and made himself comfortable. Remington closed the pocket doors and then sat beside Phoebe on the sofa and took the cup she offered him.

"It's disappointing that Thaddeus and Fiona aren't here, not for them, I'm sure, but for me. And they missed an excellent meal. Ellie sets as fine a table as my wife, and that's saying something." He waved away the comment he saw Remington was about to make. "Enough of that. We're here for business. Miss Apple? Are you certain you want to be here?"

"Phoebe, please. And yes, I am. Remington asked me, but I would be here without an invitation."

The edges of Brewer's mouth turned up. "Very well. Remington's told you everything?"

"I believe he has."

"I have," said Remington. "And Phoebe's given me something to think about." He related the conversation and Phoebe's glib, but insightful, remark that the no chin feature was like a brand. "She's right, you know. So I was considering her idea of rounding up the clan and cutting out the no chins from the rest of them, and it occurred to me that some kind of family reunion might give us an opportunity to muster the herd."

Brewer listened, thoughtful, and when Remington was done, his gaze moved to Phoebe. "Mustering the herd? That's all you?"

"I said it, but Remington's the one who realized it could be important."

Remington objected. "She's being modest. So what do you think?"

"I think there's more merit in it than any of the things I was considering on my way out. Frankly, I wasn't sure where to begin. Have you spoken to Les?"

"No. Wasn't sure if I should. I trust him, but family's family, and the Brownlee clan has considerable sprawl."

Phoebe said, "I'll talk to him."

"You?" asked Brewer. "Why?"

"Because nothing about the conversation I'll have with him will make him suspicious. I regularly make a nuisance of myself asking questions. Mostly it's about what the men are doing, how it's done, why it's done, what happens if it's not done. But I'm interested in other things, too. Where they've lived. If they have a sweetheart. I've asked about family. Les Brownlee is shyer than the rest of them. Most of the time he ducks out of the way if he sees me coming, but I've talked to him on occasion. Never about family, though. It'd be a new conversation. I can do that."

"And what about this reunion idea? Do you think you can get him interested in that?"

"I don't know. I'll have to think on whether that's the best approach. Don't worry. Something will occur to me.

Brewer and Remington exchanged significant looks and then nodded in unison.

"All right," said Remington. "You talk to Les and we'll see what happens."

Brewer said, "I reckon you're clever enough to talk a bear out of his honeycomb. Les Brownlee should be no kind of problem for you." He appreciated that Phoebe beamed at the compliment, but he couldn't help noticing that Remington beamed a little brighter.

The door to Phoebe's bedroom opened with a theatrical flourish. Phoebe wished the covers were still over her head, but her very fine dream had come to an abrupt end when she heard the light footfalls hurrying down the hallway toward her.

She pushed herself up on her elbows in time to see Fiona all but burst into the room. Oddly enough, the first thing she noticed was the change in Fiona's shape. Gone were the fashionable and torturous curves that Fiona affected compliments of an S-shaped corset that emphasized breasts and bottom and a fourteen-inch waist. Fiona's rush to greet her had left her slightly breathless, but at least she looked as if she could breathe.

Phoebe had never done it before, and she could not say why she did it now, except that it seemed that she should, and that it seemed that she always should. She pushed herself up the rest of the way and opened her arms. It was gratifying to see that Fiona didn't hesitate to rush forward and fill them.

Phoebe's head banged the headboard when Fiona bowled her over. She expelled a lungful of air, part groan, part laughter. "Wait. Fiona. Let me sit up."

"Oh, yes. Do. Do sit up." Fiona grasped her by the shoulders and pulled her up as she straightened. "Are you all right?" She searched Phoebe's face. "You are. Of course you are. And do you know what? So am I. I told him, Phoebe. I told him everything." She gave Phoebe's shoulders a small shake. "That's what he did to me. Shook me. A lot harder than I'm shaking you. Shook me loose of all of it." She dropped her hands and put one in each of Phoebe's. "He was so angry at first. So angry but so full of love that it hurt my heart to look at him. And my tongue cleaved to the roof of my mouth. It's hard to talk to a man when he's like that, like he wants to throttle you and kiss you senseless at the same time. So he shook me and it all tumbled out like dice on a craps table, and it wasn't any prettier than that sounds, but it needed to be said."

Tears spilled past Fiona's lashes in spite of her effort to blink them back. She did not try to brush them away. Instead, she squeezed Phoebe's hands even tighter. "Thaddeus told me you knew that, and that it was your idea for him to take me away from here. We had a suite at the Boxwood. Plenty of room for pacing and carrying on and making up and carrying on some more. Did you suggest that, too?"

Phoebe opened her mouth to say she had not suggested an actual room, but Fiona was going on again. "And there was a young scoundrel there who had the temerity to lock us in our suite until, he said, we could conduct a conversation that could not be overheard in the dining room. Naturally I explained to him that I had experience on the stage and knew how to project my voice, and that Thaddeus had a holler that could give rise to a stampede, but he was unmoved."

"You didn't say that."

Fiona shrugged. "Very nearly did, but we were locked in by the time I thought of it and he was already walking away. And wasn't he just whistling to himself?" She added in confidential tones, "I think Thaddeus might have paid him to do what he did, and something about it struck me as romantic."

"I'm imagining it." Phoebe slipped one hand out of Fiona's clutch and used a corner of a sheet to erase her tears. "Your nose is red."

"Is it?"

Phoebe thought she seemed unconcerned. "And your complexion is a tad blotchy."

Fiona sniffed. There was nothing elegant or haughty about it. "It can't be helped, I suppose."

"I used to think differently." Phoebe finished dabbing at Fiona's face and dropped the sheet. "So Thaddeus didn't leave you in Liberty Junction. He brought you back. Imagine that."

Fiona nodded and sighed happily. "He did. Nothing's changed and everything's changed. He loves me. Best of all, he knows how to love me."

Phoebe pointed to herself. "You told him about me?"

"Yes. He didn't flinch. He suspected. He presented me with opportunities before to tell him the truth—the last time was the night you and Remington rode out to Thunder Point—but I threw them all back at him. I didn't trust him. Not enough. You know why."

"Ellie."

"Yes." Her voice dropped to a whisper and she glanced over her shoulder before she went on. "He says I'm wrong about Ben, but it's not because he never slept with Ellie. He believes she would have told him if it were true, which I think is naïve of him, but I have made peace with it. He also said that she might not know the truth. Her husband reappeared around that time. Thaddeus thought she might leave with him, but it never happened. Then Mr. Madison died and there was no question but that she would stay. There has been nothing between them all these years."

"And you are satisfied with that?"

"I am, mostly because of what else he said."

"What's that?"

"He is giving her notice, Phoebe. It's because of the money. I told him about that, explained that I wanted to leave, and how she understood that without me ever telling her and offered me the means to go. Thaddeus was surprised, more than that, actually. I think he considered it a betrayal, so he is going to tell her to go. She will be well compensated, but he is firm that she will be leaving, and for everyone's sake, it will be done quickly. I expect she will be gone tomorrow. You will help me manage, won't you? It will only be for a few days until I can interview and hire a new housekeeper. I want someone who will help me, and help me learn, not shut me out."

Phoebe was too stunned to do anything but nod.

"Good. I felt certain I could depend on you."

Phoebe found her voice. "What about Ben?"

"Yes. Ben. Thaddeus does not want him to leave and I certainly would not ask Thad to force it. I like Ben. What he does will be his decision. That's only right." Fiona tilted her head as she studied Phoebe's face. "What? What is it? You look worried."

"I am, but perhaps not as worried as you should be. I would think twice about eating anything Ellie prepares for you before she's gone." She patted the back of Fiona's hand. "And no, Fiona, I won't be your taster."

Chapter Thirty-seven

Ellie Madison sipped tea from a pansy-patterned china cup, but she returned the cup to its saucer when Natty Rahway joined her at the table. The restaurant in the Butterworth Hotel was largely empty in the middle of the day. She thought that perhaps she should have suggested a different time, but the truth was that no matter the time of day, someone would notice her speaking to this man, a stranger to everyone, because it was so far outside the normal course of things.

"Thank you for coming," she said. "I didn't know if you would."

"I shouldn't be here." He removed his hat and laid it on the seat of the chair beside him. "But I was curious."

"I told Mr. Butterworth—he's the owner—that I was being interviewed for a new position. Was that all right?"

It was better than he hoped for when he decided to answer her summons. "It's fine. You talk first." He raised his hand, gestured to the girl hovering at another table as she talked up a cowboy, and asked for a beer when she came by. "What's happened?" he asked when she was gone.

"I was let go. After more than twenty years, Mr. Frost showed me the door. You're the first person I've told the truth. It's only been a few days, but people around here think Mrs. Frost and I couldn't get along, which is more or less the way it was. I'm satisfied with folks assuming I left on my own terms, and Mr. Frost is never going to say any different. What I don't like is anyone thinking his wife got the better of me."

"Ben?"

"He'll likely go on working at Twin Star. I have no plans to tell him what happened. He thinks the house got too crowded for me what with Mrs. Frost hovering and her sister always trying to be helpful. I took a room here for the time being. Mr. Frost was financially generous in his desire to see the last of me, so I can sort through what I want to do, where I want to go. I don't see myself straying far, and I already have offers. One of them is here at the Butterworth." She shrugged her narrow shoulders. "Managing a hotel could not be much different than managing Twin Star."

Natty's beer appeared and he took it from the waitress's hand before she placed it on the table. He shooed her away without ordering any food. "So why did Frost show you the door?"

"His wife told him I offered to give her the money she needed to go back to New York."

He whistled softly. "I see. Is it true?"

"Doesn't matter. He thinks it is."

Natty chuckled softly as he raised his glass to his lips. "Always wondered what the money was for. I figure now I know." He put out a hand to stop her from saying anything. "I'm not sure why you asked to see me. Seems strange meeting face to face after all this time. Good thing you didn't change your mind about that fussy flower hat you're wearing or I wouldn't have been able to sort you out from . . ." He briefly cast his gaze around the dining room. "From, say, that sour-faced pickle of a woman over there picking at her hash. All things being equal, I'm glad it's you."

Ellie's thin smile was cool. It did not touch her eyes. "I don't want any of what happened coming back on me, and I especially don't want my son involved. I think we can agree you were compensated handsomely to perform a service, and part of that service involved a guarantee that you would not be caught."

"Perform a service." His rough, deep voice was a soft echo of hers. He locked eyes with her and raised one dark eyebrow. "I'm not sure that's how the Putty brothers described it to me, but all right, let's call it a service for now. What's this about getting caught? What have you heard all the way out there at Twin Star? Or maybe it's been since you came to town."

Ellie did not answer the question directly. She leaned forward as though earnestly engaged in their conversation and spoke so she could not possibly be overheard. "Blue Armstrong. Let's talk about Blue. Why did any one of you think that was necessary? And don't deny involvement. I won't believe it. I heard—overheard—enough to know his murder is connected in some fashion to the robbery."

Natty stopped short of jabbing himself in the chest with a forefinger. "I don't know what you think you know, but I had nothing to do with that."

"You didn't stop it."

"I didn't know it was going to happen."

"Then you can't control them." Ellie could see that rankled. "From what Phoebe said about the robbery, it seemed you were in charge. Was she wrong?"

"No. She wasn't. But things change and Doyle and Willet are out of their minds. As they recently reminded me, they invited me to join them, not the other way around. They're not wrong. Your arrangement was with them, so what I'm wondering, since I'm the one here, is if it's still with them. What do you have in mind, Mrs. Madison?"

"I'm taking a risk here, Mr. Rahway, trusting you, but the Putty brothers are known to me and they have never inspired confidence. I realize it begs the question of why I ever came to terms with them, and the answer is time and the fact that there was so little of it. I did not sanction the robbery. Whose idea was that?"

"Doyle's, but I won't mislead you. I agreed to it. It wasn't a bad idea, merely a poorly executed one, mostly in the aftermath."

"That's probably an understatement."

"Yes, ma'am."

"You think you can fix it?"

"I can."

She studied his face, measured the confidence of the man. He didn't fidget with his beer or his mustache. He didn't look away or study some point over her shoulder. "I'm going to tell you something, Mr. Rahway, and you should take it as fact because it is. Thaddeus Frost had no interest in pursuing Phoebe's abductors. He had no interest in getting his money back. Do you know why?"

It was a rhetorical question, but Natty shook his head anyway.

Ellie narrowed her gaze and held up a single finger. "One reason," she said. "He's believed from the very first that his wife was behind what happened. He still might. He only has her word for saying that I offered her money. I never said I did. Nothing would have come of that night if the passengers hadn't been robbed. Everything that went wrong began there."

Ellie turned her finger down and tapped it against the table as she finished. "This is what I want you to do, Mr. Rahway: Make it right."

Phoebe found Thaddeus and Remington in the barn examining a hoof on one of the newer thoroughbreds. She stood back, listening to them discuss furrows and frogs and walls and whether or not the mare required a new shoe. The mare was at her ease, Phoebe noticed, but then she had the attention of two handsome admirers who wanted nothing but the best for her.

After several minutes, Phoebe interrupted. "A new shoe," she said. "A lady always wants a new shoe. There truly is no point in further debate."

Remington clapped his father on the back and they both straightened. "She's right. A new shoe it is. All the way around." He waved her in. "We saw you were talking to Les and decided to make ourselves scarce." When he saw Phoebe look around, he added, "We're alone. Johnny took off when I threatened to give him indoor work."

"I thought that might be the case," she said, smiling. "He's weeding in the garden. Fiona keeps wandering onto the back porch to check on him."

Thaddeus cocked his head toward the barn's open doorway. "What did Les have to say? Are you satisfied with what you heard?"

"I am. I wish I had been able to ask him about his family earlier, but perhaps it would have seemed suspicious so soon after the sheriff was here. It's hard to say what everyone's thinking." Phoebe held up a hand and began ticking off names on her fingers. "There are the Brownlees, but then we knew that. On his father's side going back a generation or two, you have the Petersons, the Corbells, the Driscolls, and the Finks. His mother's side is more complicated because there are a number of marriages involving cousins. The family multiplied and spread out, but there are fewer surnames. Mostly they're all Washingtons or Puttys. You'd need a chart or the family Bible to keep it straight."

She folded her fingers into a loose fist and dropped her hand to her side. "Once Les got to talking, he warmed to the subject. It seems his mother was a Putty, but he told me she did not have much in the way of good to say about her family. His mother generally described her kin as the black sheep. The larger family tends to stay clear of them. I don't know if it means anything, but I thought it was worth mentioning because he thought it was worth mentioning."

"Hard to imagine a family that size not having a few black sheep in its midst, but it could be anything that sets them apart. Did he tell you something specific? The Putty name is not familiar to me."

"Les had some colorful stories about a few of them. If I had pressed, there are probably more. He was quick to point out that none of them ever warranted a wanted notice, at least that he knew, but they're acknowledged to be a rough lot by the rest of their kin. There is a history of cattle rustling, cheating at cards, drunkenness, fighting, and ducking the law. It's this last piece that gives rise to rumors in the family of what the Puttys *might* have done."

"Hard to say if there's something there or not," said Remington. He slanted Phoebe one of his secretly amused smiles. "Did you ask about the chins and the no chins?"

"No!"

He laughed. "All right. I suppose there was no subtle way to advance the subject."

"No polite way either," she said. "Really, Remington."

Thaddeus caught Remington's eye. "You've been chastised, son. Better sober up."

Remington did, though his grin was slow to fade. "There's still the problem of rounding them up. We'll never get them all, but we have to find some means of attracting a large number of them."

Thaddeus set his arms across his chest as he nodded. "What about that reunion you mentioned?"

"It was just a passing thought," said Remington. "I can't see my way clear to making it work. It's hard to imagine how we'd get one of them to initiate something like that, and if the reason for it were understood, it would be even less likely. We need to find another way."

Phoebe said, "I've been applying myself to that very problem. I might have an idea that will work."

Remington and Thaddeus gave her their full attention right down to the identical curious arch of their left eyebrows.

Phoebe asked, "What do you think about a wedding?"

Ben finished counting head in the bottom pasture and looked over at Les Brownlee, who was close to completing his. "I have three hundred and twenty-one, give or take, for the valley. You?"

"Just under. I think we're good. Plenty of grazing room. No sign that the water supply's going to be a problem. Thaddeus will like that. Hell, I like it. Wasn't sure that we wouldn't have to cut out a spring."

"Same here. Let's head back and tell him."

Their exchanges were brief for much of the ride, most concerned Les's tuneless whistling and Ben's demand that he stop. Sometimes Les just hummed, which was almost as bad as far as Ben was concerned.

"Don't you know any melodies?" Ben finally asked. "Sing something, for God's sake."

"That'd surely put your hackles up. I'll try to mind. You ain't exactly been yourself since Ellie left, but I guess it's natural for you to miss her. I do. A few of us were talking, and there's agreement that we'll all be relieved when Mrs. Frost hires help at the house." He looked sideways at Ben. "Did you see your ma when you were in town yesterday?"

"I did. She's good. Mr. Butterworth's offered her a job at the hotel. I'll find out tomorrow if she's going to take it. I'm headed back to pick up a mail order. I have a feeling her leaving Twin Star is probably going to work out for the best."

Les nodded and knuckled his mostly clean-shaven chin. "Probably so. You think it was something about Blue's murder that made her want to move on? Couldn't help but notice that she was sad."

"Maybe it had something to do with it. Hard to know a woman's mind, especially when she's your mother." Ben eyed Les thoughtfully, and when the ranch hand glanced his way, he said, "I noticed you spent a fair amount of time in Miss Apple's company this morning. You sweet on her?"

Les's dark brown eyebrows shot up high enough to lift his hat a fraction. He blushed red to the tips of his ears. "Now why would you go and say a thing like that? Not called for. Not called for at all just because we had a chat like we were old friends."

"All right." Ben put up a gloved hand to call it quits. "So what do old friends like you chat about?"

Les shrugged. "Family mostly. Hers. Mine. Did you know she had family in the theater goin' way back? I'm talking Revolutionary War days. That's somethin', I thought. Nothing like that in my family."

"Huh. I had no idea. So you talked about your kin?"

"Sure. Why not? We've got some stories that make for interesting telling. You know the ones I mean."

Ben frowned. "Do I?"

"Sure. Mostly I was telling you about the Puttys. Remember? Oh, it's been a while back. We all were playin' cards.

Remington was off somewhere—Chicago, I think—but the rest of us were there. Can't recall how it started, but we got to jawin' about this vagrant we heard that Brewer threw in jail for showin' off his tallywacker to Mrs. Washburn in the bank."

"I have a vague recollection of that."

"Well, we started trading stories, and someone—I think it was you—asked if any of us actually knew anyone who made it a habit to run left of the law."

Ben's frown deepened. "Me? I asked that?"

"Pretty sure. Guess it's not important, but I know I talked about the Puttys. They don't know there's a *right* side to the law. Never did much jail time, though, so you gotta figure them for a little bit clever."

"Huh," said Ben. "I'll be darned. You amuse Miss Apple with those stories?"

"Sure." After a moment, Les regarded Ben doubtfully. "At least it seemed she was amused. Now that I'm hearin' you don't remember the stories, maybe she was humorin' *me*."

Ben reassured Les that was unlikely. "Entertain me," he said. "We have time, and even if I come to recollect the Putty tales, they'll be a damn sight better than your whistling."

Chapter Thirty-eight

Phoebe sat huddled in one corner of the porch swing, her skirt smoothed over her drawn-up knees. "What was I thinking?" she asked Remington. "*Was* I thinking? You were there. Did it seem as if I was conscious?"

"You were conscious."

"Maybe I was concussed."

"You were not concussed."

Phoebe snorted.

"Doubts?" he asked. A smile played around his mouth but he was careful to restrain it.

"Of course. Don't you have any?"

"No."

She blinked. "Truly?"

He shook his head and toed the floor to put the swing in motion. "None."

"Not about the marriage," she said. "The *wedding*."

"Ah, the madness." He pretended to think about it. "It will be fine. You'll see."

"Of course I'll see. I have to be there. But whether it will be fine is something else entirely. Did you know Thaddeus was going to invite everyone? *Everyone?* He advertised in the *Frost Falls Register*, the *Liberty Junction Gazette*, and the *Collier Sentinel*. People from all over the county will arrive."

"Not an advertisement. More like an announcement. I'm his only son—we think—and you're his only daughter, I'd guess you'd say, so it's natural that he'd want—" He stopped because the pointed toe of her kid boot found its target in his thigh. "Ow. What was that for?"

"You know. You said it on purpose to get a rise out of me, and you did, so I will not apologize for it, and you should stop grinning. It is not amusing. I am most definitely not your father's daughter."

He removed her foot from where it was pressing against his leg and pushed it back toward her. "All right. We are not brother and sister in any fashion and I pity the person who wonders about it aloud."

Phoebe rested her face in her hands a moment. "Oh, Lord. I shall have to shoot someone."

"Yes, well, we have that to look forward to. With any luck it will be a no-chin Putty."

That made her giggle a little wildly from behind her hands.

Remington patted her knee. "It's going to be all right, Phoebe. I swear it is. Fiona says you have bridal nerves. I didn't know what she meant, but I think I'm seeing them now."

Phoebe lowered her hands. "When did you start paying attention to anything Fiona said?"

He shrugged. "Since I realized she is going to be my mother-in-law. I am trying to make peace or at least keep it. She apologized to me, you know."

"No. I didn't."

"I don't suppose she could tell you because that would mean admitting to what she did in the first place. It was hard enough for her to speak to me about what happened. She rambled a bit, circled the thing for a while, but then she got it out. All of it. It was uncomfortable for both of us, and I am confident we will never speak of it again."

"Did she say why she tried to seduce you?"

He shivered a little, remembering. "No, and I didn't ask. I'm leaning toward her wanting to make my father jealous, but I don't need to know her reasons. And please don't say 'seduce' again. I'm done with it."

Phoebe laid a hand over the one he had on her knee. "I'm glad." She smiled a tad unevenly as her thoughts moved to what lay ahead. "How many people do you imagine will show up?"

"You don't want to know."

"I don't, do I?" She sighed. "My dress arrived. Ben was dispatched to town to pick it up. Your father again. It's incredible to me that he could choose something that I would have chosen for myself."

"He might have had some help."

"Fiona? I don't think so. She and I have very different tastes."

"Not Fiona."

Phoebe stared at him. "You? You helped him?"

"Maybe."

"You are certainly full of surprises." She laughed when he affected a modest shrug. "I don't know how the two of you did it, or when you did it, and I suppose your motives had something to do with me not changing my mind, but I don't even care about that. Mrs. Fish is coming here tomorrow morning to manage the alterations. That was Fiona's idea. She needed to fuss and would not accept that I could make the nips and tucks myself." She pointed a finger at Remington. "And you will be discharged to some far corner of Twin Star so there is no possibility of you seeing me in the dress until Saturday. Thaddeus, too. Fiona does not trust him not to peek and tell you how enchanting I look in it."

"It's disappointing, but not unexpected, and just so you know, enchanting is exactly what we had in mind."

She regarded him dubiously. "If you say so." They fell into an easy conversation, then, reviewing the plans for the reception. There were the details that needed to be discussed for any after-wedding repast, but there were additional things to consider in regard to the roundup. Fiona, who felt more strongly about observing certain refinements about the wedding than Phoebe did, insisted that Thaddeus hire a photographer to make a record of the event. Thus, there would be a wedding album and photographic evidence of the guests, particularly the no-chin Puttys. Remington and Jackson Brewer judged it was too dangerous for John Manypenny to appear at the wedding, even if he agreed to make the journey from his sister's, but having him look over

photographs seemed like something they could insist that
he do.

Nothing was sure. No one could know for certain that
the men they were seeking would be among the guests, or
if they were, whether or not they might allow themselves to
be photographed. There was no proof that the no-chins were
part of the Putty clan. It seemed unlikely that the men who
had worn the blue bandannas would appear at a reception
with those same kerchiefs dangling from their back pockets.

And yet, they were hopeful. If Les Brownlee had accu-
rately described the antics of the Puttys, there was a good
chance they'd be drawn to an event that promised an opportunity to get liquored up and carry on. There would be
dancing, carousing, plenty of food, a fair number of single
women, and what might prove to be the irresistible urge to
rub elbows with Phoebe Apple and the law. There would be
a certain kind of satisfaction in getting close to her, perhaps
even asking her to dance, confident in their anonymity.
They'd see Jackson Brewer among the guests, maybe have
a laugh behind his back, viewing him as the hapless sheriff who couldn't track them down. It was easy to imagine
them exchanging elbow jabs when they saw Remington
Frost and recalled that he had been so helpless to stop them
on the train that they had not cared whether they stepped
on or over him.

Those were the behaviors Remington and Phoebe hoped
to see, the reactions that could place them apart from others
and make them worth watching as the evening wore on. No
one was particularly worried that they would be an excess
of trouble. Few guests would arrive wearing or carrying guns,
and those that did would have them taken and put up to
prevent mishaps. Breaking with what Phoebe had called a
Frost tradition, this was not a shotgun wedding.

"He ain't to be found," Doyle said. He knuckled the flat
bridge of his nose. "You know what I'm thinking, Willet.
I'm thinking we was lied to."

"Uh-huh," Willet said mildly. "Seems so." The newspaper rattled in his hands as he shook out the creases to give it a new fold. He largely ignored his brother, which was easier to do when Natty wasn't around.

Doyle gave Willet a sour look before he heaved a sigh and leaned back on the wooden bench they occupied. The Harmony train station was hardly bigger than an outhouse. When he stretched his legs, the toes of his dusty boots touched the base of stationmaster's counter. The stationmaster was no longer at his post but had stepped outside to smoke. Doyle could see flakes of tobacco and ashes dusting the floor so it was clear the old man didn't always smoke out on the platform, but it suited Doyle just fine that the stationmaster didn't seem to care for present company. Doyle didn't much care for anyone at the moment either, including his brother, who had about as much to offer to their present dilemma as a side of beef. "Can't believe the whore lied," he said, mostly to himself. There was a large slate hanging on the wall behind the counter with the train schedule neatly printed in chalk. For lack of anything better to look at, Doyle stared at it. "Cashdollar. What the hell kind of name is Cashdollar? Fabricated. That's what it is. A fabrication. You know what a fabrication is, Willet?"

Willet did not look up from behind his paper. "A goddamn lie?"

"That's right. It's a goddamn lie. She made it up, right there on the spot. There was money on her bureau. Bills. Cash. Dollar. See? Cashdollar. It probably inspired her. She died with a lie on her lips. She'll have to answer for that when judgment's passed. I reckon a lot of other things, too, her bein' a whore and all."

"There's that."

Doyle set his folded arms across his chest. "You figure she lied to them? The deputy? Frost? The Apple girl?"

"Maybe."

"Then they don't know any more than we do."

"And maybe not," said Willet.

Doyle's hands curled into fists. "Damnit, Willet, I've got

a good mind to put my fist through that paper, and if it con-
nects with your face, then . . ." He shrugged. "You see where
I'm goin' here?"

Willet lowered the paper, gave it another shake, and
folded it neatly into eighths. He held it out for Doyle to take,
the item of interest centered on top. When Doyle showed no
interest, Willet waved it in front of his face.

Doyle snarled, snatched the broadsheet as if it offended
him, and held it almost at arm's length to see. He still had
to squint. He read it through quickly the first time and was
nearly at the end when he understood the import of what he
was reading. Once he did, he began again, more slowly. His
lips moved as he read. When he was done, his lips moved
around words that were not on the page.

"Jesus, Joseph, and Mary," he whispered. "They're gettin'
hitched."

"Yep."

"Am I readin' this right? Open invitation? Friends, family, town folk, friends and relatives of town folk, friends and
relatives of folks associated with Twin Star. That'd be mer-
chants and breeders and stockmen. Lord, from what I'm
seein', it could be the whole damn county."

"Yep."

"Les is there."

"Uh-huh." Willet held out his hand for the paper.

Doyle slapped it into his palm. "Seems like we could go
regardless, but havin' Les there makes it better, I think.
More . . ." He paused, searching for the right word. "Genuine. Like we have more reason to be there than other folks."

"Don't know about that." Willet flicked the article with
a fingertip. "It says right here that everyone's welcome to
come celebrate the nuptials. Real friendly."

"Real quick, too. Saturday. Kinda makes you wonder
why. Could be there's some urgency. Maybe there's really a
baby on the way this time." He shook his head. "She pulled
the wool over our eyes on the train, and damn, but I hate to
be taken for a fool. I wanted to drive my fist into her belly
when I heard the truth."

"Hope that's behind you, Doyle. That's not the sort of thing you'll be able to do in front of witnesses, and I figure there will be a couple hundred of them there."

Doyle shrugged. "Maybe not, but it warms me some to think about it. You reckon she'll be there?"

"She's the bride. Of course she'll be there."

"No, I mean Ellie Madison. Aren't you curious how she'll be if we show ourselves?"

"Not exactly curious," said Willet. "But I figure this wedding is a fine opportunity to remind her how things stand. That's a woman you don't want gettin' ideas in her head and speakin' out of turn. She's a loose end."

"So that's your game."

Willet nodded. "You have somethin' else in mind?"

"Maybe." Doyle pointed to the newspaper in Willet's hand. "You gotta figure that if they paid for the gal when she was just Miss Phoebe Apple, they'd pay that and more once she's Mrs. Remington Frost."

Phoebe brushed bits of hay off the bodice and skirt of her calico day dress and knocked Remington's hand out of the way when he tried to pluck more bits out of her hair. "Attend to yourself," she said, giving him a withering glance.

More amused than chastised, Remington finger-combed his hair and brushed stray pieces of hay off his shoulders, some of which drifted onto her dress.

Phoebe pointed to a spot three feet distant. "Move over there. You're making it worse." When Remington merely grinned, she scooted sideways. "I don't know how I let myself get talked into coming up here with you."

"Sweet talk. I sweet-talked you into it."

"Yes," she said dryly. "That must be it." The smile he turned on her was a shade wicked, and Phoebe was reminded that talking, sweet or otherwise, had nothing at all to do with why she was in the barn loft. "You know, you're getting to be as good as Johnny Sutton at shirking work."

"I know. The boy is an inspiration."

Phoebe tossed a handful of hay at him. "Work on that."

Remington's attempt was haphazard at best before he gave up. Leaning back, he stretched out comfortably and supported himself on his elbows while he watched her. "Ben mentioned in passing that his mother is coming to the wedding."

"I know. Fiona told me. He must have said something to Thaddeus."

"Actually, I did, but that's neither here nor there. Thaddeus had hoped Ellie would find a reason not to come, but he's not going to insist she stay away. Ben still doesn't know why his mother left—not the truth—and my father wants to keep it that way as long as Ellie does."

"I'm glad she'll be here, and only a little bit of that is because of Ben. I like Ellie, and I'm sorry it all ended so badly for her. I imagine that if I had a rival for your affections, I'd offer her money to leave, too."

"A lot of money?"

"Enough to purchase the pine box I'd put her in."

He laughed then sobered abruptly. "Wait. You're serious."

Phoebe merely raised an eyebrow.

"Well, that's something to think about." He batted away the next handful of hay that she tossed at him. "What did Fiona have to say about Ellie coming?"

"Interestingly, she wasn't bothered at all."

"So there won't be a cat fight."

"You probably should not sound disappointed when you say that."

"Noted." Watching her, he cocked his head to one side. Her meticulous grooming fascinated him. He could imagine her sitting at a vanity, her gaze looking past her reflection to where he sat on the bed. Maybe she was preparing to join him, or perhaps she was repairing the plait of hair he had unwound when she was lying beside him. It struck him anew how truly lovely she was, how indifferent she was to it, how unaffected. He couldn't say when she had ceased to make unfavorable comparisons to Fiona, only that it had happened. She believed him when he told her she was beautiful, but she liked it better when he said she was clever.

He was tempted to test those waters as she plucked a long hay stem out of her hair, but he said nothing about the fact that she beguiled him. She was certainly astute enough to divine he wanted a chance at a second tumble. He picked up the piece of hay she dropped aside and twirled it between his thumb and forefinger.

"You know," he said casually, "if you'd married me in Liberty Junction, you wouldn't have to say your vows in front of a packed house on Saturday."

"I'm aware. I've played for an audience before, so I know I'll be fine, but I'm thinking you might have stage fright."

"Maybe, but to be clear, we are not playing at anything. This is real."

Unconcerned that she was burrowing into the hay again, Phoebe threw herself at him with enough force to drop him off his elbows. She cupped his face and kept it still while hovering above him. "I know this is real. Never doubt it. Perhaps I should not have offered our wedding reception as a means to capture Blue's murderers, but it's done and I'm unlikely to have regrets if we're successful. As for the wedding itself, I have no regrets. None. Ever."

She kissed him on the mouth. It surprised neither of them that this kiss lingered. And lingered.

Without quite knowing how it happened or what he had done to provoke it, Remington got his chance at a second tumble. He took it.

Chapter Thirty-nine

People began arriving shortly after the noon hour. They came, not bearing gifts for the couple, but cold side dishes and desserts. Scooter Banks and Ralph Neighbors were in charge of the spits where the sides of beef had been turning since early that morning. The aroma of roasting meat wafted in the air and guests caught the scent of it before they sighted the ranch house.

Johnny Sutton, much to his dismay, had labored alone for days constructing enough sawhorses to support a dozen long tables. Fiona insisted on covering the rough wooden planks with blue-and-white-checked cloths. She filled jars and pitchers and little tin pails with wildflowers she'd collected and arranged them carefully on the table tops, each equidistant from the next. Phoebe doubted the waitstaff at Delmonico's took such pains to be precise, but watching Fiona being mindful of every detail had the power to blur her vision. She ducked behind the curtains in the front room before anyone saw her peeking out.

There was a general cacophony coming from the kitchen. In addition to the very recent hire of a housekeeper, the widowed mother of Jackson Brewer's wife, Fiona was also paying for the services of three young women from town to assist with the reception. Mrs. Packer, a straight-backed, no-nonsense sort of woman who would have been comfortable wearing epaulets on her shoulders and brass buttons on her cuirass bodice, kept the girls busy and attentive to their tasks when she was in the room. When she stepped away, they tended to snarl and hiss at one another like cats trapped in a bag. Mrs. Packer was away from them now. Pots banged.

Dishes clattered. Someone squealed. Phoebe avoided the kitchen.

The parlor was deserted. She stepped inside, closed the pocket doors behind her, and leaned back against them. She closed her eyes. Outside there was a swell of sound as more guests arrived. The back door opened and closed and opened and closed. Women came and went with their baskets. She could hear Mrs. Packer trying to organize the chaos, directing which platters needed to be taken out and which required to be placed on ice. Phoebe recognized Arnie Wilver's strident voice inquiring of someone if it was time to tap a keg. A chorus of women, Fiona among them, informed him the answer was no.

Phoebe looked at the clock on the mantelpiece. She and Remington were supposed to exchange vows at one thirty. She had forty-five minutes to dress. Fiona had arranged her hair earlier, swept it up in a full pompadour so that it framed her face and sat high over her forehead. Where it was upswept around the sides and back, Fiona had dotted it with seed pearls that she'd picked out of an old necklace and painstakingly glued in her hair. It was a stunning look, Phoebe agreed, but she couldn't help wondering if hay stems wouldn't be easier to remove and better suited to a wedding where the men were wearing boots, the woman were wearing banded straw hats, and cows were roasting on spits. She kept this thought to herself. Fiona would have argued that, as the bride, she was expected to occupy center stage. Phoebe was sure that was about to happen.

She was wearing all the appropriate undergarments beneath her robe. Her white silk stockings were held up by ice blue garters, the exact shade of her tightly laced corset. She wore a sheer chemisette under the corset and a frothy, silk taffeta petticoat that rustled with her every step. The rustling sound was oddly seductive and it gave her a little thrill to know that at some point this evening that sound would be for Remington's ears alone.

The knock behind her made the doors rattle. Phoebe jumped away then turned quickly to hold them closed. "Who's there?" She was tempted to peek but didn't dare.

"It's me."

"You can't be here, Remington."

"Why not? I can't even see you." He played with the doors, but it was more in the way of teasing her than out of any real attempt to part them. "Are you dressed?"

"Of course I'm dressed."

"Mrs. Packer says the last time she saw you, you were still in your robe."

"Which means I'm dressed." She could hear him bang his forehead against the doors. She glanced back at the clock. "I have time. Besides, the last I looked, people were still arriving."

"Sure, and they'll keep on arriving all afternoon. You have to understand that the early folks are mostly good friends who want to observe the marriage rites; the stragglers will be here for the revelry."

"I heard Arnie ask if he could tap a keg."

"Then you probably heard the response. No serious drinking until anyone carrying has his gun put up and we've said 'I do.' They're passing flasks, but they're also getting anxious."

Phoebe spoke directly into the narrow crack between the doors. "So am I, Remington. I'm wondering if we shouldn't get married in here."

"I'm sending in Fiona," he said in a voice that brooked no argument. "Unless you want someone else. Ellie's here. She brought someone with her, which was good of her when you think about it. They look handsome together. Would it be better to send her?"

Phoebe shook her head before she realized he couldn't see her. "No. Not Ellie. I want my mother."

Remington held his breath as the front door opened. He was aware of silence rolling through the gathering as one by one people stopped talking and turned their attention to the porch. Standing at his side, Thaddeus whispered a caution. "You're about to take the ride of your life."

Remington was sure that was true.

She was something more than enchanting. When Phoebe stepped off the shaded porch and into the sunshine, she was very nearly ethereal. Light wreathed her hair; the seed pearls turned opalescent. A becoming blush colored her cheeks pink. Her lips were a darker shade of rose. Remington suspected she had been worrying them up until the moment she opened the door, and that she had found the courage to come out anyway, made him smile.

Her white silk dress fairly gleamed as she approached. In spite of everyone's efforts, the carpet of grass the ranch hands had laid down had been trampled to virtually nothing, and the hem and train of the gown stirred puffs of dust where they dragged the ground. The cone-shaped skirt, supported by a rustling taffeta petticoat, flared wide and swung softly from side to side with each step.

The bodice fit her as closely as a kid glove, emphasizing the waist he could almost circle with his hands. From elbow to wrist, the sleeves were tight, but from shoulder to elbow they ballooned in the leg-o'-mutton style that was both fashionable and elegant.

There was an appliqué of beadwork in the bodice that extended into the skirt, a long curlicue that twisted and swirled until it disappeared into the folds of the gown. It teased the eye, winking and sparkling. It glittered, but no more than the flecks of gold in Phoebe's green eyes. That's where Remington's real attention was drawn. The first chance he had, he promised he would lose himself in those eyes.

The opportunity presented itself sooner than he expected. She stepped into his circle, closer than arm's length, and tilted her head upward. Her smile was shy, but her eyes were confident. He was prepared to drown in those unfathomable depths, but she took his hand and saved him from himself.

The ceremony was a civil one, performed by the Honorable Judge Richard Miner, the same judge who liked to play cards at the Boxwood, the one Phoebe failed to meet when he came to their table. He presided with a solemn, dignified air that he was rarely inclined to use from the bench, but then he was rarely as sober as a judge on those occasions.

He did right by them, articulating each word so they could repeat their vows clearly and with conviction. Some guests thought he sounded as if he were handing down a sentence, and some among them who were married, perhaps not as happily as others, thought a sentence described marriage exactly as it was.

Neither Phoebe nor Remington shared that view, at least not its undesirable connotations, and when it was time to give her the ring, Thaddeus had it at the ready. Remington took it from the heart of his father's open palm at the same time he raised Phoebe's hand. She held her gaze steady, her eyes awash with sudden tears. His own vision was a little misty. "My mother's," he whispered, slipping the gold band on her finger.

There were more words, then. Traditional words. Phoebe's hand was warm in his, and only he knew there was a delicate tremble in her fingers. Only she knew how hard he had to swallow before he spoke.

Buggies and wagons were still arriving as Judge Miner called for the kiss in the manner of a man lowering his gavel. To the delight of everyone, Remington swung his bride back over one arm and made the moment a memory that would last. She gasped. He chuckled. The kiss began with a matched pair of smiles, a bit secretive, more than a bit wicked. There was whooping and hollering. Young girls blushed. Young boys stared open-mouthed and envious. Thaddeus caught Fiona by the waist and pulled her close, and when the kiss did not end in a timely manner, Johnny Sutton began a round of foot stomping and clapping that others quickly picked up.

It was like thunder in Phoebe's ears, but Remington barely heard it above the pounding of his heart.

They were both laughing a little breathlessly when Remington ended the kiss and they were finally standing side by side. Judge Miner introduced the couple to another round of applause and, having completed his duties, called out for someone to tap a keg and be quick about it.

There was no formal receiving line, but it seemed to

Phoebe that everyone, or nearly everyone, sought them out to wish them well. She glimpsed Ellie Madison several times, usually in a clutch of people that included Ben and at least one of the other hands. She understood why Ellie did not approach. With Fiona and Thaddeus standing close by, Ellie's presence would have been, at the very least, awkward, and perhaps unwanted, and while all parties would have been on their best behavior, there was no good reason to tempt a drama.

Phoebe promised herself she would seek Ellie out later and make sure she was properly welcomed. Even Fiona had expressed feeling charitable toward Ellie of late; it was Thaddeus who, by his stony silence, communicated disapproval.

Remington inclined his head a few degrees toward Phoebe and whispered out of the side of his mouth. "If one more person congratulates me with a hearty clap on the back, I'm going to slug him." The words were hardly out of his mouth when Jackson Brewer sidled up and did just that. Remington smiled through gritted teeth. "I am sorely tempted," he said.

Only Phoebe understood what he meant and she ignored him in favor of greeting Addie Brewer, who she recalled was Remington's first love when he was a student in her classroom. Those school days became fodder for some good-natured ribbing at Remington's expense until Jackson swept his wife away.

Phoebe slipped her arm through her husband's. "You bore that very well. And no one was slugged. I credit your deep well of patience."

"Uh-huh." He underscored his dry response with an even drier look.

Thaddeus closed in just then. "The dancing's about to begin as long as you begin it. Les has his fiddle out. Hank Greely brought his and Bob Washburn has his banjo. I told them to set up on the porch."

People parted around them as soon as Les Brownlee scratched out the first few notes tuning his instrument. When the playing began in earnest, Remington and Phoebe were ready.

It occurred to Phoebe that they had never danced together, but that did not seem to matter. Without knowing the steps or the tune or even if she would ever catch her breath again, she held him, held on, and followed his lead through a series of spins and dips and sashays that were unlike anything she had known. It was not long before Fiona and Thaddeus joined them, and then the sheriff and his wife, and soon the center of the front yard was filled with a kaleidoscope of color as men twirled their ladies and the ladies twirled their skirts. There was enough stomping to shake the ground and enough raucous laughter to wake the dead.

Phoebe changed partners frequently, beginning when Thaddeus caught her in his arms. At first she looked wildly around to make sure Fiona was not abandoned, but then she saw Remington stepping in with no hesitation and Fiona accepting in the same manner.

Thaddeus saw the direction of her glance. "They'll be fine. Have you noticed? It is better every day."

Phoebe nodded because speaking would have meant losing her rhythm. She was not as confident of Thaddeus's lead as she had been of Remington's.

"I am to be congratulated, of course," he said. "Fiona called me a *shadkhn*. Am I saying that right?"

Phoebe nodded again.

"I thought she was cursing me at first, and perhaps she was. She didn't think Remington was right for you, or you for him, but I knew. I knew from the first. And that was when I met you in New York, not when I saw the two of you together. Not bad, I think, for an old man."

Before Phoebe could think of a response, let alone manage one, she found herself in the sheriff's arms. And so it went from partner to partner until Remington caught her again and twirled her out of the center of the circle to the edge of it. Someone—she did not know who—put a glass of beer in her hand and she drank it with the gusto of a cowboy bellying up to the bar after months on the range.

Remington lifted the glass from her hand and finished

it. He passed off the empty glass to someone walking by. "You're flushed," he said, looking her over. "And quite beautiful with it. Come on, we can sneak away for a few minutes while you catch your breath." He placed his hands on her shoulders, turned her, and gave her a nudge toward the side of the house. Once she was moving in that direction, he took a beer from Arnie, who was holding one in each hand.

"Hey!" Arnie called after Remington, watching his beer being carried away.

Remington looked back over his shoulder and grinned. "Thanks." He rounded the corner of the house, the relatively quiet corner, and found Phoebe leaning against the roughly timbered wall. "Here," he said, giving her the beer. "Go easy. It's early yet, the sun's out, there will be more dancing, and you don't want to stagger at your own wedding. That's for other people to do."

She thanked him and raised the glass. This time she was not greedy with the drink. She let him wipe a foam mustache from her upper lip. "I've seen more than a few no-chins. You?"

"Yes."

"I danced with some. One of them had a poorly set nose. I could barely stop staring."

"I know. I saw. And I didn't like it."

"Jealous? Or concerned for my toes?"

"Jealous," he said. "And concerned for your safety."

"Remington. What did you think could happen?"

"Remember the catastrophes you imagined when you were alone in Old Man McCauley's cabin? It was like that." When she laughed instead of offering sympathy, he confiscated the beer and enjoyed two large swallows before he passed it back. "Did any of them introduce themselves?"

"Tim Brownlee. He's Les's youngest brother. Another was a cousin. Ned Washington. Oh, and the flat bridge was a Putty, or a Petty. I can't be sure. He did not mention any connection to Les. He mumbled, and he was nearly as breathless as I was. Hoyle. Doyle. Royal. He did enjoy the dancing, though. You know, I had the oddest sense that I'd seen him before. It can't have been on the train, so I don't know where it could have been. I wasn't prepared for that. I'll have to think about it."

"I don't believe for a moment that his last name is Petty, and neither do you. I'm going to keep an eye on him." He set his hands on either side of her shoulders and bent his head to steal a kiss.

Phoebe touched her mouth with her fingertips. "More beer foam?"

"Nope. I was just hankerin' for a taste of your fine lips."

She laughed. "Fool."

He shrugged, helped himself to a second tasting, and then stepped back. "Did you see Ellie?"

"I did, but not who she brought. I want to be certain to speak to her and thank her for coming. I won't let on that I know the reason she's not working here any longer."

"She probably thinks we both know."

"I don't care. I'm not going to confirm it and embarrass her." She took another sip of beer and then placed the glass against her forehead. The beer was warm but glass felt cool against her skin. "Did you ever ask Thaddeus about Ellie being bought out by her husband's partners?"

"Odd you'd ask me now. I just mentioned it to him the other day when we were banished because Mrs. Fish was here for your fitting. He said it was too long ago for him to remember the details, but that it sounded right."

Phoebe frowned. "Thaddeus said he didn't remember the details?"

"I know. That sounded wrong to me, too."

"Hmm."

"I let it go. It didn't seem as if anything good would come of challenging him." He saw Phoebe was about to respond, but before she could, Mrs. Packer rounded the corner and their marginal sense of privacy was gone. The housekeeper set her hands on wide hips and took a militant stance. It was very different than what Ellie would have done, but it was equally effective. "We're coming, Mrs. Packer."

"See that you do. Your guests are milling about the tables looking to help themselves. The children can barely contain themselves, and I don't like shooin' them away. Poor dears. It isn't right. Come and get yourselves a plate so folks can have a bite before their bellies are full of liquor." She started to turn, stopped, "Oh, and there's a young fella looking for you. He was talking up Thaddeus and Fiona the last I saw him, and I think he's already been into the blueberry pie."

Remington and Phoebe exchanged surprised, then knowing, glances before they returned their attention to Mrs. Packer. They said his name at the same time. "Handy McKenzie."

Chapter Forty

"Damn if I didn't dance with her." Doyle practically cackled with glee. He poked his brother in the ribs with his elbow. "Did you see? Didn't think I did too badly. At least I wasn't stepping all over her toes. Caught her gown once, but she just swept it aside and kept on goin'. You gotta like a gal who can do that."

Willet dug Doyle's elbow out of his side and pushed his brother away. "That hurts. You gotta stop jabbing at me. I get what you're sayin' without the physicality."

"Physicality. Huh. I like that. You read that somewhere, Willet?"

"Shut up," he said tiredly. "How much have you had to drink? I saw you posing for a photograph with some young gal on your arm. You think that's wise?"

"Don't you worry about me." Doyle lifted his hat, raked his hair, and set the hat back. "You see her?"

Willet didn't ask who "her" was. He knew. "Sure did. More important, I saw who's with her."

"Huh? Doyle looked around before he recalled Ellie Madison's diminutive stature. The press of people around the tables, the roasting spit, and the liquor bar was too thick for him to find her without standing on tiptoes or stepping up to the porch. He gave up, trusted that Willet would tell him. "So? You gonna keep me on pins and needles?"

"Natty's here."

"What?" In contrast to Willet's quiet answer, Doyle's response was loud enough to turn heads.

"Would you mind yourself?" Willet hissed. "You damn

well heard me so there's no point in asking 'what' like you don't know what I said. And I don't care if it surprised you, keep it to yourself."

"What's he doin' here?" asked Doyle. "He see you? You talk to him?"

"I don't know if he's seen me. I've been doin' my best to stay clear, so you better believe I haven't talked to him."

"Damn."

"I really wish you hadn't danced with the bride, Doyle. Kinda hard to believe he didn't see that."

Doyle shrugged. It was done and there was nothing he could do about it. "Where is he now? I don't see him."

"He's got a beard. Looks a mite different than you're used to."

"A beard, eh? Don't reckon I've ever known him to have one." Doyle didn't think the beard was particularly important in locating their former partner. In contrast to Ellie Madison's petite stature, Natty Rahway was almost six feet and should have been easy to spot. "Damn, where'd he get to?"

"I don't know. I lost him. Ellie, too. They could have gone inside the house. Maybe the barn. I noticed Ellie hasn't been much for helping, so I asked about it. Casual-like, you know. Seems she left Twin Star. Not long ago, but she's here as a guest. She took a job at the Butterworth Hotel."

"The Butterworth. Huh. Ain't that somethin'?" He thought about it a little longer. "Why d'you suppose she did that?"

"Couldn't say. But I have a mind to ask when we cross paths. And we will. I'll make damn sure of it."

Phoebe sank into the chair that Handy pushed against the backs of her knees. "Thank you. Oh, sweet Lord, thank you."

Handy stepped around the chair so she could see him and gave her a wide toothy grin. "You want I should get you something to eat? To drink?"

"No." The thought of eating or drinking anything at this

point in the day made her slightly queasy. She had had her fill three times over, and in spite of the chemisette she was wearing under her corset, the stays were gouging her.

The sun had dipped behind the mountains and dusk was settling. There was a group of guests who left in the late afternoon, most of them with children in tow, but there were still dozens and dozens of people congregating in small groups of three and four, grazing at the long tables, dancing around the bonfire that Scooter and Ralph built where the spits had been. Les Brownlee and his fellow fiddlers were indefatigable with a seemingly endless repertoire of melodies at their fingertips. No one had been able to call out a song they couldn't play, or at least one they couldn't make up.

"Have you seen my husband?" Phoebe asked Handy. She liked saying "my husband" and used it whenever she could instead of his given name.

"I saw him go into the bunkhouse a while ago. Some fellows hustled him in there. Wedding shenanigans, Mrs. Tyler said, but I think there might be a card game. Leastways I heard Mr. Tyler say so, and he's gotta nose for sniffin' out a card game."

Phoebe looked around and saw that Ben, Scooter, Ralph, Arnie, and Johnny all seemed to have disappeared. Most likely it was shenanigans, but she said, "Cards? At my wedding reception?"

"Yes, ma'am."

Phoebe could not muster the energy to affect even mild annoyance. She patted the bench beside her chair. "Sit here, Handy. Is Mr. Tyler in there with my husband?"

"No. His missus got a firm grip on his arm and steered him away."

She sighed. "I suppose I'll have to learn how to do that."

"Oh, I think it'll come to you natural, and ma'am?"

"Yes?"

"I don't think Mr. Frost is going to give you much trouble."

Phoebe couldn't help laughing. Handy entertained her for quite a while, mostly with stories about his experiences at the Boxwood, and many of those were about Mrs. Jacob C. Tyler, who had returned to Saint Louis three days before the wedding announcement appeared in the paper. Except for those times when guests came by to introduce themselves and extend more good wishes, Handy happily chattered on.

Thaddeus strolled over. He pulled out a handkerchief as he sat beside Handy and wiped his brow. "I swear to you, dancing has me more tuckered than a week of roping and wrestling calves." He pointed to Fiona, who was high stepping with a new partner. "She has not lacked for attention since the music began. I know it's your wedding, Phoebe, but this is your mother's coming-out party. I should have had some kind of shindig when I brought her out here." He tucked his handkerchief away and looked around. "Speaking of inattentive and cloddish husbands, where is yours?"

"In the bunkhouse, according to Handy. I think your men are plying him with drink and feeding him the kind of wedding night stories that are not fit for female ears. It's all right, though. He'll tell me later."

Thaddeus laughed. "Handy, if you would be so kind, I sure could use a beer." Handy launched himself off the bench before Thaddeus could tell the boy he wasn't to sample any of the drink.

Phoebe watched Fiona twirl like a dervish with her partner's expert guidance. She lifted her chin in that direction. "Who is he?"

"Couldn't tell you. Too many people here I don't know, have never seen before, and am likely to never see again."

"He looks familiar," she said, studying the man as he matched Fiona's steps. He was tall, slim-hipped, and broad-shouldered. Unlike many of the men present—Remington and Thaddeus also being notable exceptions—he wore a high-buttoned, single-breasted box-cut suit, black peg-top trousers, and a black vest. Under the vest was a crisp white shirt, and above it was a high, stiff collar. In spite of his exertions, he looked at his ease and, most miraculously, managed to keep his felt derby secured on his head. His dark hair and mustache were neatly trimmed, his beard only a little less so. He could have been a professional gambler or an undertaker, Phoebe thought, but what he wasn't was a no-chin relative of Les Brownlee's. That eased her mind.

"I should cut him out," said Thaddeus. He didn't move, though. Instead, he sighed. "She looks very well on his arm, doesn't she? And he's of an age with her."

"What does that have to do with anything? Besides, I just realized why he caught my eye earlier. He was on Ellie's arm. I think he's her escort. Get back in there, Thaddeus, before there's scratching and clawing and someone's dress is left in tatters."

"But . . . my beer."

Phoebe placed her hand on his back and gave him a less than gentle shove. "Never fear. Handy will find you." She stood and continued to nudge him toward the dancing. "Likewise, I'm off to find my husband. If you have any kindness in your heart, you will not organize a search party for us."

Chapter Forty-one

Phoebe opened the door to the bunkhouse and poked her head inside. There was indeed a card game. She attempted a reproving look but couldn't manage to sustain it. The men crowded around the table were regarding her with apologetic expressions largely softened by too much drink. Chief among the penitents was the man presiding over the game by virtue of his status and his winnings.

"Hello, Judge."

"Ma'am." The Honorable Judge Miner waved a hand over the table, an invitation implicit in the gesture. "Come. Sit. Poker's a woman's game as much as a man's. Mr. Sutton will give you his chair. Go on, boy. Get up."

Johnny's chair scraped the floor as he began to push away from the table.

Phoebe opened the door a few inches wider and put out a hand to stop him. "No. Stay where you are, Johnny. Thank you, Judge. Men. I'm looking for Remington . . . my husband. I was led to believe you hustled him in here. Up to no good is the consensus. What did you do with him?"

It was Scooter who answered. "Teased him some, had a couple of shots. Mostly he humored us. Said he was going to dance with his bride and then he left."

"He wasn't exactly walkin' a straight line," said Arnie. "Not staggering, but not the straight and narrow, if you know what I mean."

"I think I do. It's all right. I'll find him. I have an idea where he'd go." She looked around the table a second time. "Where's Ben? I thought he'd be with you."

Arnie and Ralph shrugged in unison. Johnny spoke up. "He left before Remington. Said he wanted to spend time with Ellie. He's a mama's boy, that one."

This brought a hoot of laughter since the other hands often described Johnny Sutton in just that manner. Phoebe waited until the laughter subsided and young Johnny's ears were marginally less crimson. "Good night, gentlemen. Judge, don't take unfair advantage."

"No, ma'am."

Phoebe knew when she was being placated. Shaking her head, she ducked out and headed for the barn. Because no one knew what the weather would bring, the barn had been cleaned to accommodate the guests, the food, and the dancing. The stalls had not merely been mucked, they had been scoured. The horses were penned farther afield, but the scent of them lingered. Bales of fresh hay were stacked steplike against the back wall to provide additional seating, and more bales lined the interior of the stalls.

Phoebe stood just inside the door, waiting for her eyes to adjust to the dark. The barn was quiet, almost eerily so. She was more aware of the absence of the animals in a way she hadn't been earlier when Thaddeus and Remington had invited her to inspect the work. She had been able to see everything then. At the moment she was relying on her memory of the space.

"Remington?" She said his name tentatively, barely raising her voice above a whisper. It was absurd to call for him so quietly, especially when she could hear the fiddles and banjo playing across the way and the voices of the guests raised in song, but something about the barn, with its high ceiling and wide-open entrance, put her in mind of a church and she felt a certain reverence for the sanctuary.

She carefully picked her way around the scattered bales of hay and headed toward the loft ladder. There had been talk about removing it to keep guests out of the loft. It wasn't out of the question that there could be drunken mishaps, either an accidental fall or a dare to dive. Instead of taking the ladder away, they lined the loft's edge with heavy bales of hay to form a barrier. A country balustrade, Thaddeus called it. Phoebe wondered if her husband was passed out behind it now. She set one hand on a rung and hiked up her billowing skirt with the other. "Remington?"

She thought she heard a stirring overhead, but it could have been the rustle of her taffeta petticoat. She started to climb. "I'm considering divorcing you, Remington. I'm also considering shooting you. I might do both."

Phoebe had to tread carefully. Her gown had substantial weight and her white kid boots were not meant to grip anything like the narrow slats of the ladder. She did not look down, though it occurred to her that once she found Remington, the descent would be considerably trickier than the climb.

When she reached the top and could peer through the narrow opening between the bales, she was no longer so certain that Remington was behind them. She carefully made the transition from ladder to loft, mostly by crawling on her knees and yanking her gown out from under her.

Far from being passed out or in any stage of inebriation, Remington was awake and alert. As soon as Phoebe appeared from between the bales, he grabbed her under her shoulders and hauled her the rest of the way through. His hand covered her mouth before she could squeal, shout, or otherwise protest.

He placed his lips near her ear. "Shh." He felt her nod but did not entirely trust her. "I mean it, Phoebe. You must be quiet." She nodded again, this time with more promise behind it, and he removed his hand. "You have to take off that petticoat," he whispered. "It's like a scurry of squirrels passing through the underbrush every time you move. Quickly." It was gratifying that she did not question him, but she still did not move swiftly enough to suit. Remington batted her hands out of the way and reached under her gown for the ribbons that held her petticoat in place. Try as he did to keep it quiet, removing the taffeta was a noisy affair. When he finally got it off, he tossed it as far away from them as he could. Once it landed, blessed silence followed.

It lasted only as long as it took Phoebe to find her voice. "What are we doing?" she whispered.

"Waiting." He paused a beat and then added, "Quietly."

She nodded. "For what?"

He sighed. "I'm not sure."

Phoebe wondered if he thought that was a reasonable answer because she certainly did not. In deference to his command for quiet, she spoke as softly as was possible. "You have to explain that."

"Ben told me to come up here. There's something he wants me to hear. He's arranging it now. I can't tell you more because I don't know more, but he was adamant. He said it was something he had to do."

"*Had* to do?"

"Hmm. Or he couldn't call himself any sort of man."

Phoebe's eyes widened. "Ben said that?"

"Yes."

"Are you sure it wasn't liquor talking? I never saw him without a drink in his hand after the ceremony."

"Maybe, or maybe drink helped him speak his mind. Now you know what I know. Shh." Remington released her, but not before planting a kiss on her mouth. As soon as she inched away, he stretched out on his belly exactly as he had been before she began climbing the ladder. A moment later she was lying beside him, mirroring his posture right down to the way he raised himself on his forearms.

Remington's eyes had had sufficient time to adjust to the dark interior of the barn. He was helped by slivers of moonlight seeping through cracks in the walls and threading through needlelike openings in the roof. He looked sideways at Phoebe and recalled that she had seemed ethereal when she stepped off the porch this afternoon. That was even truer now. "Otherworldly" was a word that came to his mind. The gown that had gleamed in the sunshine was a cool and ghostly silver-blue thanks to the moonlight.

In spite of his insistence on silence, there was something he had to know. "Why are you here?"

As far as Phoebe was concerned, it was the wrong

question. He should have been asking why she had come looking for him, in which case she would have explained that, as his wife of less than one day, she had the right to expect that he would not wander away like a pup off its leash. It was perhaps a harsh criticism, but then she was not feeling particularly charitable, and although the kiss had been rather nice, she would not be placated so easily.

Still, she answered him because there was obviously more going on than he could properly tell her and curiosity trumped truculence. "I tried the bunkhouse first because Handy saw you being hustled off there. When the men told me you'd left, I thought of where I would go if I desired a few moments alone and was willing to shuck my responsibilities to my guests, my family, and my husband." She thought he might have winced, but she couldn't be sure. "And here you are, exactly where I would be. Or rather, where I am."

"Did I know your tongue was this sharp when I married you?"

"You should have. You kissed me often enough."

He very nearly gave a shout of laughter. What he did, though, was kiss her, long and deeply, and satisfied himself that he knew the shape of her tongue. He spoke softly, his mouth hardly a hairbreadth from hers. "I'm glad you found me."

"Are you?"

"Mm. Aside from the obvious benefits of having you this close, one of us missing from the revelry was bound to raise eyebrows, but if both of us are missing . . . Well, that's more or less expected."

Phoebe placed her hands on Remington's shoulders and pushed him back. She squinted at his shadowed features. "Don't get any ideas."

Remington rolled over and took up his previous position. "I don't know how long we'll have to wait. Did anyone see you come in here?"

"I imagine so. Maybe you didn't notice, but I'm the only one wearing white."

A chuckle rose in his throat and then lodged there as the

barn door swung open on noisy hinges. He looked over at Phoebe to make sure she had also heard it. Her head was up; she was alert. He did not bother putting a finger to his lips.

Ellie Madison stopped a few feet over the threshold. "I can't see a thing, Ben. Did you bring a lantern?"

"No. Give it a minute. I didn't want to attract attention." He held the door open long enough to allow Natty Rahway to enter then he shut it.

Natty said, "I saw the new Mrs. Frost duck in here a while ago. She didn't seem to care about attracting attention."

"Well, she's not here now. You'd know it. She glows like a firefly in that dress."

"Maybe," said Natty. "Is there another way out? I didn't see her leave."

"There's a door on the left at the back."

"Loft?"

"Yes, sir. I'll check it out if you like."

Natty brushed past Ellie and Ben and found the ladder. He gave it a shake. "Sturdy enough, but I don't think she could climb it. What I recall is that she needed a leg up to climb onto the back of a horse." He picked his way around hay bales until he found the back door. "It's ajar." He shut it tightly so he would be sure to hear it if it was opened again, then he rejoined Ellie and Ben near the entrance. "All right. What's this about?"

Ben did not hesitate. It was unimportant that they could not see him well; he lifted his chin belligerently. "I've been watching all day. Watching you, watching them. I want to know why you'd come here. No one wants your kind of trouble."

Natty stroked his beard. "I figure you're addressing me, son, and the answer to why I'm here is standing beside me. Your mother invited me to escort her."

"Is that true?" asked Ben.

"Yes."

"Why would you do that?" Before she could answer, he asked, "The others? Did you ask them to be here, too?"

"I did not. They're here same as everyone else. Thaddeus

issued an open invitation. You'd have to expect there'd be all kinds of folks showing up." Ellie found her son's arm and gave his sleeve a tug. "Why are you bringing this up now? You've had all day. It's the drink, isn't it?"

"Dutch courage," said Natty, amusement in his voice. "Why don't you say what's really on your mind?"

"What's on my mind is relieving it if you don't leave and take your friends with you." He shook off his mother's hand. "Ma, I'm going to tell Thaddeus the truth. I can't look him in the eye any longer."

"Then leave the ranch," said Ellie. "It's not up to you to come forward."

Natty's hand snaked out and he grabbed a fistful of Ben's shirt. "That's for damn sure. Do you hear what your mother's saying? It's not your place to decide anything."

Ben grabbed Natty's wrist in both hands and tried to wrestle his shirt free of the man's grip. He staggered back when Natty let go but caught himself before he tumbled backward over a bale of hay.

Ellie reached out blindly in an effort to steady her son. She caught air and nothing else. She straightened, set her hands on her hips, and took a half step forward. A full step would have put her squarely between Ben and Natty. It was not a safe place for her to be, not in the dark, and not with tempers flaring. "Enough. Both of you. Ben, you had better explain yourself."

Ben straightened his shirt and pulled the collar away from his neck. "I'm going to tell Thaddeus what I did. I don't have to involve you, Mother. I can say it was all me, all my idea. And I'm not giving up anyone else."

Natty shook his head. "I don't think I've ever met anyone as green as you. Do you suppose anyone will thank you for your confession and let you go? There's Blue Armstrong, you dumb son of a bitch, and someone's going to want to hear what you know about that."

"I can't say what I don't know."

"That didn't stop you before."

"What do you mean?"

"That line of bull you fed me about the pearl choker, how someone was trying to sell it, how it belonged to a passenger on the train. Lies. Every bit of it. But it was the first domino to fall. That makes you as responsible for Blue Armstrong's murder as the idiots who did it."

Ben wished he had brought a lantern after all. He wanted to see Natty Rahway's face; he wanted to judge the man's truthfulness for himself. Ben tried to sound certain, not defensive. "That doesn't make a lick of sense. What does the dog collar have to do with anything?"

"That's just it," said Natty. "It doesn't."

"I don't understand."

Ellie broke in before Natty spoke. "I don't understand either. What's this about a choker? Pearls, was it?"

Natty said, "The damn thing didn't exist, but because you told me it did—I'm talkin' to you, Ben—I mentioned it to the others. I wanted to see what was what, so I planned to follow Blue. That got me to the whore, and then the boys got ideas of their own. They cut me out, followed the deputy themselves, and learned it was the pear shape diamond ring that he had, not a pearl collar. They *knew* they'd sold the ring to a fellow, but they didn't get his name. He didn't have theirs either, but they figured he could give the law a pretty good description. You probably read about what happened next, or maybe you heard it straight from the sheriff. They squeezed the life out of Blue and his whore to get the name, and they got it, too. Heard it was the whore who gave it up. Blue wouldn't."

Natty shifted his weight from one foot to other and folded his arms across his chest. "If you haven't considered this, Ben, you should be doing it now. I don't know how it came to your attention that it was a collar that was stolen, but it was never that. The boys swear there was no such piece, and while they'd stare at a blue sky and tell you it's purple, I'm inclined to believe them about this. So if there was no collar, why were you so sure there was? See, if it was me, I'd be thinking someone was pissin' on my leg and telling me it was raining. But hey, that's just me."

Ellie's eyes narrowed as she attempted to study her son's features. "He's right, isn't he? Someone told you. Someone suspects you're involved. Who was it?"

"Can't be important now," said Ben. "It's a dead end. He doesn't know I told you."

"Not the point," Natty told him. "The point is you were told something that wasn't true. You weren't trusted. Maybe you weren't trusted since the first. You think of that?"

He hadn't, but he was sure that was irrelevant. He was doing the right thing, he was certain of it. With this off his chest, he'd be able to look Remington—and Thaddeus—in the eye, and he would be able to face himself in the mirror.

Ellie's voice was sharp when she addressed Ben. "There are only two possibilities. I want to know which one of them it was."

"Why?" asked Ben. "I did what you asked. Everything you asked. I told you there was no affair between Mrs. Frost and me. Whatever you saw with Remington or thought you saw, it was never like that for me. That's what started this. I don't think you ever believed me, but she was nothing but kind, and yes, she was lonely, and you were grasping at anything you could use to send her away as long as it did not reflect poorly on either of us."

"I was looking out for you. It's what a mother does. What a mother always does, unless she's no kind of mother to her own child. Yes, I'm talking about Fiona. She was not much of a sister either. That woman was so jealous of Phoebe that she couldn't see straight. Tried to pass it off as concern, but what it was, was jealousy. She did not want Phoebe anywhere near Thaddeus, and I didn't want Fiona anywhere near you.

"Fiona had the will to leave Twin Star but not the means. She confided in me, Ben, and I listened to her. Phoebe's abduction, the ransom, it was all in aid of funding Fiona's escape. I was helping her, don't you see?"

"Tell yourself that, Mother, but you had your own reasons for wanting Fiona gone. You've been in love with Thaddeus for years, maybe always, and the only person who didn't seem to know was Thaddeus."

"You're wrong, Ben. It was about you. Always about you."

"Stop. Just stop."

Natty said, "This is all very touching, but it has nothing to do with me."

"Of course it has to do with you," said Ben. "You took Phoebe from the train, set up the ransom, didn't stop those two miscreants from robbing the passengers, and worse, didn't stop them from murdering Blue Armstrong."

"Carried out your mama's plan," said Natty. "Same as you. You seem to be forgetting that most of that ransom ended up in your hands. I know because I put it there. Doesn't matter to me what Ellie wanted to do with the money. That's her business. As for the miscreants—and that might be the best word ever applied to them—they're finished. Ellie and I have reached an agreement that has nothing to do with you. Leave it be, Ben. Better that you stop threatening to open your mouth more than you already have. It's done. Or it soon will be."

Natty, Ellie, and Ben turned as one when the barn door creaked loudly and a pair of lanterns swung into the opening ahead of the two men carrying them.

Doyle raised his lantern to cast light over the intimate gathering. He smirked. "Told you, Willet. Told you I saw them duck in here."

Chapter Forty-two

Willet kicked the door hard enough with the heel of his boot to make it shudder when it closed. "You did tell me they were here. You have to wonder what they're up to standing around in the dark."

"I'm not wonderin' at all," said Doyle. "Plottin' is a word that comes to mind. Up to no kind of good, is what I'd say." He lowered the lantern so light spread in a circle around his feet. "Hello, Mrs. Madison. Ben." He stared hard at Natty. "I figured we'd cross paths sooner or later. Had the feelin' you were avoidin' us."

"Not avoiding," Natty said easily. "Just nothing to say."

Doyle snorted. Willet remained silent.

Natty thrust his bearded chin forward. "What do you want?"

"Nothin' in particular," said Doyle. "Mostly curious. Willet and me couldn't exactly hear what was being said from the other side of the door on account of the fiddles, but we sure could tell you was talkin'. Kinda contradicts that notion that you have nothin' to say."

"To you," said Natty. "Nothing to say to you or your brother."

Ellie said, "I think you should extinguish the lanterns before the light attracts attention and someone gets curious."

Willet shook his head. "We're not doing anything, so what do we care if someone comes nosing around? You got somethin' to hide, Mrs. Madison? Ben? No point in asking anyone else. Your man's always hiding something. Never knew him not to have a card or two up his sleeve."

Ben took a step sideways to be closer to his mother. "I admire your nerve, coming here today. Rubbing elbows with the law. Taking a turn with Phoebe. Chatting up Remington like you were an old friend. They'll figure it out, you know. Blue's murder. There will be justice for him and Miss Carolina, and you'll know I'm speaking the truth when they're stringing you up."

Doyle spit and wiped his mouth with his sleeve. "My goodness. Never figured you for a self-righteous prick. You thinkin' about talkin' to someone? Is that what this is about? Seems to me that if you're inclined to speak up, you might have an appointment with the hangman yourself. As far as I can tell, there are no innocents here."

Willet said, "It pains me some to tell you that Doyle's speakin' for me. I don't usually find myself in such agreement with my brother. I imagine from your perspective, Doyle and me look like a couple of loose cannons. Have I got that right?"

"Aren't you?" asked Ellie. She skewered the brothers with a sharp look. "You stole from the passengers and you had to kill to cover your tracks. That was stupid. All of it."

"That's over with," said Doyle. "Our man ain't nowhere to be found, so I guess we're clear of it." He swung his lantern a few degrees up and down. "We had a name from the whore. Turns out it was probably a lie, but no one's come forward to say different or to point a finger at us. I jawed some with the sheriff this afternoon, just because I could. You didn't see him haulin' me off to jail, did you?"

"Damnation," Natty said, shaking his head. "That's not confidence you're showin' off. That's a lack of brains, pure and simple. Willet, you really need to take your brother in hand. When he goes, it's a sure thing he's going to take you with him."

Willet shrugged. "You leave Doyle to me and worry about yourself. We have ourselves in a bit of a pickle with Ben here. Has he been talkin' nonsense long?"

"Long enough," said Natty. "Murdering that deputy put him out of sorts. That's what I'm getting from our conversation.

And he doesn't cotton to killing the whore either. It's you and Doyle that got him thinking that maybe he needs to wipe his slate clean. You know damn well that I didn't like it. Until the two of you went sideways on me, no real harm was done. Sure, Frost was out some money, the passengers were out some trinkets, and Northeast Rail was some kind of mad about the stain to their reputation. Now you got Ben thinking he needs to set it all right."

Doyle raised his lantern again, this time to shine it in Ben's face. "That's right, boy. You need to blink and step back like you was scared, 'cause if you ain't scared, I'm tellin' you that you should be. What I want to know is if you're so hell-bent on sayin' something to the law, why haven't you? Why are you here havin' a powwow about it?"

"Shut up, Doyle," Willet said. "And put that lantern down. Don't push him. Can't you figure that he wanted to talk to his mama first, maybe give her a chance to reason him out of it? He can't tell his story without involving Mrs. Madison. That's got to be weighin' on him some. That sound about right, son?"

Ellie's chin came up. "Don't call him that. He's not your son."

Willet's dark eyebrows rose high enough to furrow his forehead. He said mildly, "That put up someone's hackles."

"Get out," said Ellie. "Your mere presence is a provocation. Let me handle this."

Willet made a show of considering what she'd said. "Probably should, Mrs. Madison, but Doyle and me have plans of our own. Doyle, for God's sake, will you stop swinging that lantern?" The expression he turned on Ellie was long on suffering. "The trouble is it's hard to know how to go forward, what with this threat hangin' over our head like the sword of Damocles."

Doyle nodded. The arc of his swinging lantern was shorter now but the light from it continued to wax and wane. "Uh-huh. Like the damn sword of Clees."

Willet's mouth flattened and he shook his head as he cast a sideways glance at his brother. Almost apologetically, he said to the others, "Sometimes he can't help himself."

When attention shifted back to Willet, Doyle swung his lantern hard, high, and wide, aiming for the side of Natty Rahway's head. Natty threw up a forearm to block the blow that would have laid him out cold. He ducked, lunged at Doyle, but he never had a chance to deflect Willet's swing. The base of the lantern caught him on the underside of his chin, knocked his lower teeth into his upper ones with a crack that seemed to echo off the barn walls. The hit took the big man down and he pitched forward onto the floor and then he was still.

Ben pushed Ellie out of the way while Doyle was still admiring his brother's work. The David and Goliath moment was not lost on him and he recognized the danger Doyle's swinging lantern presented. He aimed low, driving his head into Doyle's soft belly and knocking the man off his feet. They went to the floor together, Ben on top, and wrestled for possession of the lantern and the upper hand.

Ellie and Willet jumped out of the way as the men rolled between them. Ellie made a grab for the lantern as soon as she could, but Willet knocked her arm aside with enough force to make her stagger backward. Before she could recover, he was behind her with a forearm locked around her throat. He did not try to cut off her air. He wanted her son to hear her strangled cry.

Ben did hear it. He stopped grappling with Doyle. "Let her go!" He tried to scramble to his feet, but Doyle would not surrender his hold. The lantern rolled sideways. Oil seeped onto the floor.

Willet marched Ellie toward the combatants. When he was close enough to make himself felt, he jammed the pointed toe of one boot into Doyle's side. "Ease up there, Doyle. We're done here, and he's finished." To make certain he spoke the truth, he brought his lantern down hard on Ben's head. Glass shattered, oil spilled, and flame followed the rivulet into Ben's hair. Ellie fought to get out from under Willet's arm but the pressure across her throat had become too much and it was only a matter of moments before she couldn't breathe.

Doyle shoved Ben away. "Damn, Willet, you lit him up." He slapped halfheartedly at the fire smoldering in Ben's hair.

"What the hell are you doing?" asked Willet. "Leave him." He removed his arm from Ellie's throat as soon as he felt her slight weight become heavy against him. She collapsed on the floor beside Ben.

"Hell," said Doyle. "You could've set me on fire." He was still examining his clothing as he got to his knees.

"You're fine. Get up." Willet picked up the lantern Doyle had dropped earlier and smashed it against an empty stall. This time oil dripped onto a hay bale. Flames left the lantern in a cascade and spread across the top of a bale. Where oil sprinkled the sides of the stall, flames licked the wood and slipped into the crevices. "We're going. You take the back. I'll get this door."

Ben stirred.

Willet pointed to him. "Do something about that, Doyle."

Doyle regarded Ben dispassionately and then aimed his boot at the younger man's chin. The kick was vicious. Ben's head snapped back, he groaned, and then he lay quiet as death. "Back door," said Doyle. "Got it. And Willet?"

"Yes?"

"Sorry I doubted about the guns. You were right. We didn't need them."

Remington heaved himself into the opening between the bales as soon as the Putty brothers left the barn. He pointed Phoebe to the large square door that was used to hoist bales into the loft before he remembered that it had been temporarily nailed closed to prevent accidents. "Never mind. Can you follow me?"

"Don't worry about me. Go on."

He made a rapid descent to the bottom, jumping free of the ladder when he still had five rungs to go. He ignored the fire spreading in the stall and went straight to Ben, took off his jacket, and used it to smother the flames crawling along

Ben's neck, collar, and across his shoulders. The air around Ben was filled with the acrid scent of burnt hair and flesh.

Out of the corner of his eye, he caught the last few feet of Phoebe's descent. He did not want her trying to slip past the fire in the stall for fear that her dress would attract the flames like a candlewick. "Try the back door!" he called out. He was not hopeful that she would be able to open it, not after Willet directed his brother to leave by that exit, but it was the safer option for a first try at escape. He wanted to be wrong, but when he heard Phoebe shouting for help, he knew he was not. He could barely hear her above the crackle of the flames and the fiddle music. She reappeared moments later and hovered on the other side of the fire, shaking her head.

"They've barred or jammed it from the outside. I can't budge it, and I think someone would have to be passing very close to hear me." Mindful of the fire, which had begun to crawl across the hay-strewn floor, Phoebe raised her skirt and gathered it as close as possible. She felt heat on her calves as she jumped this newly erected fence of flames. As soon as she was safely on the other side, Phoebe dropped her gown and ran to the barn door. She yanked and shoved. The door shuddered when she put her shoulder into it, but it didn't budge. Frustrated, she beat at it with her fists and called out as loud as she was able.

Remington redirected her attention. "Come here and stay beside Ben. See if you can rouse Ellie or this fellow."

"Mr. Shoulders? No. I'll tend to Ellie and Ben."

He was satisfied with that. "I'm going to get blankets out of the tack room. Don't move." He gave her his jacket. "Use this on the fire if it breaks this way. Watch that your gown doesn't catch."

Phoebe waved him away. "Go."

Remington found a stack of blankets in the tack room and carried them out. In the short time he had been gone, flames had leaped to three more bales. The surface and sides of all of them were carpeted by fire but the dense centers were still untouched. Phoebe was no longer crouched beside the Putty brothers' unconscious victims. She had purposely put herself away from them and was standing in a ring of fire that was nibbling away at the hem of her cone-shaped skirt. She was alternately beating at the flames and trying to wriggle out of the gown. Trying to do both at once was what was defeating her.

Remington rushed through the firewall that now separated them and knocked Phoebe to the floor. He snapped open one of the blankets, rolled her onto it, and wrapped it around her feet and ankles until the flames were extinguished.

"It's all right," she said, sitting up. "It's done. Help me out of this." She twisted and presented him with her back. "It happened so fast. The oil from the lanterns. It seeped into the cracks in the floorboards. They just erupt." Even as she said it, a line of fire suddenly appeared near Ellie's feet and raced in the direction of her dress. "Get Ellie," she said. "I can do this."

Remington looked at the long line of fabric-covered buttons that closed the bodice and wasn't as sure, but he also knew the futility of arguing. He left Phoebe's side to hook Ellie under her shoulders and drag her to one side of the door, well away of the encroaching flames—for now. He did the same for Ben, and then for Mr. Shoulders, though he was sorely inclined to abandon him to the fire.

Phoebe had managed to tear away most of the buttons at her back and was trying to shimmy out of the gown when Remington returned to help her. He made fists in the silk on either side of her hips and yanked hard. The fabric gave way and fell in a puddle at her feet. He didn't wait for her to move; he lifted her out and away from the skirt. She did not so much shed the bodice as molt it. In spite of the burgeoning heat from the fire, Phoebe shivered violently. He started to pull her into his arms, and God knew, that was what she wanted, but she shook her head and asked for a blanket instead.

Remington spread one open for her, and when she walked into it, he wrapped her inside. "Go wait by the door." He coughed. Smoke filled his nostrils. He breathed in a lungful. "Stay low. Find somewhere you can breathe."

"What are you going to do?"

"I'm going to try to put out the fire."

Phoebe looked past his shoulder to where the flames were sliding into a second stall. Another bale of hay erupted. "Can't you fire a shot? Someone would hear that. Where is your gun?"

"In the house."

She glanced behind her at Ben and Mr. Shoulders. "What about them?"

He shook his head. "We put the guns up, remember? So no one would get foolish."

"Let me help you, then." Phoebe did not wait to see if he would agree to it. She stripped off the blanket and side-stepped Remington to attack the fire wearing her ice blue corset, matching garters, and silk stockings.

Watching her, Remington could imagine the fire retreating in the face of Phoebe's Amazon warrior fierceness. When it didn't, he followed her into battle.

Chapter Forty-three

The Honorable Judge Miner stepped out of the bunkhouse with more money in his pockets than when he went in. It was his opinion that coming out ahead made it a worthwhile use of his time. Thaddeus Frost's fine liquor was an additional bonus. The judge recognized there were less than half the guests present than there were when he took refuge at the card table, but there was still plenty of food to be had and dancing to be done. He was making a relatively straight path for the lovely Mrs. Frost when he veered sharply to the left. Someone observing him might have attributed his sudden change of course to inebriation, but that would have been the wrong conclusion.

Judge Miner had just spied the Putty brothers. He couldn't recall seeing them earlier, or at least not seeing them present at the nuptials, but then there had been such a gathering that he could easily have missed them. There also existed the very real possibility that they would have used the crowd to hide from him. If they'd seen him, they would have been relieved when he disappeared into the bunkhouse.

Judge Miner sidled right up to Willet Putty and threw a friendly arm around the man's shoulders. When he spoke, though, it was to the sheriff. "These boys giving you any trouble, Jackson?"

"Not a whit," Brewer said. He waved a lantern over the table where the guests who had been carrying had put down their gun belts. "It's like an armory. We're trying to find a tooled leather belt and a Colt with a pearl grip. We have plenty of ivory grips, but not one of the other. Mr. Doyle Putty says it belongs to him, but I don't see it."

The judge leaned forward and poked his head around Willet so he could see Doyle. "Is that right, Doyle? You own something like that? Or could it be that you saw it earlier and thought you'd like to leave with something different than you carried in? We've talked about this sort of thing before, haven't we? At least that's my recollection." He felt Willet try to shrug him off. Instead of removing his arm, he tightened his grip under the guise of another friendly squeeze.

Jackson Brewer's gaze shifted from the table to the Putty brothers. "You familiar with these men, Judge?"

"We have a nodding acquaintance. Isn't that right? Doyle? Willet?" When neither man spoke, the judge added, "I know their daddy a mite better, but these two have passed in front of my bench now and again. Just passed, mind you. Slippery. The pair of them. What was it last time, boys? Something about welshing on a bet. Or was it about a missing side of beef? I had to throw it out because the man who brought the complaint didn't show for court."

"Interesting," said Brewer. "So, Doyle, do you see your gun on the table or not?"

Doyle shifted his weight from side to side. "No, sir, I guess I don't see it. Come to think of it, I left my gun behind."

Judge Miner nodded. "There you go, Sheriff. No gun. What about you, Willet? Were you carrying?"

Willet pointed to a scarred brown leather belt with an ivory grip six-shooter in the holster. "That's mine."

Sheriff Brewer picked it up, examined it, and returned it to the table. "I'm not comfortable passing it to you right now, but if no one else claims it by the end of the night, I'll have it for you tomorrow in my office. You can come by and pick it up. How's that suit?"

"That'd be fine," said Willet.

"Excellent." Judge Miner removed his arm from around Willet's shoulders and patted him on the back. "You boys go along now, and make sure you're riding out on what you rode in."

Jackson watched them go. "Is it my imagination, or do they look like they're struggling not to run?"

"Probably not your imagination. They have what you'd call a natural inhibition when it comes to the law."

"You sure? Doyle Putty talked to me for quite a spell earlier."

"Huh. First I heard of a Putty doing that. Mostly they try to steer clear. I probably only see them a quarter of the time I should, but on the other hand, they're probably only guilty of about half the things folks credit them with. You'll have to figure out how that adds up. I was never good with fractions."

Inside the barn, Remington and Phoebe were making no headway against the fire. They extinguished flames blanketing two of the bales, but while they worked, the fire spread to more stalls.

Remington circled Phoebe's waist with an arm and dragged her away from the heat and billowing smoke. When they were close to the door, he released her waist and set his hands on her shoulders. Her face was streaked with soot and beaded with sweat. Her eyes were awash in bitterly angry tears. She held the smoldering blanket she had been using to fight the fire in front her, one corner in each blackened fist.

Remington lowered his head, met her eyes. "Listen to me. We can't win this. We're going to lose the barn, but that's all we've been fighting to save. The fire is our escape, Phoebe. We just have to keep it from reaching us until someone on the outside recognizes what's happened. We'll be in the most danger after they remove the bar and open the door. The fire will leap this way. We won't be able to stop it. It will beat our rescuers back, and you and I will have to move quickly and be ready to take Ellie and Ben with us."

"Mr. Shoulders?"

"Ellie and Ben first."

Phoebe nodded. "I can drag Ellie out."

Remington took the blanket from her hands. "You get under the smoke. Stay beside the door, not in front of it. It won't be long." He pointed to the loft. Floating embers had ignited some of the bales forming the barricade. "The roof's next. We want the fire to break through there."

Remington waited until Phoebe crouched below the smoke before he left her side. He wrapped the blanket he took from her around his shoulders and grabbed a second one to pull over his head. Without a word of his intentions, Remington ran headlong into the wall of fire. He heard Phoebe cry out and recognized it as a cry for him not as sign that she was in danger. He ignored it.

His goal was the ladder on the other side of the dancing, crackling flames. He threw off his blankets, grabbed hold of a slat, and began to climb. When he reached the loft, he shoved several of the burning bales out of his way, and then raised the ladder to use like a battering ram against the roof. He struck again and again. His arms trembled with the weight of the ladder and the jarring force he was using to punch a hole. Wood cracked and creaked but it was impossible to know if the cause was his relentless effort or the work of the equally insistent fire.

None of it was as welcome to his ears as the sound of Phoebe heaping curses on his head. Apparently she had a list of them.

Thaddeus opened his arms to Fiona and invited her to sit on his lap. He expelled a breath when she collapsed heavily on the seat he made for her.

"Did you just *oof*?" she asked, leaning backward to get a better look at his face.

He pretended ignorance. Sometimes it was a husband's only defense. "Hmm?"

Fiona patted his cheek. "I'm going to let that go." She slipped off his lap and onto the bench beside him and promptly rested her head against his shoulder. "I am exhausted, Thaddeus, and replete, and I cannot remember when I have enjoyed myself more. Judge Miner would not release me. I had to beg him for a drink so I could sneak away."

Thaddeus chuckled. "He was resting his legs under a poker table most of the day."

"Ah, so that's where he disappeared after the ceremony. Have you seen Remington? Phoebe? They shouldn't leave without saying farewell to their guests."

Thaddeus looked around. "I don't think they've actually gone anywhere. More likely they wanted a little time away."

"That's what the honeymoon is for. Will you at least tell me where they're going?"

"After they've left. I promise."

Fiona sighed. "I don't understand why people don't trust me with their secrets when I've proven that I know how to keep them."

"You know I'd tell—" He stopped because Fiona sat up abruptly. She lifted her head and sniffed the air.

"Thaddeus? I smell—"

"Smoke," he said. "I do, too. The wind's shifted. It's coming from the bonfires."

She frowned. A sharp crease appeared between her eyebrows. "I don't think so." She jumped to her feet and began to turn. "This smells more like . . ." Fiona grabbed Thaddeus's shoulder. "Thad! The barn's on—" She didn't finish her sentence. She didn't have to. At least four people shouted it out for her.

"Fire!"

The music stopped. The band threw down their instruments, jumped off the porch, and ran full tilt toward the barn. Guests abandoned the tables, left the circle of the bonfires, and dropped their drinks. The men in the bunkhouse were moved to leave it as soon as the shouting reached them, and when they recognized the cause of the commotion, they directed people to the watering troughs and the well. Women joined the men to start a brigade.

Thaddeus caught Scooter Banks by the sleeve. "Where's Remington? Is he with you? I don't see him!"

Fiona jammed a fist against her mouth as spindles of fire arose from a hole in the roof. "Phoebe! Has anyone seen

Phoebe?" She grabbed Jackson Brewer's arm as he was hurrying past and pulled him up short. "I can't find Phoebe! She would have come running if she could. Remington, too. I'm afraid they're—" She couldn't say her fear aloud and accepted that Jackson would nevertheless understand.

"I'll see to it," he promised, and then he was running again.

Remington dropped the ladder over the side of the loft once he had opened the roof. The blankets he had used to protect himself earlier were now ablaze. Descending the ladder would be like choosing to enter one of the circles of hell. Before he took that path, he began pushing bales of hay off the lip of the loft. Although some of them were burning when he dropped them, none of them exploded into flames. Just the opposite, in fact, the thick bales smothered a swath of fire. The unfortunate consequence was impenetrable clouds of smoke.

Remington could no longer draw a breath without coughing. He grabbed the top of the ladder, swung around, and lowered himself four rungs before he surrendered to the inevitable and jumped. Phoebe might have screamed. He couldn't be sure. They were both choking on the smoke.

The bales cushioned his fall. The sleeve of his coat smoldered. He slapped at it as he scrambled over the hay bales and charged forward. He was gratified to see that Phoebe hadn't moved from where he left her. He dove for her, tunneling under the heavy layer of smoke. She kept him from banging his head against the wall.

"They have to be close," he said between coughs. "The fire's through the roof. Can you shout? Curse? Bang the walls?"

She did all of that. He rose to his knees and joined her. Behind them, the fire continued to creep in their direction. Occupied with attracting attention, neither of them saw the man they knew only as Mr. Shoulders heave himself off the barn floor and climb the wall hand over hand until he was standing on his feet.

It was when Mr. Shoulders began to cough that Remington became aware of him. "Get down! You can't breathe up there."

"Can't . . . breathe . . . down . . . there." He pounded his fists against the wall. "Got . . . to . . . get . . . out."

Phoebe tried to make herself heard over the hand she was using to cover her mouth and nose. "Do what he says. Get down! I think I can hear them. They're coming." Her intention was to keep pleading but she did not have the breath for it. She gave up and went back to pounding the wall.

Natty Rahway inched sideways and tripped over the unconscious bodies of Ellie and Ben. He sprawled on the ground, picked himself up to his knees, and crawled toward the barn door.

Remington made a grab for him and missed. He also called out a warning. It was ignored. "Get ready, Phoebe. I think you're right. They're close." He crawled sideways, found Ellie, and rolled her toward Phoebe. "Take her wrist. You'll have to move fast."

"Worry about yourself."

Remington cupped the back of her head in his palm. What he did then could hardly be called a kiss, not when his mouth was as hot, hard, and sooty as a branding iron. "Sweet Jesus, but I love you."

The door opened then. They sheltered their heads while Natty Rahway was consumed in a tornado of fire.

Epilogue

The honeymoon was postponed. Twice. Once for their convalescence, which Fiona and Thaddeus insisted on supervising at Twin Star, no matter the inconvenience to Dr. Dunlop, who had to make the journey from town daily in the beginning and then three times a week after he was able to convince Thaddeus that it was sufficient to monitor their progress. The second delay was forced on them when the Putty brothers proved to be every bit as slippery as Judge Miner had once named them. The posse was seven men strong and included experienced deputies from neighboring counties, but the brothers eluded capture for six weeks by doing something no one suspected they would do. They split up. There was talk of dividing the posse at that point, but Jackson Brewer was of the opinion that concentrating on one would eventually lead them to the other. They identified Doyle as their priority. The posse numbered eight men by then because Remington left Twin Star to join the search as soon as Doc Dunlop pronounced Phoebe fit. His residual cough kept him from receiving the same clean bill of health, but he'd had enough of everyone's hovering and coddling by then, and with Phoebe's blessing—some would say insistence—he left Twin Star to join Sheriff Brewer.

They tracked Doyle to a whorehouse in Harmony, then to a saloon in Jupiter, from there to a hotel in Lansing managed by a distant cousin who didn't hold with his nonsense, and finally found him in a Denver jail sleeping off a drunk and disorderly charge after losing at the card table in the Palladium.

Willet may well have been the cleverer of the brothers, but as it happened, he was also a creature of habit. Doyle had no compunction about telling them that, although in fairness, Remington questioned him while he was still under the influence of Rocky Mountain moonshine. Willet, they learned, returned to what was familiar, and what he knew best was the protection of the family. Although they had been to several of the Putty households previously, Willet was too well hidden. Now they changed tactics and staked out the old homestead. They ran him to earth in his mother's house just as he was sitting down to Sunday dinner. They were graciously offered to partake in chicken and gravy over hot biscuits—which they did—and as good as that meal was, it didn't sway them from taking Willet into custody once their plates were clean.

The brothers were now safely behind bars in the Frost Falls jail although not in separate cells. There was some talk that maybe one of them would kill the other out of sheer annoyance and save the town the trouble of separate trials, which their lawyers were insisting was their right since they were brothers, not Siamese twins. Judge Miner had yet to rule.

Ben and Ellie recovered more slowly. Thaddeus paid for Ellie to stay at the Butterworth, where Dr. Dunlop could attend her. Phoebe vacated her room to be with Remington, and Ben was moved back in. Ben had burns on his scalp and neck that required frequent dressing changes and the application of specially made ointments. His cough was deeper and raspier than either Phoebe's or Remington's, and for a time they all feared his lungs would not heal. Fiona stayed at his bedside for long hours. She changed his bandages, applied the ointments, read to him, performed scenes in which she occupied all the characters, and sometimes she simply sat.

No charges were being brought against either Ellie or Ben. Phoebe put forth the argument that Ellie's plan was merely an abduction for ransom. Remington quibbled with the modifier "merely," but he let it go in the interest of reaching consensus. It was Phoebe's position that if the plan had been executed as intended, she would have been the only victim, and because she was reasonably well treated and returned unharmed, which was also Ellie's plan, she felt it was her prerogative not to pursue action against Ellie. She further argued that Ellie had not hired the Putty brothers or Natty Rahway. What she had done, through her son, was make them aware of an opportunity. She did not advance them any money. On the contrary, Natty Rahway delivered money to her, again through Ben.

When she was done, Jackson Brewer regarded Remington with a jaundiced expression and asked who exactly was the lawyer in the family.

Thaddeus had slightly different reasons for not seeking a full reckoning in court. The fact that he had been wholly unaware of Ellie's deep and abiding feelings troubled him. That his ignorance might have contributed to her actions troubled him even more, and then there was the question of Ben's parentage, which he was only now beginning to wrestle with. It pained him to admit aloud that he had suspected Fiona of concocting the plot to take Phoebe hostage. Oddly enough, or perhaps not, Fiona was flattered that he thought her capable of so much scheming, and further moved by his desire not to see her exposed for it.

Phoebe could only shake her head at this line of reasoning, and when she looked askance at Remington, it was to find him similarly confounded.

Northeast Rail was satisfied to have the Putty brothers in custody for destroying company property when they tore up the tracks and for stealing from the passengers. Some of the jewelry had already been recovered thanks to Willet and Doyle's mostly accurate report of where they had sold it. Representatives from the railroad offered to plead with the judge for a lighter sentence if the brothers cooperated, and the Puttys accepted that offer.

The brothers neglected to account for Jackson Brewer, though, and the sheriff had definite ideas about what he thought was appropriate justice. The murders of Blue Armstrong and

Caroline Carolina had but one outcome as far as he was concerned. The Putty brothers could hear the construction of the gallows from their jail cells.

Phoebe and Remington were thinking about none of that at the moment. Their concerns were very much in the present. Phoebe was trying to hold on to Remington after being swept off her feet and then being ordered to close her eyes. Remington was occupied with all of Phoebe's wriggling while making sure she wasn't peeking.

They had yet to cross the threshold of Old Man McCauley's ramshackle cabin because someone had taken it upon himself to lock the door. Remington adjusted Phoebe's weight in his arms as he grappled with the door handle.

"Who the hell thought this was a good idea?" he muttered. "I swear . . ."

Phoebe chuckled, but she didn't open her eyes. "I didn't know the door had a lock."

"It didn't."

"Oh, then who's been here? Are we trespassing?"

"Hardly. I bought the place. Can you reach above the door frame and see if the idiot who put a lock on the door thought he should leave a key? Just feel around for it."

This news of ownership was surprising and actually quite pleasing. "Really? You bought it?"

"Wedding gift. Please, Phoebe, the key."

Grinning, she kept one arm around his neck and stretched the other to find the narrow ledge made by the frame. "This is a little ridiculous, you know. It's not as if I don't know where we are or that I haven't been here before. Oh, wait. I think . . . yes, got it." She fisted the skeleton key, but before she gave it to him, she raised her eyelashes just a fraction and regarded him from under their dark fan. "I'm sure there are brides who imagine honeymooning in Europe or New York or San Francisco, but I'm not one of them. This is the most romantic gesture you could have made, and I will always cherish that you did it for me." She dangled the key in front of him and closed her eyes again.

"I'm hoping you still feel that way once we're inside—if

we get inside." He pecked her on the lips, rebalanced her in his arms, and fumbled with the key in the lock. When he felt the latch give, he toed the door open and was finally able to carry Phoebe across the threshold. Looking around, he whistled softly. This was something more than he'd expected. "The elves have been busy," he said. "Very busy."

"How's that again? You cannot be cryptic when my eyes are closed, not if you hope to be understood."

"Go ahead," he said, lowering her to the floor. "Open them."

She did and was stunned into silence. While the outside of the cabin was largely the same except for some shoring up of the supporting stone columns, the interior was something altogether different. A patterned carpet in rich plum, cherry, and dark leaf green hues had been rolled out so that it occupied most of the single room's center space. The stove had been blackened and polished and now had the appearance of new. Someone had whitewashed the rough walls and painted the cupboards cherry red. There was a painted table in the same cheerful color and two matching spindle chairs. The footstool had been padded and covered in damask. An eyelet lace valance hung above a remarkably clean window, and three small tin pails filled with wildflowers, reminiscent of the table settings at their wedding, were lined up on the sill.

Old Man McCauley's sturdy, square-legged bed was gone. So was the thin, lumpy mattress. In its place was an iron rail bed with a plump mattress, clean sheets, multiple pillows, and two quilts as colorful as the carpets. Best of all, the bed was wide enough for two to sleep comfortably and cozy enough for every other thing.

"Oh, my," said Phoebe. "You think this is the work of elves?"

"Uh-huh. They go by names like Ralph, Les, Johnny, Arnie, and Scooter. Scooter has pointy ears. You ever notice that?"

She chuckled and leaned into him. "You're surprised?"

"I am." His arms circled her. "Thaddeus and I came out once to do some work on the place. That was before the wedding, when Mrs. Fish was at the ranch to do alterations and we were banished. We cleaned up, talked about what could be done to make it ready if not precisely civilized. He thought I was out of my mind for wanting to bring you up here, but I remembered what you said about having a fondness for the place, and it felt right to me."

"I'm glad. It *is* right."

"Old Man McCauley would hate what's become of it. I think he'd appreciate the bed—my idea, by the way, or at least the mattress was—but all the other touches? He'd object. I'm certain of it."

"Well, I think it's charming. All of it." She found his hand, squeezed it. "Why don't you see to the horses and then bring in the hamper Mrs. Packer prepared for us? I'll set the table. I'm thinking the elves probably left dishes for us. Les would think of that." Phoebe looked to the window and the pretty flowers on the sill. "Does Fiona know we're here?"

"She didn't, not at first, but she wheedled it out of Thaddeus when our departure was delayed." He followed her gaze to the window. "You think those were her contribution?"

"Don't you? They're her peace offering."

"You could be right."

"I am." She stepped out of the circle of his arms and gave him a gentle push toward the door. "Go. Horses first. Then food. I'm hungry." She hovered in the doorway. "Do you still have the key?" When Remington showed it to her, she said, "Good. Keep it." Then she closed the door behind him and turned the latch.

"Hey!"

"Horses," she called from the other side. "Then food." She pressed her ear to the door, heard him step off the stoop, and only then did she begin preparing for his return.

Phoebe told herself she should have known he wouldn't be gone long. The man was nothing if not optimistic, and he would not have missed the sheet she hung in the window to keep him from looking in. That all but telegraphed that she was up to no good, or alternatively, that she was up to something very good.

"Just another moment," she called out when she heard the key in the lock. She grabbed her thick plait of hair and pulled it forward over her shoulder. She hurriedly plucked at the braid, unwinding it until her hair fell freely in a cascade of waves. The black grosgrain ribbon that had held it together dangled between her fingers. Her moment was up. The latch was turning. She tossed the ribbon into the air. It was still floating to the floor when Remington stepped into the room.

"Mother of God," he whispered when he saw her standing beside the bed.

"Um, no. Not her." Phoebe's attempt at wry humor did not alight with her usual aplomb. She blamed it on the fact that Remington's eyes were hot enough to melt her ice blue corset, or at least it seemed that way. She swallowed hard. This was, after all, something he had seen her wearing before, but perhaps the threat of being burned alive had made it less provocative at the time. He looked extraordinarily provoked now.

Remington dropped the hamper. It thumped hard on the carpet, proof that it had been packed with enough foodstuffs to survive the apocalypse. In contrast, the key hardly made a sound when it fell.

"Don't move," he said. "I'm the one who needs another moment."

She blushed fiercely, though she wasn't sure why. The way he looked at her was nothing but flattering. Well, perhaps there was something dangerous there, and yes, she spied a hint of carnal villainy, but mostly it was flattering if she thought of herself as a little iced cake and him as the rascal who was intent on finishing her off in a single bite.

"This isn't the same corset," she said by way of making conversation. "The one I meant for our wedding night was scorched." She raised her left leg a few inches off the floor, turned her foot this way and that to show off the white kid ankle boots. "New stockings, too. But these are the same garters. If you look closely, you can see soot that no amount of scrubbing can remove."

"Is that right? I'll be sure to take a closer look." Remington removed his hat and flung it toward the table. It skittered across the top and stopped short of falling over the far side.

"Um. Maybe I should unpack the hamper."

"I wouldn't try it if I were you. I'm still strapped."

She bit her lip to keep from laughing outright. "Are you threatening me, Mr. Frost?"

"Is it working?"

"I haven't moved, have I?"

"Then, yes, I'm threatening you." He dropped his gun belt and made sure she knew it was still in easy reach. He unfastened the fly of his trousers, looked down at his boots, and then at Phoebe. "I'm coming to you."

Now she did laugh. He sat on the edge of the bed to remove his boots while Phoebe quelled the urge to gather up and fold his discarded clothes. "I could help you," she said to distract herself from the shirt that draped the hamper.

He shook his head. "I know what you want to do. Go on. Get them. You'll feel better for it and I will be the beneficiary of all your good works."

She kicked him lightly in the shin that was no longer protected by a boot.

"Ow. What was that for?"

"For being right." She stepped over his outstretched legs and picked up his clothes, folded them, and placed them on one of the chairs. She didn't return to the bed until he handed over his trousers. Once they were in the same pile as everything else, Remington opened his arms wide and Phoebe fairly flew into them. She pushed Remington backward on the bed and followed him down, grinning as she planted kisses at the corners of his mouth, on his chin, at his temples, everywhere, in fact, except squarely on his lips.

He caught her face in his palms, held her still, and watched the centers of her green eyes darken until the gold flecks all but disappeared. "The first time I saw you in that corset, you were as fierce as an Amazon warrior. I expected the flames to retreat just because you willed them to."

She smiled. "What a lovely compliment. And what about the second time you saw me in it?"

"Well, that was different. I guess you'd say I had a vision of the Promised Land and was preparing to atone for every sin, real and imagined, just to reach it."

"I wouldn't say that. No one would say that. Most likely that vision you had was Sodom and Gomorrah. Really, Remington, the way you looked at me, it's a wonder you aren't a pillar of salt."

His laughter shook her, enveloped her, and eventually took her breath away. Her heart stuttered. His dark eyes held her with adoration and amusement, and she was glad for both. "I suppose you could say I love you," she whispered against his lips.

One corner of his mouth lifted. "No supposing about it," he told her. "I would always say that."

Turn the page for a preview of Jo Goodman's

The Devil You Know

Available now from Berkley Sensation!

Pancake Valley was seventy-five square miles of prime grazing land, fit for raising beef cattle for the Chicago stockyards and smart, surefooted horses for cutting herds, mountain tracking, or outfitting an Army troop. The lay of the land bore no resemblance to any sort of pancake, flapjack, or johnnycake, nor was it properly a valley. But upon claiming the land in 1839, Obadiah Pancake declared its peculiar saddle shape to be a valley and so it was known from that day forward.

Wilhelmina Pancake had known her Grandpa Obie, remembered quite clearly sitting on his lap in the rocker he brought all the way from Philadelphia because he promised Granny that he would. She remembered that Granny complained, mostly good-naturedly, that excepting for the years she was nursing her sons, Obie and Willa got more use out of that rocker than she ever did.

Grandpa Obie was gone almost a score of years now, having taken a spill from a fiercely bucking mare that he was trying to break. Instead, the mare broke him, snapping his neck like a frozen twig. Willa had known he was gone before she reached him, and she had wanted to put the mare down, but Granny had stopped her, taking the gun out of her hands and holding her so tightly that Willa thought she might suffocate in that musky bosom. She hadn't, though, and was glad for those moments because it was only a few years later that Granny passed.

Some days Willa missed that bosom, missed the comfort of it the way she missed her grandpa's lap. From time to time, she sat in the rocker, but it wasn't the same, and unless Annalea crawled into her lap—and really, Annalea was getting too big to be an easy fit—Willa found sitting there to be a bittersweet experience that was best avoided.

Willa lifted her face to the halcyon sky, tipping back her pearl gray Stetson, and let sunlight wash over her. She remained in that posture, one gloved hand resting on the top rail of the corral and the other keeping her hat in place, and waited for sunlight and the cool, gentle breeze to press color into her cheeks and sweep away the melancholy.

"Use your knees!" she called to Cutter Hamill as she pulled herself up to stand on the bottom rail. "Get your hand up! She's going to throw you!" No sooner had the words left her mouth than the cinnamon mare with the white star on her nose—named Miss Dolly for no reason except that Annalea declared it should be so—changed tactics and crow-hopped hard and high, unseating her rider and forcing him to take a graceless, humiliating fall.

Miss Dolly settled, shaking off the lingering presence of her rider even though she could see his face was planted in the dirt. She nudged him once with her nose as if to prove there were no hard feelings, and then she walked toward Willa, her temperament once again serene.

Willa threw one leg over the top rail, and then the other. She sat perfectly balanced, her boot heels hooked on the middle rail, and braced herself for Miss Dolly's approach and inevitable nuzzling.

"You all right, Cutter?" she asked as she held the mare's head steady and stroked her nose. "This little lady has no use for you climbing on her back."

Cutter lifted himself enough to swivel his head in Willa's direction. "She's no lady, no matter what Annalea says." He laid his cheek flat to the dirt again. "Anyone else see me fall?"

Willa looked around. Except for animals of the four-legged kind, the area was deserted. "Happy's inside the house, making dinner if you can take him at his word, and

Zach must be in the barn, leastways I don't see him out and about. Seems like I'm the only witness, and you know I don't carry tales."

"I don't know that," he said. "I don't know that at all."

She chuckled. "Go on. Get up and shake it off." Willa could not repress a sympathetic smile as Cutter groaned softly and pushed to his knees. He rolled his shoulders to test the waters, and upon discovering he was still connected bone to bone, scrambled to his feet.

Unfolding to his full height, he shook himself out with the unconscious ease and energy of a wet, playful pup. At nineteen, Cutter still had a lot of pup in him, though Willa knew he thought of himself as full grown into manhood. She had suspected for a time that he favored her in a moony, romantic sort of way in spite of the fact she was five years his senior and his boss, at least in practice, and she was careful to treat him as fairly as she did the other hand and not encourage any nonsense.

Annalea, though, did encourage nonsense, and took every opportunity to make faces behind Cutter's back but with Willa in her open line of sight. Annalea would pucker her lips and make a parody of kissing. She also liked to hug herself and pretend to engage in what she imagined to be a passionate embrace. In the first instance, she looked like a fish trying to capture a wriggling worm; in the second, she looked like the wriggling worm. Thus far, Cutter had not caught her out, but odds were that he would eventually, so Willa saved the scold that Annalea was certainly due and waited for the more enduring lesson of natural consequence.

Cutter removed his sweat-banded hat and ran one hand through a thatch of wheat-colored hair before he settled it on his head again. He grinned at Willa. "You want me to give it another try?" he asked.

"Give what another try? Getting thrown?"

He flushed but held his ground. "I thought I'd—"

"I know what you meant. Lead her around, let her walk off the jitters, and then take her to the barn and wipe her

down. And talk to her while you're doing it. You don't talk
to the animals nearly enough, Cutter. Miss Dolly will respond to your voice if you sweeten it a bit."

Cutter regarded her skeptically but kept his questions to
himself. He dusted off his pants and shirt and dutifully
started walking toward Miss Dolly.

Willa chuckled under her breath when the mare sidled
just outside of Cutter's reach as he approached. "Sweet talk,
Cutter," she called to him.

"Is that what you want, girl? Sweet talk?"

At the sound of the smooth, tenor tones of her father's
voice at her back, Willa shifted so sharply on the fence rail
that she nearly unseated herself. "I thought you were making supper."

"I *am* making supper. Just stirred the pot. No harm leaving it alone for a minute. I saw Cutter take a fall and thought
maybe I should check on the boy myself."

"He's fine, Happy."

Simultaneous to Willa's pronouncement, Cutter yelled
over. "I'm fine, Happy."

Willa returned her attention to Cutter but spoke to her
father. "See? You have it twice over. Better go check on that
pot because it won't stir itself."

Happy shrugged, and except to reach for a flask inside
his scarred leather vest, he didn't move. "Feeling a chill,"
he said by way of explanation, although Willa had given no
indication she knew he had his flask in his hand. "So what
about that sweet talk? You lookin' for some of that from
Mr. Cutter Hamill?"

Willa pretended she hadn't heard him.

He'd been christened Shadrach Ebenezer Pancake at
birth, but family lore had it that he carried on with so much
chortling gusto that it was only right and natural that he
should be called Happy. Since he had answered to the name
all of his life, most folks did not know he had another, which
suited Shadrach Ebenezer just fine when he was a youngster,
and later, when he was a husband and then a father. But now
that he was a widower, barely a father, and usually a drunk,

he wore the name like a hair shirt, and that, too, suited him in a dark, humorless fashion.

Happy sipped from the flask, capped it, and returned it to his vest. He folded his arms and set them on the top rail a short distance from where Willa sat.

"You should have a hat on," said Willa without glancing down. "Wind's picking up."

He nodded. "Going back in directly." Still, he didn't move.

Willa sighed. "You already burned supper, didn't you?"

"I might've scorched the biscuits."

"Stew?"

"I expect most of it will be good if we don't draw the ladle from the bottom of the pot."

Willa said nothing.

Happy grimaced in response to her silence. "I swear no one speaks as loudly as you do when you hold your tongue. Wouldn't hurt at all for you to let it out. Might even feel good uncorking that bottle of mad dog temper once in a while."

"I doubt it," she said, and her words were carried away on the wind. She called to Cutter before he disappeared into the barn. "Take your time. Supper's going to be—"

She stopped as a movement a hundred yards distant caught her eye. She tipped her hat forward to shade the winking sunlight and squinted at the tree line as a figure burst into the opening and continued racing toward them. "Now what is she up to? And where is John Henry?"

Happy scratched his head. "Damned if I know."

"I wasn't talking to you."

"Well, there's no one else around, is there?" Happy was forced to move when Willa swung her legs back over the fence and jumped down. He was perhaps all of two inches taller than his daughter, and when they were eye to eye, she looked right through him. He shivered. "I swear that cold shoulder you like to give me is a damn sight frostier than any wind coming off the mountains. I got ice splinters prickling my skin."

"Another reason you should have worn a hat."

"Maybe so. But I got this." He patted his vest to indicate his flask.

Without comment, Willa turned smartly on her heels and started off toward Annalea. Cutter, she noted, had also observed Annalea coming at them at a flat-out run, and she motioned to him to secure Miss Dolly and follow her. Her father stayed where he was, which to Willa's way of thinking was a point in his favor.

In spite of Willa's head start, Cutter's long legs carried him farther and faster, and he reached Annalea a few strides before she did. Willa wondered if he regretted it when Annalea launched herself at him. He staggered backward but managed to stay upright, sweeping Annalea into his arms before she caused his second spill of the day.

"Whoa! Whoa there, Annalea." Cutter set her down, unwound her arms from around his neck, and looked her over. Her cheeks were deeply flushed, and she was breathing hard. Her pigtails had mostly come undone. She inhaled loose, flyaway strands of dark hair and her fingers scrabbled at them to keep them out of her mouth. He simply shook his head. "Ain't no one called you for supper that I recollect, so what's chasing you?"

Willa caught up to the pair in time to hear Cutter's question. "Answer him," she said, her eyes focused once again on the tree line.

"She can't talk yet," said Cutter. "Near as I can tell, she's not hurt, but she's run a ways."

Willa gave her full attention to Annalea when she observed no disturbance in trees. Nothing was chasing Annalea except perhaps her own imagination. "Is he right? You're unhurt? Just nod your head."

Annalea sucked in a deep breath and nodded hard so there could be no mistaking the matter.

"Where's John Henry?"

Annalea pointed behind her.

"So he's following you?"

"No," Annalea said on a thread of sound. "Told him to stay."

One of Willa's expressive, arching eyebrows lifted a fraction. John Henry was devoted to Annalea. That the dog would stay anywhere without her was extraordinary, if it were true. "And he listened to you? That seems . . ." She paused, looking Annalea over again. "Where's your coat?"

"Left it with John Henry."

"That's no kind of answer."

"No kind of good answer," said Cutter.

Annalea shot him a withering look. "There's a man," she told Willa, using her thumb to point over her shoulder. "I found him a ways back close to Potrock Run, and I left John Henry with him to stand guard. He's hurt, Willa. Bad hurt. The man, not John Henry. I figure we should help him, Good Samaritan–like. That'd be the Christian thing to do."

"Maybe," said Willa. "And maybe not."

Annalea nodded gravely. "I already entertained that argument, but you go on ahead and have it out with yourself."

Willa gave a small start, blinked once, and then surrendered in the face of Annalea's clear and righteous expectations. "Very well. Cutter, sounds as if we'll need a wagon." Out of the corner of her eye, she saw Annalea nod. "Go on. Take care of that while I find out what else we need." She put her arm around Annalea's shoulders and gently urged her in the direction of the house. "C'mon. You're shivering."

"He was worse cold than me. That's why I gave him my coat."

"Well, I suppose that was a kindness as long as you don't take ill. If that happens, I might say it was foolish."

Without breaking stride, Willa shrugged out of her jacket and tucked it around Annalea. "Could be I'm foolish as well." She bathed in the warmth of Annalea's radiant and knowing smile all the way back to the house.

Happy wanted to come along and see the trespasser for himself, but Willa told him plainly that was not going to happen. She left Zach in charge of making certain her father did not attempt to follow. Happy was just tipsy enough to trip over his own feet. On horseback, he was a sure danger to himself and the animal, and there was still the matter of supper. Zach, at least, could be counted on to put something on the table they could actually eat.

Cutter and Willa rode on the wooden bench seat with a shotgun resting between them while Annalea huddled under two woolen blankets in the bed of the wagon and offered directions and commentary as necessity or her mood dictated.

"I don't think there will be any call to shoot him," said Annalea. "He is not likely to give you a reason."

Willa patted the Colt strapped to her right leg. The last thing she did before she left the house was put on her gun belt. Annalea had not commented at the time, but clearly she had been thinking about it ever since.

"We don't know anything about this man, and we don't know what to expect when we reach him. It's a certainty he didn't drag himself all over creation, so it could be that whoever did that to him is still around. Better to be prepared than not. Don't make me regret not tossing you out of the wagon and leaving you with Pa and Zach."

Willa looked back at Annalea, her eyebrows raised. "You understand?"

Turtle-like, Annalea poked her head outside the shell of her blankets. She nodded once. "I think the guns are an abundance of caution."

"Nothing wrong with that," said Cutter.

Annalea harrumphed too softly for Cutter to hear, but Willa caught it and quickly averted her head before Annalea saw her lips twitch.

Cutter pointed to a split in the pine trees up ahead. The parting made a natural fork in the trail. "Which way, Annalea? Right or left?"

Annalea mumbled under her blanket and Willa interpreted. "She says left."

Cutter gave the reins an expert tug and guided the mare to the left. Under his breath, he said, "You reckon he'll still be alive?"

Willa shrugged. How could she possibly answer? For Annalea's sake, she hoped he was, so she said that.

Annalea rose to her knees and inched toward the bench seat. She leaned forward, poked clear of the blankets, and inserted her head between Cutter and Willa. "Did I tell you he wanted me to leave him where he lay?"

"No," said Willa. "You did *not* tell us that."

"I figured he was talking out of his head so what he said he wanted was of no account." She nudged the shotgun a little to one side to make more room for her head. "John Henry licked his face. It was kinda sweet, him showing partiality like that, and I judged it to be a good sign."

Willa smiled wryly. "Of course you did."

Annalea suddenly thrust an arm between the pair to motion toward the bend up ahead. "Just around there. Look, you can see the grass is trampled coming off the hillside. He was dragged that way. Probably over that patch of rocks, too, and then across Potrock because he's on this side of it. Someone sure had it in for him."

"More like some*ones*," said Cutter, following the trail that emerged from the trees and took a meandering route toward the run.

Willa nodded. She was more interested in where the trail began than in where it ended. She looked as deeply as she could into the cluster of limber and lodgepole pines. The thick, scaly trunks made it difficult to see what might be hiding behind them, and the canopy of boughs cast a shadow across the area that the lowering sun could not penetrate. The surest way to learn if someone was watching with the intention to harm was to find Annalea's stranger and tend to him.

"There!" said Annalea, waving her hand up and down. "I see John Henry! Over there." She stopped waving and grabbed Cutter by the elbow to guide him as he was guiding the horse. "Do you see him?"

Cutter did. "You stay down in the back, Miss Annalea. Under the blankets would be better than out of them."

Annalea made a face with every intention that he should see it.

Willa clamped her hand over Annalea's head and firmly pushed her down. "Do what Cutter says. We will let you know when you can get out of the wagon." Willa noted that Annalea complied, albeit with little grace. And as compliance was all she cared about at the moment, she said nothing.

Cutter had not brought the wagon to a full stop before Willa hopped down. She left the shotgun with him and walked straightaway for the circle of trampled grass, opening her jacket and resting her hand lightly on the butt of her Colt. It was only when she reached John Henry and the stranger that her hand fell away.

It was clear at first glance that the man posed no threat. What required further investigation was whether or not he was breathing. Willa snapped her fingers to move John Henry out of the way, but he remained steadfastly obedient to the orders of his mistress and stayed nestled in the crook of the man's arm.

"Call your dog!"

Willa winced as Annalea's shrill whistle split the air around her, but John Henry leaped to the extent that his short legs would permit and hurried off toward the wagon. Shaking her head, Willa hunkered beside the stranger and bent her ear toward his mouth.

"You must be the help."

Startled as much by the warmth of his breath on her cheek as she was by his speech, Willa jerked back and stared into a pair of plainly pained and singularly colored blue-gray eyes.

"Wilhelmina Pancake. Willa."

"Ah."

He closed his eyes, and Willa was tempted to check for breathing again. She motioned for Cutter instead. "Bring the bandages and blankets. We can tend to some of these wounds before we put him in the wagon." She began to lift Annalea's coat but paused when the man shivered mightily. "It's got to be done," she said. "Hurry up, Cutter." She handed off the coat and took the bandages and blankets when Cutter arrived.

Cutter tossed Annalea her coat and then bent to help Willa. He whistled softly. "It's like she said. He's in a bad way."

"He can hear you," Willa told him. "Dip a couple of bandages in the run and wring them out. I'll clean the scrapes. How do you feel about putting the shoulder back in place?"

"Squeamish."

Willa and Cutter stared at the stranger because the response had come from him, and even though his eyes remained closed, it was as if he knew they were regarding him with equal parts astonishment and wariness because he said in a voice as abraded as his flesh, "I have a say, don't I?"

Willa glanced at Cutter, who she saw was looking a bit squeamish now that the stranger had spoken, and said, "I'll figure it out."

Cutter nodded and was off to do her bidding before she changed her mind. The stranger said nothing.

"There's really no choice," said Willa. "Not if you hope to have full use of your arm again. I can help you sit up if you can't do it on your own. I promise you the ride back to the house will be easier if I fix your shoulder now."

He made a small movement that might have been a shrug or a pathetic attempt to rise. Willa took it as the latter and slipped one arm under his back. He was not much in the way of help as she began to lift, and she could have used Cutter just then to lend some strength, but she heaved and he groaned with her effort and his own, and between them he came to a sitting position.

Willa could now see more evidence of his injuries. His jacket, vest, and shirt were shredded, and beads of dried blood, like so many black pearls, dotted the length of the abrasions. Under her examination, the lean muscles of his back jumped once and then were still. She tore her eyes away and said, "Tell me what happened."

"Do you need the distraction for what you're about to do or is it for my benefit?"

"Can't it be for both those things? Besides, you are going to do most of the work."

"I am?"

Willa nodded as she studied his legs. Annalea had said one of them was turned at an awkward angle, but that was not the case now. They were lying straight in front of him, the feet slightly turned out. "Start with what happened to your left shoe."

"I don't know where my shoe is."

"Which is not quite the same as telling me how you came to lose it."

He said nothing.

"Can you draw your knees toward your chest?" He grunted softly as he showed her that he could. "Wrap your arms around your knees. Palms over your kneecaps." Because his movements were slow and cautious, and she could hear the short, stuttered breaths he took, Willa thought Annalea was right about him having some cracked ribs. She lent him assistance, making sure his fingers were laced and the thumbs were up before she released him. "Grip tightly."

He frowned in anticipation of what was coming.

Willa looked up as Cutter returned. "Find a place to stand so Annalea can't see. I don't need eyes in the back of my head to know she's watching."

Cutter's eyes darted in the direction of the wagon. "That's a fact." He stepped sideways and blocked Annalea's view. "Does he have a name?"

"Imagine so. He hasn't offered it, and I haven't asked."

"She was more interested in what happened to my shoe."

Cutter's mouth twisted to one side in a look of perfect puzzlement. He scratched behind his ear. "Is that right, Willa?"

"It is."

"I guess you have your reasons."

"That's right." She saw that the stranger's grip had loosened, and she pressed his hands together. "In a moment I want you to lean back. Not far, not fast. I'll tell you when. Cutter, stay where you are. I'm going to move behind him to cushion him if his grip fails and he falls backward." Willa dropped to her knees and then into position. She laid her hands lightly on the stranger's shoulders. "All right. Lean back now."

The first movement was tentative, testing, and Willa put some strength into her fingers so he could feel the weight of them. "More," she said. "Lean back more. I've got you."

He did, this time with more confidence. His knuckles were bloodless, but the grip remained firm.

"You can shout," Cutter said.

Willa added, "Curse if you have a mind to."

"That's right," said Annalea, stepping out from behind Cutter. John Henry appeared from under her skirt and between her legs. "There's no ears here that haven't heard the like before, and that includes Mr. John Henry. As I recall, I heard you blaspheme on earlier acquaintance."

"Jesus," he said under his breath.

Annalea nodded sagely. "That's what I recall, too."

Willa looked sharply at Annalea. "I told you to stay in the wagon. Cutter, how did she get around you?"

He flushed but held his ground. "Sneaky as a sidewinder."

"I am," said Annalea, clearly proud.

"Then bring your sneaky self over here and hold his knees." She tapped her patient on his uninjured shoulder when Annalea was in place. "You don't have to hug him that hard."

"Oh." Annalea offered the stranger a rueful smile. "Sorry."

Willa thought she heard him curse under his breath again, but it might have been intended as a prayer this time. "Keep leaning back," she told him. "That's it. Stretch. More. More."

There was an audible popping sound when the shoulder joint realigned. Willa, Annalea, and Cutter all blinked. The stranger groaned once and then was silent. A heartbeat later his laced fingers unwound, his hands dropped away from his knees, and he collapsed against Willa.

"I didn't expect him to faint," Willa said, carefully lowering him to the ground. "But maybe that's better all the way around. It will ease the ride back for him *and* us." She shooed

John Henry out of the way as the dog came forward to sniff the stranger. "Annalea, put John Henry in the wagon and fetch me a cloth large enough to make a sling." She stretched out an arm toward Cutter. "The damp cloths, please."

While Willa tended to the stranger's cuts and scrapes, the rope burns around his wrists, Cutter walked off with the shotgun to explore the clearly marked trail made by dragging the man onto Pancake land. Annalea stayed with Willa, assisting now and again, but mostly she sat cross-legged at their patient's feet, still and contemplative.

Willa tied off the sling and critically eyed her work. She looked to Annalea to invite comment. When none was forthcoming, Willa made a small adjustment to the knot and padded it with a cloth she folded into quarters.

"You are uncharacteristically quiet," she said. When Annalea had no response to that, she added, "And apparently deep in thought."

"Hmm." Annalea's eyes did not stray from the stranger. She was leaning forward, chin cupped in her palms, her elbows resting on her knees. "Do you figure him for a criminal?"

"Hard to make a judgment there. Is that what you're trying to do?"

"Uh-huh. I am wondering about the nature of his activities. It's a sure thing you don't get dragged behind a horse and left for dead if somebody ain't pissed at you."

One of Willa's dark eyebrows kicked up. "Language."

"Sorry. If somebody *isn't* pissed at you."

Willa's lips twitched, but the raised eyebrow stayed in place a moment longer. "Have you considered that Happy might know him?"

Annalea's head lifted a fraction as she frowned deeply. "Why would Pa know him?"

"Because he spends considerably more time in Jupiter than any of the rest of us."

"Yes, but mostly he's in the Liberty Saloon or the jailhouse." Her frown faded, replaced by a lopsided grin as she comprehended her sister's point. "Oh. I see. Liberty or the jail."

"Happy could have made his acquaintance in either place," said Willa. "But if it happened, I'm inclined to think it was probably the jail."

"He and Pa might have shared a cell. Wouldn't that be something?"

Willa did not hear any condemnation in Annalea's tone. In fact, she seemed unreasonably intrigued by the notion. "I was not suggesting that they shared a cell. I was thinking of the posters hanging in the sheriff's office. Happy might have seen this man's likeness on one of those." Shrugging, Willa returned her regard to the man's countenance. Where the skin wasn't scraped, it was bruised, and where it wasn't colored red and purple, it was ash. Sometime during her ministrations, the left side of his face had begun to swell. If he tried to open his eyes, he would only be able to see out of one. That struck Willa as a damn shame, although not, she reflected, for the same reasons it would strike him. She was remembering the exceptional clarity and color of his blue-gray eyes. "Right now I am hard put to believe his mother would recognize him."

Annalea nodded in agreement. "He seems worse off than when I found him. I didn't think that was possible."

Willa started to explain how that had come to pass, but her attention was caught by Cutter's shout from two hundred yards up the hillside. "What's he saying?" she asked Annalea. "And what has he got in his hand?"

Annalea had already jumped to her feet. "It's the shoe. He found the shoe."

"Lot of fussing for a shoe, though I expect this fellow will be glad of it. Wave Cutter back here. We need to go."

Annalea cupped her hands around her mouth and shouted for Cutter.

"Not what I asked," Willa said dryly. "And here comes John Henry. I'm not sure the dog knows his name yet, but he does recognize that come-to-me cry of yours. Go on, Annalea. Walk him out to meet Cutter." After Annalea and the dog hurried off, Willa spread one of the blankets on the wagon bed and another beside her patient.

"What about your name? It's the least of what we need to know, but we have to call you something." She did not really expect a response, but she did not think she imagined a shift in his breathing. Could he hear her? She pressed on, regarding him more keenly. "On the other hand, Dr. Frankenstein's monster never had a name, and truth be told, you put me a little in mind of him."

Willa waited for a twitch and was rewarded when she glimpsed his long fingers curling the merest fraction. It was something at least, although if she were being strictly honest, she had hoped that it would be his mouth that twitched. Because all things considered, it was rather a nice mouth. Not particularly amused by the odd thought, Willa reined herself in as she gathered the soiled cloths and went down to the run's gently sloping bank to rinse them. She had just finished wringing them out when Cutter and Annalea returned, John Henry quite literally dogging their footsteps.

Willa slung the damp cloths around her neck and stood. She absently brushed herself off as she approached the trio. "Did you find anything besides that shoe?"

"Bits and pieces of clothing. Evidence that there were four horses, but I think only three other men. Best as I could figure out, he rode with them for a ways, probably from town, before things took a turn. Could've been planned from the outset, and they surprised him, or maybe he had his suspicions and no choice in the matter. Plenty of good hanging trees back there, and we know they had a rope, but I can't say if that was their intention and they had a change of mind."

Willa nodded. "Lots of ways to kill a man, but if his death is less important than his suffering . . ." Her voice drifted off.

"Yep."

Cutter's laconic response prompted Willa's rueful smile. "You think you can put that shoe on him without twisting the foot overmuch?"

"Sure." Cutter immediately bent to the task.

"We are going to move him onto the blanket and carry him to the wagon. We will have to lift him over the side."

"What can I do?" asked Annalea.

Willa did not have to think about it. "You have the naming of him. Choose carefully. It's his until he decides it isn't."

Annalea straightened her shoulders and nodded gravely. She crooked a finger at John Henry and he dutifully followed her back to the wagon. She set him on the bed and climbed in, and the pair of them sat beside the stranger for the whole of the journey back. John Henry occasionally sniffed the man's privates as if they might hold the secret to his identity while Annalea teased out his name in more conventional ways, testing them one by one on the tip of her tongue. By the time they reach the ranch, she had it.

"He is Augustus Horatio Roundbottom," she announced when the wagon stopped.

Cutter asked, "Are you certain?"

"I am. I reckon he won't cotton to being addressed with any variation of Augustus or the more formal Mr. Roundbottom, and we will have the truth out of him soon enough."

Willa's smile was perfectly serene. She nudged Cutter with her elbow and whispered, "That's my girl."

Jo Goodman is the *USA Today* bestselling author of numerous romance novels, including *The Devil You Know*, *This Gun for Hire*, *In Want of a Wife*, and *True to the Law*, and is also a fan of the happily ever after. When not writing, she is a licensed professional counselor working with children and families in West Virginia's Northern Panhandle. Visit her online at jogoodman.com or facebook.com/jogoodmanromance.